Wreck upon the water
Washed up on the sand
Make a town of sea wrack
We'll call it Flotsam.

The seaside city of Flotsam grew from the wreckage of a doomed Empire. For hundreds of years it has sat beside the Blood Sea of Istar and watched as kingdoms rose and fell throughout Ansalon. It has hosted dragon armies, the vilest villains, and the greatest heroes ever to walk on Krynn.

But its days are numbered. . . .

A young wizard and his betrothed have come to Flotsam in search of the woman's father, but they soon find themselves trapped in a city caught between the machinations of a greedy dragon and the ambitions of the Dark Knights.

The heroes are forced to play a deadly game, and it's winner-take-all, with Flotsam as the prize.

THE CROSSROADS SERIES

The Clandestine Circle
Mary H. Herbert

The Thieves' Guild
Jeff Crook

Dragon's Bluff
Mary H. Herbert

CROSSROADS

Dragon's Bluff

MARY H. HERBERT

DRAGON'S BLUFF

©2001 Wizards of the Coast, Inc.

Cover art by Mark Zug
First Printing: July 2001
Library of Congress Catalog Card Number: 00-190891

9 8 7 6 5 4 3 2 1

UK ISBN: 0-7869-2623-6
US ISBN: 0-7869-1877-2
620-T21877

U.S., CANADA,
ASIA, PACIFIC, & LATIN AMERICA
Wizards of the Coast, Inc.
P.O. Box 707
Renton, WA 98057-0707
+ 1-800-324-6496

EUROPEAN HEADQUARTERS
Wizards of the Coast, Belgium
P.B. 2031
2600 Berchem
Belgium
+ 32-70-23-32-77

Visit our web site at **www.wizards.com/books/dragonlance**

For Thomas. . . .
You've waited a long time for a dedication just for you,
and in that time you have come to love books, fantasy,
and dragons as much as I do. Since you've read most of
this book over my shoulder and made several astute
suggestions, I dedicate this book to you with all my
love.

—Mom

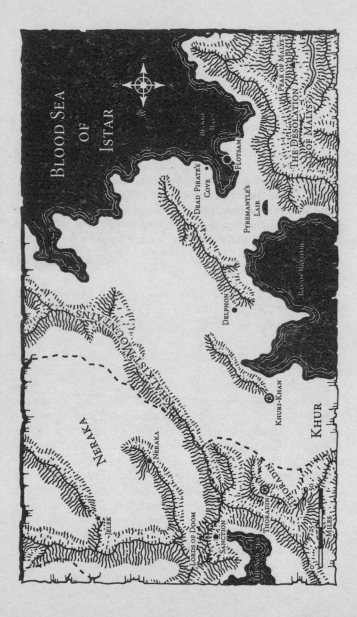

Prologue

Ulin had never liked chicken and dumpling soup. There was something about the sight of those bits of dough floating in the rich broth, or maybe it was the smell of chicken and herbs that brought back memories of bad colds, bouts of influenza, and a broken arm suffered in childhood—all dosed by his mother with bowls of hot, steaming chicken and dumpling soup. It wasn't that his mother's soups were bad. In fact, Usha Majere's cooking was almost as renowned as her skills in painting portraits. The problem lay in the fact that chicken soup seemed to be the cure-all shared by all the women in his life. Every time he came home to Solace tired, weary, sick, or downhearted, his mother or grandmother served him a bowl of chicken soup. Now his future mother-in-law had taken it upon herself to treat him with soup as well, and like his grandmother and mother, he didn't have the heart to tell her he didn't like it.

He sighed and forced himself to take another spoonful.

1

It had been seven days since he returned from his latest trip, a visit to Palanthas, and he was still bone-tired and depressed. The journey, like others before it, had been a waste of time and served only to strengthen his private misgivings. Since his return he had come to this little house in Solace every evening about this time to meet Lucy, his betrothed, and every time he walked in the door, her mother took one look at his drawn face and thrust another bowl of soup at him. Unfortunately, the soup hadn't helped much. He still felt as if he had been hollowed out and tossed aside, an empty husk.

He stirred his spoon listlessly through the broth and tried to look anywhere but at the bits of dumpling floating on the surface. The house was quiet at that moment. Lucy's mother, Ellse, was in the pantry slicing bread and cheese, while her two younger sisters laughed and played outside in the dusting of a late winter snow. Lucy had not yet returned from her work at the refugee school. Ulin slouched in his seat, and his well-cut lips curved in an expression of impatience. He wished Lucy would hurry, so he might have a chance to slip his bowl of soup under the table for her cat. That animal would eat anything.

The thought had barely crossed his mind when the kitchen door blew open, admitting a gust of chill wind and a young woman dressed in a long-sleeved tunic and skirt. A cloak was flung carelessly over one shoulder, and she clutched a piece of paper like a club in her balled fist. Anger radiated from her tense body in palpable waves.

Surprise held Ulin silent. Lucy was not a temperamental person, and he had rarely seen her in this state of rage. Her eyes had turned a deep gray-green like thunderstorm clouds, and her freckles were lost in a flush of scarlet.

A dwarf stamped in behind her and closed the door against the evening wind.

"I can't believe it!" Lucy cried before Ulin could say a word. "Look at this! Ten years he has been gone, and what do we finally get from the reprobate? A letter notifying us of his death and a request to identify the body! Why can't he just rot quietly into the ground?"

Ulin blinked as he tried to put the few facts together and figure out what she was talking about.

Lucy slammed the paper on the table, sending ripples through Ulin's bowl of soup. "Look at this! Go ahead and read it," she said. He picked it up and smoothed out the crumpled sheet as she plunged on. "He died in Flotsam during the winter," she informed her mother, who had come to see what the shouting was about. "He's dead, and we still can't get rid of him!"

"Who?" Ellse asked worriedly.

"Someone named Kethril Torkay," Ulin replied, perusing the first part of the letter. A thought clicked in his head and he glanced up at Lucy. "Your father?"

Lucy did not reply, but the drawn lines of dismay on Ellse's face answered his question. He set the letter aside, hurried to his feet, and helped Ellse into a chair. Since both Torkay women were distracted by the shocking news, he played the part of host, offering a seat to the dwarf and pouring tea for Lucy and her mother. He found a jug of something a little stiffer and fixed a pitcher of hot spiced brandy for the dwarf and himself. He placed a mug of the steaming brew in front of the dwarf and took a deep swallow of his own to rid his mouth of the taste of chicken soup.

The dwarf, bundled against the cold, slowly peeled off a muffler, a thick jacket, and a hood to reveal the dour, unbearded face of a mature female. "Thank you," she said gruffly and downed the hot drink in one long gulp.

Ulin poured another drink for her then sat down by his betrothed. He took her hand in his. "Lucy, I'm so sorry."

Lucy jerked out of her thoughts. "Don't be. The man was worthless. *That* part doesn't bother me."

Ulin felt perplexed. Lucy had trained with him as a sorceress, and for the past six months, since the destruction of the Academy of Sorcery, she had spent her mornings teaching in a school for refugee children and her evenings working for Ulin's grandfather and aunt at the Inn of the Last Home. She had grown close to Ulin and his family, and yet, not once could he remember her mentioning her father—until now. He glanced at the dwarf drinking her brandy, her face expressionless.

Lucy's anger, an emotion she could never hold for long, faded. The young woman leaned forward to rest her elbows on the table and her head in her hands. "What bothers me is this dwarf wants me to go to Flotsam to identify his body."

"What?" Ulin and Ellse burst out together.

"That's absurd," Ulin snorted. He snatched up the letter and read it this time from start to finish. The words stood out clearly on the coarse paper.

"Who are you?" Ellse finally noticed the dwarf.

"She's a lawyer," Lucy replied.

"A what?"

"A magistrate," Ulin told her. "A scribe of sorts . . . an official who deals with legal matters such as estates, wills, certificates, deeds, litigation, that sort of thing."

The dwarf pushed to her feet and bowed. "I am Chalcedony Rockdale. I have been sent by the Flotsam City Council to request a member of the Torkay family accompany me to Flotsam to identify the body."

Lucy's mother sniffled into a napkin. "What happened?"

"He was caught in a fire."

Lucy snorted. "Probably some bar fire."

Chalcedony did not respond. She watched stonily as Ulin passed the letter to Lucy's mother.

"If the man is such a rogue, why go all the way to Flotsam just to bury him?" Ulin wanted to know.

"There is the matter of his estate," Chalcedony responded, her brown eyes assessing him.

"You mean he actually had something?" Lucy asked, her tone skeptical. She stood up and paced a slow circle around the table.

"A fair amount. Enough to help our townspeople with several necessary projects. However, he left no will. Legally, no one can touch his estate until his body is identified and a certificate of death is issued."

"But why us? He deserted us ten years ago. Surely someone around there knows him better."

"Not in Flotsam. He spent most of his time in a place called Dead Pirate's Cove"—Chalcedony curled her lip up in a sneer—"and most of those people are totally untrustworthy. The town council would certainly prefer that Kethril's money stay in Flotsam, and the only way to ensure that is to have a reliable witness." She turned to Ellse and tapped a stubby forefinger on the letter still laying on the table. "The council knows it is asking a great deal—"

Ulin scooted his chair back, interrupting her with its sliding creak. "It's asking the ridiculous. Flotsam is on the other side of Ansalon. The journey will take months, and may be worthless. A burned body will not last long in any recognizable condition."

"They've buried him in the sand near town. He'll dry nicely in the heat."

Lucy couldn't help a grimace.

Chalcedony paused then went on. "The council is willing to offer you twenty-five percent of Kethril Torkay's estate plus traveling expenses if you will identify him."

Lucy studied the dwarf for a long breath. "And if we cannot make an identification?"

"You will still earn your fee."

Ulin's lips pursed in thought. This situation seemed rather odd, but then he'd always found lawyers a rather strange lot. He hoped Lucy was not seriously considering this. "Why does Flotsam's council even bother with formalities? If they truly have their hands on Torkay's estate, they could've kept it and saved themselves the expense of searching for his heirs."

"True." Chalcedony finished her spiced brandy and helped herself to another mug. "That would have been easier, but the elders of Flotsam's council have some honor, and they are trying to polish a little tarnish from Flotsam's image. They felt it was worth a try."

Lucy nodded. She looked around at her small cottage, at the worn furnishings and the empty shelves in the pantry. The three-room house just outside of Solace was comfortable enough for one or two, but since her mother and two sisters moved in a few months ago, the place had become a little too crowded for Lucy's comfort. "What do you think, Mother?" she asked Ellse. "We could certainly use the money."

Ulin started in his chair. "Lucy, you're not thinking—"

"Yes, I am," she insisted. "I am the only one who can go."

"Ulin can go with you," Ellse spoke at last. She sat still, her eyes downcast.

Resentment flared in Ulin's mind. He had just returned from one long, fruitless journey. The last thing he wanted to do was go on another. "I don't want to go to Flotsam," he blurted before he could stop the words.

Ellse lifted her head. Slow tears trickled down her seamed cheeks. "You will if you want to marry my daughter."

As quickly as it flared, Ulin's resentment died down. Lucy's mother was right. Mothers usually were. If he wanted a place at Lucy's side in the future, he needed to support her in the endeavors that meant the most to her. The gods knew she had supported him.

But he wasn't ready to give in quite so easily. "Flotsam is in Malys's domain. Reaching it will be difficult. Coming back with anything of value could be impossible."

Lucy stopped pacing and put an arm around her mother's shaking shoulders. "I know that, Ulin. Believe me, I have thought about that."

"And you still want to do this?"

"No, I don't *want* to go." She hesitated and shook her head at her own foolishness. "But if I don't bring back some token that my father is truly dead, we will never *know*. We won't be able to close that part of our lives." She slid her hand across the table and laid it over Ulin's. "Believe it or not, in all the years that my father has been gone, we have never given up the hope that he might return. We *need* to know he is dead."

Ulin's weary face relaxed in a warm smile. If it meant that much to her . . . "All right. When do we leave?"

"We?" Lucy echoed. "You don't have to come—despite what Mother said. You're still exhausted from your last trip. And what about your father?"

He closed his eyes when he thought of his father. Palin was home now, thank the absent gods. For months he had been held prisoner by Knights of the Thorn, the magic-wielding faction of the newly named Knights of Neraka. The Knights, under the command of the green dragon overlord, Beryl, had tortured and interrogated him to learn the truth about the failure of magic. Eventually they had realized he knew no more than they did, and they had released him. He had come home a broken, bitter man who quarreled with his family and friends and sank deeper into depression.

Ulin opened his eyes to meet Lucy's. "There is little I can do to help here. I'd like to go with you. I've been gone from you too long, and besides, two can accomplish more than one."

They had been so engrossed in their conversation that they had forgotten the dwarf.

Chalcedony cleared her throat. "Arrangements have been made. If you can be ready, we should leave in two days."

"Two days?" Ulin repeated. His bedroll hadn't even been cleaned from the last trip.

Lucy bounced to Ulin's side and put her lips over his mouth, cutting off his words with a deep kiss. When she straightened, the last traces of storm clouds cleared from her eyes, leaving them fresh and green. She grinned at her beloved and her mother. "This deserves a celebration. Let's go to the Inn and tell Laura and Caramon."

Chalcedony waved a negating hand. "No, I will just—"

"My grandfather makes the best ale this side of Flotsam," Ulin informed the dwarf.

"And fried ham, spiced potatoes, fresh bread . . ." Lucy added.

The magistrate drained her third brandy and bowed her thanks. "In that case, I will join you."

Still warmed by Lucy's kiss, Ulin slid his bowl of soup under the table for the cat. Grabbing his cloak, he escorted the two women and the dwarf out the door and called Lucy's sisters. Perhaps, he thought, something good would come of this. With luck, the journey might not be a total disaster.

Chapter One

Palin once said that if you could avoid pirates, marauding Dark Knights, sea dragons, the Dragon Overlords, the fickle storms, and the general vagaries of a sea voyage, a ship cruise through New Sea could be a restful and relaxing way to travel.

So far, Ulin mused, his father had been right. The weather had stayed calm, the sky had remained clear, and the ship still floated. Ulin felt more rested than he had in days, since all he had to do was loll around the deck in the warm sunshine and stay out of the crew's way.

He was performing that task well as he leaned back against a bale of fleeces, stretched out his legs, and closed his eyes. Lucy had somehow talked the dour dwarf out of their cabin for a game of cards. The dwarf, who grudgingly admitted they could call her Challie, had been civil but not friendly, and this was the first time she agreed to any social entertainment. They sat on the deck nearby, engrossed in a game of Bounty Hunter that involved a lot of haggling and betting. Ulin paid little attention. He let his mind wander back over the course of their journey so far and decided that their little party had been lucky.

After leaving word for his parents with his aunt and grandfather, Ulin, Lucy, and the magistrate had left Solace and traveled south to New Ports. Chalcedony had already arranged for a berth on an Abanasinian freighter bound east across the New Sea with a load of foodstuffs for Sanction. The price of passage was exorbitant, but Chalcedony had paid it.

The council had sent her off generously funded for this journey, and she seemed determined to get it over as quickly as possible. Berths could be few and far between this time of year.

The freighter pulled out of New Port on a favorable wind and made the haul to the island of Schallsea where several passengers debarked, and Captain Tethlin traded a portion of his winter wheat for several bales of good fleece, a commodity in demand by the weavers in Khur. They left the next day, sailing north past the Citadel of Light and around the northern tip of the island. Once past Schallsea, the freighter sailed east along the coast of Throt to keep as much distance between it and the swampy realm of the great black dragon, Onysablet. Better to risk the unpredictable depredations of the hobgoblins than draw the attention of Sable. So far, they had been unmolested by anything larger than flies.

"Ulin," Challie's voice cut through his reverie. "Come play cards with us. I think Lucy's cheating."

With a groan and a stretch, Ulin pulled himself out of his musings and moved over to join the two at their card game. "Lucy doesn't have to cheat," he told Challie. "She's too good at the game."

Lucy looked up from dealing the cards and smiled at him—that spicy, slightly devilish smile that could melt his insides. She was not a beautiful woman, not like his mother or even his auburn-haired sister, Linsha. In fact, she had been given the name Plain Lucy at the Academy, an appellation Ulin detested. While it was true she was stocky, her features were rather large, and her face was too round for conventional beauty, she had gloriously green eyes like sunlight glowing through jade and a smile that radiated humor and joy. Several days in the clear spring sun had brought out bronze highlights in her chestnut hair and intensified the galaxy of freckles across her nose and cheeks. To others she was plain, but to him she was the light that kept back the darkness in his heart.

"Are you going to sit there gawking like a moonstruck calf, or are you going to play?" Challie demanded. The dwarf slapped down two cards, face down.

Her comment startled him out of his thoughts—this seemed to be a good afternoon for daydreaming—and he belatedly looked at his cards. A lousy hand as usual.

They played for several hours, keeping score on the ship's railing with a piece of chalk.

Challie played with a dwarf's stubbornness and a careful eye for detail, and she won several important hands. She was organized, neat, quiet, and introverted to the point of coldness. It was little wonder to Ulin that she was a lawyer. Dwarves were known to value law and order, and this one practiced the essence of order from her perfectly packed bags to her simple rugged clothing. She wore no jewelry or bright colors, only a well-made tunic, brown pants and boots, and a thick coat of knobby wool. Her long brown hair fell in a tight braid down her back and the only weapon she carried was a steel axe polished to the sheen of sterling silver.

It was probably a good thing she did not carry the axe all the time, Ulin thought as he watched her toss her cards down after Lucy won a hand and left her stuck with too many cards.

"Where did you learn to play so well?" she asked Lucy.

Lucy shook her head, flipping her ponytail over one shoulder. "My father. It was about the only thing he taught me." She said nothing more, but simply picked up the cards and dealt another hand.

Ulin tried to concentrate on his game and could not. The air was too pleasant, even for the last days of Rannmont, and the ship's gentle roll over the waves was too soothing. Lucy and Challie quickly cleaned out his few coppers and smugly suggested he return to his bale of fleeces for a nap. That didn't seem like a bad idea, so he stretched out his long, lanky frame, crossed his ankles, and closed his eyes.

The sleep that seemed so close didn't come. The sun still shone clear, the noises of the ship sounded the same, and yet something seemed different, something gently persistent that he had not noticed while sitting upright. He could not explain what it was, only that it set off a small alarm in the back of his mind. His eyes opened, and he sat up. Ulin had not survived numerous journeys across Ansalon by ignoring his intuition.

Wide awake now, he climbed to his feet and went to stand by the bow rail where the wind tugged at his clothes and raised goose bumps on his arms. Salt spray kicked up by the bow splashed across his face. The ship was nearing the narrowest part of New Sea where Sable's swamp encroached so far into the shallow sea that it created a strait into the northeasternmost end of the body of water. To his left he could see the green, hazy hills of the coast of Throt, while far to his right lay a low, dismal line that marked the beginning of the swamp created by Sable out of what had been New Coast and Blödehelm. Ulin scanned the southern horizon and was very relieved to see no sign of the great black. With luck, she was in her lair, dabbling in her vile experiments or snacking on a few hapless swamp creatures.

Puzzled, Ulin looked around the ship. The crew must have noticed a change, too, for their activity had increased in just a few minutes. More sailors were topside, clearing off the deck and scrambling into the rigging. Captain Tethlin shouted orders from the wheel, and in the crow's nest, the lookout stared fixedly to the west.

A sudden gust of wind caught the ship, and its lurch to the right threw Ulin off balance. As he braced himself against the rail, it occurred to him what he had felt: a change in the movement of the ship. Instead of a rhythmic rise and fall over the swell, the ship was taking on a decided roll sideways over a changing wave pattern. The wind and waves were swinging around to the northwest.

"What's the matter, Ulin?" Lucy called.

He studied the western horizon and saw with a twinge of alarm that the sky was no longer clear. "It looks like our good weather is about to end."

Lucy and Challie joined him at the rail, and together they watched a formidable line of cloud gathering across the sky in an angry gray wall.

"Move it, folks!" a seaman shouted. He and another sailor grabbed a bale of fleece from the pile on the bow and hauled it toward an open hatch.

"Captain says clear the deck," the second man ordered. "That means you."

There was nothing to do but obey. Lucy and Challie picked up their cards and cups. Ulin pulled up the blanket they had been sitting on, and the three followed the other passengers down into the small cabins under the raised upper deck at the stern.

As soon as they were in the small cabin he shared with the women, Ulin went to the porthole and threw it open. They were lucky to have one of the few portholes on the passenger deck, even if it was small, hard to open, and showed signs of too much rust. Ulin craned his neck to get a better view of the sky and was not reassured by what he saw. Already the clouds had overtaken the western sun and turned the afternoon light to gray gloaming. The roll of the sea increased noticeably.

"Can't the captain pull over or something?" Lucy asked. There was a tremor in her voice.

"Pull over?" Ulin repeated, turning around to explain that ships just can't pull over like a wagon. He saw the look on her face, leaped for the chamber bucket, and shoved it under her chin just in time.

Her greenish look of apology silenced the remark he was about to make about weak stomachs. He had forgotten she'd never traveled on a ship before.

With Challie's help, Lucy climbed into her bunk and crawled under the blankets. Ulin emptied the bucket out the porthole and tied it securely to the safety rail in easy reach.

Challie looked on with a grim expression then crawled into her own bunk. For a while Ulin sat beside Lucy in silence and listened to the growing fury of the storm. Thunder rumbled like a charging cavalry, and the wind wailed around the ship and through the rigging. They heard thumps and strange bangs, shouts and running footfalls as the crew hauled in the sails and battened down the hatches. As the rolling motion of the ship grew worse, so too did the darkness until their cabin was darker than night. Outside they heard the rain begin to fall in battering torrents.

"We're so close to Sable's swamp," Lucy breathed. "What if we're blown aground?"

Ulin tried not to think about being at the mercy of the treacherous black dragon. "If Captain Tethlin is as good as I think he is, he'll use the wind to blow us through the strait."

"I hope you're right," she said weakly.

Ulin pushed his stool closer to her bunk, and they leaned together, grateful for company in the pitching darkness. "Tell me again why we're doing this?" he asked, trying to keep his voice light.

She made a sound like a strained chuckle. "Because I lacked adventure and excitement in Solace," she replied. "Attacks by Dark Knights and draconians, the destruction of the Academy, the loss of my magic abilities, the constant strain of dealing with refugees and worrying about Beryl aren't enough. I wanted more! I need to make a name for myself if I am going to marry a Majere. Why not brave the dangers and travails of a trip to Flotsam?"

Her words took him totally by surprise. He swiveled around and stared at her through the darkness. "You're joking . . . right?" he demanded. Most of her tirade had to be a joke! Surely she didn't mean that part about making a name for herself. A flicker of lightning glinted off her eyes and for an instant he saw she was grinning—or grimacing.

Her hand clasped his arm. "Of course, I'm joking. I'm doing this because . . . my father. If he is truly dead, then I will bury him with decency. If he's not, then I am going to find him and kill him myself." A groan escaped her as the ship took a nasty pitch over a wave. After a moment, Lucy pointed a finger at Ulin. "I know you're doing this—"

Ulin cut her off. "Because I love you."

"And because Flotsam is on Blood Bay." She managed a faint smile at the guilty start she felt jerk though his muscles. "Confess. I know it. There is a trove of ancient magical artifacts to be found on the coast of the Blood Sea of Istar and you are hoping to find some."

"It's worth a try. For my father," he admitted, his voice more bitter than he intended. "I don't believe even a god-crafted artifact is going to help us any more, but if I could find something that still functioned . . . maybe it would snap him out of his terrible depression."

Ulin was cut off by the sound of groaning. Giving his arm an apologetic squeeze, Lucy grabbed for her bucket.

The ship's pitching movements were miserable now. And dangerous, Ulin decided when a stool crashed into his shins then rolled across the floor. He staggered to his feet and practically fell across the cabin into his bunk. The bunks were more like narrow cupboards built into the wall than real beds, but on a tossing ship they were safer and had straps to help hold in the occupants. Ulin pulled his blankets over his shoulders and wedged himself in. He was too tall to stretch out comfortably on the bunk, but for once his length was an advantage and helped keep him in place.

Sleepy as he had been on the upper deck in the sun, sleep would not come now in this pounding, rolling darkness. He lay on his side for hours watching lightning flash through the small porthole and listening to the cacophony of the ship battle her way through wind and water. Although the gods had departed the world before his birth, Ulin's parents had made sure he was raised with the knowledge of the gods' identities, history, and sacred ways. Some day, they hoped, the gods would return. Ulin would often say prayers to the gods in the feeble hope they were still listening, but in his mind a strong core of common sense, or pragmatism, or bullheaded obstinacy refused to believe they listened, let alone cared. He toyed with the idea of saying a prayer now for his companions' safety and the continued well-being of the ship, then he cast away the thought. The gods were gone and many ships had been lost at sea despite endless streams of prayers and curses. He might as well save his breath.

Lightning and thunder cracked simultaneously outside, and for a second, silvery-green light flared through the porthole. In a blink it was gone, followed by a sudden cessation of any light through the porthole. Abruptly, the ship began to lean to starboard.

Challie cursed as the table and the other stool broke loose and crashed into her bunk.

"It's just a big wave," Ulin called to reassure them all. "It'll pass."

But it was not passing quickly enough. Groaning like a wounded animal the freighter rolled farther and farther to the right until Ulin feared the ship would never recover. He knew tons of water were pouring over her decks, pulling her deeper into the grip of the sea. If she reached horizontal and her masts hit the water, she would founder and sink in moments.

Frantically he held on to the straps while his bunk tipped toward vertical. Seconds passed like hours. A new sound caught his attention, a rusty creaking noise that came from their porthole. Alarmed, Ulin let his body slide toward the edge of his bunk until he could see the porthole. Just as he peered around the bunk wall, the metal hinges gave way and the portal flew open with an explosive crash. A column of dark water shot through the hole into their small cabin, drenching Lucy and Challie.

Lucy, Challie, and Ulin scrambled out of their bunks. Shouting wordless oaths, they fought their way across the tilting deck toward the porthole. In the intense darkness, Ulin groped for one of the stools. He found one and tried to jam the round seat into the hole. It was a close fit, but the pressure of the water wrenched the stool out of his hands and threw it across the room where it floated in a growing flood of seawater.

"Try magic!" Lucy shouted over the uproar of storm and struggling ship.

"No!" Ulin made a grab for the second stool. His foot slid on the steep wet flooring and he crashed into the water by the wall, sputtering invectives. Challie slipped and fell with him.

"Ulin, please at least try it! We can't stop the water with just a stool."

Challie hauled herself up by the bunk. She could see nothing in the black cabin, but she could feel something. "She's coming back!" she cried.

Her two companions realized she was right. As the wave passed, the ship slowly righted herself. The force of the water pouring into the room abated, and the tilt of their cabin returned to a more normal upright position. The flood of water against the wall spread out to cover the whole floor.

Wind and rain still poured through the hole, soaking what little bit of Lucy was still dry. She tried to close the porthole cover, but the hinges were twisted and useless,

17

and the force of the crash had broken the thick glass. There was nothing they could do with that cover.

Ulin sloshed through the cold water, carrying the stool. He jammed it into the opening as another wave, a smaller one this time, slammed into the ship. Seawater poured into the hole and pushed the stool away.

"We need something to hold this in place," Ulin gasped.

Lucy helped him shove the stool back in place. "Try magic. A seal of some sort."

"It won't work. Spells rarely work for me anymore," he muttered between his teeth.

She bit back a retort. There was no point arguing with him. The wild magic Palin Majere had "discovered" years ago was failing for them all. For almost two years the followers of Goldmoon's mystical magic of the heart, the students of the Academy of Sorcery, even the great Dragon Overlords saw their powers weaken and dwindle away. No one, not even Palin, knew why their magic was failing, and that confusion and disappointment ate away at the elder Majere, and in a lesser degree at his son. Both of them had worn themselves to exhaustion traveling across Ansalon in search of answers and in hope of finding magic artifacts that still functioned. For his trouble, Palin had seen his beloved Academy of Sorcery destroyed and had been held prisoner by the Knights of the Thorn. His hands were forever broken and twisted by their questioning. Ulin, while he had not been physically tortured, had lost almost everything that meant something to him. His world had come unraveled. He had virtually given up his studies of magic and only the hope that he could help his father kept him searching for something for which he had lost faith.

But Lucy was an optimist. Despite everything that had happened, she had not quite given up hope that her abilities to wield magic would some day return or that Ulin would somehow find an answer. Until then, she would continue to encourage Ulin, try her spells, and hope for the best.

Ulin knew this, and he recognized the set determination on her face. A groan so soft only he could hear it escaped from his clenched teeth. He didn't think there was much hope for success. Most of his spells failed utterly, but he would try for her. He had been, after all, a Dragon Mage and the Assistant Master of the Academy of Sorcery. He knew the spells. He was comfortable with the glorious feel of magic coursing through his veins, warming his blood and tingling on his skin. He just could not force the power to work for him as it once had, and the empty, bitter feeling of disappointment was almost more than he could bear.

Steeling himself, he put his hands down on the bottom of the stool seat and pushed it into place over the open port. The spell he decided to try was a simple one, one he had performed countless times with little effort: a basic wizard lock that would seal the wood seat to the wooden frame of the porthole. Ignoring the pitch of the ship and the water that sloshed around his ankles, he took a deep, controlled breath and released it. He willed his body to relax and his mind to focus solely on the wild magic he could feel around him.

The power was still there, in the wood of the ship, in the water around him, in the force of the wind and waves that surged against the struggling ship. It was this continued presence of magic that made Ulin so frustrated. It was there within his grasp, tantalizing and mocking, yet every time he tried to form a spell and bend the magic to his will, something seemed to pull a plug and drain the power away, leaving him weak, empty, and somehow diminished.

This time was no different than countless other times. He formed his spell, focused on his magic, and felt it fade from his grasp like smoke. There was nothing he could do to stop it. He dropped the stool in disgust. Something tickled his neck, and he swatted at what felt like insects brushing by his neck. Probably mosquitoes, or maybe fleas from the bunk. He couldn't tell in the dark. It seemed odd he hadn't noticed fleas before.

"I'll find the carpenter's store," he said, his voice terse. "We'll nail it in place."

Lucy nodded once and sank back on her soggy bed, too disappointed and seasick to stay upright.

"Maybe this will help," Challie offered. From under her wet pillow, she handed Ulin her small, perfectly balanced hand axe, beautifully wrought and sharpened to a deadly edge. A leather sheath protected the head of the axe, and finely woven strips of leather covered the handle.

Ulin offered his thanks and hurried to his task. From previous explorations on the freighter, he knew where to find carpenter's store just off the galley one deck below. The difficulty lay in making his way over the wet deck. Theirs was not the only porthole or hatch that had given way under the weight of the giant wave, and sailors struggled above and below decks to keep the bilge pumps working, to find and repair the damage, and to check the cargo. The ship's carpenter was already in his small storeroom handing out iron nails, boards, rope, and caulking to the crew.

He listened to Ulin's tale of the porthole, then thrust a handful of nails in his direction. "Take these. Find something to nail over the hole. I'll be along soon as I can—if we don't sink first!"

With the nails, a stool seat, and Challie's axe, Ulin accomplished what he could not do with magic. The porthole was blocked and the relentless rain and seaspray pouring into their cabin dwindled to mere trickles.

To everyone's relief, the huge wave that broadsided the ship proved to be a rogue, and the rest of the waves that night were not enough to overwhelm the tough freighter. When dawn came, gray and wet, the storm moved on to the east and blew out its fury over Sable's vast swamp. The ship was left in its wake, her crew battered, soggy, and thankful to be alive. By noon the sky was a serene sapphire.

Ulin and Challie pried the seat cover off the porthole to let the sunshine and warm breeze pour into their wet cabin. Hours of mopping cleared out the water on the floor. They carried their soggy belongings and bedding outside and, with Captain Teflin's permission, spread them out on ropes and the rigging. They carried a weak and shaky Lucy out on deck, too, and propped her in the sun. Her normally healthy complexion was a sickly shade of white, and her thick chestnut hair hung in lank strands, but she smiled at the sun and quickly fell asleep.

With the ship now floating on a calm sea, the ship's cook prepared hot food. His galley boy brought a tray out to Challie and Ulin on deck where they had settled down for a long-needed rest.

Ulin took one look at the thick, steaming soup and groaned. "Chicken and dumpling," he groaned. "The gods save me from chicken and dumpling."

Challie's brown eyes lit with unexpected humor. "Be thankful, Ulin. They almost did. You nearly became seafood yourself."

He snorted, but he took the bowls from the puzzled boy and served Challie. With a look of resignation on his lean face, he dipped a spoon into the broth and took a long, suffering sip.

Chapter Two

L insha was right, Ulin decided. Sanction was a beautiful city.

From where he stood with Lucy and Challie at the rail of the freighter as it sailed into serene Sanction Bay, Ulin could see most of the broad valley of Sanction Vale set like a green gem in a half crown of towering volcanic peaks. The city's tall towers, walls, and buildings of pale stone filled much of the valley and gleamed in the early morning sun like alabaster against the stark red flanks of the three Lords of Doom, the majestic, and still active, volcanoes that ringed the city with fire.

Ulin's sister, Linsha, had spent years in Sanction, and after her return to Solace had described its charms to him in long and admiring detail. She told him of the inns and taverns, the gardens and shops, the large Souk Bazaar where virtually everything that was for sale on Ansalon could be found. She described the City Guards in their scarlet uniforms and the Governor's Palace set like a white fortress upon a northern hill. Her descriptions had been so complete that Ulin found his eyes searching the city and its harbor for landmarks he felt should be there.

"It is so lovely," Lucy said beside him. Her eyes were wide with curiosity. "Look at those volcanoes. They're smoking!"

"Yes," Challie agreed. "It's not bad, for a city under siege."

Sadly, Sanction had been a city under siege for a long time. The Knights of Neraka—the Knights who had, until recently, called themselves the Knights of Takhisis—had changed not only their commander and their name in the past year, they had also changed their strategy concerning Sanction. For years they had wanted control of the port city but had contented themselves with minor attacks and blockading the only two major land routes into the city while they studied the policies and activities of the powerful, magic-wielding lord governor, Hogan Bight. However, when magic began to fail all over Ansalon, the Dark Knights' new leader, Morham Targonne, decided the chance to defeat Lord Bight had finally arrived. He launched a major offensive against the city's fortifications that nearly overwhelmed the valiant City Guard, still weakened in numbers by the plague that decimated the city three years before. Only the fierce determination of Lord Bight and the courage of the Sanction defenders had kept the dark forces at bay. Eventually, even Lord Bight was forced to admit the city needed help. Against his better judgment, Lord Bight acquiesced to the demands of his frightened city council and made a pact with the Knights of Solamnia.

As far as Ulin knew, little had changed in the city since the arrival of the Solamnic relief force. The Knights of Neraka still beat at the eastern gates, and the city's defenders still held them to a stalemate. At least the harbor was still open. Although the Dark Knights tried to blockade Sanction Bay, Lord Bight's forces and the Solamnic Knights managed to keep the seawall open. It was the only

lifeline to the rest of Ansalon still remaining to the belea-
guered city.

Through this lifeline, Captain Tethlin had brought his
ship into Sanction Bay under cover of early dawn. Now, as
the sun rose over the mountains, he maneuvered her into
the port.

Rigged with only enough sail for guidance, the freighter
slid through the crowded harbor and took her place at the
largest of Sanction's piers, the southernmost Long Dock.
Dockhands caught the freighter's ropes and pulled her
snug against the pier for unloading. Immediately, the
Harbormaster's aide hurried on board to check Captain
Tethlin's manifest and cargo and give the crew permission
to unload.

The three travelers watched the bustling activity for a
few more minutes then went to their cabin to collect their
belongings. Ulin was about to close their door behind him
on their way out when Captain Tethlin came bustling
down the narrow corridor to see them off.

A big man, he beamed down at Challie and tousled her
hair. "Quite a cruise, eh?" He chuckled.

Although Chalcedony was a head shorter than Lucy,
she was older than Ulin and Lucy combined and she did
not appreciate big people who treated her like a child.
With quiet dignity she drew back from the captain's reach
and gave him a glare fierce enough to melt the brass on his
buttons.

Captain Tethlin never noticed. "So, Ulin, are you staying in Sanction? Do you plan to meet the lord governor?"

Ulin had considered introducing himself to the city's
governor, Lord Bight, simply for curiosity's sake. Linsha
had described Hogan Bight in such glowing terms that Ulin
had to admit he was intrigued by the man who had roused
such loyal friendship in his sister. But while Linsha had
told him about Sanction and its governor, she had never
explained to his satisfaction what she was doing there for
the Solamnic Knights or why she had had to leave Sanction

so precipitously. Perhaps it would be better to leave that stone unturned. He decided, too, to stay anonymous. Challie had told him they would have to travel to Flotsam with the Khurs, and the Majere name was well known and would not be welcome among the Khurish merchants and traders that ran their caravans to Khuri-Khan and Flotsam. The Khur tribes were known to deal with the Knights of Neraka and their ilk and would not hesitate to kidnap or murder.

A brief shake of his head answered the captain's question. "We'll look for a caravan going east."

"That won't be easy. Very few get out of Sanction past the Knights of Neraka. Their blockades are growing stronger by the day. In fact, I wouldn't be surprised if they close off this port within a week or two. We were lucky to get through this time." He stroked his beard with a callused hand. "You ought to follow those bales of wool." He pointed to where several sailors were hauling the bales of wool fleeces onto the dock. "They're going to Garzan the rug maker in the Souk Bazaar. He has managed to send out caravans several times this year. If he can't help you, maybe he'll know someone who can." Tethlin shook Ulin's hand, bowed over Lucy's, and waved to Challie. "Farewell and good luck to you!" he called, already hurrying back to work.

The three stood in the corridor with their bags and packs and stared at each other. They had been so occupied after the storm they had not had time to discuss the details of making arrangements in Sanction.

"Where to?" Ulin asked Challie.

"His information is as good as mine," replied the dwarf. "I talked to Garzan about a caravan when I was here last month. We will speak to him."

"Lunch first," suggested Lucy. "After two days of keeping my head in a bucket, I'm starving."

Ulin agreed. "Lunch it is. We'll find an inn, leave our bags, and go look for Challie's rug merchant."

"And the Souk Bazaar," added Challie. "We'll need a tent, some clothes suitable for the desert, and provisions for the trip: weapons, probably horses . . ." She strode purposefully for the gangplank.

Ulin and Lucy exchanged a humorous glance and hurried after her.

* * * * *

From the Long Dock they were directed to Shipmaker's Road, the main east-west road that bisected the city from the teeming harbor district to the huge guard camp on the eastern side. Along the road, they were told, they could find everything they needed, from inns and taverns to shops and the Souk Bazaar.

Just outside the towering city wall they found a small inn named the Brimming Barrel that offered good beer, hot meals, and a few clean rooms. The innkeeper was a retired guardsman who kept the inn more for his pleasure than necessity and strove to ensure his customers were as comfortable as he. While Ulin, Lucy, and Challie ate their midday meal, the keeper answered their questions about Sanction and filled them in on the latest news about the siege.

"The Solamnics," he grumbled. He rubbed a towel over a clean tankard and slid it down the bar to join a line of others. "They've been here over six months now and damned all they've done so far. Lord Bight called 'em to help after the Knights of Neraka stepped up their attacks on the eastern fortifications. At first we thought they'd sweep in, kick the Dark Knights out of here, and save the day." He made a rude noise. "All they want to do is sit on their armored backsides and 'study the situation.' Lord Bight must be ready to burst a blood vessel."

Ulin remembered something else his sister mentioned about Sanction. "Whatever happened to the bronze dragon that saved the city during the plague?"

The innkeeper shook his grizzled head. "Haven't seen it in a long time. Word around town is the dragon's dead, probably killed by that black bitch, Sable." He broke off to polish another tankard. "Too bad. We could really use that dragon about now."

After their meal the three travelers left their cloaks and bags behind and walked out onto Shipmaker's Road. Sanction had one of the most diverse populations in Ansalon, and every one of its inhabitants seemed to be out in the streets. The paved thoroughfares thronged with carts, wagons, horses, and draft animals. Pedestrians and peddlers, hawkers and laborers crowded the wooden sidewalks. City Guards in their scarlet uniforms patrolled the docks and alleys and walked on the high city wall, while squads of Solamnic Knights marched through the busy streets.

Following the innkeeper's advice, Ulin and the women made their way through the traffic to the Souk Bazaar and the waymeet of the north-south road. There they turned onto the Street of Weavers that bordered the southern edge of the great square.

Garzan the rug maker had a large shop at the Souk Bazaar and a warehouse on the south side of the city. He was a prosperous merchant, able to afford a warehouse on the inside of the city wall and a large contingent of laborers, haulers, drivers, and guards. What he lacked on that particular afternoon was a cook. His caravan was almost ready to depart, but the night before his cook had enjoyed one too many flagons of ale at his favorite tavern, tripped over a kender trying to "borrow" his purse, and fallen hard against the stone-flagged floor. His subsequent broken arm and concussion had left him unable to fulfill his duties.

Garzan was livid.

By the time the noon sun poured golden light across the smoking volcanoes, everyone in the Souk Bazaar knew Garzan was looking for an experienced cook who could leave the next day. Few thought he'd find one.

Lucy, Ulin, and Challie heard the news shortly after they walked into the rug merchant's shop. Garzan was there, talking to his overseer at the top of his substantial lungs.

"The fool fell over a kender. A kender! Can you believe it? Drunk as a farmer on mushroom spirits. If he survives the blow to his head, I just might throttle him and finish the business." Garzan stood behind the board that served as a display table and counter. Rolled rugs lay in stacks about him while others hung like tapestries on the walls or lay in piles on the tables around the big room. A second man stood beside him, his dark bearded face thunderous.

"Where will I find another cook so quickly?" Garzan continued. He brought a meaty fist down on the board with a crash. Suddenly he saw Ulin and his companions, and anger evaporated from his face to be replaced by a large smile. A Khur by birth, Garzan was a stocky man with swarthy skin, black hair to his shoulders, and mustaches of impressive length. His mercurial temper was known to all who dealt with him, as was his habit to drive hard bargains.

"A pleasant afternoon, good people. What may I do to help you? Would you like to see a rug?" he offered, waving an expansive hand at his wares.

Challie bowed her head in greeting. "I am Chalcedony of Flotsam. It is not rugs that bring us to see your inestimable self, my good sir, but fleeces."

"Ah, yes! So you wish to inspect my fleeces. They are the finest Schallsea wool. Excellent texture, long fiber . . ." He went on at some length describing the qualities of the wool.

Ulin and Challie let him talk in spite of their own impatience and Lucy's increasing fidgets. Khurs loved to talk, to sing, to tell tales, and to bargain, often in extravagant tones and phrases. Even dwarves had learned the hard way that it was not polite to interrupt a Khurish merchant in the midst of establishing a deal.

The merchant carried on for several minutes then asked the nature of their business with fleece.

"In truth, good sir, we do not wish to purchase the fleece. We wish to travel with it." Challie replied with a bland smile. "If you are kind enough to remember, I talked to you last month about a return journey to Flotsam."

Garzan's left eyebrow rose upward. "Indeed. So, you inquire about my caravans? How far do you intend to go?"

"We are traveling to Flotsam," Challie replied, her words clipped with barely suppressed annoyance.

"Ah." A speculative light lit the merchant's eyes. "Yes. Caravans are the only way to reach that fair port from Sanction without months of sea travel."

Ulin bowed in respect. "And we heard yours were the largest, the safest, and most prestigious."

Lucy fought to keep a grin off her face. They'd heard no such thing, but she was beginning to understand the process of negotiation with a Khur.

"It is unfortunate you did not hear that I no longer allow passengers on my caravans," Garzan said with mock gravity. "You must understand, the trail we must take to bypass the siege forces is long, the way is dangerous, and the tribute we must pay to her Magnificence, Malystryx, is exorbitant. Every beast and wagon I send is fully laden, every driver and guard who attends the goods must work to their utmost to see to the safe arrival of the caravan. Passengers are a hindrance and a nuisance."

Undismayed by the Khur's words, Ulin cut off Challie's indignant exclamation with a chop of his hand. He said smoothly, "Even ones who pay well?"

Garzan rubbed his chin thoughtfully. "Perhaps if there was something you could do . . ." he said, studying the trio before him.

Ulin, Challie, and Lucy exchanged puzzled glances. Working for their passage had not occurred to any of them. What could they do for a caravan? Challie was short, even for a dwarf, and knew nothing useful about driving a

freight wagon. Lucy was pleasant-looking and totally in-
nocuous, and Ulin was lean and gawky. All of them were
dressed in plain, travel-worn garments with nothing more
than daggers and one small axe between them. Not one of
them could pass as a guard, mercenary, or even wagon
driver. Just what did the merchant have in mind?

Garzan fastened his gaze on Lucy. "Can you cook?" he
asked.

Lucy chuckled. "I can barely boil water, but he can."
She pointed to Ulin. "He was raised in an inn."

Ulin blinked as pieces began to fall into place. Truth-
fully, he had not been raised at the Inn of the Last Home.
He'd had his own home with his parents and sister, but he
had learned many of his grandmother's recipes and secrets,
and he *could* boil water.

"Is this true?" Garzan demanded, his excitement barely
suppressed behind his sharp gaze.

Ulin lifted his hands in a dismissive gesture, "I am training to be an alchemist, yet in truth, the only differences between the two arts are the ingredients and the final
results."

The Khur merchant leaned over the table between
them, his eyes shadowed by his heavy brows. "You need
conveyance to Flotsam. I need a cook. Perhaps we can
make a deal agreeable to all . . . ?"

Challie crossed her arms and kept her face blank. If Ulin
was willing to do this, she would not argue. The wages
they earned would save the city council a fat fee. "What
would the job entail?"

"I have a cook wagon already outfitted and stocked. The
caravan leaves tonight at midnight. You must be able to
drive a wagon and cook enough to feed at least twenty-five
people. You may be called upon to tend injuries, fight brigands, and perhaps"—he pointed a finger at Lucy—"defend
yourselves. My men will respect you if you feed them well,
but if they do not like the food, they will not hesitate to tell
you about it with their fists or knives."

"Fair enough," replied Ulin.

Garzan clapped his hands, and an older woman poked her head out through a curtained doorway behind him. "Bring kefre and cakes for five!" he ordered. "Writing a contract is hungry business."

In a few minutes Garzan, his overseer, Ulin, Lucy, and Challie were seated around a small table in the back room. The elderly woman served them strong, black kefre—a drink made from the bark of one of the few shrubs that grew in the Khurs' desert homeland—in tiny cups and plates of cakes with bowls of honey for dipping.

Lucy was still hungry after her bout of seasickness and plunged into the fare with gusto. Challie ate sparingly and, for once, let Ulin do the talking.

The men sipped their beverages and exchanged pleasantries for several minutes before Ulin asked, "I am curious to know. How do you take your caravans past the Knights of Neraka? Haven't they been guarding the passes for years?"

The rug merchant nibbled his honey cake and chuckled as he wiped away the crumbs. "It is as I thought. You are new to Sanction."

"Just passing through."

"Ah. Well, the Dark Knights covet this city for themselves, but they are not yet strong enough to take it. All they do is sit in the passes and prevent honest travelers and merchants from passing through."

"But not dishonest ones?" Ulin remarked with a glimmer of a smile.

Garzan leaned back in his chair and twirled one end of his mustache through his thumb and forefinger. "Not the *clever* ones. We of the Khur have our own trails and our own ways over the mountains. If the Dark Knights know of our paths, they do not interfere. They owe us too much for their own trade to want to annoy our chiefs."

Ulin nodded once. "Glad to hear it. So . . . what are your terms?"

A long and, to the women, somewhat tedious discussion followed about fees, wages, tasks for Ulin's two "helpers," and the length of the contract. Garzan's overseer swiftly wrote the terms on a piece of parchment as they were agreed upon.

"Most of the train is bound for Khuri-Khan," Garzan informed them. "However, some of the wagons will be added to another smaller caravan that will proceed to Flotsam. Sadly, we do not send many caravans there anymore. Since Malys destroyed their harbor facilities, their business has fallen considerably."

"I can imagine," Ulin said.

Garzan rose to his feet and opened his arms wide to include them all. "A safe journey, my friends. May the wind always blow at your back and your axles stay strong."

Ulin, Lucy, and Challie rose and bowed their thanks.

The second stage of the journey began.

Chapter Three

"D o you ever keep a journal of your travels?" Lucy asked Ulin one afternoon. They were driving the wagon at the end of the caravan on the last leg of their journey from Delphon to Flotsam. Ulin and Lucy sat on the driver's seat while Challie took her turn trying to nap on the pile of bedrolls behind them.

Lucy squirmed her abused backside to a different angle on the seat—not that it made much difference. The seat was little more than a board nailed across the front of the cook wagon and was probably used as an instrument of torture in Khurish prisons.

Ulin gazed at the distant horizon, his golden brown eyes lost in a world of private speculation and memories. When he did not answer right away, Lucy nudged him and repeated her question.

He heard her this time. "A journal? No, I've never had time. Why?"

"Because if you were writing one now, I have several

words I would like to include."

"Such as?"

Lucy swiped her sleeve over her sweating face. "Hot."

"Dull," Challie called from the back.

"Painful," Lucy added. She held up her hands to examine the new calluses on her hands.

"Cold," said the dwarf.

Lucy began to tap her hand on the sideboard and chant.

> "Sweat at noon.
> Freeze at night.
> Endless wind.
> Nothing in sight.
>
> "Dunes of sand.
> An empty waste.
> We cook for the Khurs,
> Who have no taste."

She was rewarded by a dry chuckle from the rear.

"I'll be sure to write that down," Ulin said in tones as arid as the land around them. Things were getting bad when drivel like that was entertaining. Not that he disagreed with them. Their choice words for his imaginary journal were well chosen and could be repeated every day for the past twenty-eight days.

In the beginning, the journey had started with some variation and interest. The caravan slipped out of Sanction in the dead of night on a bleak path that skirted the large camp of the Knights of Neraka, who guarded the east pass. From there, the caravan wound through the Khalkist Mountains just north of the ogre realm of Blöde. The path was narrow and rough, full of ruts and rocks and holes big enough to break an axle, but it *was* a road. It wound beside a narrow, rushing river for some miles then began the steady and arduous climb over the high mountains.

It was then that Ulin began to develop a real respect for the drivers of the wagons and the small, tough oxen that pulled them. There were ten cargo wagons in all, with narrow beds and canvas tops that held a mixed cargo of fleeces, bags of pumice, a large box of wool dyes, and a few cases of delicacies such as dried mushrooms, bottles of Sanction wines, and dried fruit. Each wagon had a driver who drove his four oxen with only a whip and his voice, a skill Ulin could not master no matter how often he tried. Fortunately, Akkar-bin, the caravan master, took pity on his oxen the second day and produced a pair of bay draft horses for the cook wagon. Ulin ignored the brands of the Dark Knights on the horses' hips and did not ask where they came from.

In addition to the drivers, there were four assistants and ten heavily-armed guards who rode nimble-footed Khurish horses at the head and rear of the train. Including Ulin and his companions, the caravan had a respectable number of twenty-seven, a number large enough to discourage all but the largest bands of brigands.

Ulin struggled for several days before he learned the knack of cooking for so many hungry people. After the second night of burned potatoes and skimpy helpings, the swarthy Khurs warned him he had one more night to prove himself or they'd stake him to a boulder and leave him for the vultures. Ulin took no chances. He cooked a simple stew based on one of Tika's recipes, and he tripled the ingredients. The Khurs devoured all of it and gave him a reprieve for one more night. Each night it was the same. He would cook vast amounts of something simple and filling, and the Khurs would eat it and give him one more night's reprieve.

It did not take long for Ulin and his "helpers" to establish a routine. Every morning before dawn, he, Lucy, and Challie fetched water, lit a fire, cooked gruel, bacon, and fry bread for breakfast, harnessed the horses, scrubbed the pans, packed the wagon, and drove through the day over

the mountainous roads. At dusk they set up camp, built a
fire, fetched the water, cooked the dinner, cleaned the
dishes, tended the horses, and prepared for the next day.
After a few hours of sleep they repeated it all over again.
Ulin could not imagine how one man could do it alone.

Once the caravan descended from the mountains, it entered the desert wastes of the Khurs and the arid domain
of the red dragon overlord, Malystryx. The work routine
continued much the same. Only the landscape changed
from rock and mountain to sand, barren hills, and scattered oases that were hot by noon and shivering cold by
night. The drudgery of work and travel continued, with
only one short break when the caravan reached the city of
Khuri-Khan and paused for a day while the caravan master
reorganized his master's wagons and drivers and sent the
new train on to Flotsam.

Ulin often wondered during the long hours of driving
through the dreary, dun-colored landscape of what used to
be Balifor, if this was worth the intensive effort.

Now that the trek was almost over, he could say "possibly" it was. They had saved some of their coins and earned
enough to buy a wagon for the return to Sanction. They
were all toughened by the work and the difficult travel, and
they had learned a few things from the Khurs: how to prepare kefre, how to spice a stew so it burned off several
layers of one's tongue, and how to wrap a burnoose to stay
on in a sand storm.

Best of all, to Ulin's mind, Lucy had learned to cook. At
least she could start a fire and boil water now. Together,
they made a good partnership.

"Akkar-bin is coming." Lucy broke into his thoughts.

Ulin straightened and saw a rider trot his horse down
the file of wagons toward them. Akkar-bin, the caravan
master, looked grim when he wheeled his stallion around
beside the cook wagon—but then Ulin had never seen him
look any other way. The man was the most laconic, humorless barbarian he had ever met, and not once on the

long trip from Sanction had he seen him laugh. At least Akkar-bin wasn't arrogant or contemptuous of the foreigners in his caravan like some of his guards. He was too emotionless for that.

"The point guard has found sign of draconians," Akkar-bin said without preamble. "We'll stop early tonight." His horse sprang forward, and he rode back up the line without further explanation.

Lucy watched him go. "Wonderful. I suppose that means we won't get to the watering hole tonight, which means no water." She swiped her sleeve across her forehead again, wiping the dust and sweat off in muddy streaks.

Ulin made no comment. The news of the draconians did not surprise him. He knew bands of draconians, goblins, ogres, brigands, and exiles roamed the desert. Some were in the service of Malys and patrolled her extensive holdings. The more desperate ones were out for their own survival and attacked likely caravans or travelers at every opportunity. The caravan guards had seen indications of some of the marauders before, but this was the first time Akkar-bin decided to stop the caravan before sunset. Not that Ulin faulted him. He knew from experience that draconians—the foul, sentient spawn that were hatched years ago from corrupted eggs of good dragons—were ferocious fighters. The caravan would need to prepare.

Behind the caravan the brassy sun dropped slowly toward the blurred horizon where the desert faded into a sunburned sky. There was no wind, so the dust stirred up by the wagon wheels and oxen hooves hung like smoke over their heads. In three hours time it would be dark. If the draconians were out there, they would probably attack after nightfall.

Ulin scanned the desert. The land all about was drab: faded browns, tans, reds, and shades of sand. Seen from afar the desert looked like a wide, featureless plain, but in fact it rolled and rippled in solid waves, a tidal pattern engraved into the land by the wind. Here and there, tumbled, twisted ridges of rock broke through the sand and provided meager shade for the stunted, scanty shrubs that struggled to grow. It was a land that required determination to survive.

As Ulin studied the line of far hills to the east, he noticed a hint of green where late spring rains on the coast encouraged grasses and low trees to grow. They were so close to Flotsam, he fancied he could smell the sea breeze, yet he knew their proximity was part of their danger. The caravan was barely twenty miles from Blood Bay, which was close enough to the coast for marauders to find shelter but too far for travelers to expect help. If only the caravan could just keep moving until they reached the streets of Flotsam. Ulin was more than ready for this journey to be over.

Ulin raised his gaze to the vast darkening sky and studied it like a man hungry for something he cannot find. There was no sign of Malys. The monstrous red was probably in her volcanic lair in the midst of her Desolation to the southeast of Flotsam. But Ulin was not looking for her. He searched for another dragon: a gold named Sunrise who had become his friend, his soul mate, and his partner in magic. Sunrise had helped him years before in a confrontation with Malys and had saved his life more than once, but when magic began to fail, something happened to the young gold. For no discernible reason, Sunrise vanished without a trace. Ulin was still puzzling over the missing gold when his young wife and their two children died in a terrible plague, leaving the young mage empty, aching, and reeling from his losses. Even then Fate was not finished with the son of Palin Majere. A year later the forces of the green dragon, Beryl, destroyed the Academy of Sorcery—with some inadvertent help from Ulin—and captured Palin. Only Lucy with her strong heart and her shining, green eyes had held him back from the abyss of despair. Although he was forced to accept the painful truth that his wife was gone, Ulin could not quite believe or accept that Sunrise was dead. Somewhere, sometime, Ulin hoped he would look up and see the dragon's golden form winging toward him.

He let out a slow breath. It would not happen this day. The sky remained empty, and his hope remained unanswered.

About an hour before sunset and far short of the planned stop at the water hole, the caravan master brought his wagons to the top of a broad hill and had them draw together in a circle. In the last light of day the tribesmen gathered all the dried dung and dead brush they could find for a fire. They cut thorny bushes and formed them into a corral for the oxen. The horses were watered from the precious store of barrels kept on the wagons for emergencies, then they were fed and tethered inside the circle of wagons.

Ulin and Challie lit the fire and hurriedly prepared a quick meal for the men while Lucy took care of their draft horses.

They were scrubbing the pans with sand in the lingering light of early evening when Akkar-bin approached them.

His cold eyes regarded them for a moment before he spoke. "Have you weapons to defend yourselves if the draconians attack?"

Lucy glanced up from where she was kneeling in the sand and hefted the large iron skillet she had been cleaning. "I was taught by a master," she said, her expression and voice completely serious.

Ulin knew exactly what master she was referring to, for he had seen his grandmother clear the Inn at closing time with a similar "weapon." He almost laughed when he saw Akkar-bin's face. The Khur's humorless gaze stared at Lucy as if he thought she had slipped into dementia.

"We have only small weapons," Ulin said, drawing the man's attention away from Lucy. "Is there a sword I could borrow?"

Akkar-bin grunted a reply and jerked his hand toward the wagon containing the shipment of swords. "Take one from the crate. They are straight blades intended for a customer on the Blood Coast. They will be easier for you to handle than our scimitars."

With another blank look at Lucy he turned on his heel and strode away.

Lucy snorted a suppressed laugh. "That man is hopeless. There are rocks in the desert with more imagination."

"Maybe," Ulin agreed. "But he does know his business. I don't know why you bother trying to goad him."

"He's a challenge," Lucy replied, her grin wicked.

Ulin left the women scrubbing pots and went to the wagon Akkar-bin had indicated. With the help of the driver, he found a long crate labeled WOOL DYES near the top of the load. Curious, he pried off the lid. Inside was a layer of hand-sewn bags containing various colors of dye. Beneath that lay perhaps a dozen swords, carefully wrapped in lengths of thick felt. Ulin pondered just who this customer was—a fuller who kept his own army? The driver winked and handed him several swords to try.

After a few minutes of hefting and testing, he found one to his liking and thanked the driver. Although Ulin was competent with a scimitar, he preferred the straight blade of a good broadsword, and this one seemed to be a fine one with a good leather grip and excellent balance. He carried his new sword back to the cook wagon and helped Lucy and Challie settle things for the night.

It proved to be a long and tense night that ended uneventfully with a red sun pushing above the skyline at dawn. There had been no sign of draconians or anything else threatening, and the caravan remained unmolested. Weary and relieved, Ulin and the girls fed the Khurs and prepared to get underway.

The caravan made good time that day, stopping only once at a tiny watering hole to refill the barrels and water the stock. The guards remained alert both before and behind the caravan, and Akkar-bin sent out scouts to keep a watch for signs of marauders. Near midday the caravan master called a halt at a small oasis already occupied by a clan of nomads. The safety afforded by the additional numbers of fighting men more than compensated the caravan for the fee charged by the clan chief for use of the wells. That night the Khurs slept well after thoroughly enjoying the services and refreshments offered by the tribesmen.

Heads were aching the next morning when Akkar-bin roused his crew and got them moving. Ulin had to treat several minor injuries won in fights the night before and a number of hangovers brought on by the powerful Khurish liquor. Nevertheless, the wagons were on the road in short order and headed east for their final push to Flotsam.

* * * * *

Perhaps it was the afternoon heat that bore down on them, sapping their strength and dulling their senses. Perhaps it was the effects of celebrating the night before. Or maybe it was the lack of sleep or the relief brought on by the impending end of the journey. Whether it was one factor or a combination of several, the effect was a lethargy that settled over the entire caravan several hours after noon. The men's voices stilled until the only steady sounds from the train were the jingling of the harnesses and the plod of the oxen's hooves on the sand-covered road. The drivers dozed on their seats.

The rearguard, annoyed by the cloud of dust kicked up the oxen, gradually dropped farther and farther back until the occupants of the last wagons could no longer see them. Akkar-bin and the point guards fought their drowsiness and tried to stay alert, but their attention was wavering when the caravan entered a short ravine between two tall hills.

The cook wagon rolled along at the rear of the caravan as usual. Lucy drove this afternoon while Challie sat beside her and Ulin slept in the back under the shade of the canvas cover. Lucy breathed a sigh of gratitude when they entered the ravine. Red rock walls reared over their heads and cast the narrow trail into shadow. It wasn't much of a change, but any interruption from the fierce sun was welcome. She glanced back down the trail and still could not see the rearguard through the hanging clouds of dust, nor could she see much in the ravine ahead. The head of the caravan was lost from sight among the steep walls of stone.

The first indication of trouble they heard was a thud on the side of the wagon.

Challie looked over her side and cried, "Lucy! That's an arrow!"

Abruptly, the air seemed full of arrows, dropping down from above. Several passed close to the women or slammed into the wooden slats of the wagon. One struck their wheel horse on his flank. He screamed in fear and pain, and both horses reared in panic, causing the wagon to jerk and pitch.

Just ahead, the driver of the freight wagon slumped in his seat. His oxen stopped in their tracks, blocking the path.

A shrill scream followed by several more pierced the hot, dusty air. Many voices shouted now, from behind and ahead and from above.

Ulin jolted upright as Challie fell backward over the seat and landed on top of him. "What's happening? What's going on?" he shouted, still groggy from sleep.

The canvas cover of the wagon blocked his view, but it did not stop the arrows. Two ripped through the cover and embedded in the wooden cupboard. Cooking pans fell from their hooks in clattering clangs. Challie lay flat, gasping for breath.

"We're under attack!" Challie shouted. She tried to roll off Ulin and grab her axe.

"Ulin, help me!" Lucy called, her voice full of urgency.

Ulin struggled through the bedrolls and over Challie. He snatched his sword and climbed over the seat.

Lucy had both hands on the reins and fought to control the plunging horses. Her face was pale under her sunburn, and her lips were pressed into a bloodless line.

Behind them came more shouts and muffled curses. Some voices Ulin recognized as draconian, while others seemed human but used a language he did not know. Someone screamed a Khurish insult and the clash of weapons rang in the dust and haze. A riderless horse careened by. The roar and crash of fighting sounded along the line of wagons, too, yet Ulin and Lucy could not yet see who was attacking the caravan.

Clutching his sword, Ulin jumped down, ran to the horses, and grabbed their bridles to calm them down.

"Lucy!" he heard Challie shout. "Back here!"

Ulin's heart leaped to his throat. He let go of the horses to rush to her aid, when something big and heavy dropped out of the sky. Large, leathery wings flapped, washing a foul odor into his face, and a screech of fighting rage pierced his ears as a Kapak draconian glided down from the rock wall and thudded to the ground by the horses. It crouched for a second on all fours then rose to two legs, its wings fanning the dust.

The Kapak's lizardlike face split in a hideous grin. With a swift movement, he slashed his sword across the throat of the nearest horse, and warm blood sprayed his muscular chest and face. The horse staggered against his teammate and fell, dragging the frenzied bay with him.

Ulin backed away, his eyes on the big creature. By the gods, he hated draconians. This was a particularly ugly one with a mane of coarse dark hair that fell across its head and shoulders, bulky muscles, and thick coppery skin. It wore no clothes or armor. Only a festoon of necklaces and chains hung around its thick neck, and a Solamnic knight's helmet, several sizes too small, perched on its horny head. Its wings clapped together across its back, and with a yowl of glee, it raised its bloody sword and sprang after Ulin.

The young man raised his sword to ward off the blow, but he knew better than to face a Kapak's venomous saliva and curving claws without so much as a shield. He needed help, and he feared desperately for Lucy. Step by step he backed away from the wagon, keeping the draconian's attention focused on him.

The beast stamped after him, its lips curled over sharp fangs in a hungry snarl.

* * * * *

Behind the wagon and out of Ulin's sight, Lucy and Challie had their hands full.

A man, a Khurish exile by the look of his ragged robes and rusty scimitar, rushed the back of the cook wagon, waving his blade to intimidate the two women who quailed in the wagon amidst the bags and boxes of food. He grinned foolishly at their fear and put a hand on the tailboard to swing himself up into the wagon.

A silver axe flashed in the hand of the dwarf and slashed into the Khur's hand between his middle fingers. He reared back and his mouth opened to release a screech of pain just as Lucy lifted two iron skillets and slammed them together with his head in between. He collapsed back to the ground and did not stir.

Challie and Lucy had only a moment to celebrate before they heard the pounding of horses' hooves from the ravine behind them. Three of the rearguard riders stormed into view through the dust and shadows, closely pursued by two humans on horseback and a second Kapak draconian wearing a battle harness and carrying a mace.

One Khur, riddled with arrows, barely clung to his terrified mount, and even as Lucy and Challie pulled back into the shadowy interior of the wagon, the Kapak bounded up beside the horse and raked a clawed hand across the Khur's face. The rider fell shrieking into the dirt, convulsed into a rigid arch, and died. The draconian hissed with pleasure and smashed the man's head.

The last two guards saw the cook wagon and kicked their horses toward it, perhaps hoping for shelter or a place of defense. Swift as they were, the mounted brigands were faster. The outlaws raised their scimitars and rode down the guards. Swords rang and flashed in the hazy light. A horse screamed. The two Khurs had their own swords in their hands, and they fought back like frenzied wolves.

Lucy sucked in her breath as she watched them. She realized the Khurs were not going to make it to the wagon. If they fell without seriously wounding their attackers, she and Challie would be left facing two armed men and a Kapak with only an axe and a couple of iron skillets.

She didn't have much time to think or worry. The second Khur toppled from his saddle, his body split across the abdomen by his enemy's scimitar. The brigands shouted insults at his corpse and turned their full attention to the last man.

Lucy did not wait any longer. She reached into a barrel and pulled out a handful of small, reddish potatoes. Closing her eyes, she forced herself to concentrate on a spell she remembered practicing time and again. Originally, the spell had been used as a joke in the slow, sleepy hours of late nights at the Academy, and a few times she had used it to discourage vermin or drive away a would-be burglar. It was simple. It was basic. It was effective. But she had never tried it on something as big as a draconian.

Fiercely, she forced away all distracting sounds and focused on the magic around her. From the wood, the earth, the dust, she drew the energy and shaped it to her will. It had to work, she promised herself. It had to! She forced each word of the spell into the magic and, to her surprise, she felt the power respond. It did not fade from her grasp or dissipate into emptiness. Like a long-lost friend it surged into her embrace, warm, familiar, and oh, so welcome. Desperately, she poured the magic fire into her handful of potatoes and felt them become fiery hot to the touch.

"Lucy, hurry!" Challie's voice rose in fear.

Lucy opened her eyes and saw the two men circling their horses in front of her. Their bearded faces leered at her.

The Kapak squatted behind them, his leathery wings folded, his copper skin splashed with blood. His eyes glowed a bilious green as he tore the limbs off the bodies of the Khur guards and searched their clothes for valuables.

Lucy hurriedly dumped her hot potatoes into the skillet before her fingers burned. Worry and fear made her hands shake. The potatoes didn't look quite right and felt much hotter than she remembered. The magic had worked, but something was wrong.

Then she had no more time. The two men dismounted and clambered up the tailboard of the wagon, daggers in their hands.

Challie cursed in Dwarvish.

Her heart racing, Lucy threw a potato at the nearest attacker. It struck him on his leather vest and burst like an overcooked baked potato: hot, mealy, and steaming. Lucy gasped in dismay. The man grinned and reached up to brush it off, but before he could touch it, a strange expression covered his face. The pale potato bits flared white hot, and where the potato stuck, flesh and fabric burst into flame. The man screamed a hideous, racking cry of agony and fell back, flailing at his burning body. His companion stared in horror.

Challie's mouth fell open as she watched the man writhe in the dirt. She knew Lucy had been a sorceress at one time, but she had never seen anything like this.

Lucy didn't have time to see the final effects of her potato bomb. The second man drew back and attempted to thrust his sword into the interior to reach her. Another potato left her hand and burst on his neck and shoulder.

The results were just like the first one. The split tuber burst into a brilliant white light that sizzled and hissed, setting the man's clothes on fire. He beat frantically at his clothing, tried to tear it off, then he, too, collapsed, a screaming, smoking ruin. The first man was already dead. A hideous stench filled the air from the scorched corpses.

"Gods!" breathed Lucy. This wasn't exactly what she had intended when she formed this spell.

Just then the Kapak looked up from its task of stripping the dead bodies. Its hooded eyes met Lucy's and its breath hissed between its teeth in a snarl.

"You're next," Lucy muttered. She snatched up the last two potatoes, ignoring the heat that singed her fingers, and clambered down from the wagon. In the distance, somewhere down the ravine, she heard the ring of weapons and the shouts of fighting men. Far away, so soft she might have imagined it, she thought she heard the baying of hunting horns.

Her head lowered, her arm drawn back to throw, Lucy advanced toward the draconian. She needed a good shot, for she had only these two potatoes left, and her aim was notoriously bad.

The Kapak's next move was so quick it caught her by surprise. It sprang sideways on all fours, then rose to its full height and leaped at her, its wings spread like a great cloak. That was its worst mistake.

Lucy had no time to adjust her aim. Her teeth gritted, she hurled the small potato at the beast and heard a soft splat before she dropped to the ground and covered her head with her arms.

The draconian sailed over her body and crashed to the ground. Crouching, it sniffed at the potato bits on its right wing and shoulder. Its lips curled into a grimace of pain just as the potato began to smoke. In seconds the draconian was enveloped in white fire. Hideous, piercing shrieks burst from its twisted snout. Kapaks never died neatly, and this one was no exception. While Lucy and Challie watched, its smoking body slowly stilled in death and began to dissolve. A dark, loathsome liquid oozed from its body, forming a puddle close to the wagon. Swiftly the entire body broke down and vanished into the liquid.

The ravine suddenly became very quiet.

Lucy thought she would vomit. She gingerly clutched the last potato and took several deep breaths. "No!" She called wildly to Challie who wanted to climb down. "Stay away from that liquid. It's acid. Go out the front. We've got to find Ulin."

She hurried around to the horses and found one dead in a pool of blood. The other lay trapped beside it, nearly dead itself from terror and exhaustion. There was no sign of Ulin.

Clutching her axe, Challie came up beside her. "Where is he? Why is it so quiet?" she asked softly, afraid to speak any louder.

Lucy's answer came out like a sob. "I don't know." She hurried forward up the line of wagons.

Chapter
Four

They passed three stalled freight wagons before they heard angry voices and the hissing snarl of a draconian just ahead. One of the Khur drivers lay dead on the ground near his wagon, his face and neck ripped open.

An inarticulate sound escaped Lucy's lips, and she hurried forward. The trail curved slightly, the rock walls blocking her view until she passed the third wagon, then the defile straightened and widened enough for several wagons to pass abreast. There the sun slanted down into the valley and illuminated four fighters: two Khur drivers, Ulin, and the second Kapak draconian. Lucy skidded to a halt and put out her arm to stop Challie.

The men did not notice the women at first. They circled the beast, using their swords to keep him within their circle. None of them had a shield. They were panting and drenched with sweat, and they looked exhausted. The draconian growled and stamped as it flapped its wings. It had only a long dagger, but Lucy could see from its unhurried movements and regular breathing that it was just biding its time until one of the men made a mistake.

"Lucy, keep away!" she heard Ulin yell.

"No, Ulin! Listen!" she cried. "Back away! All of you!" She edged toward them, the potato burning hot in her hand. "I made a spell. It worked! Just get away from the Kapak."

The Khurs did not understand her. They stayed where they were, too close to the Kapak for her throw her weapon. Ulin understood, but he did not believe it.

"That's impossible," he yelled, one eye on the draconian and one on Lucy. "How could a spell work now?"

Lucy ignored the faint derision she heard in his voice. "It just did," she insisted. "Now, get out of the way!"

She made her demand in Common, loud and urgent, and this time the drivers understood. They shot a startled look at the woman, then at Ulin, and stumbled back out of her path, leaving a gap in their defenses.

The opening was what the draconian was looking for. Giving a roar of defiance, it whirled to face Ulin, snapped its tail like a whip, and lunged to bury its claws and blade in the pale man's chest. Ulin managed to avoid the viscous thrust and twisted out of the way of the draconian's attack. Pivoting, the draconian sprang into the air, beating hard with its wings to lift itself up over Ulin's head, and again it launched itself at the man.

The force of the draconian's attack slammed Ulin to the ground. He fell hard, and the creature pounced on top of him, its heavy weight forcing the air from his lungs. Slavering and growling, it tried to stab him with the dagger as he struggled to defend himself.

Lucy screamed and threw her potato hard and fast against the draconian's back. The tuber burst into white pulp against its dark, muscular back.

This strange new attack from the rear startled the Kapak. He sprang to his feet to face Lucy, his wings flat against his back. Then the pain hit him.

Lucy saw the smoke and the white fire ignite on his back, and she dashed to Ulin's side. "Come on," she told him. "Get out of its way. It's going to die."

Her urgency propelled him to his feet and sent him running out of range. He knew all too well what happened to dead Kapaks. The drivers, Challie, Lucy, and Ulin watched, awed and fascinated, as the draconian's burning body collapsed and slowly dissolved into a smoking pool of acid.

"Great gods!" Ulin exclaimed. "Lucy, how did you do that?"

She looked up at his face, her green eyes filled with confusion, excitement, and a glint of fear. "I'm not sure. I—"

"*You* did that?" A new voice exclaimed. "Boys, it looks like we've found ourselves a sorceress."

Startled, Lucy and Ulin saw a troop of warriors halted on the trail, staring at the puddled draconian and her with various expressions of awe and surprise. Akkar-bin and three of his guards were with the troop and looked equally stunned.

Ulin had seen some mixed bands in his life, but he had never seen a troop as strange as this one. He counted fifteen in all: five Khurs on horseback, two kender on ponies, a wild elf, three men of indeterminate background, and two dwarves in light armor. All were heavily armed and all wore a silver emblem on their tunics that looked something like a wolf's head.

Their leader sat on a tall gray horse, his lean handsome face tanned by the sun and his pale grayish clothes immaculate. His hair was silver, though he appeared to be young, and his ears bore the slender points of a person with elven blood. He beamed at Lucy and dismounted, revealing an athletic grace and energy that confirmed his youth.

"Spread out," the leader ordered his band. "Search for the rest of the brigands." Talking excitedly among themselves, the warriors split into groups and moved off to obey their commander. He made a straight line to Lucy, bowed over her hand, and said, "My Lady Sorceress, this is indeed an honor. May I introduce myself? I am the Silver Fox, Captain of—"

"That's impossible," Ulin snapped. "You're too young." He immediately regretted his outburst.

The man turned his wide smile to Ulin and bowed to him as well. "I am too young," he agreed affably, "to be the original Silver Fox, but I am the third man to bear that name. We're trying to keep the reputation going, you see. The revered resistance leader, the dreaded scourge of ogres, goblins, and draconians, the vaunted master of the Thieves Guild, the roving ranger of the desert realms . . . The Silver Fox, feared throughout Malys's realm." He flourished his sword and struck a dramatic pose.

Lucy laughed and Challie rolled her eyes.

Ulin felt his annoyance toward the man fade a little. It was difficult to dislike someone who saw such humor in his situation—as long as the man kept his distance from Lucy. He moved beside her and took her hand, making it clear where his loyalties lay. Lucy cast a twinkling glance at him.

"Please excuse my manners," Ulin said. "It has been a busy afternoon."

"I noticed. And who are you?" asked the Silver Fox, his eyes on Lucy.

"I am Lucy, late of Solace. This is Challie of Flotsam, and my betrothed, Ulin, also of Solace. It is a pleasure to meet you, the, uh . . . sir . . . Silver Fox."

Her emphasis on "betrothed" did not escape the man's notice. The half-elf dipped his head once in acknowledgment and winked at her. "Call me Lysandros. That's my own name." He turned to the dwarf and gave her a brief nod. "Chalcedony, it's good to see you back."

Akkar-bin chose that moment to approach. He looked grimmer than ever. "Get back to the cook wagon, you three. We will pull out as soon as the wagons can be readied."

The resistance leader turned slowly on the caravan

master. All affability vanished behind a cold, angry mask. "You were a fool to take your caravan on this short-cut. You know this is a favorite ambush site."

In unison Lucy, Challie, and Ulin turned accusing eyes on Akkar-bin.

The Khur drew himself up. "We hadn't seen sign of the draconians since yesterday," he said defensively. "I was trying to save time."

"Lucky for you, we've been watching for your caravan," Lysandros said, his pale eyes unblinking. "Lucky for you, you had this sorceress."

Akkar-bin's mouth worked over words he wanted to say. His face hardened, then he turned on his heel and went back to his men.

"Captain!" a pair of shrill voices shouted. "Captain, you've got to come see this!" The two kender dashed up to the half-elf, their topknots bouncing with excitement.

One kender, slightly taller than the other one, spoke first. "There's four dead men over there and another pool of acid."

"And a dead horse!" the second kender added rapidly. "Someone slashed its throat!"

"And body parts," the first finished. "There's blood everywhere, and the stench is awful!"

Lysandros held up a hand. "Slow down, boys. You talk so fast. I didn't catch all that."

Instead of a reply, the kender grabbed the Silver Fox's belt and hauled him toward the rear of the caravan.

Ulin, Lucy, and Challie followed.

"Four dead men and another draconian?" Ulin said so only Challie and Lucy could hear. "What in the name of Paladine did you use?"

"Well," Lucy hesitated. She was reluctant to admit she was as confused as he was. "I think one of the men they saw is the dead driver. The bandits killed the rearguard."

"Yes, but another draconian?"

"And three brigands," Challie put in.

Ulin blanched. "But what did you use?"

Lucy threw out her hands. "Potatoes! I was trying to create that old hot potato spell. It was the only thing I could think of. I just wanted to drive them away."

"*Potatoes?*" Ulin repeated. "What happened to them?"

"I don't know. I worked the spell as I always did, but something changed it."

They reached their cook wagon and saw a large group crowded around the back. The stink of the dead draconian's puddle already ripened in the hot air, and flies gathered on the slashed throat of the dead horse.

Lucy was relieved to see someone had cut the bay horse loose from his dead teammate and had tied the lathered animal to the back of the next wagon. She was not willing to view the carnage again behind the cook wagon, so while Ulin went to see, she untied the horse and walked him to relax his muscles.

Ulin came back after just a few minutes and fell into step beside her. "I don't know how you did it, but I am so proud of you." He chuckled. "And there I was trying to keep one Kapak away from you."

"For which I love you beyond words." She slipped her free arm through his.

He felt the nearness of her body so close to his, and an urge filled his mind to wrap his arms around her and hold her so that nothing could ever take her away from him. Not plagues, nor magic, nor draconians, nor even the gods. His fear for her, and his fear of more loss and grief, fed the urge until it took all his strength to keep his arms at his sides and his stride steady. "I could not bear to lose you, you know. Not now."

"I know," she said simply. She had met him when he was still mourning for his wife and two children dead from the plague. She had stood by him when the Academy he loved was destroyed, and she had watched him suffer through the disappearance of his father. She knew what she meant to him, and although the depth of his need for her scared her sometimes, it gave her the strength to wait for him to heal.

Together they walked the horse in companionable silence until he was cool and could be reharnessed alone to the cook wagon. That accomplished, Ulin reluctantly left her to help the Khurs bury their dead.

Meanwhile the Silver Fox and his troop helped Akkar bin put the caravan in order. Word spread fast about Lucy's battle, and everyone came at some point to see the bodies and the pools of dead draconians. A great deal of whispering and hushed talk went on, and more than one warrior came to stare at her in speculative interest until Lucy threatened to get her skillet and bash the next person who eyed her. Of course, the kender thought that would be fun to see and fetched the skillet for her. After that the men kept a respectful distance.

As soon as the bodies were removed, Lucy and Challie put the cook wagon back in order with the enthusiastic help of the two kender. Lucy made sure Challie's axe and their personal belongings were kept out of sight of the inquisitive young duo.

The kender took an immediate liking to Lucy and introduced themselves. The tallest was Cosmo Thistleknot, a cousin, he claimed proudly, of the renegade kender leader, Kronn Thistleknot. The other was a year or two younger and went by the name of Pease Stubbletoes. Both kender had hair the color of honey oak. Their eyes, like bright brown acorns, glinted at her behind rosy cheeks and fields of freckles. Both wore tan-colored tunics and breeches without a kender's usual clutter of pouches and overfilled pockets. Both were personable and insatiably curious, and yet Lucy noticed the two seemed not so frivolous. There was a serious, harder side that ran through these two like a vein of iron. They had grown up in the shadow of the red dragon overlord and had heard the horrific tales of the destruction of their homeland, Kendermore. They knew what few kender ever learn: fear and the will to fight. They were also very proud to be riding with the Silver Fox.

"He likes to be called Captain Fox when we're out trooping," Cosmo told the women.

"So what is this troop?" Lucy asked, hanging the skillets back on their hooks.

Pease tapped the silver fox emblem on his tunic. "We're the Vigilance Committee."

Cosmo swatted his arm. "We're the Vigilance Force," he corrected his friend. "The Committee meets in town."

"Which town?" asked Lucy.

"Why Flotsam, of course. We have a very active underground organization," Pease told her. "We fight ogres, defend caravans, raid the Dark Knights' patrols . . ."

Cosmo's foot flew out and kicked his companion's shin. "Shhh!" he whispered loudly. "You're not supposed to tell anyone!"

Pease rubbed his arm and glared at the other kender. "We can tell them. They're not Khurs or Knights of Neraka. That one's Chalcedony—obviously, she already knows. And *she's* a sorceress." He didn't add "so there!" but it rang as clear as a bell in his voice.

"My name is Lucy," she told them.

The kender broke off their argument and bowed politely.

"If you are going to stay in Flotsam, you must come visit us," Cosmo said. "We have the most disheveled hovels in town."

Lucy checked in surprise at his choice of words. She opened her mouth to say something, then closed it again and thought better of opening that topic of conversation. Kender could talk all day on some of their favorite subjects, and at the moment she was too tired to listen.

"Who's the tall man who likes you? Is he a sorcerer?" Pease asked as he pulled out drawers in the food cupboard.

Lucy came behind him and closed them again. She smiled a sad smile. "He used to be. His name is Ulin."

From outside, the captain's voice called his riders to mount, and to Lucy's relief, the kender hastily jumped out of the wagon to fetch their ponies. Several spoons, a bag of salt, and a tin of hot pepper disappeared with them, but Lucy didn't mind.

* * * * *

It was early evening before the wagons were ready to roll. Two drivers and seven guards had been buried by the road. The wounded had been bandaged, and the dead bandits were dumped in a gully for the scavengers. In the failing light of sunset the caravan set off under the escort of the Vigilance Force.

The miles rolled slowly by, and gradually the desolate hills gave way to grasslands dotted with copses of scrub oak, cedar, and wild olive trees. Trees in greater number had grown there once, until the powerful magic of the red dragon had changed the landscape and the weather and turned the lands into waste.

The single moon rose, shining and full-bellied, and cast a silver light on the dim trail. It was fully dark when Lysandros brought the caravan to a watering hole and called a halt. They were only eight miles from Flotsam, but the animals were weary and the wounded men needed rest. Ulin and his helpers made an easy meal, using all the remaining supplies left in the cook wagon. Everyone enjoyed the beans, spiced potatoes, flat bread, and bacon.

Dawn came, clean and clear and warm enough to promise another hot day. The caravan left shortly after daybreak and took the road over the grassy hills toward Flotsam.

Lucy drove, for Ulin had been pressed into service driving one of the freight wagons. Although he still could not manipulate the whip like the Khurs, Akkar-bin put him in the last ox wagon, knowing that on this gentle road, the oxen would simply follow the others. The caravan master then told Lysandros and his company to ride at the rear while he and his remaining guards rode at the front of the train.

Lysandros lifted one elegant eyebrow at that effrontery but chose to ignore it. He sent most of his riders on to Flotsam while he and a few others rode alongside the wagons.

Lucy soon realized why. As soon as the caravan was well underway, Challie tugged at her sleeve and pointed, and when Lucy looked around, she saw the captain riding his big gray close beside her. His silver gray hair shone in the early morning light, and his pale blue eyes gleamed like forget-me-nots against his tanned skin. A saber hung at his belt, and a silver horn was fastened to his saddle. He did not look up at her or say anything at first. He rode as if lost in thought and unaware he had pulled so far forward, yet Lucy saw him cast furtive glances at her, and she wondered why. She was honest enough with herself to know she was no beauty, so why was someone as dashing and handsome as the captain studying her so intently?

She saw Ulin glance back and frown at the rider. She could not resist giving him a smile and a wave. "So"—she turned to the captain—"you are a resistance leader and the master of the Thieves' Guild? That's an interesting combination."

The half-elf lifted his chin, his mouth curved in good humor. "In this region, the two jobs go well together."

"Are you related to the original Silver Fox?"

He rested his hand lightly on the hilt of his saber and nodded. "I am his youngest son. My oldest brother was the second Silver Fox until the Dark Knights caught up with him. We never found his body. Only this sword, which belonged to our father . . . and the dismembered bodies of his troop."

Lucy hid a grimace. She had lived in a free realm for so long that she could not imagine what life was like under the merciless control of a dragon overlord. She wondered for a hundredth time why her pleasure-loving, irresponsible, rogue of a father had come to Flotsam, and if he had really died in that fire. She heard Lysandros ask her a question, and she pulled out of her thoughts.

"What are we doing here among the Khurs?" She flipped her ponytail over her shoulder and laughed. "It was the only way we could get to Flotsam. I have come to find my father."

He looked up at her obviously intrigued. "Your father is in Flotsam? Who is he?"

Lucy was so busy shifting her attention back and forth from her task to her companion that she did not see the hard look Challie fired at the resistance leader. "It would be more accurate to ask who *was* he? The magistrate came to tell us he died. She asked us to come to Flotsam to identify a body."

Lysandros pretended to ignore the dwarf and said in a startled voice, "You traveled all the way from Sanction to identify a body?"

"Actually," Challie informed him coldly. "We've traveled all the way from Solace."

Both of the captain's eyebrows rose to his hairline. "Solace? But that's . . ."

"Ridiculous?" Lucy offered. "Foolhardy? Dangerous?"

"I was thinking 'far away.' What sort of man engenders such devotion in his family that they would risk so much for his corpse?"

"One who doesn't deserve it," Lucy replied. She caught the startled look on his face and gave her shoulders a slight shrug. "Maybe you knew him. His name was Kethril Torkay."

An odd, rather strangled sound forced itself past Lysandros's tight lips. His face turned the strangest shade of red. "Are you all right?" Lucy asked in genuine concern.

"I'm sorry," he managed to sputter. "Something just disagreed with my stomach. Excuse me, my lady." Making wheezing noises, he reined his horse around and trotted off into the dust.

"I hope he's not sick," Challie said in her driest tone.

"I'm sure he's fine. He probably just choked on the memory of my father," Lucy replied. The corners of her mouth turned down, and her hands tightened on the reins.

Challie's expression softened. "Surely your father wasn't that bad to you."

Lucy snorted. "He was a cheat, a con-man, a gambler, a womanizer, and a fake. He abandoned his wife and daughters, and he never bothered to write or visit or do anything to prove that he still cared about them. I'm glad he died a miserable death." Her voice hardened with each word until she was spitting them out like nails. The sudden intensity of her feelings took her by surprise. She had tried for years to bury her anger and resentment toward her father, and she thought she had been moderately successful, yet all it had taken was the reaction of a stranger and the sympathy of an acquaintance to jiggle loose her poorly constructed defenses. She closed her mouth with a snap and stared down at the rump of the bay horse.

The dwarf looked around, startled by Lucy's outburst. "Maybe he was, Lucy, but surely he must have had something positive about him to attract your mother. She seems to be a very nice person. Even if he did nothing else good, he fathered you and your sisters."

Challie's unlooked-for solicitude touched Lucy and surprised her. She shrugged, feeling slightly embarrassed. "I'm sorry. I shouldn't explode like that. He wasn't that awful. That was the problem. He had just enough good qualities that we all adored him. I just wish I could have seen him one more time." She fell silent, and her thoughts flowed back into the few memories she had of her father.

Chapter Five

Flotsam lay on the southwestern edge of the Blood Sea in the shelter of Blood Bay. It owed its name and much of its existence to the ancient kingdom of Istar whose Kingpriest awoke the wrath of the gods and brought cataclysm upon Krynn. His fabled city sank to the bottom of the Blood Sea where it was lost beneath the great Maelstrom. Bits and pieces, trash and relics washed ashore along miles of coastline, but due to the currents and the curves of the shoreline, much of the flotsam washed into Blood Bay. Drawn by the hope of valuables, the lure of magic artifacts, and ready availability of building materials, a diverse collection of people settled in the area and named their town with simple honesty. Flotsam had gone through many changes since its founding. It had been a pirate hideout, a dragonarmy base, and a flourishing port. Now, under the merciless rule of the Red Marauder, about two thousand of its surviving citizens eked out a rough existence as best they could.

Because of the town's isolation, the population considered the arrival of a caravan from Sanction and Khur a big event. The Silver Fox's men had spread the word that the wagons were due by noon, so when the wagons wound down out of the hills and into the valley of Flotsam, most of the residents came out to greet them.

At the dusty end of the caravan, the cook wagon crested the low ridge and started down the long slope. Lucy reined her horse to a halt and stared down on the valley below. The port lay in a cup-shaped vale surrounded by bare hills that ended in bluffs at the water's edge. A small but deep harbor sat like a blue bowl on the eastern side of the valley, and on the east side of the bay sat the Rock, a thumb-shaped, rugged headland that projected out into the bay and rose more than thirty feet above the water. The Rock was a natural fortress and formed Flotsam's strongest defense and shelter from the rough storms that plagued the Blood Sea.

In the midst of this valley, curving around the circular bay like an old dump, stood the most ramshackle, disreputable excuse for a town Lucy and Ulin had ever seen. For a moment they were struck dumb by what they observed.

"I've seen gully dwarf towns that look better than that," Lucy finally remarked.

Challie shrugged. "It certainly fits its name."

"Welcome to Flotsam, ladies!" Lysandros called. He waved cheerily as he cantered his horse past the wagons. "I'll see you in town." He and his men rode on past the caravan and down the road where they disappeared among the rowdy crowd waiting to greet the newcomers.

Lucy slapped the reins to urge the horse forward, and they followed the other wagons down the hills. They passed a few farms with fields newly plowed for spring planting. Some gentle slopes were rowed with grape vines and olive trees, and here and there a few cows and sheep grazed in small pastures beside the farmhouses. For the most part, the land around Flotsam sat empty and ill-tended.

Ruins of burned-out cottages and the gray skeletons of wrecked barns were scattered across the valley, attesting to the numerous depredations of Malys. The closer the caravan drew to the town the more the years of damage became apparent. Crumbling cottages and outbuildings sat in ruins beside the road, some nearly lost in tumbled vines and overgrown weeds. A few huts and hovels looked inhabited, but they were ill kept and shoddy.

On the freight wagon, Ulin glanced back at Lucy and saw the expression on her face. It probably mirrored his own. His grandfather, Caramon, had been in Flotsam many years before when the Blue Lady's dragonarmy made the town its headquarters, and he remembered some of his grandfather's tales about the town. He looked to find some of the landmarks Caramon mentioned, yet nothing looked the way he thought it should. Where the city wall and its guard towers once stood, he saw only the rubble of its foundations and cut stones scattered across the fields. Where the busy wharves had been, there was only empty water and the bones of old pilings. Two wharves had been rebuilt to service the fishing fleet and the few merchants that sailed in, but the breakwater and its beacon had been destroyed and most of the warehouses were ashes. What was left of Flotsam after thirty years under Malys's iron claw was perhaps half the original population and the seediest, most dilapidated collection of shops, tenements, taverns, and bawdy houses Ulin could imagine.

The people who hurried out of these buildings to welcome the caravan were hardly any better. The denizens of Flotsam were almost as varied as Sanction's, including various humans, kender, and a scattering of half-elves, wild elves, dwarves, hobgoblins, ogres, and gully dwarves. The difference was that while Sanction's people looked fed and prosperous under their circumstances, these people were ragged, thin, and harassed.

They seemed happy enough at the moment, though, as they cheered the caravan's arrival. Children ran to the wagons and clung to the sides for a ride into town. Ulin found himself with five boys of varied ages hanging like sprites on the wagon and two more riding his oxen. They all grinned and waved to him.

Ulin returned their greeting and tried to look pleased. He combed his fingers through his wind-tangled hair, straightened his loose robes, and waved back to the people. It would be good, he thought, to claim the father's body and get out of Flotsam as soon as possible. Maybe, if their luck held, they could return to Khuri-Khan with Garzan's wagons within the next few days.

Following Akkar-bin and his guards, the wagons rumbled into Flotsam past the razed city walls and between the jumble of crude buildings. Years before, in more prosperous days, the streets had been paved with stone. In recent times, however, the stones had been removed for repair or rebuilding purposes, and now the streets ran dry and dusty through out the town. A few wooden sidewalks lined the main road, and a group of enterprising storekeepers had put up water troughs and hitching posts in front of their crude storefronts.

In the center of town, located just behind the wharf area, was the town's marketplace where a few struggling merchants, farmers, and fishermen came to sell their wares in canopied stalls or open carts. Akkar-bin, ignoring waves and greetings, led his wagons to the open market and parked them in two rows of five. With the skill of long practice, the drivers quickly set to work. Several set up Garzan's colorful booth while the rest unhitched and led away the oxen before anyone could offer to buy them or try to steal them. The Khurs took no chances with their transportation.

Ulin pulled his wagon into line with a sigh of relief. Wearily, he applied the brake and dropped the whip. His small passengers dropped off and came around to accost him. Their grinning faces looked up at him hopefully, and their hands reached out to him.

"Spare a few coppers, sir?" implored the loudest of the lot. "Just a few? We haven't eaten in days,"

Akkar-bin strode over to them before Ulin could respond. His whip cracked in the air, scattering them in all directions. "Be off, ye greedy little street urchins!" he yelled.

"Master Akkar!" Lucy's voice snapped with the speed of the Khur's whip. "How dare you? They are just hungry little boys."

Akkar-bin coiled his whip and shrugged. With more patience than Ulin would have given him credit for, he replied, "Mistress Lucy, they are merely emissaries. If you give them even the tiniest copper, they and every other child in town will be hovering around you every time you set foot out a door. They are incorrigible beggars."

Ulin jumped down from the wagon to forestall further argument from his tenderhearted betrothed. "Master Akkar," he said, "It is time to complete our business."

The caravan master nodded and drew a leather bag out of his voluminous waistband. "Your coins, as stated in the contract. The sword must be returned, of course."

"You may keep the sword, Ulin of Solace, as a gift from me," a familiar voice called out. The Silver Fox appeared behind Akkar-bin. He had changed out of his sand-colored clothing to a faded blue tunic trimmed with gray fox fur and flowing pants. A dingy yellow burnoose hid his silver hair and pointed ears. Several men were with him, and one carried a small ironbound chest. "The price as agreed with Garzan," Lysandros said, indicating the box.

The Khur shouted an order to two of his drivers. Moments later they returned, carrying the crate of "Wool Dye" Ulin had opened.

Ulin's eyes narrowed. So, the Khur merchant who dealt with the Knights of Neraka also sold arms to the rebels in the red dragon's realm. The man's reach was wide indeed.

Lysandros opened the crate in front of Akkar-bin and lifted a corner of the dye bags. He nodded with satisfaction and passed the small chest to the caravan master. "Tell Garzan we will take more when he can send another shipment."

The Khur turned to go, his business finished, when Lucy caught his arm and indicated the bay horse hitched to the cook wagon. "Master Akkar-bin, I would like to buy that horse." She ran hand down the animal's neck. "We will need a horse for the return journey, and I have become rather fond of this one."

The old Khur's expression did not change. "The horse is stolen. If it wasn't for your help with the bandits, we might have lost the caravan. Keep the horse." Pivoting on his heel, he strode away to supervise the unloading of the cargo.

Lucy watched him go, her lips parted in surprise. "I guess that was his way of saying thank you."

The captain chuckled. "Knowing Akkar-bin, that was the closest thing to a compliment he's ever given. Just don't let any Dark Knights see that brand."

Ulin pulled the sword out from under the wagon seat and laid it with the others in the crate. The half-elf watched, his arms crossed. "I gave that weapon to you, Ulin. Do you refuse it?"

The young Majere bowed. "I am grateful, but I do not want to be obligated to someone in a town I must leave so quickly."

Lysandros's rich laugh filled the space between the wagons. "Whether you go or stay, you will need a weapon around here. Keep it. Do not worry about obligation."

Annoyance flickered in the back of Ulin's mind. He did not want to accept a sword from this man, for honor demanded that he find some way to repay the rebel leader for this generous gift, but to refuse it now would be an insult. Hiding a scowl, he belted the sword to his waist and tried to appear pleased.

With a brief bow, the captain bade farewell to the newcomers, and with his men, he blended into the crowd with the skill of a pickpocket.

"Thought he'd never leave," grumbled Challie. "Now, bring your gear. There are some people who want to meet you."

"Does this have anything to do with my father?" Lucy asked wearily.

"It does. The city council has been waiting for some time, hoping to meet you. I thought they could give you news about him, perhaps tell you more about how he, uh, died."

Lucy said nothing. She and Ulin eyed the magistrate for a moment then looked at each other and hoisted their packs to their backs. Wordlessly, they followed the dwarf out of the marketplace and into the streets.

Lucy, keeping a firm grip on her horse's halter, brought up the rear of the little group as the magistrate led them along a street that followed the curve of the harbor. Clusters of rickety one-story buildings sat on both sides of the street. Each had a crude name painted above the door, and from the racket of raucous voices, loud music, and the occasional crack of breaking furniture, the buildings were taverns and gaming houses with several gaily painted bawdy houses for variation. The businesses and streets in this area were busy even at this time of day with hawkers, pickpockets, barkers, and a rowdy clientele that did not seem to have much else to do in the day's heat.

Ulin and Lucy stared at the streets and buildings in a mix of distaste and amazement. Every edifice in town appeared to be hastily thrown together from whatever building material was available at the time. One enterprising tavern keeper had hauled an old wrecked carrack out of the water, cut off her masts and rudder, planted her keel in the dirt, and opened for business under the name of The Ship Wreck. Other people used crates or old ship timbers, stones from the city walls, canvas, and even whale bones to construct a hodgepodge of homes, shops, and businesses. Nothing was the same, and nothing looked strong enough to survive a good wind.

The other characteristic of Flotsam the travelers noticed immediately was the smell. In the heat of early summer on a windless day like this one, the odors rose from the town in powerful waves that assaulted the nostrils of new arrivals who had not had time to become inured to the stench. Ulin recognized the smells of tar, horse manure, refuse of all kinds, dead fish, and poor sanitation before he gave up and tried to breath through his mouth. He just hoped the sea breeze would pick up very soon.

Following the curve of the harbor, the small group soon arrived at a complex of large stone buildings on the northwest shore, directly across the water from the Rock. Most of the outer buildings had collapsed into rubble, but the main wing still stood. Scorched by old fires and missing part of its roof, it remained a silent testimony to the skill of its original builders.

"This used to be the barracks of the Black and White armies stationed here before the Chaos War," Challie said before anyone could ask. "Malys has burned it several times, but I think it has protective wards built into the walls. It won't fall down."

"What is it now?" asked Ulin.

"Our lord mayor uses it as his city hall."

A laugh welled out of Lucy. "This place has a mayor?"

The dwarf nodded, her dark eyes unblinking. "To give him credit, he tries."

The title of lord mayor triggered a memory in Ulin's mind of another detail from his grandfather's tales. "What happened to Highmaster Toede?"

"Who?" Lucy said.

"He was a hobgoblin who wormed and kicked his way into a position of power in the service of the Dragon Highlord." Ulin explained. "He was lord mayor of Flotsam for years."

Challie agreed with his description. "The old monster died about five years ago after Malys razed his manor and everything else on the Rock."

Ulin found his gaze searching the rocky headland for landmarks he'd heard about. Nothing was there. The Rock had been stripped bare of Tocdc's two-story manor, the inn called the Saltbreeze, the treasury, and every hut, house, shed, or outhouse all the way down to the wharves at its base.

"The Red Marauder has been rather hard on this town," Challie observed.

An obvious understatement, thought Ulin.

A party of four waited for them on the step in front of the old barracks. They greeted Challie warmly then turned to meet the two new arrivals with barely concealed relief.

Challie made the introductions. "Ulin, Lucy, this is Lord Mayor Efrim Getani and the Flotsam City Council."

Mayor Efrim bowed stiffly, and Ulin feared for a moment the mayor would not be able to straighten up again. The man was at least as old as his grandfather and not nearly as hale. His fragile body swayed within his red robes that seemed several sizes too big for him. Pushing on his cane, he managed to lever himself to an upright position and bestow a toothless smile on everyone. A thin beard framed his narrow face and continued in a ring of white around his bald head.

"Mayor Efrim was a pirate once," Challie said, eyeing the old man with a glint of irritable respect. "He and my grandfather fought together."

"Saved your life, too, you old rascal," Efrim said through toothless gums.

"And he thinks I'm my grandfather," the dwarf added to her two companions.

"I, however, suffer no such delusions," said the second man. He was much younger, perhaps in his fifties, and the only portly man they had seen so far in Flotsam. His round face sweated profusely in the hot afternoon sun, and he constantly wiped it with a damp handkerchief. He took the mayor's arm to help support him. "I am Geoff Aylesworthy of the Flotsam City Council. I am also the owner of the Jetties, the finest inn in Flotsam. Please allow me to reserve two rooms for you at my establishment."

"Take them," suggested Challie. "He's not kidding. He does have the best inn since the Saltbreeze burned down. I've had a room there for several months."

"And a stall, too?" Lucy asked.

Aylesworthy mopped his face again. "Of course. It will be my pleasure to have you stay."

"HowlongareyouplanningtostayinFlotsam?" inquired the third person. Shorter than Challie, the diminutive, bright-eyed male was a gnome with rich brown skin, a snowy-white beard braided in two braids, and a large nose. He had a small lantern tied to his stiff hat and a fistful of small tools on his belt. His clothes were dusty and smudged with something gray. Like most gnomes, he tended to talk so quickly his words bumped and ran together into a bouncing stream of words.

Mayor Efrim held a skinny hand to his ear. "Notwen, if I've told you once, I've told you a thousand times. *Slow down.*"

"Only until I identify my father's body," Lucy answered before the gnome had to ask again.

A glance, so swift Ulin almost missed it, passed among the council members.

"Ah, yes. Kethril Torkay," the fourth elder said in a voice meant to be comforting. "A fine man. We shall miss him, dear."

Lucy curled her lip. "You didn't know him then."

The innkeeper chuckled. "We all knew of him, Lady Lucy. He was a man of many talents."

"Quite," she replied dryly. "Then can you tell me where his body lies?"

Again that lightning swift look of communication passed between the elders. Aylesworthy barely nodded.

"Unfortunately, we have suffered a miscommunica-tion," said the fourth council member. She was an elderly lady, almost as old as Mayor Efrim, but her body was not as frail, and when she tilted her head to look at Lucy, Ulin saw the clear glint of a sharp intelligence behind her deep set eyes. Challie introduced her simply as Saorsha.

"We don't know exactly where he is," Mayor Efrim said. At least he had the decency to look red-faced and embarrassed.

Lucy's green eyes darkened. This was difficult enough without these four old politicians acting stupid. She reached into her pack and pulled out the worn, folded letter her family had received. She flipped it open and waved in their faces. "You asked us here on this trumped-up tale to view my father's remains," she said angrily. "Now where is he?"

Ulin, wary now, studied the faces of the elders and the dwarf around him to note their reactions. If the blank look Challie gave the council was feigned, then the dwarf was a consummate actress. The rest of the council appeared worried and very uneasy. About what? Ulin wondered.

Mayor Efrim recovered first. He puffed out his thin chest and replied, "He has been buried, of course."

"Of course," Lucy said, her voice heavy with sarcasm. "We know that."

"Oh. Um, where did they bury the body?" Efrim fumbled and turned to the innkeeper.

Aylesworthy fluttered a pudgy hand. "That is the problem, remember Mayor? We don't really know. We asked our usual burial detail to put the corpse in a safe place." He sighed. "They hid it so well, they cannot remember where they put it."

"How convenient," Lucy muttered. "What do you plan to do about this difficulty?"

Mayor Efrim spread out his hands in a reassuring gesture. "Search for him, of course! We haven't done so yet simply because we were not certain you would accept our offer. Please! Allow us to find his body for you. It should only take a few days, and it would be our pleasure to have you stay in our town."

Lucy pursed her lips and studied the elders. Something was not right with this situation. She knew the elders were not being entirely truthful with her, and she could sense Challie had something to hide, too. But what? If her father was not dead, why bother lying about it? And if his body was truly missing or destroyed, why couldn't they just admit it?

It was too confusing. She was hot, tired, and weary of travel. She could see the exhaustion on Challie's face, too, and the hollows under Ulin's eyes. They all needed rest. If the city council was willing to help her, she could give them four or five days to prove it. If she didn't have her father's body by then, or at least a reasonable explanation of his disappearance, she would take matters into her own hands. She looked up into Ulin's eyes and saw the same suspicious glint she knew must be in her own. He tilted his chin down and winked once, and she knew without asking that he would accept whatever decision she made.

Lucy extended her hand as if to seal a deal. "Thank you, Mayor Efrim. I accept your offer."

Chapter Six

Innkeeper Aylesworthy was as good as his word. He hurried away after the meeting on the steps, and by the time Ulin, Lucy, and Challie had walked to the Jetties on the south side of Flotsam, he had two adjoining rooms and a stall cleaned and ready for them. The Jetties proved to be a ramshackle, sprawling building that looked like it had been thrown together by shoving several different houses together and tacking on a few sheds for good measure. Its main room and bar occupied the central space in an edifice faced with chunks of stone mortared together like a puzzle.

In spite of its haphazard appearance, the Jetties was neatly tended, and the ale, while not up to Ulin's standards, was acceptable. Lucy looked over the two small rooms and the newly swept stall, nodded her acceptance, and paid the innkeeper for four nights.

Pleased that she would pay in advance, Aylesworthy clapped his hands for his kitchen help and ordered a tray of food to be sent to their rooms immediately.

When Lucy returned, she found Ulin standing by the bed, staring out the small window. Without saying a word, Lucy stood on her tiptoes and kissed Ulin's cheek, then took her belongings into the second room.

In the months since Ulin had pledged to marry her, he had been the proper gentleman: affectionate, loving, supportive, and faithful, but he refused to set a date to confirm their vows, and not once had he let his affection heat into honest passion. Lucy knew his reluctance was not due to her. He loved her and wanted to be with her, but he had thrown a shield around his heart. Some day, she believed, he would move beyond his fear and grief and take her to be his wife.

Footsteps thudded down the hall and a small familiar figure burst into her room carrying a laden tray. The kitchen help proved to be Pease Stubbletoes. Grinning from ear to ear, the kender set the tray on a small table and poured mugs of cool ale. The plates he brought were lavishly laden with fresh bread, goat's cheese, chunks of fried fish, and spice cookies the size of saucers.

"My ma is the cook here," Pease said proudly. "She's the best in Flotsam, so Master Aylesworthy lets me help her. When I'm not riding with Captain Fox, of course," he added with equal pride.

Ulin came in to join them, and Lucy soon saw why the trays were so full. Pease had invited Challie, and as soon as the dwarf came to the table, he plopped down on a chair beside them and joined in, confident that he was already a best friend and did not need an invitation.

It was a pleasant meal full of kender chatter and gossip. Ulin and Lucy learned much about Flotsam's history of the past five years, of the Jetties and how its previous owners died in a fire after one of Malys's visits, and of the people who lived in the town.

"We have all kinds," Challie told them. The good food and plentiful ale had warmed her usually stiff conversation skills. "Pirates, smugglers, farmers, miners, shopkeepers, shepherds, tribesmen from Khur, fishermen, and—"

Pease jumped into the conversation, "And refugees and mercenaries. There are a couple of dwarves and lots of kender. Notwen is the only gnome in these parts. He's a tinker. He's always playing with machines and building stuff. And we think Saorsha was with the Legion of Steel. She's always helping people. She's one of the leaders of the Vigilance Committee."

Ulin sat a little straighter and asked, "Who else is on this committee?"

"Oh, the captain, of course," Pease answered. "Master Aylesworthy, at least two other innkeepers and the blacksmith. Ma is, too. Lots of people in the Thieves Guild and the Fishers Guild help the committee by passing on news or standing watch on the observation posts."

Ulin hoped that Pease was not as talkative to others. If he repeated some of this to an undercover Dark Knight, he could get half the town arrested. "Are you on the Committee?" he asked Challie.

The magistrate leaned her chair back to a comfortable angle. Her stern face relaxed. "Not officially. I did not want to get involved, but after the dragon crushed my house, I began looking at Flotsam with a different perspective. This place kind of grows on you . . . like a fungus. Now, I do what I can. "

The talk continued until the plates were empty and there was nothing left but a cookie or two. At last Lucy sat back and sighed. "You know what I would like now?" she asked no one in particular. "Some kefre. I've been around Khurs for so long, I've gotten used to it."

"I haven't," Challie said, making a face. "That stuff tastes like old bark."

"It is old bark," Ulin laughed.

"Ma has a kefre pot. She keeps it for the Khurs who stop by. Do you really want some?" Pease wiped a napkin across his freckled round face and hopped to his feet. He

tucked the last cookie into a pocket "for later" before looking up at Lucy. "I hope you can stay for a while. Captain
Fox said you could be a big help."

Ulin and Lucy looked at him in surprise. Challie stared
at the empty fireplace.

"What is that supposed to mean?" Lucy demanded.

The kender suddenly looked flustered. He dropped his
napkin, and a flush spread slowly up his face to meet his
brown hair. "Oh, I don't know . . . really. Just something
the Captain said. He, uh, he eats downstairs some nights.
You could ask him then."

Pease abruptly scooted out of his chair and picked up a
tray of dirty dishes. "I'll just get rid of these." He flew out
the door, his topknot bobbing behind him.

Lucy rubbed the bridge of her nose. She could feel a
headache lurking on the edges of her skull. "The sooner
we get out of this town, the better," she grumbled.

Ulin agreed.

* * * * *

After a cup of kefre and a nap, Lucy felt much better.
By evening she was ready to go to the common room for
supper. They found Challie at a table in the busy room
beside one of the few narrow windows, and they accepted
her invitation to join her. The place was almost full with
locals, Khur tribesmen, and a few nondescript humans
whose background and livelihood were anybody's guess.
Aylesworthy stood behind the bar, pouring wine and tapping ale.

Lucy and Ulin hoped to find Lysandros there, but the
innkeeper informed them the captain had left on a sur-
veillance ride. He assured them that steps were already
being taken to find the missing corpse. Lucy thanked him
for the lunch and asked him to let them know when the
captain appeared.

The newcomers' arrival drew the attention of the

customers and more than a few stamped and cheered for Lucy. The story of her fight with the bandits and her spell for deadly potatoes had already spread around town. To Lucy's amusement, the tale had already grown in telling to include several draconians, a horde of bandits, and potatoes that incinerated like dragon's fire. One Flotsam merchant was so impressed that he sent a flask of wine to her table with his compliments. Lucy smiled her most enigmatic smile and accepted the gift. It never hurt, she mused, to have an aura of mysterious power.

The trio ate their meal and watched the crowd, but when Lysandros did not return after several hours, Lucy and Challie went to bed. Ulin stayed for a while longer, nursing the same cup of wine. He stared into the flame of the lamp on his table, his mind years away in memories sharp and sad. The weaving flame reflected in his eyes, yet shadows darkened the hollows of his face. No one tried to approach him. At last, when the bar was nearly empty and the barmaid was clearing off the tables, Ulin tossed back the dregs of his wine and went to his room. He made certain Lucy's door was locked then sought his own bed. Even then, sleep was long in coming.

* * * * *

The three travelers spent a lazy morning the next day. For the first time in over a month, they did not have to rise early to start fires, or feed grumbling tribesmen, or set out on another long day of travel. Pease brought another laden tray to Lucy's room and joined his new friends to break the fast. Lucy and Challie indulged in a bath in the inn's tiny bathhouse, then spent the rest of the morning washing their laundry with the help of Bridget Stubbletoes, the best cook in Flotsam. She was tall for a kender, nearly Challie's height, and more serious than most. Her face and arm were disfigured from scars suffered in a fire she endured as a young girl when Malys destroyed her village.

She had lost everything in that attack but her will to survive. Lucy liked her from the start.

After the midday meal Bridget and her son took the two newcomers on a brief tour of Flotsam and the city market. The sun shone hot in a clear sky and glittered off the water in the harbor as they walked through the maze of streets. A slight breeze stirred the dust but did little to lift the odors in the streets or disturb the flies that hovered over the refuse piles.

Many people were outdoors in spite of the heat, and the travelers quickly learned that the story of the fight against the bandits had spread all over Flotsam—that and the news that Lucy was Kethril's daughter. Too many folks recognized Lucy and stopped to welcome her to Flotsam and to talk about her feat or her infamous father. Others waved and called greetings. She wasn't sure what to make of her new celebrity status in a town like Flotsam, so she just waved and greeted people with a calm smile.

Ulin took her hand and gave a quick squeeze. "Looks like you've made a name for yourself," he teased, reminding her of what she had said on the ship.

She sighed in mock seriousness. "It's not enough. I should at least rescue a lady in distress or wipe out a troop of Dark Knights."

He swept a hand around to include the busy streets. "Give this town of storytellers another day or two and they'll have you doing that and more."

Still chuckling, Lucy and Ulin followed Bridget as she led them into the marketplace. The two travelers trailed behind the kender while they went from one booth to the next buying foodstuffs for the inn. They studied the different varieties of food available: fragrant spices and herbs, stacks of dark kefre bark, bags of dried beans and grain, boxes of figs, olives, and brightly colored corn. Several farmers had brought late winter cabbage, yams, and potatoes out of storage.

They stopped to visit Akkar-bin and check on the progress of the caravan master's business. His wares were nearly gone and had been replaced by goods he had purchased in Flotsam to sell along the road to Sanction. He agreed to take Lucy and her party back with his caravan, if they were ready to leave when he was. He refused to wait, so Ulin and Lucy could only hope the council would hurry.

After Bridget bought a box of his dried mushrooms, they bade farewell to the Khur and moved on to visit the fishmongers. Along the street closest to the wharves stood the fishers' booths, filled with the day's catch of shellfish, crabs, and fish unique to Blood Bay. The small boats of the town's fishing fleet were already back from the early morning catch and had just completed their unloading. Their hawkers' shouts filled the air over the voices of other merchants and the shoppers.

The mongers knew Bridget, and instead of rolling their eyes and guarding their wares as merchants usually did in the presence of kender, they welcomed her warmly and offered her the best of their catch. She bargained with skill and complete knowledge of her needs, and soon she had her son and Ulin laden with parcels and bags.

"Sometimes the fishermen deliver to the inn," she told them, "but why pay extra when I have willing hands to help?" She gave Ulin a bright smile.

They wended their way back through the market toward the inn and nearly reached the street when a horn blared a long, strident warning from the Rock.

Every person in town froze. Sounds immediately died into a silence, tense and wary.

Ulin and Lucy looked about in surprise. Lucy saw with alarm that Bridget was shaking.

"What—?" asked Ulin.

"Not yet!" Bridget hissed. "Wait. Listen for it." She clutched her basket so hard that her knuckles turned white.

The sickening fear struck them all at the same time, like a wave washing over the town. People cried out and fell to the ground as a huge shadow swept over the sun. Lucy and the kender cowered, but Ulin had experienced the hideous terror that emanated from evil dragons, and although his knees quaked and every instinct screamed at him to hide, he remained on his feet. He forced his eyes to the sky and saw a monstrous red shape flying high and fast toward the southeast. The dragon was returning to her lair in the Desolation.

"Malystryx," he spat the name.

Bridget whimpered.

As quickly as it overwhelmed them, the dragonfear faded from their hearts, and the shadow vanished south. From the Rock came a second horn call, signaling the all-clear. In a heartbeat the noise and activity resumed throughout Flotsam as if nothing had happened.

"Shards of the Gem!" Lucy exclaimed. "Does that happen often?" She dusted off her own skirts and moved to help Bridget to her feet.

"Too many times," Bridget replied, her voice shaky. "That's why the Vigilance Committee keeps a watch on the Rock."

Pease nodded vigorously. "Yup. Even a little warning is better than none. So if you hear two quick blasts. Run for it."

Ulin glanced dubiously at the rickety buildings around him. He had fought Malys once from the back of the dragon Sunrise and would have died were it not for the speed and courage of the gold. Malys was a monster who stretched over four hundred feet from cruel snout to tip of tail. The titanic beast's weight would flatten the shoddy little buildings without the use of her scorching breath, sharp claws, or scything tail. In Flotsam, there was nowhere safe to run.

"I hope she doesn't come here any time soon," Lucy breathed, putting a voice to Ulin's heartfelt sentiment.

There were no more alarms that day, and life went on in the port town. As evening approached, the activities in the taverns and gaming houses became rowdier and the streets grew more crowded with the rougher elements. The farmers, shopkeepers, and families quietly withdrew to their own hearths and bolted their doors. By sunset the market was deserted and the taverns overflowing.

The Jetties seemed to draw a better behaved crowd, yet even it filled to capacity with noisy people eating Bridget's food and drinking ale as fast as Aylesworthy could tap it. A pair of musicians passing through agreed to play for an evening in exchange for a room and a meal. Their tunes on pipe and drum kept the common room lively late into the night. Ulin and Lucy stayed for a while, hoping to talk to someone on the council or the Vigilance Committee, but Aylesworthy made himself too busy to talk and no word came from the Silver Fox or the elders. Eventually, Lucy retired, leaving Ulin to his ale and his shuttered thoughts.

* * * * *

Their third day in Flotsam began much like the first. Pease brought their meal on a tray and stayed to join them. As soon as the dishes were washed and the morning's chores finished, the kender offered to take the travelers up to the Rock to see the observation post. Only Ulin decided to go. Lucy wanted a bridle for her horse, and since Challie had several errands to do, she offered to accompany Lucy to the marketplace.

Lucy and Challie walked north on the wooden sidewalks along a street that seemed to have no name. Challie told Lucy the road bore the original title of Market Street, due to the street's eventual destination. They stopped at the blacksmith's shop to deliver a deed written in Challie's careful hand and picked up a packet of papers from an older couple living in a tiny hut tucked between two brothels. Eventually, wending their way through the busy morning traffic, they soon spotted the crowded marketplace. Wains, booths, and stalls stood in rows between beaten dirt paths on the market grounds while jugglers, minstrels, and other entertainers played for coins and attention along the perimeter. Hawkers carried trays laden with food or trinkets and wandered among the customers.

Lucy and Challie browsed for a while among the stalls, admiring the handiwork of local craftspeople. They soon found a leather worker, and Lucy bought a simple bridle with a snaffle bit for the bay horse. She thought about purchasing a saddle, then changed her mind. They might need the money for a wagon, if her agreement with the council was successful.

"What do you think I should call him?" Lucy asked Challie while they walked back through the market. She had the bridle slung over her shoulder and her purse tucked firmly in her sash belt.

"I don't know. Why do you bother to name a horse?"

Lucy rolled her eyes. "He's just a plain draft horse, but he deserves a name."

Challie's face screwed up with good humor. "Call him Akkar-bin."

"No, the horse has more personality. How about . . ." Lucy looked back and saw Challie stopped in place, staring between two small booths at something in the next aisle. She took a step back to see what the dwarf was looking at. Shouting erupted close by and several large crashes rattled the booths. Lucy saw a huge, muscular man with blond hair burst into view. He joined a second, smaller man who stood close to the stall in front of Challie. Lucy realized he was scooping bracelets and rings and small gems into his bag. The proprietor lay on the ground unmoving.

With a nasty laugh, the big blond man kicked the unconscious jeweler and pulled the booth apart with his bare hands. Two more laughing men ran into sight, their arms full of stolen goods. Booth owners and customers scattered in all directions.

The blond man suddenly saw the two women. "What are you staring at?" he roared, and in one abrupt movement, he leaped straight through the gap and pounced on the dwarf. He snatched her arm in one huge hand and backhanded Lucy.

The force of the blow sent her reeling into the cart of a vegetable vendor. The cart tipped over, spilling vegetables everywhere. Pain exploded in her head. She heard Challie scream, but she could not force her body to respond. Desperately, she struggled to her feet and staggered over the vegetables. Her vision swam, and for a moment Lucy thought she would vomit. Somehow, she managed to stay upright in spite of the blood that ran from her nose and forehead. One eye was already swelling shut.

She heard Challie scream again, and fury as white-hot as dragon rage erupted within her. It burned away her dizziness and fired the embers of her strength until she could stand upright and see what was happening around her.

The blond man held Challie upside down by one foot and was shaking her violently. The other thugs were snatching everything of value they could carry, and no one seemed to be doing anything to stop them.

The smaller man caught sight of Lucy on her feet. Gloating, he snatched her sleeve and hauled her close. "Give us a kiss, girlie. Then maybe we'll have some real fun."

Lucy felt her fingers tighten around the leather straps of the bridle still clutched in her hand. She wrenched away from him and whipped the bridle around. The metal bit slammed into his mouth, cutting the flesh and breaking teeth. He fell to his knees, and before he could recover she snatched a clay bowl and smashed it over his head. He sagged to the ground without a sound.

"Hist!" someone cried. "Sorceress! Here, take these!"

Lucy turned at the sound of the voice and saw a young woman crouched behind the spilled cart. The woman held out her hands as if making an offering. On her open palms were three large reddish potatoes. For a moment Lucy stared at them, wondering what on earth she was supposed to do with those, then the memory of her spell and an idea ignited in her thoughts at the same time. It was crazy, but it was worth a try. She snatched the potatoes like a gift from the gods.

Raising the tubers above her head, she faced the brigands and began to chant the incantations to Ulin's spell in a loud and firm voice. With a prayer that she could force the magic to work again, she focused on the power she could feel around her and drew it carefully into her incantation. She almost completed the spell when something soft as gossamer tickled the back of her neck. Although she tried to ignore the sensation and concentrate on her spell, she felt the magic falter and fade. Several unladylike words passed through her mind, and she had to swallow hard to hide her frustrated disappointment.

"Great bullocks, Grethor!" one of the thugs shouted. "That's the sorceress who killed those dozen draconians."

Lucy molded her expression into a mask of stern anger. She lowered her arms, and held a potato ready to throw at the big man holding Challie. He stood stared at her, eyes wide and mouth hanging open.

"Put her down this instant or die," Lucy demanded.

Dazedly, he opened his hand and dropped the dwarf to the ground where she groaned and lay still.

Lucy wanted to run to Challie, but she dared not take her eyes off the brigand. "Now, tell your men, all of them, to put the goods down and lie on the ground, or I will burn you all."

Such was the power of Lucy's reputation—thanks to the storytellers in Flotsam—that the three men took one look at her face and the potatoes in her hand and obeyed instantly. All of them dropped to the ground and spread their arms and legs. One of them whimpered.

Help suddenly appeared from all directions. Booth owners, vendors, and customers crawled out of their hiding places or came hurrying back, and in short order they had all four men trussed and taken away under guard. The young woman under the vegetable cart gave Lucy some water and strips of fabric for her face and helped her revive Challie. The battered dwarf cursed intermittently then laughed at Lucy's potato trick

"Did the spell work this time?" she whispered to Lucy when they were alone.

Lucy gave her head a small shake. She kept the potatoes tucked in the crook of one arm. "I don't think so. They're not hot like the last ones, but I don't think I'll try them out here. I'd hate to ruin my reputation."

Challie tried to smile through her split lip and started bleeding again. "I wish you had fried that beast," she groaned.

Lucy put an arm around her companion as much for her own support as Challie's. The dwarf was not seriously hurt, but she suffered several severe bruises on her legs and face, abrasions on her forehead, and a sprained ankle. All Lucy wanted to do now was go back to the Jetties and lie down.

"Young woman, you are a marvel," she heard someone say close beside her.

Lucy glanced up with one good eye and looked into the kind, intelligent gaze of Councilwoman Saorsha, the older woman Pease thought was a retired member of the covert Legion of Steel. Looking into Saorsha's aged face, Lucy could well believe the kender was right. This close Lucy noticed details she had not paid attention to before. Saorsha's skin was wrinkled and spotted, but it was the toughened, weather-beaten patina caused by years of living in wind and rain and burning sun. Her eyes were bright, blue, and piercing, and her hair had been cut short into a fluffy cap of waving white. When she offered a hand to

Lucy to help her stand, her grip was firm and strong. Her hands bore the old callouses of a sword-fighter.

Lucy allowed herself to be pulled to her feet. Her head felt as if some evil dwarf stonecutter was trying to split her skull with a dull wedge. Slowly, so she wouldn't lose her breakfast in front of the councilwoman, she bent over and helped Challie stand.

All at once applause and cheering burst out around them. Startled, Lucy saw dozens of people gathered, clapping and smiling and calling her "Sorceress." She blinked and her free hand flew to her battered face.

"You'd think they'd never seen a mage before," she muttered. A little attention was nice, but this was getting embarrassing.

"Actually we haven't seen one in a long time," Saorsha told her. "Malys killed all the ones she could find, and once the magic started to fail, those few that were out here left to find answers elsewhere." She lifted a hand and indicated the people around them. "You have brought them a gleam of hope."

Lucy watched the crowd slowly disperse. "Hope for what? Another good story?"

"Even stories can lighten fear. But enough, you've had quite a blow to the head. You need rest and a soothing drink. Come with me. I have my pony trap close by, and it would be a pleasure to take you back to the Jetties."

Considering the long walk back to the inn with Challie's sprained ankle, Lucy accepted. Between them, they supported Challie for the short walk through the market to Saorsha's pony and cart. The cart was barely large enough for three, and the little pony hardly looked big enough to pull one old woman let alone Lucy and Challie. But as soon as they all squeezed on and Saorsha took the reins in her firm grip, the pony started forward without hesitation.

Challie sagged against Lucy and closed her eyes. Lucy wanted to lean against something, too. Now that the attack was over, the reaction and shock were settling over her in a cloak of lethargy. Unfortunately, the narrow seat had no sides or back, and she did not think it would be wise to lean against the driver, so she sat upright and tried not to concentrate on her pain.

"I was wondering," she asked, "why does this town have no guard or law enforcement? Do you have any laws here?"

The councilwoman gave a rueful shrug. "Of course, we do. Mayor Efrim has been trying for years to clean up this town. The problem is we have very little authority. Every time we organize a guard, try to repair the city walls, build towers, or do anything that could be construed as organized resistance, either our Dragon Overlord sweeps in and incinerates the town or she sends a unit of her Dark Knights to put us in our place. That's why the Vigilance Committee and the Force are strictly volunteer and why we keep them covert." She sighed. "And unfortunately, that's why brutes like those feel free to come into town to loot and assault innocent folk."

"So why do you stay?" Lucy asked. She could not see Saorsha out of her right eye, so she turned her head to look at her with the left.

The old woman did not answer at first. She clucked to her pony, her blue eyes as hard as gemstones. "My husband is here, and my daughter. Up yonder." She pointed toward the edge of town.

If Lucy squinted hard enough she could just make out a far hill dotted with mounds and stony cairns.

"Aye," Saorsha said softly. "Malys killed my husband ten years ago. My girl died of a fever that swept through here. I could leave, I suppose, but I have nowhere else to go."

Lucy's lips curved upward in understanding. "And nowhere else where people need you."

The councilwoman tipped her chin up to acknowledge the truth of Lucy's statement. "Even old women like to feel they can be useful."

The pony stopped by the stone front of the Jetties, and Pease raced out to help, effectively ending the conversation. Saorsha walked with Lucy and Challie into the inn and saw them settled with cool drinks while Bridget fussed over their injuries, but she declined Aylesworthy's invitation to stay.

Just before she left, she touched the innkeeper's arm and said, "We shall meet for a game of Dragon's Bluff tonight. Downstairs."

Aylesworthy simply nodded.

Pease bounced to his feet. "Me, too?" he yelped.

Saorsha's piercing gaze did not leave Lucy's face. "Not this time. I want to invite Lucy."

Challie managed a dry smile. "You may not want to play with her. She is very good with games."

Saorsha turned at the door and gave Lucy another brilliant glance. "I'll wager she is."

Chapter
Seven

Lucy would not have considered going to the common room that night if it hadn't been for Saorsha's odd invitation. She felt terrible, and in spite of Bridget's cool compresses and poultices, her face had swollen like an overripe melon. Whatever attractive qualities she had were now lost in the bruised and puffy flesh that covered the right side of her face. Yet she could not forget the searching look in Saorsha's eyes and the invitation to play a game downstairs. As far as she could tell, the inn had no downstairs.

Ulin was not enthused about her going. He was still shaken by their mishap and the extent of their injuries. He laughed at her description of the hot potato spell, but he could not help feeling helpless and angry when he thought of Lucy and Challie at the mercy of four brutal ruffians.

Both accepted the assumption that the invitation was not about a game of cards. The people involved were the same ones the kender mentioned as members of the underground Vigilance Committee. The question in both their minds was why Saorsha wanted Lucy to attend. They agreed to eat in their rooms, and if the Committee wanted Lucy, someone could tell her when and where, and they would attend together.

Ulin passed on their request to Pease. The kender soon returned with a tray of food and wine and a large hourglass.

In a blink or two the table was laid. There was hot soup, cold meats, half a ripe cheese, and biscuits—plain food, but tasty and nourishing. Pease set out more candles, lit lamps, and set the hourglass on a low table.

"Turn the glass twice," he instructed them, "then, if you please, Madam Saorsha and Master Aylesworthy beg the courtesy of your presence for a game. I will come get you." He bobbed his head and hurried away.

Ulin speared some meat onto his plate. "Did she give any reason why she wanted you?" he asked for the third or fourth time.

"No," Lucy replied patiently. She poured a glass of wine and sipped it. "She just invited me to play Dragon's Bluff."

"That's a high stakes game," he mused. "It requires strategy, skill, and some deception to win. I wonder what they're up to."

The two hours that followed seemed long and dreadfully slow. Ulin and Lucy ate a leisurely meal and talked while the sand trickled down and the evening turned to full night. When at last the top of the hourglass was empty, Pease knocked quietly on their door. Lucy unbound her hair and let the heavy chestnut locks fall across her battered face. Taking Ulin's arm, she walked with him to the door and down the corridor behind the kender.

Silently—for once—Pease led them through a small hallway and into the kitchen. His mother glanced up from her place by a low stove and nodded to them. They filed quickly through a door and descended down a wooden staircase into the cellar filled with barrels of ale, racks of wine, and a large cooler. The walls, floor, and ceiling of the room were lined with stone, which helped to cool the underground room and provide some protection from fire above.

Of course this place would have a cellar, Lucy thought. Is this the downstairs Saorsha referred to? She rubbed her sore neck and looked around, but she saw no one else.

Pease came to a stop by a large barrel resting on a stand against the far wall. "Here. We go through here," he said happily. He pried off the round lid and pointed into the interior.

"You first," Ulin said.

The kender agreeably crawled in on hands and knees and disappeared into the darkness. Ulin and Lucy could hear the numerous pouches on his belt jingle and rattle as he moved, then they heard a thump and his voice called back, "Come on! It's easy!"

"It's easy for you to say," Lucy grumbled as she worked her way into the barrel. She wondered if there wasn't another, easier way to get where they were going, for while the barrel and the tunnel behind were barely large enough for the two humans, she could not imagine the stout Master Aylesworthy hauling his frame through there.

The round tunnel passed through the wall and went straight for several yards before it ended in another darkened chamber. As soon as Ulin and Lucy climbed out, Pease carefully closed the exit with another wooden cover.

"It's shut," he said aloud.

A lantern was uncovered, and a dim light filled the room. A table, four straight chairs, and three people were all that could be seen. The chamber was utilitarian and unadorned.

"Thank you for coming," said Saorsha. She gestured to her companions, Lysandros and Geoff Aylesworthy. "You know my friends."

Ulin studied each one in turn. "You are the Vigilance Committee."

"All the ones you will meet tonight," Lysandros replied. "Have a seat." He sat down in the dealer's position, spread out a game board, and began to shuffle a deck of cards.

Saorsha and the innkeeper took their places at the table, leaving only one seat. Ulin held it for Lucy then stood like a silent sentinel at her back, his golden eyes hooded in shadow and his face unreadable.

"You know how to play?" Captain Fox asked.

Lucy crossed her arms and studied the board. Dragon's Bluff was a complicated game involving cards, a game board with marked spaces, dice, and markers. In the center of the board, she was interested to see a red dragon figure perched on the winner's space marked LAIR. There were several variations of the game using either good or evil dragons. The object of the game was to steal the dragon's treasure while either "killing" or outwitting your opponents without being eliminated yourself. The red dragon was the most difficult dragon to defeat.

"Seven cards to a player," she replied at last. "High cards take the tricks and move the markers forward. Bets on all hands. Winner takes all."

"Ah, her father's own," Lysandros joked.

"No, I am not," she said, her voice cold and deliberate. "You brought me down here to play this game. Tell me why."

The captain winked and dealt the seven cards to each player. "Kings are high and dragons wild. The stakes are set at ten silver coins apiece." He flipped a card over from the dealer's pile. "Ah, the suit of hearts is trump. Players, pick your markers and place your bets."

Aylesworthy made the first play, and the game commenced. Unwillingly, Lucy joined in, hoping they would explain themselves sooner or later. She flubbed the first two hands out of sheer irritation, leaving her silver marker sitting in the start box, but soon she settled down and began to play with a vengeance. Her marker moved steadily toward the dragon's lair. Her pile of coins gradually increased from a stack to an impressive pile, until one by one her opponents were forced to drop out of the game.

During the last few hands only Lysandros remained. He played his cards carefully and trumped her enough to move his marker and win back several coins. Lucy said little. She sat perched on the edge of her chair and watched him steadily with her one eye through the strands of her long hair.

While the game continued, Saorsha studied Lucy like a master studying a prospective apprentice. When Lucy finally slapped her cards down and took all of the Fox's coins, a slow smile of satisfaction spread across her worn face.

"Now," Lucy said forcefully. "I have played your game." She knocked the little red dragon from its lair and placed her marker on the winner's place. "Tell me what you want or we will leave this moment." Using the hem of her tunic for a pouch, she scooped up the pile of coins and rose to her feet.

Sarosha folded her hands on the table in front of her and glanced at the two men. Both gave her a brief nod. "You must think this whole thing is rather silly," she said to Lucy. "Actually, we use this game as a test."

The captain crossed his arms and leaned back in his chair. "Dragon's Bluff is not only a good measurement of an opponent's concentration and determination, but it is also long. The game gives Saorsha here time to put her abilities to the best use."

Both Ulin and Lucy looked at the old woman warily. "What sort of abilities?" Ulin asked.

Quiet pride filled Saorsha's face. "I was born with a natural talent to read a person's character. The only drawback is I cannot see through a person's façade in the first few minutes. I need to be close to sense the good or evil, the compassion or hatreds, the fears and strengths that lie in a person's mind. Oh, don't worry," she assured them. "I cannot read thoughts. I only see images of someone's spiritual aura."

Ulin frowned. "You're a Sensitive? Did you ever train as a mage or a mystic?"

"I was a legionnaire, a calling I excelled at. The Legion appreciated my skill, but its leaders knew I did not have a strong enough talent or the self-discipline to wield magic. I preferred helping people in my own way."

Lucy felt for the chair behind her and sat down again. "So what is your point to this?"

"We would like to offer you a job, young woman," Aylesworthy said.

"What?" Lucy and Ulin spoke together. Neither one had expected this.

Lucy pushed her hair back. She was so taken aback by their intentions that she did not know what to say first.

"You are exactly what we need," Saorsha told her. "Compassionate, strong, determined."

Lucy's lips tightened to a thin line. "So is Ulin. Why didn't you ask him?"

The councilwoman smiled gently at Ulin without a hint of disappointment or condescension. "He is as you say and more, but his strengths are in a flux at the moment, while you have the advantage of a powerful reputation already in place that will work for you even when the magic fails."

A start of surprise jolted through Lucy. "You know about the potatoes?"

"I watched you today in the market. I saw a look of annoyance flash across your face when you realized the spell had not worked, yet you did not quit. You bluffed your way through and won."

Lucy looked at the cards still spread across the table. "Like this game." She blew out a breath of air. "What do you have in mind?"

Lysandros moved forward to rest his elbows on the table. "We would like you to be our sheriff."

Mutual shock stilled the words in both Lucy and Ulin. They stared as if the woman and the two men had taken a sudden and complete leave of their senses. No one said a word through a long and pregnant silence.

Ulin was the first to speak. "That's impossible. We did not come here to stay."

Lucy stood up again. "I came to identify my father's body. We intend to leave the moment I have seen him."

"Lucy, please, just listen," Saorsha implored. "You have seen how much we need help! This need only be temporary. Just a few weeks at best. Until after the Visiting Day festival next month. The tax collector is coming to collect our tribute to the red dragon, and it is always chaotic, for the kender have their picnic and the "Hiyahowareyou" gathering, and the riffraff always get drunk. The citizens resent the taxes, and"—she threw up her hands—"we need someone to keep the peace, to calm things down, to get the collector and his unit of Dark Knights out of here with a minimum of fuss."

"We will pay you handsomely," Aylesworthy added.

"And do everything in our power to help," said Lysandros.

Lucy clutched her tunic with its hoard of coins and stepped away from the table closer to Ulin. "Thank you for your confidence in me, but the answer is no."

"You don't have to decide now," the old woman pleaded. "Think about it."

The captain echoed her sentiments. "Please consider our offer. We need you."

The lantern light shone gold in Ulin's eyes as he turned his head to face the half-elf. "Why don't you do it?"

Lysandros flashed a roguish grin. "I am too well known. When the Dark Knights come, I hide."

"What he's saying," Aylesworthy rumbled, "is there is a price on his head."

Ulin thought of his father in the brutal hands of the Dark Knights and stifled a shudder. "I understand your danger," he said to the captain, "and it is not one I wish on Lucy. She said no, and I agree."

Saorsha, Aylesworthy, and Lysandros traded looks of resignation.

Pease Stubbletoes stepped out of a corner where he had been sitting and watching. He had been so quiet that Ulin and Lucy forgot he was there. "Shall I take them back?" he asked the Committee.

At their affirmative reply, he took Lucy's hand and led her back to the round hole in the wall. Ulin followed more slowly. Just before he ducked into the exit, he turned and regarded the three Committee members. "We plan to leave whether you produce a body or not," he said, his voice filled with steel. "I don't want Lucy mixed up in this." Then he vanished into the darkness.

The small chamber was quiet for a few minutes before Saorsha sighed and climbed stiffly to her feet. "Well, it was worth a try. She has such potential."

Aylesworthy glowered at his empty purse. "It was an expensive try."

Lysandros's chuckle drew their attention. "We've come too far to give up on her yet." He held up his left arm and shook it until a flat piece of paper slipped out of his jacket and fell to the table. It was a dragon card from the deck they used. "We still have that other card up our sleeves we can play."

"But will she take it?"

"The gods willing and the creeks don't rise," Lysandros replied, using an old expression.

Aylesworthy shrugged. "We have nothing to lose."

"Then do it," Saorsha ordered, and she blew out the lantern.

* * * * *

"Where is it?"

The question, shouted at the top of dwarven lungs, jolted Lucy wide awake. Loud thumps, strange bangs, and a steady muttering of a very annoyed voice echoed through the wall from the next room. Lucy pried one eye open and rolled over on the bed.

"Challie!" she demanded loudly. "What in the name of the absent gods are you doing?"

More thumps, a few scrapes, and the sound of furniture being shoved around the room sounded through the wall.

"Oh, did I wake you?" Challie shouted. "Sorry." She did not sound contrite in the least. The noises suddenly stilled, and from the hall came the crash of a door being flung open hard enough to hit the wall. "Pease! You sticky-fingered little son of an orc! Where are you?" Her footsteps thudded away.

Lucy rubbed her stiff neck and climbed very slowly out of bed. She dressed in a clean tunic and her favorite pair of baggy Khurish pants. During the fight the day before, she must have pulled muscles in her neck and shoulder, for any movement there sent fiery pain shooting through her back and head.

She was trying vainly to pull on her boots when Ulin knocked at her door and came in. He looked as tired as she felt, and she wondered if he had slept at all that night. Recognizing Lucy's difficulty, he hurried to her and helped pull on the boots.

Voices echoed down the hallway, and footsteps pounded toward the room. Challie barged in, a kender in her right hand.

"Where is it?" she shouted, giving Pease a shake. A red flush stained her cheeks, and her brown eyes were thunderous. "Tell me you took it!"

Pease turned a wide, innocent face to her. "Took what?" he squeaked.

"My axe, you dunderhead. The silver one. It was my father's. It's missing, and you probably took it."

Pease's bewildered sense of innocence was plain, but that meant little in a kender. The small kender were blessed with a lighthearted nature and a childlike spirit and cursed, some said, with an inability to take things seriously and a tendency to acquire things that did not belong to them. They did not steal—never steal—yet small items had a tendency to disappear, only to reappear later in a kender's pouch or pocket or box of personal treasures. Kender liked to borrow things or save them for later or simply have them to admire, and if asked they would always return what they borrowed or offer it as a gift. The dour, serious-minded dwarves found kender irritating to say the least, but few people had the strength to stay mad at a kender for long.

Challie was no exception. She knew anger was not really effective against kender, so she drew a deep breath to calm down and changed her tactics. She let go of Pease's collar and said in her politest voice, "It's my favorite axe. About as long as my arm with a head of bright steel and a silver haft. I would really like it back."

Pease scratched his forehead and shrugged. His face scrunched up in thought. Challie crossed her arms, and her foot began to tap the floor.

All at once his face burst into a brilliant smile. "I don't know about *your* axe, Challie, but *I* have one like it. I'll show you." He bolted out of the room.

"I thought you might," Challie said.

They only had to wait a few minutes before Pease came running back. "It's my bestest best axe, Challie, and I want you to have it," he said.

She took her father's axe out of his hands. Biting back several harsh comments, she managed to thank him with a modicum of grace as she fastened the axe to her belt. "Now," she said. "How about a noon meal for Lucy?" She shooed him out the door.

Lucy straightened. "Noon? I slept until noon?" She went to the open window and saw the truth of Challie's words. The sun was directly overhead. A warm breeze wavered over the roofs of the town and stirred dust devils in the streets. The road in front of the inn was nearly deserted except for a pair of donkeys laden with broom brush, a few pedestrians, and someone running headlong toward the inn. A pensive Lucy stuck her head out the window for a better view. The runner looked familiar. He raced to the inn's front walk, skidded onto the walkway, and vanished through the front door.

"Ulin, I think something's happened," she said.

"I'm not surprised. We can't seem to get through a day here without some incident."

The runner, one of the men who had ridden with the Silver Fox to help the caravan, hurried to their room, his face sweating and red. "Please come, Sorceress. Mayor Efrim asks for you."

"Is it important?" Ulin demanded. "She is not recovered from yesterday."

The messenger saw her bruises and her swollen black eye and winced, but he did not leave. "It is the burial detail. They had some trouble, but they found the body."

"The gods be praised, they have a body," Ulin muttered. Belatedly he looked at Lucy and saw the tension in her eyes. He bit back the next sarcastic remark and subsided into a more supportive silence.

"All right, I'll come." Lucy pulled out her burnoose and wound it loosely around her head so that part of it encircled her face like a veil. Followed by Ulin and Challie, she hurried after the messenger.

The man led them outside into the noon heat and trotted rapidly north past the marketplace and around the harbor to the old barracks. By the time they arrived, Challie was limping again and Lucy's head throbbed with fatigue and the pain of yesterday's injury.

"What's the hurry? The man's dead!" Ulin snapped to the messenger as he helped the women sit down on the stone steps of the city hall. "Why didn't you tell us we had to come this far? They could have ridden the horse."

"A thousand apologies," the man said, looking contrite. "I did not know you had a horse." He hurried indoors and soon returned with Mayor Efrim and a pitcher of water.

The mayor poured the water into cups for the three. "I'm sorry, Lucy," he said, handing her a cup. "I didn't realize you were feeling ill."

"She wasn't until now," Ulin replied, since Lucy was too busy drinking water to answer for herself.

The mayor flapped a hand, his seamed face deeply concerned. "I do apologize. The men we sent to retrieve the body ran into a spot of trouble. Two were injured, and this was as far as they could go. Actually, I was hoping one of you had training as a healer."

Lucy stared over the rim of her cup. "What sort of trouble?"

"Do you mean this town doesn't have a healer?" Ulin said at the same time.

The mayor shrugged his thin shoulders and tried to answer both questions. "A couple of hobgoblins, early this morning. Unusual this close to town. And not anymore. The best we can do is a midwife or Notwen."

"Notwen? The gnome?" Ulin exclaimed. "You're joking." He considered gnomes to be a nuisance at best, a menace at worst. One with a desire to practice first aid sounded truly frightening.

"Not really. Notwen is not your average gnome. He tinkers with everything. One month it's machinery, the next it's construction, the next it's alchemy. This month it happens to be healing. He's had no training, but he tries."

"Where are your men?" Lucy asked.

"Inside. They came from the north road and made it this far."

Everyone trooped inside. The double doors opened into a wide corridor that passed a short row of offices on either side and led into a large hall. The hall had been recently renovated, but even new roof rafters, some bright wall hangings, and a thorough scrubbing could not completely remove the scorch marks of an old fire or camouflage the smell of fire-heated stone. A long table sat in the middle of the room near a huge fireplace that was empty and cold.

Daylight gleamed through long, slender windows on the north side of the hall.

The four diggers of the burial party were by the table. One sat on a high-backed chair, one lay on his back on the floor, and two stood by a wrapped bundle, the length and width of a human, laying at one end of the long table.

"I sent for the rest of the council," Mayor Efrim told them. "They should be here any moment."

Lucy and Ulin spared only a glance for the corpse as they hurried to the wounded men. The man in the chair, an old Khur by his swarthy skin and black hair, held his hand clamped over his face. His teeth were clenched shut and sweat stood out on his skin. His other hand gripped the armrest of his chair with a strength that could have torn the chair to pieces if he'd tried. A long, bloody gash stretched from his wrist to his elbow and went through the muscle almost to the bone. Beside him stood Notwen.

Notwen held a steel needle and a long trailing length of thread in one hand, and with the other ran his finger along a line of text in a huge tome that lay open on the table beside him. He read a few lines, nodded, and stabbed the needle into the man's arm. Despite the man's clenched teeth, a whimper of pain escaped him.

Ulin stared at the gnome, aghast. He had been forced to learn rudimentary healing techniques on his journeys, but he had never seen anyone try to stitch a gash with three feet of thread and no notion about what they were doing. He jumped forward and snatched the gnome's hand from the needle. "What in the name of Mishakal do you think you're doing?" he shouted.

The Khur started like a wild horse. His eyes flew open and he stared pleadingly at the mayor.

Notwen gazed up at Ulin through a pair of large spectacles perched on his wide nose. His blue eyes were intent and filled with concern. "Oh, are you a healer? Could you help? I am trying to learn the basic skills of first aid, and no one around here is willing to show me. I have this book

I found in my library, but it's so much easier to learn through hands-on experience, don't you think?"

"Unless you happen to be the patient," Ulin pointed out.

The Khur nodded his agreement.

The gnome stroked his beard. "True. I guess it's fortunate that one was passed out."

Ulin and Lucy took a close look at the unconscious man on the floor. His pant's leg had been cut away to expose a laceration on his upper thigh, probably caused by a slash from a sword. The wound hadn't been bandaged yet, and in its present condition, Ulin doubted it could be. The gnome had stitched it closed, and while his unpracticed stitches were close enough together, he had tied them off in a tangled weave of knots and ornate bows the likes of which Ulin had never seen.

"Could you redo these knots?" he whispered to Lucy. "I'll try to help the Khur."

She nodded, her expression struggling between sympathy and laughter. She beckoned to Challie, and they put their heads together over the prostrate man.

Ulin turned back to the gnome and the Khur. Patiently, he showed Notwen how to cut a workable piece of thread, wash the needle in strong alcohol, and clean the wound.

The gnome watched avidly and did his best to help. While he worked, he talked in a fast, enthusiastic stream of comments and questions. "This book says to use horse hair in an emergency, but there weren't any horses nearby, so I used this thread we make from cotton. Can you really use spider webs to stop bleeding? And marigolds to make an astringent? Why are you stitching his muscle together before you stitch the skin? Do you make bows, too? Do you need some wound powder? I made some following a recipe in this book. It called for the mold on old bread. It's supposed to stop infection. Have you ever trained with the Mystics? Do you know how to use the power of the heart? I don't, but I'd like to try."

Ulin tried to follow his monologue and answer questions when he could, but after a while he lost track of the gnome's endless conversation and focused on the Khur's arm. The wound had been bound shortly after it happened and there was little swelling to worry about. The skin went back together fairly well. By the time he was finished, he thought the Khur would have a scar but would retain most of the use of his muscle—as long as the hobgoblin's weapon that caused the slash was not poisoned.

When he finally sat up and cut the last knot, the Khur sighed with relief. "Thank you, Friend of Sorceress. You have my lasting gratitude."

Ulin laid the needle down. "It should heal well," he said. "There was little swelling."

"How fascinating!" murmured Notwen, peering closely at the closed wound. "If it does become gangrenous, will you allow me to watch the amputation?"

The Khur's groan was lost in a commotion at the entrance. Saorsha and Geoff Aylesworthy arrived at the same time, both breathless and agitated. The innkeeper was dusty from a hurried ride back to town from his small brewery. The elderly woman still wore an apron and smears of flour from her baking. Their eyes went directly to the wrapped body on the table, then they huddled with Mayor Efrim in a close, fast-talking group. Challie joined them.

Ulin and Lucy wiped their hands clean. They exchanged a brief, searching gaze of silent support, then Lucy clutched the small knife she had used to cut the thread for the stitches and walked down the length of the table to stand by the silent form lying so still in its dirty shroud. The two quiet guardians inclined their heads to her and backed away to a respectful distance, leaving room for Ulin. The council fell quiet, staring at Lucy with an obvious intensity.

Ulin watched Lucy's hand poised over the cords that bound the chest. He glanced up and saw with a start of surprise they had a much larger audience than he expected. People in twos and threes slipped in the door and gathered quietly around the room. He recognized members of the Vigilance Force, the blacksmith, and people from the market and the common room at the Jetties. Apparently, quite a few people in Flotsam wished to see if Lucy recognized this corpse. He returned his gaze to Lucy and saw her hands shaking.

Notwen trotted up beside her, his small face alive with interest, and he climbed up on a chair to see better. "It's all right, Miss Lucy," he said soothingly. "The body still stinks, doesn't it? But it should still be identifiable. He died from the force of the explosion *before* the fire."

Ulin stiffened in his place by the table. "No one said anything about an explosion."

The room remained breathlessly silent.

Lucy's eyes narrowed, and as Ulin opened his mouth to say something more, she forestalled him with a quick slash of her knife against the binding cord. "Let's see who this is, then we'll ask the questions," she said.

Ulin subsided back into his watchful pose while Notwen leaned forward to help Lucy. Together the gnome and the woman severed the ropes and unwrapped the rotten stained strips of cloth that encased the body.

Notwen was right. The body stank. Four winter months in the desert sand had not been enough to completely desiccate it or deter the worms and insects drawn to the smell of decaying flesh. By the time Lucy reached the last layer of foul cotton next to the corpse, everyone in the room wished the dead man had been left outside.

Lucy's full lips curved in a grimace of disgust. Ulin scarcely breathed.

"Look at that!" Notwen said brightly. "The worms burrowed into his eye sockets, but what's left of the face is intact."

Challie appeared at Lucy's side and thrust a mug in her hand. Lucy caught the smell of wine, rich and red, and she took the mug gratefully and downed the contents in one long swallow, hoping the wine would soothe her stomach before she embarrassed herself in front of the townspeople. She took a firm grip on her resolve and looked carefully at the sunken face of the corpse.

The spectators held a collective breath.

Ulin held himself very still as he watched Lucy pull away the shroud from the shoulders, arms, and torso of the body. From what little Ulin knew or guessed about Kethril Torkay, the corpse appeared to be a close match. It was a human male, white-skinned, about six feet in height, with light brown hair liberally sprinkled with gray, and a creased face with a close-cropped beard. The explosion that had killed the man had apparently blown behind him, for the back of his skull was crushed and flattened. The nose and much of the flesh on the forehead, cheekbones, and chin was eaten or burned away, and the man's clothes showed tears and scorch marks. Would it be enough?

Ulin could see the intense concentration on Lucy's pale, battered face, and he recognized a momentary flash of indecision. He wondered what would she say. Was this her father? Did she know for sure? He knew she would not lie, even for the inheritance. Lucy had more integrity than most people, but could she be certain one way or another? Gripping his hands behind his back, he looked on while she lifted the body's arms and studied each hand. She carefully laid the limbs back in place, covered the corpse again, and moved away. He accompanied her, with Challie and Notwen, as she approached the city council.

"That is not my father. I don't know who you have or why you thought it was Kethril, but it is not he." Her words were strong and clear, and to Ulin, sounded slightly relieved.

The hall erupted with dozens of voices talking and shouting all at once.

"Are you certain?" Mayor Efrim asked over the noise.

"Very. I know my father was born with a stunted fore-finger on his left hand. He always wore gloves to disguise it, but his family knew. That body has normal finger bones."

The old mayor sighed deeply and collapsed into a chair. Aylesworthy turned pale under his tan, and even Challie and Notwen shared expressions of concern and dismay. Saorsha sat beside the mayor, her face buried in her hands.

Lucy and Ulin glanced at each other in surprise. They expected disappointment, but the loud, angry voices from the crowd and the obvious despair on the faces of the council went beyond mere thwarted desire for a dead man's estate.

"What is going on?" Ulin demanded. "This is more than an accidental death by fire and an unclaimed inheritance. What are you people trying to do?"

Noise from the onlookers subsided as the townspeople waited for their council to respond. For once Notwen was quiet, and it was Challie who finally explained the truth.

"We really did not know if that was Kethril Torkay. We only know him by reputation around here. Even now, I don't know if we should be pleased or frightened out of our wits that this is not he." The magistrate stood before them, her arms crossed, her face stonily professional. "The accident happened last winter during an attempted robbery. We don't know exactly who was involved besides Kethril, but we do know they managed to steal most of the contents of our city treasury before the mishap."

Lucy's face paled then grew hot. She knew her father was underhanded and self-centered, but she never thought he would stoop to robbing an entire town.

"How do you know he was involved?" she asked.

"One of his cohorts identified him as the ringleader. Unfortunately, that thief died from his injuries sustained in the fire." Challie crossed her arms and added, "The explosion was not intentional."

Ulin cleared his throat. "I understand," he said, "Your

anger and concern with the robbery and your desire to identify this body. But surely there are people in that town you mentioned—Dead Pirate's Cove—who could have known Torkay missed part of his finger. Why did you have to bring us all the way from Solace?"

Saorsha sighed deeply and, with an effort, pushed herself to her feet. She straightened her back and faced Lucy and Ulin. "There probably are people there who know Kethril that well, but we need more than someone to identify him. We need help."

Ulin did not like the sound of that. There were too many nuances, too many possible things that could go wrong in those three simple words. His gold eyes darkened under his lowered brows.

Challie read his expression correctly and took up the tale in her cool, unemotional tone. "The money stolen was the collected taxes and tribute due to our overlord, Malys, money that will soon be collected by her tax collector, the red dragon known as Fyremantle."

Ulin's brows dropped into a deep frown. "Another red dragon."

"Unfortunately, yes," Challie confirmed. "He is one of Malys's underlings. If he doesn't destroy the town, Malys will—unless we pay the tribute."

"When are the taxes due?" Lucy wanted to know.

"In three weeks. On—"

The date clicked into place in the puzzle of the conversation Lucy had had with the Committee two nights before. "On Visiting Day," she said, cutting off the dwarf.

"Yes," Saorsha sighed. "That is our annual tax day."

Ulin felt the spectre of disaster looming over his shoulder. He thought he had a very good idea where this conversation was leading and it made his stomach crawl. "Do you have the amount due?" he asked quietly.

Saorsha said, "Of course not. Oh, we have the taxes from the last four months but it is not nearly enough to make up for the missing funds. This is not a prosperous town. We scrimped and saved for eight months just to put together the amount demanded by the Overlord."

Lucy looked horrified. "That's why you wanted me to be sheriff? To face Malys and tell her you don't have the taxes?"

"Oh, the gods forbid, no, Miss Lucy!" Mayor Efrim climbed to his feet. "As Saorsha said, we really do need help. We just thought . . . we *hoped* . . . if this wasn't your father, maybe you would be decent enough to help us find him. We still have three weeks. If we could find him or the stolen funds, we could still make our deadline."

"How do you know if the daughter of Kethril Torkay is decent enough? How do you know I might be willing, or even capable enough, to help you? How did you know he even has a family?" Lucy demanded, her voice rising. Her good eye turned that stormy shade of green Ulin had learned to respect.

The council members looked at one another in resignation. "When we heard from a good friend of Kethril's that he had a grown daughter in the Academy of Sorcery, we had Challie check into it," Mayor Efrim replied. "We are desperate, Miss Lucy. We are willing to go to any lengths to save this town."

A silence settled over the group. Lucy stood too stunned to say more. No one moved. Only Notwen shifted from foot to foot and watched the scene with fascinated eyes.

Lucy finally wavered and dropped into another empty chair. "Ulin," she said wearily, "what do we do now?"

Chapter Eight

"I'm happy you asked me," Notwen said, beaming up at the tall, lanky man.

Ulin didn't feel he should say *there wasn't anything else better to do,* so he returned a cooler version of the gnome's smile and replied, "Saorsha told me you could show me the treasury."

The gnome, mindful of Mayor Efrim's constant reprimands, tried to speak his words slowly and deliberately so the human could understand. "There really isn't much left of it, but I'd be happy to show you the ruins."

They had met at the foot of the Rock near the wharves at noon. It was another cloudless, sunny, hot day in Flotsam, and Ulin was out of sorts. He and Lucy had argued quietly and at length since they left the city hall the day before. Lucy refused to leave without some due thought to her father's alleged villainy and Flotsam's predicament. Ulin just wanted to pack and go before things got worse. *If* he could have firmly believed the city council was telling them the truth and *if* he had been alone, he would have given serious thought to offering help. But Lucy was with him, and he had a bad feeling about all of this. Two dragons, missing taxes, robbery, death, and citizens who couldn't seem to keep their story straight. He had a hard time believing they'd send someone all the way to Solace just to look for a relative of the thief on the vague chance that person might help out of a sense of second-hand guilt.

Akkar-bin offered them a place in the caravan returning to Khuri-Khan, but, to Ulin's disgust, Lucy turned him down. The Khurish caravan left that morning, and Ulin had watched it go, his thoughts worried and unhappy. Their one sure mode of transportation and armed escort had moved on without them, and no one in this forsaken dump of a town seemed to know when the next caravan would arrive.

Feeling surly, Ulin walked around the streets of Flotsam for hours until a short, white-haired figure wandered into his path. Saorsha's comment came to mind. Hot, tired, and bored, Ulin decided to ask the gnome about the burned treasury.

Notwen turned toward the docks and took Ulin around the harbor road toward the barracks. Ulin was startled then dubious when Notwen led him though the large double doors of the city hall and into the main corridor. No one had mentioned the treasury was in this building. But the gnome kept walking past the office of the mayor, down the corridor, through the great hall, and out a back hallway to a walled courtyard.

"This is the old prison and work yard," Notwen explained as he trotted into the hot sun. "It was built by the dragonarmy years ago. It's only accessible through the barracks."

Ulin looked around. The prison was a one-story stone building with barred windows and a single entrance. There were no prisoners inhabiting the damp, cramped cells—only spiders and cockroaches the size of rats. The only impressive aspect of the building was the fact it was still standing.

"The treasury is, uh, *was* over here." The gnome showed Ulin to the corner of the courtyard opposite the prison. The damage quickly became apparent. What looked like a shadowed doorway into the building under the wall walk proved to be a doorless entrance into a gutted room, scorched and scored by a powerful blast. The floor had collapsed into a deep pit eight to ten feet deep, and the inner dividing walls had been burned away, destroying part of the old kennels and a bake house.

The smell of burned wood and stone permeated the narrow room, as well as an odd smell that reminded Ulin of something he couldn't place. A thin chill crept up his back. This blackened room reminded him too much of the ruins of the Academy of Sorcery after the attack of Beryl's minions. He shoved that thought aside and stepped into the room. He was both impressed by the thieves' audacity and puzzled by their methods. He studied the room carefully from blackened ceiling to collapsed floor, while Notwen moved cautiously around the edge of the pit and examined the walls from behind his large spectacles.

"This doesn't make sense," Ulin said. "If thieves did this, why is Lysandros so eager to help the council? Why does he want a sorceress like Lucy to be sheriff?"

"Because the Thieves' Guild had nothing to do with this," Notwen replied. "It was an outside job, and the captain is furious. He would split Kethril in half with that sword of his if he could find him."

"Why? For horning into his territory?"

"No! For putting the town into such a crisis! The Thieves' Guild here may be sticky-fingered and greedy, but they would never do something to endanger the entire town. They live here, too."

"Hmm . . ." Ulin squatted in the doorway and tossed a pebble into the dark pit where the floor had been. "How did they pull this off? In the city hall of all places. Weren't there guards?"

"Of course, we posted guards outside. They never saw a thing until the room blew up in their faces." Notwen pushed his spectacles back on his nose, leaving a smear of soot from his grimy fingers. "As for the theft, I can't say for certain how they did it. I can only go by the clues. Take the pit, for example. There is no lower level beneath this section of the barracks, so I have surmised Kethril and his cohorts dug a tunnel beneath this room and removed the contents a little at a time. The tunnel apparently collapsed in the explosion."

Ulin lifted a single eyebrow. Whether he liked it or not, he found himself intrigued by the gnome's interpretation of the theft. It was a heinous deed, but the machinations behind it were interesting. "What was in here? Ingots? Loose coins?"

The gnome peered down into the pit. "Mostly loose coins and odds and ends like jewelry, plate armor, swords, a few fine daggers, things like that. This town has to scrape up every bit just to meet Malys's demands. My guess is Kethril only had a few men to help and it took several nights to remove the pile. I think, in order to keep us fooled, they replaced the valuables with fakes."

"Why do you say that?"

"Someone on the council came in here every day to add deposits or check the inventory." Notwen patted the wall beside him. "I noticed these walls are spattered with bits of fool's gold and lead," then he pointed down at the hole. "If you look carefully you can see broken glass and bits of cheap twisted metal in the rubble."

"Fool's gold . . . good gods," Ulin muttered. He didn't have to ask what would have happened if the theft had gone unnoticed until the city council presented the false coin to Malys's collector, Fyremantle. Red dragons were anything but understanding. A slow anger began to simmer in Ulin's gut. What kind of a man could put his own greed before the safety of an entire town?

"Is there any chance this Kethril got caught in his own explosion?" Ulin suggested.

Notwen scratched his head. "I don't think so. We looked through the debris, and we only found the bodies of the guards and two thieves. There was no trace of anyone else."

The young man stared deep into the darkness of the hole. "What if Kethril set off the explosion to kill his cohorts and mask his escape with the treasure?"

"We thought of that," Notwen sighed. "I just don't know. The explosion happened down there in the tunnel, and its blast started the fire, but I haven't discovered yet what set it off or why." The words were barely out of his mouth when his face suddenly brightened. "I've taken some samples to my laboratory. Would you like to see?"

Ulin hesitated. He was hot, tired, still feeling out of sorts, and most gnome labs usually involved noxious smells, clouds of odd gases, and the imminent danger of an explosion. And yet . . . the puzzle of the treasury piqued his interest. He had studied the effects of explosives at one time, and his interests leaned toward alchemy these days. Why not take a quick look at Notwen's samples? Solving that puzzle could prove useful in the future if Lucy decided to stay. Besides, if the lab proved too dangerous, he could always leave.

"All right, thank you," he replied.

"It's this way," Notwen said. He led the way out of the barracks, skirted the docks, and trotted up the path that climbed the slope of the promontory called the Rock.

The road was wide enough for handcarts, donkeys, and pedestrians, though it was little used any more by anyone other than the Vigilance Force, who maintained a constant watch from its height. After the first time Malys leveled the buildings on its top, a few stubborn people tried to rebuild the Saltbreeze Inn and the lord of Flotsam's manor, only to see their efforts destroyed in seconds during another of Malys's visits. Since then the Rock had remained bare in deference to the Overlord's opinion. Even the Force's look-outs stayed concealed behind a camouflaged observation post.

Ulin remembered the stripped and wind-blown surface of the Rock from his previous visit, and he wondered where Notwen could possibly hide an entire laboratory.

The little gnome led him past the crest of the path and to the side of the headland where the rock bulged out like the belly of a pregnant woman. A level, bare space and some stones were all that marked the foundations of Toede's old manor and its walls.

Ulin stopped and stared around, his arms crossed. A sea breeze stirred his chestnut hair. "Now what?" he asked, too curious to be annoyed.

"OverhereUlinIfoundthisayearafterToededied."

Ulin held up a finger. "Wait. Wait, slow down again."

"Oh, sorry. Sorry. I do that when I get excited." Notwen's blue eyes were vivid against his golden-brown skin. He waved a small hand and headed to the edge of the ruined building where a few shattered blocks of stone were scattered over a layer of dirt and sand. "Stand back," the gnome warned, and he pushed one stone about a hand span to the left to reveal a weathered bronze lock. Pulling a key from his pocket, he inserted it and turned.

A loud rumbling, grating noise erupted from the ground at Ulin's feet, and he leaped back in alarm. Dust rose in clouds around him. The sound grew to a roar, and suddenly a huge block of stone lifted out of the dirt.

Notwen watched proudly. More rumbling, creaking, and grinding of stone on metal thundered around them. Slowly and noisily, the block of stone lifted straight up until it was clear of the old floor. Still the noises went on, louder than before. The huge slab lifted ever higher until a three-foot gap yawned underneath the massive weight of the stone. The sounds ground to silence, the stone halted in place, and the dust settled slowly around the hole.

Ulin stared, amazed. The slab, nearly one-foot thick,

had been lifted horizontally out of the foundations by what looked like four columns, one at each corner of the slab. He glanced at Notwen questioningly.

"Hydraulics," the gnome grinned "I'm working on a way to lift the slab completely out of the opening, but I haven't completed all the calculations to compensate for its thickness and weight."

Ulin had to admit he was impressed. He'd never thought much of gnomes. Tinker gnomes were notorious among the other races of Krynn for building large, overly complex machines that failed more often than not. Although they were often bright, curious, and endlessly imaginative, they were cursed by the god Reorx so they could never master the inventive genius of their quick minds. And yet, Ulin remembered hearing a tale about a group of gnomes who had been freed of the curse at the end of the Chaos War. They came to be called thinker gnomes, and they scattered across the world seeking wisdom and knowledge. They did not look different from their tinker cousins, yet they were master inventors and perfectionists whose smaller, less flashy constructions usually worked.

The mage watched Notwen walk to the slab and disappear into the dark depths underneath, and he wondered if indeed this bright-eyed fellow in the orange tunic was a thinker gnome.

Ulin eyed the stone warily. It seemed sturdy enough. Using utmost caution, he sat on the brink of the opening and swung his legs through onto a wooden staircase that led down into darkness. He barely breathed while he slid his long torso through and drew his head under. Hurriedly, he crawled down the steps until his head was clear of the stone and he could stand upright.

"Come on down!" the gnome's voice called. Light flared golden yellow some twenty feet below.

Ulin stepped down between the columns. The walls of the stairwell consisted of packed dirt and rubble braced with wooden beams. Beneath the stairs, Ulin could just make out the complex gears and cables of Notwen's hydraulic machine. Slowly, he went down toward the light.

The bottom of the stairs ended in a narrow corridor, stone flagged and arched overhead. The corridor had been carved out of bedrock by skilled hands and led directly to a wooden door that stood open into a room blazing with light.

Ulin hesitated a moment. The rock slab opening into the earth, the working machinery, the corridor leading into a room as bright as day—this was not at all what he was expecting. In spite of his depressed mood, he found himself intrigued and more than a little curious. He hurried into the room and stopped with a sudden jolt.

The chamber was huge. A great round circle cut out of the living rock, its ceiling was domed and painted white with a mural depicting the ancient runes and symbols of the gods. Ulin stood on a railed balcony that circled the upper portion of the room and contained a row of bookcases. Looking closely at the shelves he saw every imaginable form of print on books, scrolls, vellum, parchment, paper, linen, and even tablets of clay and wax. Lamps hung on sconces from the walls, and overhead, suspended from the ceiling, hung a chandelier of glowing oil lamps set behind reflective lenses.

Ulin walked farther into the room and saw a circular stair leading down to the floor below. Tall cupboards, gilded with gold, stood upright between more shelves crowded with an incredible clutter of stuff. On the few bare spaces of wall left hung clocks of every description, size, and shape, their ticking filling the air with a steady drone. A water clock occupied the space near a large fireplace. Other instruments of time, navigation, survey, and drafting lay scattered on heavy worktables or piled on shelves. Everywhere Ulin looked, he saw tools, artifacts, colored glass bottles, crocks and jugs, knives, candles, dishes, maps, and odd things he could not begin to identify.

Notwen was nowhere to be seen, so Ulin walked down to the bottom floor. Curious, he threw open the doors of the first cupboard he came to and drew a breath of astonishment, for on its set of shelves he beheld an alchemist's treasure: scales and weights, a mortar and pestle, stone bowls, rows of neatly-labeled bottles and boxes. He saw yellow brimstone, sulfur, saltpeter, white lead, vials of mercury, and nuggets of pure silver. There were little bottles of arsenic, viper's poison, distilled toad, cock's eyes, larger bottles with animal specimens neatly preserved—tangled webs of jellyfish tentacles, clippings of mermaids' hair, and many more substances he did not recognize.

He heard a sound behind him, and he turned to see Notwen appear through another door pushing a wheeled tray bearing plates and bottles.

"How did you find all of this?" Ulin asked. He flung out his arms to include the entire chamber. "How could one person collect so much?"

The gnome pushed his tray to the fireplace and arranged two leather chairs beside it. "Come eat. I'm hungry." He settled Ulin comfortably in a chair, filled two flagons with cold cider, fixed two plates of food, and sat down on a shorter chair to enjoy his meal. It wasn't until his plate was empty that he leaned back against the worn leather padding and answered Ulin's question.

"I wish I could say I collected all this, but as I said, I just found it. I've added my own things, of course, but the books, the Istar artifacts, and the chamber were here."

Ulin's interest spiked at the mention of artifacts, but he said nothing.

"I've studied some of the papers and manuscripts left down here," Notwen continued, "and I believe the collection belonged to a black-robed mage who worked for Highmaster Toede for years. Toede helped him add to it, of course, probably hoping the mage would add to his treasury in return."

"Why didn't Malys destroy it?" Ulin asked. "Or add the artifacts to her own collection?"

"She hasn't found it yet. I think the chamber is protected like the barracks with magical wards. When the red dragon attacked the manor, she destroyed the original entrance and filled the basement above with rubble. Fortunately, the original flooring remained and the chamber is still intact."

Ulin pointed toward the ceiling. "Why don't you replace that slab with a concealed door of bronze or something easier to open?"

"So it won't be easy to open—or find." Notwen shuddered. "Can you imagine the kender down here? And who would hesitate to plunder a gnome's laboratory if all you had to do was open a door?"

"Point taken." Ulin finished his cider and set the flagon aside. He felt better now that he'd eaten. He hadn't realized how hungry he was until the food was placed before him. "Would you show me your collection?"

Happiness glowed on Notwen's face, and he bounced eagerly to his feet. He took Ulin by the hand and led him to the first table, made of stone and used for working with volatile substances. The surface was stained and pitted by constant use. Notwen ran his hand over a particularly large pit blasted from the table's surface. "Knowledge is obtained by study and practice," he said, then chuckled. "I practice a lot."

Ulin's thoughts went back to memories of the laboratory at the Academy of Sorcery, to the chambers of Huma's Tomb where he met Sunrise for the first time, and to other places where he had learned and practiced the art of sorcery. The little gnome may not cast spells or know the intricacies of wielding magic, Ulin thought, but his philosophy of knowledge and his pleasure in its gathering were so similar to his own that the young mage felt drawn into the conversation.

The two soon lost all track of time in the discussions that filled the afternoon. They talked about healing remedies from Notwen's tome, argued about metallurgical experiments, and examined every bottle and box in the laboratory.

Notwen proudly showed Ulin the clocks he had made and demonstrated each gear and weight and clock face. "Beneath the magic and superstition, there is a clock-work precision to the way the world works," he proclaimed. "I want to find that precision and learn what makes it tick."

Ulin found the words matched his own unspoken need. He had tried magic and that had failed him. Now he wanted to look for something deeper, something more basic and profound that would be unchangeable, irrefutable, and perhaps eternal. In his studies of magic he had never taken the time to see how ordinary things worked, or why. He had been too involved in learning spells, and for a while he had excelled at his chosen craft. Then came the failures, the terrible losses, the bitterness, and the fear . . . until he could no longer face the torment of the endless disappointments. All he had left was himself—his own intelligence, imagination, and strength, and slowly he was beginning to stretch out his abilities to learn the depths of capabilities he never realized were there. Notwen was right. Behind the veneer of magic was an entirely new world to be explored, tested, and studied, a world more reliable and eternal than the realm of faulty magic. His mind filled with these thoughts, Ulin studied Notwen's clocks with new and fascinated eyes as if he had never seen a gear or pendulum before.

Time passed swiftly in the gnome's laboratory, and in spite of all the clocks around him set to the same time, Ulin did not realize how long he had stayed until he looked at one particularly large clock on the wall and saw the small hand on the number eight. His eyebrows flew to his hairline.

"Lucy is going to have a fit!" he exclaimed. "Notwen, I must go."

The gnome started at the man's outburst. "But why? If

you are hungry, I will fix a meal. I keep food in a small pantry here. There is no need to go yet."

"Yes, there is! My friends don't know where I am, and I have been gone all day. One in particular will be very angry."

Notwen's small face creased in thought. Gnomes were often too busy to worry about social and personal obligations, but Notwen had met Lucy. "Ah, the Sorceress. It would not be right to anger her. Will she allow you to return?"

The irony of his simple question did not escape Ulin. While he deeply respected Lucy's abilities as a mage, *he* had always been the one in the forefront: the son of Palin Majere, the assistant director of the Academy of Sorcery, one of the few dragon mages on Krynn. People had come to him for help and advice. They had looked up to him. Now most of that was gone, and by a strange twist, he was being called "Friend of the Sorceress" and treated as her bodyguard or shadow. He didn't know whether to laugh or bury his head in his arms and weep. He was not an envious man by nature, and he would never begrudge Lucy the honors she deserved, yet the changes in his life had left him raw and badly shaken.

Keeping careful control of his voice, he thanked Notwen for his hospitality and accepted an invitation to return, then he hurried up the wooden stairs and crawled out into the fading light of evening.

A vigilante hurrying toward the slab almost stepped on his fingers. "Ulin!" he gasped. "I'm on watch tonight. I saw a patrol of Dark Knights ride into town, so be on your guard. They're Malys's men, very unpredictable." Before Ulin could reply, the guard shouted down the stone hole. "Notwen! Knights in town!"

Ulin backed away as the machinery began to grind. The stone slowly dropped into place with an echoing boom. By the time he looked up, the guard had returned to his post, and he was alone on the windy rock. He kicked some dirt over the cracks between the stone until the slab was indistinguishable from the others. If he hadn't seen the block with his own eyes, he would never guess the entrance was there. He couldn't wait to tell Lucy about the laboratory— once she got over being mad at him.

He took a quick survey of the town while he hurried down the path. Dusk cast a heavy gloom over the weather-beaten old buildings, but everything seemed normal. The taverns and pleasure houses were crowded, the market was nearly deserted, and the city hall was dark. Lights glowed in the windows of houses and tenements, and columns of smoke rose from dozens of kitchen fires to drift west into the grasslands on the wind from the sea. There was no sign of the Knights' patrol. Ulin hoped fervently he could reach the Jetties and get out of sight before he was spotted. He did not want to risk a confrontation with the Knights of Neraka.

All too soon he discovered his wish was in vain, for when he approached the ramshackle old inn his hope sunk into dismay. Five saddled horses stood tied to the inn's hitching post. Each one wore a skull-shaped brand of the Dark Knights on its hip. Although the front door stood open and lamps were lit, no one was in sight, and the inn was strangely silent.

A commotion rose out of the walled stable yard to the rear. Ulin could hear the nervous clatter of a horse's iron-shod hooves on the stone paving and the shouting of angry voices. One of the voices was Lucy's. Ulin broke into a run toward the door.

Without warning a small figure pelted out of a side entrance and slammed into Ulin's stomach, knocking the air from his lungs.

"Oh, it's you!" squeaked Pease. "Ulin! You must come. The Knights have arrested Lucy."

Chapter Nine

His first inclination was to burst into the courtyard and start laying about with his sword until Lucy was free and all those who dared touch her were dead. Fortunately, his common sense prevailed.

He snatched the kender's tunic and hauled him into the concealing shadows of the side door. "How many Knights are there? What did they arrest her for? Where is Challie?"

Pease, trembling, tried to answer all the questions at once with a tangle of words. Ulin had to shake him again to rattle some sense back into his head.

"There are two Knights holding Lucy in the courtyard. The other three threw everyone out of the common room and are searching the inn." Pease's words tumbled out. "Challie's with Lucy in the yard. I was sent to look for you."

"But what did they arrest her for?" Ulin demanded to know.

"Horse stealing. They found her horse in the stable, and that snitch of a groom told them whose it was."

Ulin muttered a few words that caused Pease to gape at him. "Is there another way into the courtyard besides the gate?" he asked.

In reply Pease took his sleeve and led him around the inn. Ulin caught a glimpse through a window into the empty common room and saw two of the Knights kicking over tables and passing a jug back and forth. He ducked down behind Pease and followed the kender through a shrubby patch of gardenias into an alley behind the stable.

It was nearly dark by that time. Dense shadows filled the alley, hiding the refuse piles and the rats that scattered among the trash and old debris. The kender cautiously picked his way along the alley to a postern gate set in the wall that surrounded the stable yard.

"Master Aylooworthy likes to keep this locked," Pease whispered, "but I haul manure out here, and I often forget to lock it up again."

From the powerful smell and the feel of the ground beneath his boots, Ulin could easily believe the part about the manure. He held his breath as Pease tried the door handle. It turned quietly, and the postern opened.

The kender stuck out his arm to stop Ulin from hurrying in. Wordlessly, he put his finger to his lips then pointed to his right and waved a hand.

Together they slipped into the courtyard and, moving right, slid unseen behind a pile of straw bales under an old, sagging plank roof. They peered around the bales and saw Lucy, Challie, and two guards standing in a pool of light that poured out of the open inn door. A very nervous and embarrassed groom held the halter of the big bay draft horse.

Ulin's stomach muscles twisted into knots. Lucy appeared unhurt, but she stood between the two Knights as rigid as a lance, her face flushed with outrage. Her clothes had been mussed, and her hair fell unbound over her shoulders.

The Knights wore dented breastplates marked with the death lily of Takhisis and a strange red emblem Ulin could not identify in the dim light. Scraps of armor covered their arms and legs. He noticed their trappings looked worn and battered, and he thought if they were truly attached to Malys's unit, then she did not keep them well attired. They were, however, well armed. Each Knight bore a short sword, an axe, and a dagger, and one had a crossbow slung across his back.

Ulin's hand tightened around his sword hilt. For once, he was at a loss about what to do. He had no armor or reinforcements and only one sword. If he could even approach the two Knights without endangering Lucy, the first clash of weapons in the courtyard would bring the other three running, and Ulin was not fool enough to believe he could successfully take on five highly trained soldiers. He understood, too, the danger he could bring on the townspeople of Flotsam. The Dark Knights and their mistress would not overlook a deliberate attack made on one of their patrols, and their retaliation could be deadly.

Ulin shifted nervously. He needed an idea, and he needed one now.

Something moved to his right. He eased back from the straw bales and saw several forms slide through the postern gate and position themselves in shadowed hiding places.

Pease put his mouth close to Ulin's ear. "Cosmo went for help. Wait and see what happens. Do you think she'll use her magic?"

"I doubt it," Ulin breathed. He knew the Knights would kill her in an instant if they thought she was trying to cast a spell.

Several minutes dragged by, and no one moved or said a word. The Knights continued to stand close to Lucy while the silent watchers waited in breathless suspense.

A burst of raucous laughter inside the inn shattered the quiet. It was followed by the innkeeper's voice raised in frightened protest. The other three Knights stamped out of the inn, shoving Master Aylesworthy before them. The portly man tripped over a loose stone and fell to his knees.

The leader of the patrol, a stocky, black-haired woman, put her fists on her hips. "An appropriate gesture, Innkeeper," she sneered. "Stay there until I tell you to rise." She pushed close to Lucy and glared at her like a cat eyes its prey. They were nearly the same height, and their eyes met and locked. Lucy did not blink or look away, but regarded the officer with cool disdain.

"Knight Officer," Challie began, "I demand to know why my client—"

The woman cut her off with a sharp jerk of her hand. "I am Knight Officer Jesic Venturin of the Third Talon. You have been caught in the possession of a stolen horse." Her gaze nailed on Lucy's face.

"Who said it was stolen?" asked Lucy.

The Knight Officer's hand cracked across Lucy's bruised cheek. "You will take care to watch your tone."

Lucy's choked cry of pain brought Ulin's anger to a boil. He would have surged out of his hiding place if Pease hadn't caught his sleeve.

"Not yet!" hissed the kender. "Not unless there is no choice."

Ulin subsided. He was beginning to see why this kender rode with the Silver Fox. He forced his attention away from his anger and concentrated on what the Dark Knight was saying to Lucy.

"This brand says the horse is stolen. In the rare instances that the Knights of Neraka sell a horse, we alter the brand."

Ulin bit back a groan. No wonder Akkar-bin had been so willing to part with the animal.

Lucy bowed her head to look contrite. "Knight Officer, I know nothing about the horse's past or its brand. It was given to me as part of my wages for a job."

"What job?" Venturin demanded.

"Well, I—"

"She accepted the position of sheriff for our little town."

Two people stood silhouetted in the doorway of the inn. Together they shuffled in, frail and bent over their walking sticks, their white hair ghostly in the torchlight.

The five Knights made no move toward the two, in fact they relaxed their tense positions and moved slightly apart. Aylesworthy shifted cautiously out of the way.

"Mayor Efrim." Knight Officer Venturin curled her lip.

The old man and his companion stopped by the Dark Knights and made ridiculously low bows. Shuffling their feet and swaying, they managed to stand upright again.

Behind the straw bales, Ulin watched the scene with interest. He recognized the other person as Saorsha, but he had not seen the councilwoman look so elderly and bent before.

"Knight Officer Venturin, what a delight to see you again," the mayor's voice quavered across the stableyard. "I apologize for any difficulty you are having. What may we do to help?"

Venturin twisted on her heel to glower at the mayor. "Explain your earlier comment, old man, and do it quickly."

The mayor flinched under the crack of her voice. "This woman agreed to be our sheriff, for a few weeks only." He lifted his trembling hands as if to ward off a blow. "Just to help keep the peace during the Visiting Day Festival."

Venturin snorted. Her black, cold eyes turned to Lucy. "This? This soft piece of gutter trash is your new sheriff? She looks better suited for one of the pleasure houses—one of the cheaper ones."

The other Knights snickered. Lucy did not move. Only her last reserves of self-control held her still and silent.

Saorsha spoke for the first time in a voice soft and compliant. "We like her, Knight Officer, and she gets along well with the townspeople—especially the kender. Our agreement is for such a short time." She smiled a hopeful smile, her gaze and posture totally inoffensive.

"Like the previous sheriff," Venturin commented dryly. She snapped back to Lucy. "You are new here. When did you arrive?"

Lucy had been watching Saorsha carefully. Now that the Knight Officer's attention was back to her, she adopted the elder's submissive behavior by dropping her gaze to the ground and relaxing her stiff posture. "I was with Akkarbin's caravan. I was his cook's assistant. When he left here, I stayed. Their"—Lucy had trouble getting the words out— "offer was hard to refuse."

"An offer including the horse?"

Saorsha answered, "Yes, your honor. We bought it from the Khur for her to ride around town."

"Hmm. Very official looking. Very stupid." The Knight walked around the big bay horse, running her hand along his flank. "Did it not occur to you to check the brand?" Her voice lost its rough edge and became silky smooth.

Saorsha and Efrim glanced at one another. "The Khur gave us a bill of sale, Knight Officer," Efrim explained, "and this brand is different from yours. We never thought—"

"Of course you didn't," Venturin interrupted, her voice full of false resignation. "And now I am forced to arrest your new sheriff. Too bad. Horse stealing is a hanging offense."

Mayor Efrim kept his eyes lowered as he reached for a bag of coins tucked into the script that dangled from his belt. "Your honor, perhaps we can reach an agreement that will save you the inconvenience of hauling a prisoner to your base, trying her, and finally burying her. You are a Dark Knight. Could we buy the horse from you?"

The Talon leader paused to go through the pretense of considering the offer. She pursed her thin lips and studied the horse from tail to chunky muzzle before she finally shrugged. "It could be done. Do you have the original bill of sale?"

Ulin tensed behind his straw bale—the Khur had left no bill of sale—but Mayor Efrim drew a piece of coarse paper from his script and held it out. Venturin snatched it from his fingers.

"Hmm. Akkar-bin again. He travels to and from Sanction for that oily Garzan the rug maker. He should know better," she growled, perusing the paper. "You paid ten silver pieces for this horse to that Khurish thief. Consider that a fine. Pay me ten silver pieces, and I will alter the brand and validate your bill of sale."

Validate it she might, but Ulin knew those ten pieces of silver would never see the coffers of the Knights of Neraka. That much was evident in the way the Knight held out her hand for Efrim's coins.

"Sheriff," she snorted derisively, "enjoy your stay in this flea-trap." Drawing her dagger, she strode to the horse, and before anyone could stop her, she slashed her blade twice across the brand in an X-shape. The horse squealed in pain and jumped sideways into the groom. With a jerk of her head toward the door, Knight Officer Venturin walked out of the stableyard, followed by her Talon of Knights.

The people left behind remained still. No one made a sound or moved. They listened to the clump of boots on the inn floor, the loud voice shouting commands, and finally the thud of hooves in front of the inn. Challie followed quietly behind to be certain they were truly gone.

At last she stuck her head out the door. "They've left," she announced.

The silence in the stableyard turned into an uproar. Ulin burst from his hiding place and rushed to Lucy. She was so relieved to see him safe and unharmed that she threw her arms around him and buried her head in his shoulder. Pease dashed into the kitchen and came out with Bridget, both talking at once in high, excited voices. Innkeeper Aylesworthy climbed to his feet and leveled a ferocious glare at his groom.

Saorsha slowly straightened to her full, erect height. "That viscous brat of an ogre's offspring," she muttered as she examined the bleeding wound on the horse's hip.

The silent bystanders in the stable spoke a few words to Pease then melted back into the darkness of the postern gate. Only Cosmo stayed to see the fun.

Lucy recovered from the shock of the moment and thrust herself away from Ulin. "Where have you been all day? I was worried sick!" she shouted at him over the hubbub in the inn yard. In a blink she switched her anger to the old mayor and added, "And you! What possessed you to tell that harpy I was your new sheriff? If she comes back here, she'll expect me to be fulfilling my duties. I didn't accept your offer!"

"We know that, dear," Mayor Efrim replied. "I was simply trying to give you an official capacity that would allow me to offer her a bribe. We do it all the time." His rheumy eyes glinted with a humorous twinkle. "The trick to dealing with those Dark Knights is to act as harmless and ineffectual as possible, then they don't bother us very much." He chuckled. "That's why the council made me mayor."

Lucy drew back and put her hands on her hips. "And is that why you want me to be sheriff? Because I look harmless and ineffectual?"

Aylesworthy tucked his hands in his belt and shook his head. "That was part of it. That Knight Officer you just met is one of the most arrogant and condescending harpies you will ever meet. If she hates men, she hates women more and considers any woman out of the Knighthood to be little more than trash."

"But we know better," Saorsha told her. "This town believes you to be fair-minded, courageous, and best of all, a sorceress. And this town is all that matters."

Ulin crossed his arms and asked, "Where did you get that bill of sale?"

Mayor Efrim grasped the paper between thumb and

forefinger and gently waved it in the air. "The convenience of living in a town that collects many talents: false coiners, herbalists, con-men, pick-pockets, and forgerers. There is a talented young man, part elf I think, who can copy anything. He did this for us yesterday. We were going to give it to you for that horse as soon as it was convenient."

"You mean as soon as I said yes," Lucy remarked. "I feel like I'm being herded into a pen."

Saorsha wiped her hands on the coarse apron tied around her waist and patted Lucy on the arm. Her smile was genuine when she offered it to the girl. "You have every right to refuse. We cannot force your hand, nor do we want to. A reluctant, resentful sheriff is no good to us. But please, Lucy, we need you. Just for a little while. Even if we can't find your father or the money, there are still so many ways you could help."

"To make amends, you mean," Lucy grumbled.

Challie stamped out of the inn into the yard to join the conversation. "To be honest, Lucy, we did not think about the sheriff's position at the time I left to find you. That idea came after the ambush on the caravan. When you handled the draconians and then the brigands so easily, we jumped at the chance to make you the offer." She made a soft sound like a derisive snort. "In this town we take what we can get when we can get it. Even for a few weeks."

Lucy looked at Ulin, her round face filled with confusion, but he did not know what to tell her. As much as he wanted to protect her, she was a grown woman and not yet married to him. Ultimately the decision was hers.

Lucy dropped her gaze to Challie, who merely shrugged, then she looked at the three town councilors and the kender who watched her hopefully. The whole idea seemed preposterous. What did she know about being a sheriff? She had come to this town to identify her father's body, not capture brigands, settle fist fights, and face dragons. Yet hadn't she already killed two draconians and been responsible for the capture of four brigands? She hadn't been looking for trouble, but it had still found her. What if she could use her reputation to help these people, even for just a few weeks? How hard could it be? Her rational mind told her: Don't be absurd. You're not a law officer or a trained knight or anyone else truly capable of handling this job. True, her heart replied, but what a challenge!

Most of what she had said to Ulin that stormy night on the freighter had been a joke, but she had to admit to herself that the sentiments were drawn from the truth in her heart. She did miss the excitement and challenge of her studies in magic. Teaching children by day and serving beer at night did not compare to the fascinating and sometimes dangerous art of wielding magic. There was, too, a small and persistent part of her mind that trembled at the thought of marrying a Majere. What if she wasn't worthy? How could she, a mere student and babysitter, hope to compare with someone like Ulin? She wanted to do something important, something that would prove to herself, if no one else, that she could be capable and strong enough to hold her head up among Caramon, Tika, Palin, Usha, Linsha, and most of all, Ulin. Perhaps this unlikely offer from the Flotsam City Council was what she needed.

As for her father, she was honorable enough to do her best to alleviate the consequences of his crime, but in the end, if circumstances came down to a final confrontation with Fyremantle or Malys, she would not endanger herself or Ulin. She owed him that much.

"I have several conditions," she said at last.

Ulin swallowed a groan.

"Name them," Aylesworthy assented.

"I want the authority to punish offenders as I see fit. I want the authority to hire deputies. I want your complete support and that substantial fee you mentioned. Last, if you are going to keep me busy here, I want you to make every effort to find my father. He deserves to be hanged."

The councilmembers looked relieved. "That's fair," Mayor Efrim agreed.

Ulin drew a deep breath and resigned himself to Lucy's decision. In his head he knew she was right, but his heart quailed at the danger she could be putting herself into. He put his hands on Lucy's shoulder and drew her close. "I have a condition of my own to add," he said, staring into her beautiful green eyes. "If you're sure you want to do this, I will do everything I can to find your father, but I want your promise that we will leave for home after the festival whether I have found him or not."

Lucy spit in her palm and held out her hand to him. "Deal."

They shook on the solemn promise then turned to the trio of elders. The offer was accepted and the terms agreed upon.

Much to Lucy's droll amazement, she was now the Sheriff of Flotsam.

Chapter Ten

It did not take long for news of Lucy's appointment to spread through the town. As soon as day broke, a line of petitioners and curiosity seekers began to form at the Jetties's front door. It grew progressively longer with every passing minute. Master Aylesworthy opened his doors early to the let the crowd into the common room, but he refused to let anyone talk to Lucy.

"In good time, my friends," he told them all while his serving girls sold biscuits and cold ham and mugs of weak ale.

Councilwoman Saorsha and Mayor Efrim were more informative. They arrived in Saorsha's pony cart two hours after sunrise just as the crowd in the inn was starting to grow restive. The councilwoman swept into the common room, Mayor Efrim trailing in her wake.

"You may see our new sheriff this afternoon at the Sheriff's Office," she informed everyone. "Not until then." Over the groans and protests she had to shout to be heard.

"We still have to swear her in. At noon on the steps of the city hall."

Grumbling loudly, the crowd dispersed into the hot street until the common room was virtually empty, except for the three elders and two serving girls.

Pease burst in, a streak of boundless energy. "She's up! She's up! Challie says they'd like a tray."

"Invite her to join us in here," Alyesworthy instructed the kender.

"Them, you mean," Mayor Efrim said gently.

"Yes, yes, of course. The whole lot."

The kender took that, of course, to mean himself, too, and as soon as Lucy, Challie, and Ulin entered the common room and sat at Master Aylesworthy's table, Pease grabbed the chair closest to Lucy and joined in.

"Lucy, I want to be your deputy," he said in an enthusiastic voice.

Her weight had not even settled into the seat before he asked her. She didn't answer right away but cast a look at the innkeeper to judge his reaction.

Aylesworthy gave him an emphatic shake of his head. "You already have enough to do. Your mother needs your help and—"

Pease's noisy protest drowned him out.

"And," Challie's voice cut him off abruptly. "She already has a deputy. Me."

Aylesworthy, Lucy, and Ulin turned to the dwarf in surprise. Her manner was usually quiet and reserved, yet she met their questioning eyes with a determined stare. "My duties as magistrate often coincide with that of sheriff. I can manage both, and I feel I owe you the help."

"Thank you," Lucy said. "I would like that."

"But what about me?" insisted Pease. "I want to help, too!"

Lucy laughed. "You might be helpful with the festival. How about a compromise, if Master Aylesworthy is agreeable? You may be a deputy, but you'll work only on the days your mother and the captain approve."

The kender grinned winningly at the innkeeper. Ayles-worthy paused for a long moment, and when he shrugged his acquiescence, his face was vaguely troubled.

Challie rolled her eyes while the kender cheered.

* * * * *

Well-fed by Bridget's good cooking, the group left the Jetties at midmorning and made the long walk to the city hall. Townspeople, seeing their city councilors and the new lady sheriff, joined in until the small party became a noisy procession of kender on foot and donkeys, women of various professions, barbarians in their flowing robes, card players, fishermen, farmers, shopkeepers, and sprinkled through the crowd walked several half-ogres, some elves, and a few dwarves—a fair representation of Flotsam's population. Gossiping, laughing, and filled with curiosity, the spectators followed Lucy and her entourage to the old crumbling barracks where they stopped on the worn, stone steps.

Mayor Efrim raised his hand for silence. "My friends, if you can be patient, we will have the swearing-in ceremony at noon, and the Sheriff will begin her duties at that time."

Numerous rowdy calls and shouts met his pronouncement, but the Mayor turned his back on the crowd and ushered Lucy, Challie, and Ulin inside.

Ulin hung back a little. This was Lucy's day, and while he wanted to be with her, he did not want to get in the way. The last one through the door, he glanced back over his shoulder, wondering if the crowd would follow them into the building. He caught a glimpse of a tall man in faded robes speaking to the two half-ogres who had trailed the procession through town. Both rocklike faces nodded a quick assent, then the two figures climbed the stairs and took their places on either side of the door. Ulin's gaze caught the eye of the man in the robes, and they nodded briefly to each other before Lysandros blended back into the crowd.

The mage turned back indoors, satisfied. Half-ogres were powerful and ferocious fighters. Most people would think twice about trying to force their way past them. The presence of the half-ogres satisfied Ulin on another level, too. While he didn't entirely trust or like this resistance leader, he had a grudging respect for the half-elf's courage, daring, and abilities. If the Silver Fox was going to be in the background, ready to lend his aid to Lucy, Ulin would feel easier about leaving her for the time it took to find Kethril Torkay. Reassured, he hurried to catch up with the group.

Once inside the big barracks, Mayor Efrim showed Lucy and her companions the courtyard in back, the old prison, and the ruined treasury.

Ulin stamped a roach into the dirt and asked a question he had thought of only now. "Where are those four brigands Lucy stopped the other day?"

"Lysandros's men lashed them and left them in the desert to fend for themselves." Mayor Efrim replied quietly. "He helps us when he can."

"What happened to your previous sheriff?" Lucy asked, looking around the empty courtyard.

Saorsha, Aylesworthy, and Mayor Efrim avoided each other's eyes. "He died a few months ago," Saorsha said sadly. "Natural causes."

"Yeah, he just naturally—" Pease started to say. His words abruptly cut off as Master Aylesworthy took an unfortunate trip over a stone and crashed into him. By the time Saorsha and Lucy picked up the kender, set him on his feet, and dusted him off, the conversation had been smoothly changed and the group moved toward the Sheriff's Office.

Located near the front doors, the office was little more than a large room with a battered wooden desk that had seen many better days, one brass oil lamp, two chairs, and a barred holding cell built into the far corner. There were no personal items possibly belonging to the previous sheriff—no decorations, not even a rug on the bare wooden floors.

"It's rather plain," Saorsha admitted, "but it's functional."

"Boring is more to the point," Challie said under her breath.

Lucy tore her eyes away from the bleak, impersonal room and stifled a shudder. "It's close to noon, let's get this over with."

They went back outside into the hot noon sunlight. The crowd had grown larger, giving the impression that half the population of Flotsam had turned out for the brief ceremony to welcome the new sheriff. People pressed in close to the foot of the stairs and gathered in the roadway to watch.

Mayor Efrim held up his hands for silence. The onlookers, curious, obeyed until only the cry of seagulls broke the silence. "Raise your right hand and repeat after me," he said to Lucy. "I give my oath to serve the city of Flotsam, to uphold the city laws, to keep the peace, and preserve the unity of its inhabitants. I will not abuse my power or authority beyond the law, nor will I break my oath. I solemnly swear."

Lucy lifted her eyebrows as if to say, "That's it?" and loudly repeated the oath so all could hear. Cheers and shouts burst out from the watching crowd.

"Good luck, Sheriff!" she heard one voice yell. "You're going to need it!" Others laughed and made more comments she could not hear clearly over the hubbub.

Saorsha, Ulin, and Pease gave her hugs. She was about to ask Mayor Efrim to give the oath to her two deputies, when she became aware of an odd thudding noise. People in the crowd heard it, too, and immediately turned around to look at the harbor.

A strange small craft was moving across the water toward the small dock that served the city hall. The boat had a wide hull, a single flat deck, and a small cabin that was smoking profusely. There were no sails or masts or oars, only the strangest contraption in the stern that turned like a mill wheel and appeared to be driving the boat forward. Notwen leaned out of a cabin window and waved at the crowd.

A pale glitter of interest flickered in Ulin's eyes. Spurred by curiosity, he walked down the stairs and pushed his way through the people until he reached the rocky edge of the harbor and the dock. He clambered onto the dock just as the odd craft pulled along side. He heard a whoosh of steam and the knocking sound stopped just as the boat bumped into the wooden piling. Notwen ran out of the cabin and threw Ulin a rope. The gnome grinned his thanks as Ulin snugged the boat close to the dock and tied the rope to a stanchion.

The gnome ducked back inside and came out trailing a long dirty-looking rag. His blue eyes shining, he took Ulin's proffered hand and clambered onto the dock.

Ulin wanted to ask him questions about the boat, the steam, and the odd wheel in the back, but Notwen jogged off the dock toward the group on the stairs of the city hall. The onlookers parted for him, their expressions a collection of awe, respect, tolerant humor, and some suspicious dislike.

The gnome paid no heed. Breathlessly, he climbed the stairs, Ulin close behind him, and stopped in front of Lucy. His small face was red with exertion and excitement, and his white hair stuck out everywhere.

"If this is what I think it is," he said to Lucy. "I want you to have it." He held up a dirty, faded strip of cloth about three feet long.

Lucy and the others eyed it askance. "You're kidding, right?" Challie asked.

"No, no. I found it in a clutter of old stuff in my laboratory. It must have belonged to Toede's wizard. I don't think it's just a rag. It's disguising itself, but it will only respond to a magic-wielder." He thrust it forward. "Take it, Lucy."

In the brief moment that Lucy hesitated to touch the dirty thing, Ulin almost snatched it out of Notwen's hands. He suspected what the rag was, and every fiber of his being itched to touch the cloth and feel it respond to his power. Biting his lip, he laced his fingers behind his back and controlled his desire to claim it. It was too late for him. Besides, Notwen had brought the cloth to Lucy, and if it proved to be what Ulin suspected, she would need it more than he would.

"Take it, Lucy," Ulin said softly. "You might be surprised."

She gave Notwen a hesitant nod of thanks and gingerly took the cloth from his hands.

Everyone stared at it as if they expected it to grow wings and fly away, but nothing happened. The cloth lay in her hands, unchanged and unresponsive. She held it up in her hand and shook it. Still, nothing happened.

Notwen looked distressed. "I thought for sure . . ."

"Try casting a spell, Lucy," Ulin suggested, "Just a small one."

"Do you know what this is supposed to be?" she asked him.

"I think it is more than just cloth, but it may be dormant. You need to wake it up."

Lucy's eyes grew large. " 'Wake it up?' " she repeated dubiously. She held it out at arm's length. The change in distance did nothing to improve its worn and tattered appearance. She might have wadded it up and shoved it in her belt if Notwen hadn't looked up at her with those imploring blue eyes and Ulin hadn't shifted from foot to foot like a child drawn by a new toy. "A spell, huh?" she muttered. "What if it doesn't work?"

Saorsha and Aylesworthy looked on with interest. "What do you have to lose?" the councilwoman pointed out.

Good point. Lucy studied the old rag while she searched her memory for a simple spell, one of the easy ones she learned as an apprentice perhaps. There was an old cleaning spell she remembered that could be used for removing stains from fine fabrics. This cloth could hardly qualify as fine fabric, but if it was something else—something sentient?—maybe it would appreciate a cleaning. Closing her eyes, she concentrated on the words of the spell and began the familiar process of drawing the power to her. A breeze wafted gently by, and she felt the cloth stir in her hand. Her eyes still closed, she hummed the words of her enchantment in her soft alto voice.

There was a sudden gasp as everyone took a gulp of air at the same time. Startled voices cried in amazement. Lucy opened her eyes and gasped herself. Two brilliant jewel-like eyes gazed up at her from the length of cloth that was no longer dirty, tattered, and faded. Instead the fabric had transformed to a glowing shade of emerald green and shimmered in her hands like silk shot with silver.

"I don't think my spell did that!" she exclaimed in raw surprise.

Notwen capered around her. "I was right. It is. It is!"

"It is what?" Challie asked, her eyes huge. She reached out a tentative finger and touched the cloth. Its diamond eyes turned to stare unblinking at her, but it wrapped its trailing end protectively around Lucy's arm.

The movement startled Lucy more than the color change, and she held the thing on her outstretched arm as if it were a large, poisonous spider. "What is this?"

The cloth immediately turned yellow.

Ulin smiled, pleased for her. "It's a Vizier's Turban. They're extremely rare and totally harmless. Put it on your head."

"Are you serious?"

"Very. They love to be worn as hats, or veils, turbans, scarves . . . what have you. They're symbiotic creatures. They attach themselves to wizards and sustain themselves on the power used to summon magic."

Lucy almost balked in spite of Ulin's calm words, for the thought of putting a strange living creature on her head to feed off her magic powers was rather frightening. "Will it do anything to me?" she asked cautiously.

"No," Notwen said, his face full of delight, "in fact, it will help you. That's why I brought it. Vizier's Turbans give their partners a greater resistance to magic and an enhanced ability to cast spells."

Pease jumped up and down, trying to see around the humans. "Put it on, Lucy, put it on!" he clamored. His cry was taken up by the spectators still crowded around the steps. Soon everyone was shouting, "Put it on! Put it on!"

The look in Ulin's eyes finally made up Lucy's mind. If he approved of this thing so much, it could not be that dangerous—she hoped. She would have given it to him, but she didn't want to hurt the gnome's feelings. Slowly she lifted her arm and let the creature slide down her upper arm to her shoulder. Once there, it slid around her head, curled over her brown braid, and took the shape of a small, feminine looking turban pinned together with two oval jewels. Happily, it settled in place and gazed down on the world around it. Its yellow color faded to a peaceful blue that matched the color of Lucy's tunic.

A smile spread over her face. "It told me it is pleased!" she said, her tone rich with wonder. "This creature's telepathic."

Ulin held out his hand to Notwen. "Thank you," he said.

The gnome took the mage's hand in his own small one. "My pleasure. I brought something for you, too," he said, and he pulled out a small parcel hastily wrapped in a shred of old linen.

Ulin took the small object and carefully unwrapped it. A pair of wire-rimmed spectacles fell shining into his fingers. "Pink lenses?" he asked dubiously.

"Rose, actually," Notwen said. "They are Truth-seers. They are spelled to see through magic disguises and deceptions. I thought they might be handy when we go look for Kethril."

Ulin stiffened. "We?" he repeated, his eyes narrowed.

The gnome pointed proudly toward the boat. "Dead Pirate's Cove seems like a good place to start. It's just across the bay. It takes two days if you ride a horse, but it only takes a day if you ride in my boat."

Challie snorted in disbelief. "That thing goes in open water?"

"I haven't tried it in the sea yet, but I've crossed the bay a time or two," Notwen answered.

"When could we leave?" Ulin asked. He stared thoughtfully beyond the harbor entrance to the wide bay glittering in the afternoon sun. Although he'd had little time to give any thought to how he would find Kethril Torkay, he began to see some merit in Notwen's offer.

The gnome lifted his slight shoulders in a shrug, "Now?"

"How about tomorrow?" Lucy suggested firmly. "You need time to pack, to collect supplies, to talk to Lysandros about this Dead Pirate's Cove, and to pick some men to go with you."

"Tomorrow it is," Ulin agreed. That would have been his answer anyway. He wanted to stay in Flotsam long enough to see Lucy settled into her new job. "But," he added, "I don't think we need extra men. Too many people might scare off your father before we can get close. Who would be suspicious of a fisherman and a gnome?"

Lucy eyed him while she debated the usefulness of arguing with him, then she nodded once. "All right. If you two try the Cove, I'll ask Lysandros to check some the outer-lying areas. And Mayor," she rounded on Mayor Efrim, "if anyone in this town knows or hears anything about Kethril, they'd better tell me. Offer a reward."

The mayor blanched but nodded. The city could ill afford a reward, but what difference would it make if Flotsam vanished into ashes?

The excitement over, the crowd dispersed, most going back to their work or pleasure. Some stayed and formed a line in front of the group on the steps. Many of them were the same people who had come to the inn at daybreak, and the looks of determination on their faces told Lucy that these would not leave so easily this time.

Lucy sighed. "You'd better deputize Challie and Pease," she said to Mayor Efrim.

"And the half-ogres," Saorsha suggested, pointing to the two silent sentries. Their thick lips pulled back in rough grins of acceptance.

The mayor quickly gave the oath to Challie, Pease, and the half-ogres whose names Lucy did not catch, then the entire party traipsed into the city hall to open the building for town business. Lucy discovered the mayor and his councilors had offices right across the hall from hers, a proximity she quickly learned to appreciate.

The first complainants barged in before Lucy and her deputies had time to make themselves comfortable in the stark room.

"His worm-ridden sheep broke into my arbor and destroyed ten healthy bearing vines!" yelled the farmer, his face livid from the remembered destruction.

The shepherd thrust his face close to the other man's and yelled right back, "Well, maybe if you could tell a sheep from a goat, you'd know it was Widow Brownly's goats that ate your vines!"

Pease shook his head wearily. He'd heard this argument before in the common room at the Jetties. "Tell Hanley to put up a fence," he whispered to Lucy.

"Enough!" Lucy bellowed, effectively cutting off the argument. Her turban flared red with streaks of orange. "Now, if you please," she said in a more normal tone of voice. "You." She pointed to the farmer. "Anyone silly enough to have an arbor without a fence deserves some depredations. Put a fence around your grapes and don't come back here to complain until it's finished. And you," she turned on the shepherd who choked on a snicker. "Help him build it and keep your sheep away from his fields."

"What about Widow Brownly's goats?" he sputtered.

"I will talk to her. Make a note of that, Challie."

And so it went the rest of the afternoon. One after another, Flotsam citizens came to lodge complaints or protests about everything from watered ale and improperly set scales at the market to trespassing, a horse theft, forged coins, stolen goods, a missing donkey, an abusive landlord, and unpaid wages. Lucy would listen to the complaint, and more often than not either the gregarious kender or the magistrate knew about the incident and could offer some insight. The council provided her with a scroll listing the laws on Flotsam's city charter, and although she tried to be fair and impartial, she had to consult with the mayor several times on certain points of the law before she could settle a dispute or make a decision.

Meanwhile, Challie took notes, collected fines, and filled out papers when needed. The half-ogres made everyone check their weapons at the door.

Notwen fixed the lock on the holding cell, then decided to go back to his boat to prepare it for the voyage across the bay. He paused once at the door and looked back to see Lucy sitting behind the desk, the turban perched contentedly on her head while it watched the goings-on with avid interest in its faceted eyes. A surge of worry and sadness flashed through Notwen's mind. This situation made him uncomfortable, but he had done his best for her. The rest was up to the sorceress.

He waved to Ulin and ducked out, his mind already on fuel requirements, tools, parts needed, supplies, and instruments. His regret faded into the background behind the anticipation of the journey. He couldn't wait until the next day.

* * * * *

Ulin stood behind Lucy as her silent bodyguard through the entire long, noisy afternoon. What he observed reassured him—as much as he was willing to be reassured. He

144

still did not like Lucy in this position. Too many things could go wrong, and yet he saw nothing that afternoon that Lucy could not handle one way or another. The problems were minor, the people tried to cooperate, and most seemed satisfied with her decisions. Several even came to congratulate her or just to visit and found her warm and approachable. The farm girl with the vegetable cart in the market brought her a bowl of potatoes, and smiling, she set it on Lucy's desk in a prominent position. Lucy chuckled and left the bowl in place. The potatoes posed a silent reminder of Lucy's arcane power.

The golden light of sunset was fading into the western hills when the last citizen left the Sheriff's Office and Lucy and her companions were able to close the door and go back to the Jetties for a long awaited meal. When she suggested leaving someone on duty, Mayor Efrim wearily waved off the idea.

"People know where to find you if there's an emergency, and the Vigilance Force is keeping watch from the Rock." He shook his head and his wispy beard swayed in the evening breeze. "We don't expect you to keep this town peaceful and free of crime every hour of the day. It is too rough for that and would require a force of deputies larger than we may safely have. Just knowing you're around will keep some of these rowdies in line."

Lucy was too tired to argue.

* * * * *

Ulin, Lucy, and Challie had their evening meal in their room that night, for once not accompanied by Pease. His mother had put him to work in the kitchen. He brought them a tray covered with dishes and mugs and a pitcher of beer, and after setting their table, he wistfully bade them good night and returned to his duties. They ate well and gratefully and cleaned the plates down to the finish.

Mary H. Herbert

Afterward, Challie went to her room, but Lucy and Ulin sat back in their chairs and savored a last few hours together. They talked quietly for a time about little things until their conversation inevitably turned to the events of the day.

Flotsam's new sheriff grinned ruefully and put a hand on Ulin's. "I know you're not happy about this, but believe it or not, I enjoyed today."

His fingers caught hers and held them tight. "You are a redoubtable woman, Lucy Torkay. I think you have no clear idea of your real ability or potential. Maybe this job will show you what you are capable of doing."

To his surprise, she blushed a warm shade of pink that put roses in her cheeks and made her all the more self-conscious. Her chin dropped, and her lashes swept down over her green eyes.

In that moment Ulin found himself on his knees beside her. He wrapped his arms around her and held her so close she could hear the rapid beating of his heart. "I love you," he whispered, all of his need and desire and fear concentrated into those three words. "You don't have to prove anything to me."

"But I have to prove something to myself," she said, so softly he barely heard her.

He kissed her, long and possessively, with an intensity she had not felt in him before. At last he pushed himself to his feet. Trembling, he touched her hair, her cheek, her shoulder, then turned and hurried to his room. The door closed quietly behind him.

Chapter Eleven

Evaporating the few clouds that tried to form, the sun soared high in the great blue arch of the sky and shed its brazen light on the dancing waters of Blood Bay. Small waves pushed by a light wind from the west rolled by the broad side of the small boat and rocked her gently as she steamed slowly north. Notwen's engine chugged noisily in the cabin and kept a steady rhythm to the beat and splash of the paddle wheel.

Ulin could not get enough of Notwen's contraption. From the time they cast off early that morning, he had been in the cabin studying the steam engine, its boiler, and the stack under the deck to see the shaft and cogs that turned the wheel. He hadn't been this intrigued with something since his days of experimenting with alchemy in the laboratories at the Academy.

"It's crude," Notwen told him. "I based it on some of the experiments other gnomes have tried. You've probably never heard of the ship the *Valiant Aftershock the Ninth*.

Most people haven't. A fine ship powered by a steam turbine. Unfortunately, they couldn't figure out how to stop it." He tapped a quill pen on his forehead, leaving a smear of ink in his white hair. "The engine was too large to be practical, so I took their idea, scaled it down, and added a few of my own. That's why I call it *Second Thoughts*. Let me show you."

For hours they pored over his designs until Ulin understood the basic principles of steam power and the potential of its tremendous energies. Now that he saw its practical application, he could not believe how simple it was. Water, heat, steam, expansion, condensation. He had seen it all in his alchemy experiments, yet he had never thought of harnessing the power of steam to drive a machine. Now that the idea was planted in his mind, he felt ideas popping like corn kernels on a hot skillet. Notwen's engine was crude, Ulin saw, and the paddle wheel was inefficient for the task, but what if he tried . . .

He grabbed a scrap of parchment on the worktable in the cabin and began to scribble and sketch some of his notions. Notwen peered over his shoulder. When he saw what Ulin was doing, he grabbed his own pen and offered suggestions. They became so engrossed in their arguments and discussions that they paid no attention to the boat's course or the fact that the wind had strengthened and was gradually pushing them steadily to the northwest.

They paid little heed to the passage of time, and the sunlight was slanting vertically through the tiny windows of the cabin when the crash came. One moment Ulin and Notwen were standing at the table, talking over the throb of the engine, and the next a rending, splintering impact sent them sprawling on the floor. Frantically, Notwen reached for the boiler and threw open a valve. Steam hissed into the air, and the paddle rumbled to a stop.

"What was that?" Ulin demanded. He could not see through the clouds of steam that filled the small cabin, but he could feel something wrong. The boat seemed high at the bow, and it rocked slightly as if caught on something. He rubbed the small of his back that had made hard contact with the wall and managed to scramble to his feet. The deck tilted at a definite angle.

Notwen clambered upright and opened the cabin door. Wind rushed in and swirled the steam away. Now they could see what they had hit.

"Great departed gods!" Ulin exclaimed. "Where did that come from?"

Notwen's hands tore at his hair, and his face became a visage of woe. "Ohno, ohno, ohno! TheislandsthewindsIforgot!" he wailed.

"Slow down!" Ulin remonstrated. "Forgot what?"

"I forgot to adjust our course according to the wind speed and tides. We're in that little string of islands almost in the mouth of the bay." He hurried outside, Ulin close on his heels. Together they stared in dismay at the bow of the boat and the island that lay beneath it. It was not much of an island, being the tail end of a small string of islets that consisted mostly of rock, moss, seaweed, shrubs, and birds. Fortunately for Ulin and Notwen, the *Second Thoughts* had missed the large, sharp-edged ridge of rock on one side of the island and plowed bow-first into a tiny strip of pebbled beach at the foot of a tall outcropping.

Ulin hoped the damage was minor. When he glanced over the bow, he thought at first the boat had simply run aground and all they had to do was push it off the beach. "Can't we just back it off?" he asked.

Notwen hopped over the railing to the beach and bent close to the bow for a more thorough investigation. "The boat can't back up on her own. I haven't figured out how to put the engine and gears in reverse," he answered as he scraped away some gravel. Suddenly, he groaned and flopped to his back in the wet gravel. "The bow struck a half-buried rock. There're at least two planks smashed and several others sprung loose. It will leak like a sieve if we can't seal it. We're doomed!" he wailed.

Ulin glanced around the barren little island and thought
they were definitely inconvenienced, but hardly doomed.
They had tools, supplies, and water to last for several days,
and the two of them certainly had the skills to repair a
small boat well enough to carry them to the mainland. He
could even see the faint dark line of land on the distant
horizon. When he tried to reassure Notwen, though, the
gnome sat bolt upright and clutched the tools around his
belt as if someone was about to steal them.

"You don't understand." His voice rose with fear.
"Things live on these islands. Evil things! Creatures that
don't like invaders. Oh, they're hideous! They'll tear us
limb from limb and feed us to the sharks."

The mage felt a definite uneasiness creep into his
thoughts. A chill ran down the back of his neck and spread
over his entire body. Could the gnome be right? There were
some truly fearsome things that lived in the warm waters
of Krynn's oceans. What if something vile resided on this
scrap of an island? The two of them had only one sword, a
handful of tools, and their wits to combat an enemy. Those
assets might fix their boat, but they would hardly make an
impression against something like a pack of koalinth, ghagglers, or even an irritated, territorial sea-lion.

Ulin clambered over the rail and helped Notwen to his
feet. "What sort of creatures do you mean?" he asked,
trying to keep his voice light.

"I think he's talking about us," a feminine voice said
from the jumbled rock nearby.

Keeping his hands in plain sight, Ulin turned toward
the speaker. When he saw what lounged on the rock about
ten paces away, he felt his jaw drop open. A young woman
rose gracefully to her feet and walked toward him. Perhaps
undulate was a better description, he thought, for he had
never seen any female move with such a supple, rippling
stride as this one.

Long silver hair flowed down her shoulders and back
like a waterfall caught in the moonlight. Beneath the hair

she had a narrow face with a pointed chin, high cheek-bones, and a small nose. Her lush body curved sensuously under an iridescent garment that clung like a second skin and barely covered the important parts. She raised her arms and began to sing a seductive tune in the rolling language of the sea.

Notwen gave a squeak of alarm and bolted for the boat's cabin. Ulin could only stare, mesmerized, his arms limp at his sides, his mouth open.

She glided to him, her sea-green eyes locked on his. The late day sun glistened on her wet body and enhanced the aquamarine coloring of her fair skin. Rapturously, she lifted her hand and touched his wavy brown hair. Her fingers trailed like silken fire along his hairline, down his neck, and along his jaw. Both hands framed his face and pulled him close.

An inarticulate sound escaped him, but he could not move. His entire body ached to touch her. Desire rose like a wave within him and warred with caution in his head. He knew what this woman was, what she was doing to him. He remembered Lucy and how much he loved her. None of that mattered. His limbs trembled with his need, and his heart pounded in his chest. All he wanted was to—

The woman pressed her beautiful body against him from head to toe, and her full lips sought his. She gave him a long, probing arduous kiss until he was gasping for air.

Strangely, though, instead of feeding the fire that burned in his loins, the woman's physical touch cooled him. His desire for her ebbed away on a tide of remorse, and he drew back as his cherished feelings for Lucy resurfaced.

The woman abruptly dropped her arms and stepped back from him, her face puckered in an annoyed pout. "Shells and spines," she said peevishly. "It failed again!" She threw her arms up, a gesture of dismay, and sank down on a boulder.

Ulin blinked. He still felt very warm, but the strange surge of passion was gone, leaving a hollow place in his gut. Although he was relieved, a fragment of his male ego was as disappointed as the sea-maiden.

"I don't understand," she cried. "I am a sirine. My song is supposed to be irresistible. Why did it fail? Who are you?"

"My name is Ulin. Unfortunately, I am not the reason your magic failed." He held out his hands and examined his long fingers that once wove spells with such skill. "Mine is gone, too."

She cast an oblique glance at him. "Are you telling me that this . . . difficulty is affecting humans, too?"

"Humans, elves, dragons, everyone . . . Sometimes the magic works. Sometimes it doesn't. Even Malys doesn't understand the reason this is happening."

"What a nuisance. So what were you, a wizard or something?"

He smiled a crooked smile that did not touch his eyes. "Or something."

The sirine sighed and fell silent. Her silence lasted only a minute or two, and in the flick of a fish's tail her mood changed again. Suddenly she giggled, causing ripples to flow through her ample figure. She was a young sirine and quite luscious in her scanty garment. Ulin, looking closely at it, saw it was made of fish scales that glistened in iridescent shades of blue and green. Guiltily, he tore his eyes away.

She giggled again. "Too bad the magic didn't work this time. You're quite—"

"Hold it there!" a shrill voice demanded. "Don't move!" Notwen glared over the boat's railing, a crossbow cocked and ready in his hands.

Ulin rushed in front of the sirine. The crossbow shook alarmingly in the gnome's trembling hands. "It's all right, Notwen. She can't entice us. Put the weapon down."

The gnome glared at the sea woman, unconvinced.

She waggled her fingers at him and winked. "Don't worry, little man. I wouldn't have hurt you anyway. I just wanted some company."

He looked from the woman to Ulin and back again then slowly lowered the weapon.

"Uncock it," Ulin reminded him.

Silence followed as the three wondered what to do next.

"Well," Ulin said when the quiet grew too uncomfortable. "Let's get this boat fixed."

The sirine put a hand on his thigh. "I don't suppose you'd want to . . . anyway?" She tilted her head toward the concealment of the tumbled rocks and offered him an enticing wiggle.

He took her hand off his leg, clasped it between both of his, and kissed the back of her hand as an apology. "No. I am betrothed to a woman I adore."

Notwen crossed his arms and announced, "And *she's* a sorceress."

The sea-woman flounced to her feet. "Oh, fine. Her magic works and mine doesn't," she sulked, as if that explained everything. "Just who is this paragon of magic?"

The gnome tilted his nose up and replied haughtily. "Her name is Lucy. She's Kethril Torkay's daughter."

Although Ulin hardly expected the sirine to recognize the name, he was startled to see a strange mix of emotions flit across her delicate face, a mix of confusion, anger, and curiosity. Irritation won out in the end, and she blurted, "Go then. Fix your noisy little craft and get off my island." She turned on a dainty heel to leave in a huff, but Ulin caught her arm.

"Won't you stay and talk to us?" he asked. A small part of him still felt sorry for disappointing her, and he wanted to make it up to her somehow. After all, she hadn't planned to drag them underwater and devour them. He hoped to satisfy some of his own curiosity. He knew little about the aquatic women that lived in the warm seas. Most preferred solitude and would take strong measures to defend their islands. A few, like this one, were more sociable and would mate with human, elf, or merfolk males to produce a child.

She hesitated at the warmth of his overture. Ulin was often too distracted to notice his effect on people, but he could be quite charming at times. "Go fix your boat," she said softly, a half-smile curving the bow of her mouth. "I will go find something to eat."

"I don't you suppose you have any caulk, do you?" Notwen inquired.

With a flip of her hair, she waded into the water and dived under the waves. For a few moments, Ulin was able to watch her swim through the clear water, as sleek and swift as a dolphin, before she disappeared into a forest of seaweed.

"Hmph," Notwen commented. Females of any sort had never interested him. They were all too illogical.

Using the tools onboard, Notwen and Ulin levered the boat off the rock and dragged it up the beach far enough to examine the damage in the hull. After much discussion, they decided to patch the damage rather than replace the boards. A more permanent repair could be made later after they returned to Flotsam. They cut lengths of board from the cabin itself and nailed them into place over the breach. The results were hopeful. All they needed to complete the job was some sort of waterproof sealant to fill in the cracks. The *Second Thought's* compact cabin was lined with cupboards, cabinets, and bins all neatly stocked with food, water, fuel, blankets, tools, nails, rope, and lanterns, but while they searched the boat from bow to stern for something—anything—they could use, they found nothing.

Notwen scratched his head, frustrated by this lack of foresight. "I must make a note for the next time: Bring pitch."

Ulin bit back a retort. Venting his irritation on the small gnome would hardly help their situation. He hadn't thought of bringing caulk either.

A few stars glimmered in the twilight sky when they finished nailing the boards, and with nothing further they could do, they lit a small lamp and fixed a meal of salted fish, biscuits, and wine. To avoid attracting bugs or other unwanted pests, they lit no other lamps or fires, and they stayed on the boat to eat their meal.

A splash outside brought them both to their feet. Something pulled itself onto the boat, causing it to rock slightly, then footsteps padded across the deck. Notwen's hand slid toward his crossbow.

The sirine thrust her dripping head through the door and smirked when Notwen jumped back in alarm. Her amusement quickly changed to worry. "Here. I found this in a shipwreck near the coast." She tossed a slimy, weed-covered wooden container to Ulin. "You may stay the night, but in the morning you must go. Quickly. Go to the mainland as fast as you can."

Ulin heard a new note of urgency in her voice that had not been there earlier—an urgency and fear that went beyond the desire to be rid of unwelcome visitors. "What is it? What's bothering you?" he asked.

She only shook her silvery hair. "Something bad may be coming. I am not certain yet. Just go." And she slipped away without another word.

"What's in the keg?" Notwen asked, relieved the girl was gone again.

Ulin turned the soggy thing over in his hands. Whatever it was, it had been underwater long enough for seaweed to grow and worms to begin their feast in the wood. It was very heavy, too. He set it carefully on the worktable and used a pry bar to break the lid loose. Together he and Notwen peered inside at the thick, black, viscous substance inside. "Pitch," they said in unison.

They wasted no time pondering what to do next. Something had spooked the sirine, and neither the man nor the gnome wanted to find out firsthand what it was. While Notwen lit a small brazier, Ulin transferred as much of the pitch as he could to an old copper pot and set it over the coals to warm. While they waited for the pitch to soften, Notwen tended the fire in the boiler of his engine. He banked it for the night and piled cut wood close by, in case they had to fire it in a hurry.

As soon as the pitch was pliable, Ulin chopped a piece of rope into bits and added the fiber to the pitch to give it body, and using an old scrub brush, he slathered the pitch over the patch on the bow.

They took turns standing guard until a few hours after midnight when the high tide reached its crest. Ulin woke Notwen to help him maneuver the *Second Thoughts* off the shingled beach, and while Ulin pushed at the bow, the gnome scraped away sand and rocks from the keel. At last the boat pulled free of the shore and floated in the water of the bay. They anchored her there and watched through the remaining hours of darkness to see if the patch would leak.

Before long the sun ascended from the sea, surrounded by thin, scarlet-tinged clouds, and the air grew warmer. Ulin looked for the sirine so he could say good-bye and offer his thanks, but he saw no sign of her. The rocky bit of island remained empty save for its birds and barnacles.

The bay was calm that morning. A light breeze ruffled the water into little wavelets and tickled the dolphins that sported in the swell. Ever so gently Ulin and Notwen swung the *Second Thoughts* around to point her bow out to open water, fired the boiler, and started the paddlewheel turning. The boat started slowly and gradually gained momentum as she left the island behind. Notwen was very careful not to repeat his mistake of the day before. He found their location on his map and carefully plotted a course that would take them northwest toward the nearest land, then west along the coast to the cove where the settlement they sought was located. Ulin pottered with the steam engine, devising experiments in his head that dealt with steam, temperatures, and pressures.

Neither one of them noticed the pale form that slid out of the rocks on the island and dived into the water, nor did they see that same form glide through the water behind the boat all the long way to the northern shore of Blood Bay.

* * * * *

If Flotsam bore a resemblance to a heap of debris washed ashore after a storm, Dead Pirate's Cove looked like a ship's graveyard. The cove itself was a difficult place to find, for its narrow entrance was protected on the east by a high ridge of barren hills and on the west by a salt-marsh that clogged the mouth of a narrow sluggish river. In more prosperous years, pirates had used the river and its marshy delta as a hide-out and had left remnants of their passing: a few old shacks on the dunes north of the marsh, an abandoned longboat, the burned ruins of a galley, its blackened ribs still poking though the sand. It wasn't until Captain Grimborne Reever arrived, however, that the cove earned its accepted name.

Legend told of Captain Reever's magnificent treasure and how he hid it in chests ensorceled with spells and buried it somewhere in the cove. It was no sooner buried than he poisoned his entire crew and left their bodies as guardians for his fabulous prize. Unfortunately for Captain Reever, the dead pirates resented their captain's greed and bloody-minded selfishness, and their spirits harried him until, in a fit of madness, he drove his ship aground on the mud flats and ran screaming onto his sword. After that people still came to Dead Pirate's Cove to hide or escape, but more came to hunt for the treasure. A few old pirates, seeing the way the wind was blowing after the arrival of Malystryx, took their ships to the cove, hauled them ashore near Captain Reever's abandoned craft, and formed their own small settlement. It was rough, it was crude, but it was theirs. Others joined them, and in time the settlement became a village of sorts with its own collection of taverns, gaming houses, shops, and houses built out of pieces of old ships, mud and reed, or whatever was handy. If anyone ever found the captain's treasure, they never confessed, for their lives would not be worth a bucket of warm spit. The red dragon had spies everywhere and would know of the find before the first piece of steel or the first gem reached the light of day. Of course, that knowledge did not stop people from hoping—or looking on moonlit nights.

A few small boats and an old caravel were anchored in the cove when Ulin and Notwen arrived late that night. They maneuvered the *Second Thoughts* past the sandbars and the anchored craft and took her to the sole pier that extended out from the marshy shore into the water from a boardwalk worn gray by time and salt spray.

The strange noises emanating from the steam engine drew a small crowd from the boardwalk and the shacks that lined the cove's so-called waterfront. The spectators held torches and lanterns and made vociferous comments on the noise, the steam, the smoke, the reliability, and the appearance of the little craft.

Notwen blithely ignored them. While Ulin jumped to the dock and tied the boat fast, the gnome shut down the boiler, released the steam, and banked the fire.

"Suffering seahorses!" a gruff old man shouted from the boardwalk. "What do you call that thing?" He limped down to the dock, his lantern swinging beside his wooden leg.

Notwen stepped out of the cabin and drew himself up to his full height of three and a half feet. "It is a fire-powered hot box and boiler with a steam-driven rod and gears that convert vertical motion to horizontal motion through a system of shafts and cogs that turn a paddlewheel, making sails obsolete."

The old man on the dock stared down at him. "Forget I asked." He turned to Ulin, hoping for briefer answers. "This is my dock. You have to pay to tie up here." Ulin gave him the response he wanted by pulling out his coin bag and paying the full amount without a quibble. The old man cheered up enough to recommend an inn when Ulin queried. "The Loathly Dragon," he grunted. "It's the only inn in this mud hole."

Ulin, with Notwen close behind, followed the old man along the dock and up a slight incline to the boardwalk. The crowd, unable to see very much in the darkness, quickly broke up and went off to their previous pursuits. With a gnarled finger, the old man pointed the way to the inn then quickly ducked into his hut and slammed the door. Ulin immediately understood why people did not linger in the open in this place. The proximity to the marsh made the settlement a prime lure for mosquitoes and biters of every kind. Smoking torches burned along the paths and at the edges of the village, but nothing seemed to slow the clouds of mosquitoes that swarmed everywhere.

Ulin squinted and fanned his face as he hurried toward the inn. There were no roads laid out in this haphazard community and no real planning. Paths followed the layout of the buildings and branched off in every direction. Sidewalks had been built over the muddy places and here and there a rope bridge stretched across the open spaces between the old ships or the few two-story buildings. There were few lights to attract insects, and all the doors were closed. Those windows that were open to catch the light wind were screened with layers of cheesecloth or netting.

At the edge of the settlement, Ulin saw the Loathly Dragon perched on a foundation of old pilings. It was a squat, solid building made of thick stucco and mud bricks to withstand storms and heavy winds. Shutters covered the windows, and a wide porch stretched across the front. Someone with a sense of humor had painted the face of a large red dragon on the white stucco around the door to give the impression that guests entering the door were walking into the mouth of a dragon.

He and Notwen entered the inn, closing the door behind them. Customers in the busy common room barely paused to study them before they went back to their drinking and entertainment. The innkeeper came to offer his services. Yes, he had one room left, his best. He asked a ridiculous price, but Ulin was too tired to haggle. He needed sleep, and he wanted to be up early to begin their search for Kethril. He paid for the room, two nights in advance, and asked for a tankard of ale to be sent to their room. Notwen asked for cider. Smiling at such generosity, the innkeeper escorted them to the room personally and delivered not only the drinks but thick, hearty sandwiches as well. The two travelers partook of their meal, crawled under the mosquito netting on the bed, and fell into a deep, well-earned sleep.

Chapter
Twelve

"Y ou slimy sack of rotten squid squeezings!"
"Squid squeezings? Squid squeezings!"
Lucy heard the words repeated in rising tones of rage.
She hurried faster along the sidewalk. This was the second
time in one day she had been forced to go to this particular
gambling house to quell a disturbance. It was getting tire-
some. She pushed open the swinging doors and marched
inside, her face a mask of displeasure. To her silent grati-
fication, the shouting in the crowded room suddenly
stopped. Only the two quarrelers did not seem to notice
her presence. They fought with fists and feet in a scrab-
bling pile on the floor. Lucy strode forward and wrenched
the two fishermen apart. She had learned in her brief
tenure as sheriff that common sense, fairness, firmness,
and an unbreachable façade of self-confidence were the
best measures to deal with the denizens of Flotsam. If she
slipped with the slightest hint of self-abasement, they
would chew her up and spit her out for fish bait. Once

again her attitude paid off, for the two men looked up at her wide-eyed and made no more attempts to smash each other's heads on the floor.

She stood, her feet apart, hands on her hips, and glared at the owner of the house. She wore what she considered to be her uniform, a dark blue pair of baggy pants, a loose, dark tunic belted at the waist, and her Vizier's Turban, which took delight in matching its color with her mood. At that moment it was a somber shade of steel blue like a thundercloud. Its diamond eyes flickered with distant lightning.

"Andur," she spoke sharply to the owner. "I will not tell you again. If you cannot keep the peace in your house, I will close it down."

Andur, a thin short little man, bowed to her, although his sharp, narrow eyes watched her constantly. "I do apologize, Sheriff. My bouncer quit two days ago, and I have not been able to find another."

"No more excuses. This is your business. You should be able to handle your own problems. If you need a bouncer, hire one of these louts." She pointed to the fishermen on the floor. "They seem to have plenty of free time and muscle."

"I'll take it!" one of the men said eagerly. "I need another job."

"No! I'll take it!" his belligerent opponent insisted. This man had obviously had too much to drink. He pushed himself to his feet and stood swaying in front of Lucy, his expression bellicose.

Lucy curled her lip. If she had a match, she thought, she could set fire to his breath. "Step back," she said calmly.

Instead he stepped closer and loomed over her like a large wall. She suddenly realized how big and solid this young man was, and how drunk. His eyes were bloodshot and bleary. Spittle dribbled out of the corner of his mouth, and he could barely stand upright. It seemed only his animosity kept him on his feet. "I don' like you," he slurred in a loud voice. "You come 'ere and start ord'rin' people around. You're a nuisance, a squeakin' little female with a fancy hat. I could crush you like a bug." So saying he drew back his fist.

The other fisherman lunged at him, but he was too far away to reach the man in time.

Lucy had only a second or two to react. She raised her hand and murmured her spell, praying to herself that it would work this time. She had practiced it time and again in the privacy of her room until the words and the manipulation of the power were instantaneous, yet in spite of all her practice, she could only make the spell work in about half the attempts. She would not know if it had worked this time until the man's fist stopped or struck her. Using all of her self-control, she stood still and watched his huge knuckles coming toward her face.

She felt the Vizier's Turban suddenly quiver, and the glorious flood of magic flowed through her, enhanced by the creature's innate ability. Half a moment later the man slammed his fist into an invisible wall, mere inches away from her nose. A slow creamy smile spread across Lucy's face. One never knew when a mage's shield would come in handy.

The man's features screwed up into a grimace of surprise and agony. Dumbfounded, he dropped to his knees in front of her, cradling his hand and blubbering. The crowd looked at her in awe.

Lucy felt the Vizier's Turban snuggle closer around her head. If it had had vocal chords, it would have been purring. Instead, it thought to her, *Nice spell. Good magic. May we do it again?*

She reached up to tuck a strand of hair back under the turban and gave it an affectionate pat. *Thank you, Vizier. We will try again soon.* Although these silent conversations with her hat seemed odd, she was beginning to enjoy it.

The first fisherman reached his companion and hauled him to his feet. "I'm really sorry, Sheriff. He gets this way when he's drunk."

"If you want the job, get him out of here," snapped Andur. "Then come back. We'll talk."

Lucy quickly dispelled her shield and gestured to the door. "Take him to the jail. Someone can look at his hand, then he can dry out in one of our cells."

Laughter lightened the tension in the room. She nodded to the owner and strode outside into the early evening. It wasn't until she had walked several blocks away that she ducked into a shadowy alley, leaned against a wall, and took a deep, cleansing breath. Oh, gods, what if that spell hadn't worked?

She heard someone walk into the alley behind her and clear his throat. Startled, she pushed away from the wall and turned to face the interloper, her hand reaching for her dagger.

Lysandros touched his fingers to his forehead in a mock salute. His tanned face split in a wide grin, and he said, "Sorry to surprise you. Having a rough day?"

Lucy leaned back against the wall with a little laugh. "You wouldn't believe. And I thought this job would be easy."

"There's nothing easy about this town." He jerked a thumb toward the street. "Do you have time to take a break? There's a little place around the corner that sells the best cider and fried pies."

She nodded, grateful for his invitation. "I'd love some kefre. Surely this place won't fall down in the next twenty minutes or so." In the dim light of the alley she thought she saw a strange expression cross his face that looked to her like regret and pain, then it was gone and she wondered if she had seen it at all.

They walked side by side along the sidewalk to the next street over and, as the half-elf had promised, found a small bakery that sold fried pies, kefre, and cups of cooled cider. Taking their treats outside, they sat on a bench beside the shop where they could see the people passing back and forth and enjoying the cooler breeze from the sea.

"So tell me about your day," Lysandros suggested.

Between bites of her pie, Lucy described her very long and stressful day. "We started this morning making visits to those people I had received complaints about—the widow and her grape-eating goats, the tenants with no rent, the merchants with the overweight scales . . . the list seemed endless. Then I had to sit on Mayor Efrim's court and listen to more complaints. Then I had to stop several fist fights, arrest four drunks, and stop a horde of Khurs who thought it would be funny to gallop their horses down a busy street and scare everyone." She shook her head. "I will never again take the town guards in Solace for granted."

A faraway look came into his pale eyes. "Solace," he murmured. "I've only been as far as Khuri-Khan. Tell me about Solace, and every place in between."

So she did. While the night crept over the town and the lights and torches began to glow like stars, she told him about the vallenwoods and the town of Solace that grew up in the branches of the great trees. She described the Academy of Sorcery and its fall—without mentioning her connection to the Majere family—and she talked about Schallsea and Sanction and the long trek across the eastern wastelands. He sat enthralled, asking questions once in a while and gazing at her mobile face.

When she finally wound to a stop and sat quietly beside him, she felt much better. Her body had relaxed, and her mind had had a chance to look elsewhere for a while. She turned to thank him and saw again that strange look of regret.

"I can't believe I'm doing this," he muttered, as if to himself.

"Talking and eating pies?" she exclaimed, astonished at his reaction. "It was your idea."

Her words snapped him out of his reverie, and his charming smile came flashing back. "Not this at all, my Lady Sheriff. This has been a treat and a pleasure. Thank you. Nevertheless"—he bounced to his feet—"duty calls. I received word earlier today that another caravan is headed our way. We must leave to keep watch for it. I came to tell you that patrols have been sent out to seek word of your father, and if I hear anything, I will send word." He bowed over her hand and strode away, his dark robes billowing in the night wind.

She watched him until his form disappeared in the darkness. What was that all about? Why did he seem upset about something? She climbed slowly to her feet and filed her concern away for later when she had the leisure to ponder it. Lysandros was an enigmatic, complicated character, and a busy one at that. Perhaps he would tell her in time what was bothering him.

"Lucy! Lucy!" A high-pitched, kender voice interrupted her thoughts. It was Pease, on duty with her that day. "Lucy, there you are!" he cried, sliding to a stop in front of her. "One of the shopkeepers caught two kender pocketing some of his wares. He wants you to arrest them this instant. I know them. They wouldn't steal." He grabbed her hand and tried to drag her along the street.

Lucy sighed, envisioning a long and vociferous argument between the aggrieved shop owner and the kender. There went her hopes for a quiet evening.

* * * * *

Lucy's third and fourth day as the Sheriff of Flotsam went much like the first two. She was busy from sunrise to late in the night, when she could finally stagger to her bed in the Jetties and sleep for a few hours before starting again. The council and the mayor helped her as much as they could, and the Vigilance Force acted as invisible guards around the town, but there was only so much they could do. Most of the responsibility of keeping the peace fell on Lucy and her deputies. Challie had become her right hand, keeping notes, filing complaints, collecting fines, and running the organization of the Sheriff's Office. Pease and his friend Cosmo were Lucy's eyes and ears. They were familiar with almost all of the permanent residents of Flotsam. They recognized the strangers and knew almost everything that went on in the town. They also took care of the prisoners in the cells, brought food from the inn, and ran errands. Lucy didn't know what she would have done without any of them.

In making her mental list of beings she was indebted to, she felt she should also include the bay horse and the Vizier's Turban. The big bay from Sanction still favored his hip where the Dark Knight's dagger wound was slowly healing, yet he carried Lucy without complaint and exhibited a resigned patience whenever she left him at a hitching post. She didn't bother to tie him. She just flipped the reins over the bar and left him to wait, knowing he would still be there when she returned. He saved her hours of walking and served as a good listener when she needed someone to hear *her* complaints without interruption.

As for the turban, it served as a constant reminder to the townspeople of Lucy's authority and power. More than one perpetrator backed down when faced with the turban's glittering eyes and changing colors. To Lucy, its friendly, enthusiastic presence was a balm to her feelings whenever one too many irate persons yelled at her or called her some ugly name and she was tempted to let her fury explode. Not only could it sense her strong emotions, it seemed to have the ability to soothe them if it desired. Already, after only four days, she was ready to pledge her eternal gratitude to Notwen for his gift of the turban.

She tried not to think of Notwen and Ulin very often. They were always in the back of her mind, of course, but if she let them into the mainstream of her thoughts, they stayed there like large boulders, blocking everything else, and she found herself distracted, irritable, and intensely worried. She should have been used to Ulin's absences by now, but she missed him this time more than ever before and yearned for his quiet, comforting presence. She could only hope he would return to her soon, with or without her father.

On the fifth day, the Silver Fox and his Force escorted another Khur caravan into Flotsam. The captain disappeared the moment the caravan hove into sight, but the populace turned out to greet the wagons and to visit the market where the Khurs unloaded their wares. This caravan originated in Khuri-Khan and carried predominantly Khurish goods: rugs, dried figs, olives, saddles, lengths of beautifully woven fabrics, pottery with the traditional blue motifs, and silver jewelry from the mountains. Lucy and her deputies had their hands full keeping the drunks in line, curbing the acquisitive tendencies of the kender, and ensuring that everyone followed the rules of the market.

To make matters more complicated, the Dark Knights returned.

Lucy saw them at the edge of the crowded market, riding their horses slowly along the perimeter. Knight Officer Venturin rode at the head of the Talon on a night-dark horse, her visage as grim and dark as her steed. None of the Knights wore armor in the heat of the day, but all were heavily armed and clad in leather cuirasses. The people in the crowded street made way before them.

The Knight officer seemed to be looking for someone, and Lucy did not need a crystal ball to figure out who. Quickly, she pulled off the turban and thrust it into Challie's arms. "Take this and get out of sight," she hissed.

The dwarf barely had time to dodge behind a laden wagon before the Dark Knight spotted Lucy, wrenched her horse around, and rode it into the busy market irrespective of the people and goods underfoot. Lucy hurried to meet them, hoping to cut them off before they caused too much damage. Taking her cue from her last meeting with the Talon leader, she bowed low before Knight Officer Venturin.

Venturin's mouth twisted into its habitual sneer. "I see you are still playing your charade of sheriff."

"Yes, Knight Officer." Lucy kept her eyes on the ground. She felt such an intense desire to plaster this Knight with one of those flaming potatoes that she was relieved she did not have one. The temptation would have been too hard to resist.

The Knight made no move to dismount. She sat on her horse, and her eyes swept the faces of the people around them. Most of the market-goers moved away to avoid the Knights, while those close by studiously ignored them and maintained masks of occupied innocence. Knight Officer Venturin snorted, a sound short and unpleasant, and turned back to the woman standing in front of her. "We are looking for a man, a half-elf to be exact."

Lucy shrugged. "There are several of that blood around here."

The Dark Knight spurred her horse forward until she forced Lucy back against a cart. Drawing her sword, she leaned past the horse's neck and shoved the point at Lucy's throat. "Don't be stupid," she suggested in cold tones. "I am looking for the leader of the resistance in this area. He is tall, fair-haired, and goes by the name of Lysandros. I have heard from my sources that he has a liking for you."

Lucy could not hide a start of surprise. She guessed the half-elf harbored feelings for her of some kind, but to realize the Knights of Neraka knew about it alarmed her.

Venturin chuckled. "So it is true, to some extent at least. I will keep that in mind. Meanwhile, little sheriff, remember this: There is a price on his head. You can profit from that knowledge or suffer. The penalty for aiding a fugitive is death."

Lucy could only nod. The black horse fidgeted under his tight rein, bringing his hooves very close to her feet. His hot breath fanned her face, and his heavy muzzle was only inches away from her nose. The edge of the cart pressed painfully into her back.

Venturin laughed and jabbed the tip of her sword just enough to pierce the skin on Lucy's neck, then she backed the horse several steps. "If Lysandros shows his face in this town, just hoist a flag from your city hall. My spies will see it and send me word. It is worth your miserable little life to obey."

Lucy bowed again without saying a word. Wheeling their horses, the Dark Knights rode out of the marketplace and back to the road. "Challie!" Lucy called. "Find Pease and have him tell the kender to keep an eye on those Knights. I want to know where they go and when they leave town." Challie nodded, tossed the turban back to her, then hurried away to find Pease.

The tension slowly eased, and the noise and bustle of the market resumed. People crowded around Lucy, talking to each other and congratulating her for avoiding trouble with the Dark Knights.

"You'd better hoist that flag," a hoarse voice murmured in her ear.

Her brows lowered, she turned to the speaker and saw a bearded man in fisherman's clothes standing close behind her. Fish scales clung like iridescent raindrops to his arms and stained leather apron, and his clothes stank of fish and bait. It wasn't until she lifted her gaze to his pale blue eyes and saw the laughter in their depths that she realized who he was: Lysandros.

"She said, 'If Lysandros shows his face in this town . . .'" Lucy replied tartly. "Well, I don't see Lysandros's face, only the ugly mug of a fisherman who presumes to give advice to the Sheriff of Flotsam."

"Well spoken, Sheriff," drawled the fisherman. "Cripes, but you're a cool one around that Knight."

Lucy sniffed her disdain. "She's just lucky I didn't have a potato handy."

Lysandros grinned at her for a moment, then he sobered and remarked, "I heard what she said."

"The fact that someone close enough to you to know your feelings is reporting to the Dark Knights bothers me."

"Not the fact that I hold deep feelings for you?" he asked.

The even tone of his voice made her uncomfortable, for she could not tell if he was joking or totally serious. She lifted her head to meet his eyes and said, "I hope those feelings are like mine, the affection for a good friend."

He stared into the green depths of her gaze and saw the unshakable truth of her words. She offered nothing more. He nodded once and turned away before she could recognize the disappointment in his heart. Perhaps, considering the future, that was for the best. He took a step back from her. "A very good friend," he agreed. "So stay out of the path of those Knights, if you can."

"You, too," she replied. "And watch your back."

He moved to go, changed his mind, and turned back. "What would you say to having pies and cider with a friend tonight? Same place?"

She lifted the turban to her head and set it in place. Lysandros noted with satisfaction that the symbiotic creature turned a pale shade of blue, a contented color. It wasn't a hot, passionate red, but it was better than, say, a fiery orange or an angry black. Lucy tucked her thumbs into her belt and assumed a slouching pose. "I'd have to say yes. See you at dusk." She swaggered off into the crowd to meet the next crisis.

Captain Fox watched her until her blue-clad figure was lost in the throng.

Chapter
Thirteen

U lin and Notwen began their search for Lucy's father shortly after midday. They had slept late despite the heat and the noise in the village, and when they woke, they were ravenous. After a breakfast of bland chowder and watery ale, they made a careful inquiry about Kethril Torkay.

The innkeeper looked at them askance. "Sure, most people around these parts know Kethril. Most people live to regret it."

"As have I," Ulin replied heavily. "I must repay a debt of gambling. However, I cannot pay him, if I do not know where he is."

A laugh burst from the old innkeeper. "If you say so, boy. I would tell you if I knew. He has stiffed me on a debt, but truth is, no one's seen Kethril around here for some months. Rumor is he's dead." He nodded toward the door. "You can try some of the other places. Maybe you'll be lucky."

Notwen and Ulin trudged outside. They paused in the warm sunlight while Ulin drew the Truth-see glasses out of his pocket. He hesitated a moment, staring at the fine wire and pink lenses. He knew they should work. They had been crafted in the Fourth Age with magic granted by the gods, magic that was still reliable even after the departure of the gods. But he hesitated, torn by an illogical reluctance and a sense of foolishness. One reason he had come to this region was to look for artifacts—so why did he have a powerful desire to crumple these spectacles and hurl them into the bay? It wasn't the spectacles' fault his magic no longer functioned. Ulin sighed and forced his feelings aside. If this Kethril was as clever as everyone thought, he and Notwen would need all the advantages they could garner. He put the glasses on.

If the spectacles worked, it was not immediately apparent. The rose lenses did nothing to improve the squalor and decrepit condition of the town, nor did they reveal anything out of the ordinary. What he saw, Ulin decided, was what he got.

He and Notwen decided to start their inquiries in the taverns and gaming houses along the ramshackle waterfront then work their way through the brothels and shops of the back streets. The first tavern they visited was built into the hold of one the old ships. A ramp led up to a door cut in the hull, and inside tables and a bar had been set up on the lower deck. The place was nearly empty, and the few customers at the bar were a mean-looking, surly lot. If they knew anything about Kethril, they were in no mood to tell.

Notwen and Ulin moved on. At the next establishment, the name of Kethril Torkay brought an instant reaction from one of the patrons.

"That conniving son of a jackal!" a powerful-looking Khur barbarian shouted. "He cheated me! I will have his tongue! His hands! His eyes will decorate my dagger!"

"Yes," Ulin said patiently, "but do you know where he is? We were told he was dead."

"Dead!" The barbarian slammed his mug on the table. "Not that we have heard. Hey, Kalim, have you seen that whoreson Kethril?"

The person he addressed raised his head from the bar and gazed blearily at nothing in particular before shaking his head and dropping it back on the bar.

The Khur stamped to Ulin, his expression bellicose and very inebriated. "If you find him, tell me. I have vowed to slit his throat."

"Stand in line," Ulin muttered. He led the drunken Khur back to his table with promises of instant notification should Kethril Torkay be found. After depositing the man in a chair, Ulin hurried out with Notwen.

They tried several more taverns with equal success until they reached the end of the small waterfront. From there they followed a different path past several run-down houses and a dilapidated shop to the next establishment: a gaming house made of mud bricks and stucco.

The owner, a tall red-haired woman of middle age, met them at the door and welcomed them inside. The shaded interior was cool after the humid heat outdoors, and fans, turned by several children, helped keep the air moving. Customers obviously appreciated the house's amenities, for the tables were nearly full of patrons playing everything from dice and khas to Bounty Hunter and Dragon's Bluff. Serving maids bustled around the tables serving beverages and snacks.

"What interests you today, gentlemen?" the red-haired owner inquired. "We offer dice, cards, khas, games of chance, games of skill . . ."

Something about the woman prompted Ulin to drop his story of an unpaid gambling debt and try something closer to the truth. "A game of Hide and Seek," Ulin answered. "We are looking for someone who was reported dead. His family is very concerned."

She considered them for a long moment then held up a hand, its fingers encrusted with rings. "Perhaps you would like a water reading? Through the oracle glass certain things can be foretold. Loved ones can be located."

Ulin and Notwen glanced at each other, interest on both their faces. Ulin had never seen an oracle glass, although he'd heard of them. He was intrigued to see how one worked.

The fortune-teller led them to a separate room enclosed with carved screens and hung with purple cloth. She sat them both in chairs beside a round table and took a seat herself. A clap of her beringed hands brought a young girl to her side. "Bring water, and be sure you filter it three times. It must be pure." She leaned back in her high back chair and studied the man and the gnome as the girl hurried away. "A curious partnership," she said softly. Her fingers drummed on the armrest. "No. Do not talk. Let me read you for myself." Her voice was husky and curiously soothing. Red-gold lashes framed her deep-brown eyes and matched the color of her hair piled on top of her head.

She reached under the table and brought out a perfectly round glass bowl, clear and nearly flawless, and set it on a three-legged stand in front of her. As soon as the girl returned with a pitcher of water, she took the pitcher and poured its contents into the bowl. The girl quickly withdrew, and the three were left in silence.

Ulin sat still, his fingers steepled, his face devoid of any feeling or reaction. Notwen fidgeted in his chair, hoping for a closer look at the oracle glass. So far, all either of them could see was clear water.

The woman hummed to herself, her eyes on the glass, her hands flat on the table. She appeared to be deep in concentration on the interior of the bowl. "Young man," she intoned at last. "You are more than you seem. You have lost much, yet your heart is strong. You are seeking . . . how intriguing. I see a dragon, a gold dragon. It carries you, but it weeps."

Ulin's fingers closed around each other in a grip so tight

his knuckles turned white. "Is there more?" he asked in a strangled voice. "Can you tell me where he is?"

"No," she said. "The oracle glass cannot be perfectly controlled. I only interpret those images that form. Let me try another." She stirred up the water with a glass rod and waited for a new image. "Who else are you looking for? Perhaps a name?"

"Kethril Torkay."

The fortune-teller clapped a hand over the glass and stared at her two customers. "Why are you looking for him?" she demanded.

"For the reason I told you. His family received a letter informing them of his death. They just want to know the truth."

She relaxed slightly, and her hand moved from the bowl. "I see truth in your eyes. Besides, that lying knave did mention a wife and children somewhere. I thought he was just lying to get out of marrying me." She smiled then, revealing large white teeth and a dimple on her powdered cheek. "*This* reading is free." She stared back into the water. "I do not see a grave. There is a hole of some sort, an excavation perhaps, but no grave. He is in it, very much alive, moving boxes I think."

Ulin pursed his lips, thinking about what she said. "Are these images of the past or the future?"

"Could be either. The oracle glass does not interpret time as we do."

"So Kethril may be alive?"

"Probably."

"Where do we find him?"

The woman shook her head. "That I cannot say. He has not been here for months. If he had visited me, he probably would be dead."

Ulin snorted a laugh. "He certainly knows how to make friends."

"That's the problem. He does. He is the most charming, delectable man who ever crossed my threshold." She sighed eloquently. "Also the most self-centered, untruthful, conniving rogue who ever set foot in Dead Pirate's Cove, and that's saying a great deal." She tapped a fingernail on the glass and gazed thoughtfully at the tiny rings that spread across the water. "There is one possibility. He is an inveterate gambler. If he is still in the area, he could be sneaking over to the *Golden Carp*. It's a riverboat used as a gaming tavern upriver. They move it whenever they feel the itch, so it could be anywhere along the river between here and Four Horse, where the river gets too shallow for boats. Maybe ten miles upstream."

Ulin dropped a steel coin on the table. "Take it anyway, and thank you."

Notwen bounced on his seat. "But what about me?"

She smiled at him. "Ah, I almost forgot. The gnome with the inventive mind." She peered into her glass again. "You have a good friend here. I think he will save your life." She shot a look at Notwen over the glass. "But beware a red dragon."

Notwen barely heard her. He climbed up in his chair and peered over the glass. "What do you see? How do you summon these images? Is the power in you, the water, or the glass?"

The fortune-teller waggled a finger at him. "Oh, no. That's giving away my secrets." She lifted her glass away from his inquisitive hands. "Suffice to know that my images are reliable. It is up to you to find their worth."

Ulin pulled Notwen away from the table and plopped him on the floor. They offered their thanks to the red-haired woman and made their way to the next establishment. For the rest of the day they talked to the citizens of Dead Pirate's Cove, but no one could give them any more information on Kethril. The man had vanished from the settlement four months ago and not even the few people who called him friend knew where he was.

With only the sketchy information from the red-haired woman, Ulin and Notwen returned to the Loathly Dragon hungry, tired, and dispirited. They rested that night and early the next morning, they made their back to the *Second Thoughts*. Under the amused scrutiny of a dozen witnesses, they poled the boat backward until they could turn her toward the river, then they lit the boiler and got underway. Slowly, they steamed toward the mouth of the river.

The particular advantages of a shallow-drafted, broad-bottomed boat and a paddle wheel soon became apparent in the silt-filled waters of the river. The boat wove a tortuous route through the saltmarsh, past sandbars, mud flats, and banks of waving marsh grass. In many places the water was shallow even in high tide and barely passable with the paddle boat. A deep-keeled sailboat would never have made the passage.

Ulin steered the small boat while Notwen kept the boiler hot and the engine working. They made several wrong turns and had to work their way back to the main current, and twice Ulin had to jump out and pull armfuls of weed, dead grass, and muck from the blades of the paddle so it could turn without too much stress on the cogs and the engine. In spite of the extra miles, the *Second Thoughts* left the marsh behind shortly before nightfall and chugged slowly up the meandering river.

In this rugged, barren land, trees only grew along the river in a thin ribbon of green that barely screened the reds and browns of the eroded hills. The riverbanks lifted high above the water in some places and slid down into silt bars and beds of reeds in others. The water, what there was of it, was silty brown and sluggish. "Too thin to plow, too thick to drink," was a common description in that region. About the only creatures who seemed to appreciate the river were the long-legged wading birds and the mosquitoes.

It was near full dark when Ulin and Notwen looked for a place to tie up for the night. The *Second Thoughts* chuffed around a bend, and Notwen was about to steer it toward a likely looking cove when Ulin's head lifted and he gestured fiercely for Notwen to shut down the engine. Steam hissed from the relief valves, and gradually the little boat drifted into silence.

Ulin pointed ahead to a thick grove of willow and cottonwood shielding the next bend in the river. Barely seen through the new canopy of spring leaves, the yellow light of torches flickered.

Silently as possible, Ulin and Notwen poled the boat into the side cove, made her fast, and banked the fire. Together they slipped through the underbrush toward the lights until they could see through the trees to the riverbank beyond the curve. There sat a large, flat-bottomed boat anchored fore and aft in a broad, deep river hole. Lamps were already lit on the deck, and light shone through the portholes. Several men stood guard at the gangplank. It was the *Golden Carp*.

They swiftly worked their way back to the *Second Thoughts* and finalized their plans.

"He may not come. He may not even be around here," Notwen pointed out while Ulin washed the mud off and changed his clothes.

"I know."

"It may be several days before he appears."

"I know."

"He won't want to be caught," the gnome added worriedly. "He's got to know the city council will hang him if they get their hands on him."

"I know," Ulin said. He finished wrapping a sash belt around his waist and put his hands on Notwen's shoulders. "I'll be careful, and I'll have you to watch my back." He slid the rose glasses over his nose and tucked several small packets into the folds of his belt. When he was ready, they doused the single candle, closed the door, and headed for the *Golden Carp*.

A black night had settled over the river when they approached the gangplank. A narrow ramp had been tied to the bank and extended to the upper deck of the boat. Ulin saw now that the boat was really a barge meant to be towed up or down the river, probably by mules or a horse. Five or six canoes and several flatboats were tied near the shore, and a picket line under the trees held five horses. Voices rang from the open widows of the barge, and somewhere within someone was playing a lute. Badly.

The guards met them at the gangway. "If you plan to play," one demanded, "you must show us your money and check your weapons at the door."

"And if we don't plan to play?" Ulin inquired.

"You will leave," the second replied in a tone that brooked no argument. "Now."

Ulin had not brought his sword, guessing this would happen, but he turned over his dagger and drew out his coin bag to show the guards his coins. He did not mention the knife in his boot. They waved him through, searched Notwen, and let them pass.

Trying to look nonchalant, Ulin wandered toward the bar. Notwen stayed close behind him to attract as little attention as possible. The main room of the gambling boat was arranged with tables and chairs set about them. A large bar made from heavy planks and saw horses sat at the bow-end of the room. The room was smoky and disheveled. The few brass lamps that hung from the ceiling beams did little to dispel the gloom. Sawdust covered the floor. Perhaps fifteen to twenty people—mostly humans, a few dwarves, and two small baaz draconians—sat at the playing tables or stood by the bar. Kender were not allowed in the door.

A tired-looking woman in a stained dress served mugs of beer and spirits. She saw Ulin and said, "What'll it be? Beer or *torquil?*"

Ulin winced. The beer was bound to be bad in a place like this, and *torquil*, a rot-gut fermentation of some cactus-juice preferred by the Khurs, gave him a fiery headache every time he tried it. "Beer," he said. At least his head would not explode.

She slid a coarse stoneware mug across to him. "What's with the funny glasses?"

"Pink eye," he growled.

She shook her head and took his coin without another word. He was right. To a palate raised on Caramon's brews, this beer was bad. He drank it anyway, leaning back against the bar, and he studied the customers one by one. First he looked at each person over the rim of the spectacles then through the rose glass. He saw no difference.

He sat for perhaps two hours nursing his beer and watching the activities. People came and left, new games were started. Notwen wandered over to a khas table by the door and soon became engrossed in a game with a trapper. There was still no sign of anyone in a disguise of any sort or anyone even close to Kethril Torkay's description. Ulin knew he couldn't sit at the bar much longer without buying another beer or joining a game. The bartender was giving him evil looks and the serving woman suggested several times that he order another drink or leave.

The leaving option sorely tempted him. The lute player had not improved with time and had given Ulin a pounding headache. The beer was foul. Then again, if he didn't throw some money around, the guards might get suspicious and not allow him back on the boat another night. He glanced around at the game tables to find something he could play, and at that moment, his decision was made for him.

Three Khurs staggered in the door arm in arm, laughing uproariously. They were full of gaiety, comradeship, and raucous pleasure, and obviously full of beer or something harder. They spotted a table under one of the brass lamps and unceremoniously dumped its occupying drunk in a corner and claimed it for their own.

"Torquil!" bellowed the tallest man with an eye patch and a full beard. "Torquil for my desert friends."

Ulin's eyes narrowed at the odd phrasing. Carefully, he studied the man over the rim of his spectacles. When he tilted up his head and looked at the same man through the rose-colored lenses, the difference was striking. The black hair, swarthy skin, rugged features, and bearded countenance of the tall man blurred and faded to reveal a white-skinned, fair-haired man with paler eyes and smoother features—an exact match of Lucy's description. As if to complete the identification, the "Khur" raised a gloved hand to bring out a deck of cards and slap them on the table.

After all the miles he had traveled to find this man and all the stories he heard, Ulin found it very strange to see the man himself sitting in a rickety chair, moving and breathing, very much alive. The disguise was excellent. Too good to be simple false hair and skin dye. Ulin wondered if Kethril was in the possession of certain magic artifacts. Lucy never said her father was a mage, but maybe he'd learned enough to wield the old magic in artifacts.

"It's him, isn't it?" Notwen murmured at his elbow. "He won't come easily."

"No, not yet," Ulin agreed. "He won't come willingly, and he may have friends in this place. I have an idea, though." He showed his teeth in a feral grin. "I owe myself this one."

Chapter Fourteen

In a hushed voice, Ulin told Notwen what he intended to do. The gnome bobbed his head in understanding and, as instructed, drifted off to melt into the background.

Ulin removed the pink spectacles. He checked the layers of his sashed belt to be certain the small packets were still there and easy to reach, then he took his mug and sauntered over to the table to watch the card game.

The men were playing a variation of Bounty Hunter, a high stakes game that involved skill and a high measure of luck. Silently, Ulin placed himself where he could see Kethril's cards and his hands, and where, if Kethril paid attention to his peripheral vision, he could be seen by the gambler.

Ulin watched the game through a number of hands until he began to understand how it was played. He also noticed Lucy's father won steadily. The man seemed to have an innate knowledge of when to bet and when to fold.

He played carefully, planning each move in advance. His opponents played hard, trying to beat him, betting more and more heavily as the game progressed, and their faces turned redder and more annoyed every time the "bounty" of coins and trinkets moved to Kethril's pile. Ulin also noticed that Kethril rarely touched his mug, while the others drank a steady stream of torquil. He was a cool player, without a doubt.

Finally, a rotund Khur in dark robes slammed his palms on the table to end his play and stamped off to find a more accommodating game. The other one grimly held his seat and passed the cards to Kethril for a new game. A third player saw the empty chairs and came to join them.

The gambler cocked his head slightly to see Ulin. A brown eye twinkled at him from under a black arched brow. "There's one chair left. Are you going to play or just gawk?"

Ulin gave a shrug, pulled out a fat bag of coins, and plopped it on the table with a solid chunk. "I don't know this game. Could you tell me the rules?" He took the chair vacated by the Khur and pulled up to the table beside Kethril.

The other Khur smirked. Here was his chance to recoup some of his losses. The new man, an old mercenary by the look of the scars on his face and the knotted muscles under his leather vest, helped himself to the pitcher of torquil and shoved the pitcher over to Ulin. "Help yerself," he grunted.

Kethril said nothing. His features were set in an expression of casual interest that revealed nothing.

Close beside him now, Ulin could see him better in the dim light. Even in his disguise he was tall, slim in the waist, broad-shouldered, and powerfully built. He wore a tunic, an embroidered vest, and long, tight-fitting pants all of rich and expensive fabrics. His hands were long and his fingers moved like those of a highly practiced wizard as he shuffled the cards, cut the deck, and began to deal seven cards to each player. As soon as the cards were dealt, he put the rest of the pack in a pile in the center of the table and turned one face up.

"Four suits in this deck: Leaves, winds, swords, and moons. Mage cards are high, ones are low. Fates are wild. We'll play a copper a point for one hand so you can see how to bet, then we'll shift back to silver."

Ulin nodded. It didn't really matter. He had never had the time or the desire to learn how to play cards well, and he usually had abysmal luck. The important part was to get into the game. They played the first hand, and as he expected, Ulin lost a few coppers. The mercenary added the meager pot to his dwindling pile and swigged down another mug of torquil. The second Khur sank into a drunken gloom.

The game continued. Gradually, the riverboat filled as night drew on. Ulin was vaguely aware of the background din of loud, indistinct voices, the rattle of crockery and bottles, and the stamp of boots on the sawdust floor. In the far corner, a worn-looking girl took the place of the lute player and played listlessly on a lap harp, singing songs no one listened to. The air grew thick and very warm. A few more lamps were lit.

Every once in a while Ulin looked up and caught a glimpse of Notwen leaning into a shadowy corner and watching the activity at the game table. The game was progressing as Ulin hoped. He and the other two were losing heavily, while Kethril continued to win. He noticed a pattern in the hands that Kethril dealt. The three playing would win a few paltry bounties to keep them interested, then Kethril would win big. Ulin felt like a fish on the line of a master angler. Although he couldn't swear to it, he guessed Lucy's father was cheating somehow, but his hands and fingers moved so skillfully that it was impossible to catch every move.

The mercenary watched the cards like a hawk and dealt his turn with ferocity, as if he could intimidate the cards into showing him some mercy. The Khur grew more sour and morose with every hand.

At last the mood at the table took the turn Ulin hoped for. The mercenary slapped down a Mage of Winds on a particularly large bounty, and his lips split in a thin grin. The Khur groaned, and his head dropped into his hands, but before the mercenary could claim his prize, Kethril shook his head in mock sympathy and slowly laid out a Shinare, a goddess of wealth card.

A howl rose from the mercenary. "You son of Hiddukel! You thieving—!" He flung his cards down and hurled himself across the table at Kethril.

In the ensuing tussle, Ulin took advantage of the distraction to withdraw a small packet from his sash, sprinkle the contents over the coins remaining in his bag and give the bag a quick shake. For good measure, he dumped the remaining fine gray powder into the pitcher of torquil as he swept it out of harm's way.

"Gently, sir, gently," he chided, setting the pitcher aside. He caught the mercenary by the shoulders and hauled him off Kethril and the mess of coins and cards on the table. While his back was to Lucy's father, Ulin slid two cards surreptitiously into his belt. The mercenary was too drunk to put up a real fight, and he slumped back into his chair looking murderous.

"Feddor, my friend, you are tired and your cards are atrocious tonight." Kethril suggested gently. "Wouldn't you rather try again some other night?"

"Piss on you," the mercenary snarled. "One more game, gambler. Your luck can't be that good."

Kethril turned to Ulin and offered him a knowing, man-to-man look of approval as Ulin straightened up the mess on the table, poured torquil into everyone's mugs, and picked up the cards to deal the next hand. When the cards were dealt, Ulin looked at his and allowed himself a sound of satisfaction. While the Khur and the mercenary watched avidly, he dumped his remaining coins out of the bag and onto the pitifully small pile of coins in front of him.

Kethril leaned over and punched him jovially on the arm. "You play well, young man, and without rancor. A true games master never allows emotion or anger to get in the way of his play."

"We shall see," Ulin muttered aside. He laid the first card down, a paltry two of leaves. The others quickly followed suit.

It didn't take long for Ulin to lose most of his money. His luck was worse than normal, and he intentionally made mistakes that allowed the other men, especially Kethril, to win his coins. He began to scowl and to move in clipped, angry gestures. Sweat gathered on his face from the thick, hot air in the room, but since it added to his appearance of agitation, he made no effort to mop his skin. The air made everyone thirsty, too, so even Kethril drank deeply from the pitcher of torquil.

The minutes ticked by while the game progressed to its end. Ulin watched each man intently and waited for the first sign that his powder was taking effect. At every opportunity he wiped his own fingers on his pant's leg. Then Kethril shook his head. He frowned and held his cards at arm's length as if he could not focus on them.

Ulin shot a look at Notwen and barely nodded. The gnome's face answered with such a look of mischievous anticipation that Ulin had to fight back a laugh. Out of the corner of his eye, he watched Notwen slip a pitcher of beer off a table when no one was paying attention and make his way toward their corner. It was his turn to play, so Ulin held his opponents' attention by frowning at his cards, tapping his last few coins with a fingernail, and making the most of a pretended internal debate. Finally, he tossed in the last of his silver coins. "Three silvers for the Prince of Thieves," he said.

The others looked at him oddly. "The Prince of what?" Feddor mumbled.

"Wrong game, my young friend," Kethril said lightly. "That's Dragon's Bluff."

All at once a small figure tripped over something on the floor and fell forward beside Kethril. The wet, warm contents of the pitcher slopped over the gambler's lap in a frothy wave.

Kethril sprang to his feet, a curse on his lips. As he did so, Ulin also rose, and with a deft movement, he transferred the two cards in his sash to the table in front of Lucy's father.

The Khur and the mercenary were too inebriated to see the blurred motion of Ulin's hand, but they did not miss the sight of the two cards fluttering down to the tabletop in front of Kethril as if they had just fallen from his vest. Their eyes bulged in fury.

"I knew it!" Feddor bellowed at the top of his lungs. "You're cheating!" He lunged to his feet, or tried to. His head lolled over his shoulders alarmingly, and he staggered sideways into the Khur. The Khur pushed him away and climbed to his feet, then his face turned blank, his eyes rolled into his head, and he pitched forward onto the table, scattering coins and cards in every direction. The table collapsed under his weight.

Kethril just stood there, his eyes glazed, his expression dumbfounded.

"Grab the coins," Ulin hissed to Notwen, and he tossed him the empty coin bag.

"You!" the mercenary continued. "You filthy Khur! You thieving scum!"

Heads turned, and people stopped what they were doing to watch the fun. Feddor took a wild swing at Kethril's head, misjudged the distance, and staggered forward into the gambler. He kicked Kethril instead, and Kethril punched him. Both men went down in a wild tangle.

Cheers rose up around them. Ulin stayed back long enough for the two men to land a few punches. By the time he intervened the fight had lost almost all momentum through alcohol and drug-induced exhaustion. He leaned over, grabbed a fistful of Kethril's embroidered vest, and hauled the man out of the mess. Feddor, lying on his back by the table, protested weakly, but he didn't move even when Notwen scrambled over him carrying the bag fat with coins.

Ulin saw movement through the crowd and realized the guards were coming to break up the fight. Hurrying, he dragged Kethril to his feet and pulled his arm across his shoulders. "Let's go. You've had enough fun for one evening," he said loudly.

The gambler glared at him blearily. His neat, fastidiously clean clothes were covered with sawdust, dirt, and dark patches of spilled beer. The eye patch had slipped, exposing a bloodshot eye, and the other eye was beginning to swell. "Who are you?" he groaned.

Ulin smiled wickedly and did not answer. He held the man's arm tighter and twisted it behind Kethril's back as the gambler started to struggle. He dragged Lucy's father forward through the crowd toward the door. Patrons laughed and made ribald comments about the drunken state of the filthy Khur.

Two guards suddenly blocked Ulin's way. "What's going on here?" one demanded. Short swords appeared in their hands.

"You're a little late," Ulin remarked. He kept his voice casual and his expression inoffensive. "My companion here had a disagreement with Feddor over there. It's over, and I'm taking him to sleep it off."

"And who are you? We've never seen you here before," said the second guard.

"Of course you have. I've been here for hours."

The guards looked confused. In a moment the bartender came through the press of customers to join them. "This Khur is a good customer of mine," he declared to Ulin. "I don't want him in no trouble. What are you doing with him?"

"I'm his future son-in-law," Ulin replied in all honesty. "His daughter sent me to find him. She's the new sheriff of

Flotsam." A sudden surge of pride at those words took him by surprise. He savored its flavor.

"The sorceress that killed all those draconians?" the bartender asked, impressed. "And you will take him home like that?"

Ulin shrugged. "He would not come before. Would you, honored father?"

The gambler made no reply—not that he could. He had passed out completely, and his entire weight sagged against Ulin's side, causing the younger man to stagger.

Ulin was beginning to feel dizzy himself from the small amount of powder he had handled on the coins. It was time to go before Notwen was forced to deal with two large unconscious men.

"Need some help?" one of the guards offered.

Relieved, Ulin transferred some of Kethril to the guard, and together they hauled him out the door. Notwen scooted ahead and made it back to the boat in time to light a lantern and fire up the boiler. He was waiting when Ulin and the guard carried Kethril onto the boat and dumped him on the deck. After commenting on the odd little boat, the guard accepted Ulin's generous tip and headed jauntily back to the *Golden Carp*.

As soon as he was out of earshot, Ulin scooped out a pail of river water and plunged his hands in. "Wash your hands quickly," he told Notwen. "That powder is potent."

The gnome obliged, and for good measure he dumped the bag of copper, gold, and silver coins in the water and washed those, too. "What is this powder? How did you get it on the coins so fast?"

Ulin dumped the used water and scooped out another, which he poured over his head to help counter-act the dizziness that still swirled in his brain. "I may be a lousy card player, but I was a good mage, and I learned a few tricks from my uncle Raistlin." He didn't realize the significance of what he'd said until he shook his head and opened his eyes to see Notwen staring at him with bulging eyes.

"Raistlin was your uncle? The finest, most mysterious archmage in Krynn was your uncle? Then you must be a—"

"A Majere, yes," Ulin finished for him. "But not here. In this realm I am only Ulin from Solace."

Notwen drew a long shivery breath. "Oh, yes, of course. No one shall hear of it from me, but . . . wow. Sheriff Lucy must be something special if she is going to marry you."

Ulin chewed his lip and rubbed his aching temples. "I'm thinking it is the other way around."

They poled the *Second Thoughts* away from the bank and pointed her bow downstream. While Notwen steered, Ulin dragged Kethril over to the side and tied his hands to the rail. He searched the man's clothes from collar to boots and pulled out an array of small weapons, loaded dice, a few odd coins, and a well-worn medallion of white gold bearing an image of a man with two faces. Ulin felt the telltale tingle of magic from the medallion, and he smiled with certain relish while he removed the medallion from Kethril's neck.

The transformation happened immediately. The dark hair and beard faded to dark blond grizzled with gray, the skin lightened to a well-worn tan, and the craggy features smoothed into a handsome visage with a long, straight nose and a broad upper lip. The sleeping man did not move a muscle as Ulin tossed the medallion, the weapons, and the dice overboard.

The night was quite dark, for there was no moon and a new ceiling of cloud obscured the sky. Far to the northwest, lightning flickered in sheets through a dense bank of darkness. The wind had died to a breathless stillness that hung heavy on the muggy air and did nothing to discourage the hordes of mosquitoes. As long as the paddleboat chugged down the river, the numbers of biters stayed tolerable, but the moment the boat stopped at the mouth of the marsh, clouds of insects moved in. Ulin and Notwen debated the wisdom of navigating through the maze of sandbars and twisting channels at night, then decided against it. They did not know the channels well enough to risk the passage. They moored the boat in a backwater and closed the shutters and door of the cabin. Ulin took pity on Kethril and moved him into the meager shelter of the cabin and covered him with a blanket. The cabin was hot and stuffy and not entirely insect-proof, but it was better than sleeping in a cloud of blood-sucking, stinging mosquitoes.

Near dawn, a brief thunderstorm moved through in a gust of wind and a few rumbles of thunder. The rain pounded on the roof of the cabin for about half an hour before it moved on to blow itself out over the bay. By the time it left, the mosquitoes had sought refuge elsewhere, and a rising sun slowly bleached away the night.

Ulin and Notwen got underway early, for they wanted to stop at Dead Pirate's Cove for supplies and more fuel. With luck and some good weather, they hoped to be back in Flotsam late the next day, two days at the latest.

The morning was fresh and still pleasant after the rain, and the river's current ran toward the bay as the tide swept out to sea. Kethril showed a few reluctant signs of consciousness, so Ulin dragged him back into the sunshine and tied him to the railing.

He tied the last knot and was straightening when Kethril's eyes peeled open and revealed irises as green and vivid as Lucy's. The gambler squinted up at Ulin. "You have ruined my reputation at the *Golden Carp*," he said in slow, painfully enunciated words.

"Oh, I doubt it," Ulin said cheerfully. "From what I've heard of your reputation, there was nothing there to ruin."

The man groaned and tried to move, only to discover his hands were tied. He stared blearily around at the marsh and the boat and finally leveled a glare back at Ulin. "Where am I? And what is that infernal racket?"

Ulin squatted beside him. "You are on the *Second Thoughts*, bound for Flotsam. That racket is the engine. If you really want to know more about it, I'll send Notwen the gnome around to tell you all about it."

"A gnome!" Kethril moaned. "Oh, gods, spare me. My head is fit to burst. That chatterbox would finish me off." He paused and blinked a few times as if assessing what Ulin had told him. "Why am I here? What is the meaning of tying me up like this?"

"I agreed to bring your body back and I will. Dead or alive is up to you."

"My body back. Why? What are you, a bounty hunter?" Abruptly he stopped. Ulin, carefully watching his face, saw the light of realization spread into his eyes. "Of course," Kethril breathed. "Last night, on the boat. Someone mentioned my daughter. What is she doing in Flotsam?" The full ramifications of his predicament exploded in his clearing mind, and the shock waves twisted his features into a mask of despair. "Oh, departed gods, I don't believe this!" he shouted. "Flotsam! They'll kill me!"

Ulin rose to his feet and said coldly, "Probably." He turned on his heel and went to help Notwen with the boat.

With the aid of the tide, the *Second Thoughts* pushed her way through the marsh and paddled down the main channel toward the cove. Ulin thought the river seemed quiet and strangely empty of boats or people for midmorning. There was no one in sight, and even the marsh birds seemed subdued. He went to stand by the bow and shaded his eyes with his hand to scan the shore and look for the distant settlement.

The old shipwrecks and rickety buildings were still out of sight behind a low hill when Notwen called to Ulin, "There's smoke over there."

Both Ulin and Kethril turned their heads and saw thick gray smoke billowing into the sky from somewhere behind the hill. "That's from the Cove," said Kethril worriedly. He straightened and pulled until he worked himself to his knees, then he peered ahead, his entire body tense.

The paddleboat steamed slowly past the hill, around a gentle curve, and entered the open water. Dead Pirate's

Cove came into view. Ulin and Kethril strained to see the town and what trouble there might be. The first thing they saw were two fishing boats burning on the water.

"The gods speed us," Kethril gasped first. "Get us out of here! Hurry!" he bellowed to Notwen. "It's ghagglers."

Notwen squeaked in alarm and threw the engine into full steam. Ulin had only brief glimpses of the burning settlement, of bodies in the sand, and worst of all, of people herded onto the dock at weapon's point by large, two-legged monsters. Those glimpses were all he needed. His mouth dry, he dashed into the cabin, belted on his sword, and threw more fuel on the boiler fire. Ghagglers, he thought, fear burning in his belly. Cruel, blood-thirsty, and utterly without mercy, the sea species of sligs were the terror of the marine waters. Why, oh, why did they have to stumble on this place?

"Cut me loose!" he heard Kethril shout. "Cut me loose!" Ulin did not hesitate. There was no chance even Kethril Torkay would try to jump ship with the feared sea-sligs close by, and he needed all the help he could get. He dashed outside, sliced the rope binding the gambler's hands, and thrust an oar at him.

Kethril looked over Ulin's shoulder and turned pale. "They're coming after us." He struggled to his feet. "Bloody fiends. They must be desperate to be so close to shore."

"Go, go, go!" Ulin yelled to Notwen.

The gnome leaned on the wheel to turn the boat away from the cove. The engine rumbled and steamed, and the paddlewheel thrashed like a mill wheel gone mad. Ulin grabbed another oar and paddled from the bow as fast as he was able.

But they were too late. Only a fully rigged clipper could outrun a pack of ghagglers on the hunt in shallow water. Ulin glanced down once and stifled a cry. A dark, gray-green body flashed through the water like a porpoise and disappeared under the boat.

"Notwen, get out of sight!" Ulin screamed.

Clawed, horny hands grabbed the gunwales and three hideous faces peered over the edge at Kethril and Ulin. Kethril flattened one with an oar, but a fourth reared out of the water and snatched the oar from his hand. Ulin drew his sword. He brought the blade arching down on the hands of a sea-slig and knocked it screeching back into the water. Two more swiftly slithered up the sides of the boat and tried to crawl over the rail.

Without warning a horrendous sound slammed across the deck. Startled ghagglers ducked back into the water, and both men stumbled back from the edge of the deck. Steam poured from the cabin as the paddlewheel groaned to a halt. Like a kite broken loose from its string, the *Second Thoughts* sheered sideways from its course and began to drift with the wind across the bay.

The unexpected and abrupt change in movement threw Ulin and Kethril off balance. As they struggled upright, Ulin saw something brown flash through the air toward Lucy's father. He lunged forward to grab him when a similar something dropped over his own head and entangled his arms. A net as strong as steel and reeking of decay was jerked around his body. Tiny barbed hooks sank into his clothes, his hair, his skin, and he was pulled off his feet. He saw Kethril collapse under another net, and he saw the man's body yanked off the boat into the water. A tremendous wrench knocked the air from his lungs. Before he could draw another breath, Ulin was pulled off the boat, and the warm, salty water closed over his face.

Chapter Fifteen

L ucy stiffened. A taut, frightened expression settled over her face, and she froze in place, her hands poised over the pile of plums she had been admiring. Her skin bleached to a deathly pallor.

Bridget, Pease, and the fruit vendor looked at each other, puzzled by her reaction. "Are you all right, dear?" Bridget asked in her most motherly tone.

Lucy shook her head. Her knees gave way, and she sank down on a nearby barrel. On her head the turban faded to a sickly gray. "I just had the strangest feeling that something is wrong." She rubbed her aching temples.

The market around her was unchanged. It was still noisy, crowded, and bright with light and color. She had spent the morning collecting fees, calibrating scales, and visiting with people. There was absolutely no reason for this cold, sickening feeling that had sunk its claws into her belly and head.

The older kender paled. She drew back under the awning and scanned the skies for any sign of the red dragon. Pease, who was accustomed to his mother's reactions, put his arm around her shoulders. "I didn't hear the horn, Ma. Maybe Lucy meant something else."

As quickly as it had come, the odd sickly feeling subsided from Lucy's mind, leaving only an aftertaste of fear. "I don't know what it was or where it came from. I've never felt anything like that before." She let out a long, cleansing breath to help ease her pounding heart. Some of her color slowly returned, and as it did, the turban brightened to its customary shimmering blue. Lucy cocked her head and looked north where the bay glittered in the midday sun and stretched out to an indistinct horizon. "I hope Ulin is all right," she murmured.

Bridget's nervousness retreated when she did not hear the signal horn. Her body trembled once as if to shake free of the fear, and she came to stand by Lucy. Her round face crinkled with concern. "I'm sure he is fine. He is a strong lad, well used to taking care of himself. But you . . . Lucy . . . I . . ." She hesitated, stumbling over something she wanted to say. Her eyes sought the sky again. "You be careful," she finally managed to say in a whisper Lucy could barely hear.

"Sheriff Lucy!" An irate shopper stomped up to them. "Come check the baker's scale. I think he's shorting the bread again!"

"Back to work," Lucy said, trying to sound cheerful. She bought a handful of plums from the fruit vendor and followed the complainant through the market with Pease and Bridget close at her heels. Only once did she pause and look again to the north. "Hurry back, Ulin," she prayed.

* * * * *

The *Second Thoughts* drifted silently out of the cove on the tide. Held by the current it drifted far from land and was soon caught by the warm water currents of the bay. The ghagglers, suspicious of the strange noises and fumes that emanated from it, left it alone and let it drift beyond their caring after they took the men. For hours it remained silent and seemingly empty. A few seagulls perched on the cabin for a while before winging away after a shoal of fish.

At long last, a shining wet head popped out of the water near the still waterwheel. A slim hand touched the paddles and eased noiselessly up the side to the gunwale. A sleek, shapely body slid out of the water and climbed easily onto the deck. Trailing wet footprints, the girl walked to the bow and back along both sides of the cabin. Her delicate nostrils flared at the powerful odors of ghagglers, burned wood, and stressed metal. Finding no one on deck, she opened the cabin door and peered inside. The little room was a mess of spilled tools, scattered charts and maps, tumbled wood, and broken crockery and bottles. The girl tiptoed into the room, her face woebegone.

"Is anyone here?" she asked, not really expecting an answer. The ghagglers never left potential meals behind if they could help it. She pivoted around to leave when a tiny rustle caught her ear, just the faintest sound of something brushing against wood. On silent feet she crept to the wood box near the engine and peeped over the edge.

A white-haired gnome took one look at her, screeched in terror, and tried to burrow deeper into the tumbled stack of fuel.

"Oh, it's you," she said.

Notwen peeped through his fingers up at the aqua-marine face and the sea-green eyes of the sirine. He was so relieved to see a familiar, unthreatening face—female or not—he hugged a length of wood to his chest and gave her a small smile.

"Come on," she offered him a hand. "Come out of there and tell me what happened. Where is Ulin?"

Notwen's smile evaporated. He ignored her proffered hand and pressed back against the wall. "Sea-sligs." He could barely get the words out. "Ghagglers attacked Dead Pirate's Cove this morning," he said full of misery.

She shuddered. "I was there after they left. It was horrible."

Notwen could barely nod. "They saw us coming out of the marsh and chased us. Ulin told me to stay out of sight. That's all I know. I haven't seen him or Kethril since then." Unshed tears glinted in the corners of his eyes.

The sirine's hand went to her mouth, and her clear eyes grew huge. "Kethril Torkay? You found him? He was on this boat? Those sea-sligs took him?" In a whirl of silver-green hair, she twisted toward the door and bolted out before Notwen could answer any of her frantic questions.

"Wait!" he cried. "Don't leave me!" But his words were lost in the sound of a splash as the sirine dived into the water. Dismayed and still badly frightened, Notwen stayed huddled in the box.

* * * * *

If this was death, Ulin decided he did not want any part of it. He never imagined death could be so cold and painful. First was his head. From the pain that thundered behind his eyes, his skull must have been split wide open. Beneath his head, his entire body felt weightless, yet it ached and shook with a strange ague, and his skin felt as if he were being stabbed by hundreds of tiny knives. His mind reeled from the unreality of it. He thought his eyes could be open, but he saw no light, only an intense darkness so thick that there were no shadows or definition of anything.

What happened to the bright light, the blissful release, the cessation of pain he'd always heard was the transition to death? Had it all been a nasty lie?

He vaguely remembered the net falling over his body and the terror he felt when he was dragged under the water. He could not remember coming back to the surface. Therefore, he should be dead. But this death felt like a dismal nightmare.

"Hey, you. What did you say your name was?"

The voice, hoarse and strained, came out of the darkness to his right. It sounded vaguely familiar, and he tried to search his memory for a face to fit the voice. The effort of thinking cleared a little of the fog from his mind and allowed the reality of his current predicament to seep into his awareness. He wished it hadn't. There was something to be said for semi-consciousness. A name floated into his thoughts. "Kethril," he whispered.

"Ah, no. I think that's my name. At least it was when they stuffed us in this pleasant little hole."

Ulin tried to put his feet on something and discovered he couldn't. Panic welled up in a choking wash of confusion and fear. He thrashed wildly only to find that his body from the neck down was submerged in salt water. His hands and arms were bound behind his back, holding him nearly immobile, and what felt like a heavy metal collar was clamped about his neck to keep his head in a rigid upright position above the water level. The collar was attached to a heavy chain that must have been fastened to the low ceiling.

"Easy, easy," said the voice close by. "Be still and let yourself wake up. You took quite a nasty blow to the head on a rock when they were dragging us in here."

There was something reassuring and sensible about the voice in the darkness. Ulin clung to Kethril's words and forced his fear back until he could calm his wild struggles and slow his frantic breathing. He spit some salt water out of his mouth. "My name is Ulin," he said at last.

Kethril chuckled, a hollow sound that echoed in the space around them. "That's better. Short, useful, and yours."

"Where are we?" Ulin wanted to know.

"An underground cave not far from the cove. I don't know how the ghagglers brought us here without drowning us, but I sure wish they had."

Ulin tried to sort that out through the pounding pain in his head. "Why?"

The man hanging beside him paused for a moment then said, "Because the ghagglers usually kill their victims right away for food. The only ones they bring to their lair are those they plan to torture for fun or use in their games."

Ulin did not like the sound of that. "Oh." He could think of nothing more to say, so he hung in the water and concentrated on the pain in his head. He wished he had some of his sister's mystic abilities. Linsha had been trained by the Mystics of the Heart to use the power of mysticism to heal her own minor aches and wounds. In fact, he wished she was there now with a joke on her lips and a key to this collar around his neck. With her talents, she could've eased his headache *and* gotten them out.

"Back at the gaming boat," Kethril said out of the echoing blackness. "What did you mean when you said you were my future-son-in-law?"

"Ah, you remember that? Your daughter Lucy and I are betrothed."

"When are you getting married?"

Considering his position at that moment, Ulin wasn't sure there was an answer to that question. "We, uh, haven't set a date," he said honestly.

"Why not?" the father of the bride demanded. "Didn't you come all the way from Solace together? Why didn't you marry her first?"

Ulin had to admit to himself the thought had not occurred to him. He wondered belatedly if it had occurred to Lucy. He did not think he appreciated the tone of this line of questions, so he tried one of his own. "How did you know we came from Solace?"

"News about the new sheriff spread quickly. I didn't know who it was though."

"Would it have made a difference if you had?" Ulin asked irritably.

There was a long silence before Kethril replied. "I don't know."

"Aren't you the least bit interested, a little curious about your own daughter? She's quite a woman, you know." Thinking about Lucy helped take his mind off his own misery, so he continued to talk to Kethril. He told him about meeting Lucy at the Academy of Sorcery and their years together as friends. There in the cold wet dark with the band of metal digging into his jaw, he described the arrival of the magistrate and the letter and their long trip to Flotsam, and last of all he told Lucy's father how she became the Sheriff of Flotsam.

After a while his spate of words trickled to an end, and he closed his eyes and let his mind drift. When Kethril did not respond, Ulin decided the man probably had passed out from boredom. He knew he'd talked too much, and sentimentality hardly seemed a trait Kethril Torkay would possess. Lucy's father couldn't have been interested after so many years separated from his family.

But he was wrong.

"You should marry her, boy. As soon as possible."

Although his voice was still hoarse, Ulin thought he heard a touch of wistfulness or perhaps sadness in Kethril's words. Ulin did not bother to reply. All this talk had exhausted him, and the collar around his neck hurt abominably.

He held still for a while and wished he could go to sleep. Unfortunately, the cold water was not inducive to relaxation. He felt chilled to the bone, and he knew if that condition continued his body temperature would drop and he would become lethargic, delusional, and eventually he would die. Somehow, in spite of the pain and exhaustion, that thought annoyed him. He did not want to die. He wanted to take Kethril to Lucy and say, "Here he is, now let's go home, get married, have children, and grow old together." He wanted more than anything in the world to live long enough to tell Lucy how much he loved her—just her. For the first time he accepted that the ghosts of his first wife and their son and daughter were still faithfully in his heart, but they were just those: memories, ghosts, pieces of his past that he would treasure. They were not of the present or the future. That was Lucy.

Ulin felt a new jolt of strength course through his limbs. Both his wrists and ankles were tied with something that felt like rough, dried seaweed, but if he could get his hands free, he might be able to unlock the collar around his neck. Drawing his knees up to his chest, he tried to work his tied hands down and around his legs. It was easier thought than done. His muscles were stiff and numb from the cold, and although most of his clothing had been removed, his bound arms barely fit past his long legs. After much splashing and struggling, he finally squeezed through the circle of his arms and hung for a minute gathering his breath.

"What are you doing?" Kethril asked from the dark.

Ulin coughed out a mouthful of water. Instead of replying, he raised his hands above the water, closed his eyes, and chanted a soft incantation. It was a basic spell, one of the easiest works taught to beginners, and one he had been able to do since he was a little boy. Like most of his spells, he hadn't been able to perform it properly since the trouble with magic began, but maybe just this once, it would work for him. He drew in the ancient power, forced it to his will, and set the spell into effect. Nothing tickled his neck or buzzed in his ear or drained the power away. The magic coalesced into a small ball and began to glow in the darkness of the cave just a few feet away from his head. He saw its glow through his eyelids and gave thanks. Ulin opened his eyes. The sphere of greenish light stayed in place and shed its soft illumination on the black water. It would stay there as long he willed it to remain.

"That's a useful talent," Kethril remarked.

Ulin snorted. "Beats card games."

Kethril suddenly laughed, and his humor rang in the small chamber. "You're no player, that was obvious. And that reminds me, how did you pull off that little trick with the sleeping powder?"

"A few things I learned from an old alchemist and my uncle." Ulin swung around so he could see Kethril. Gods, he thought, if the man looked that bad, how awful do I look? Lucy's father hung from a similar chain-and-collar restraint that held his head slightly above the water. His eyes were sunken into deep pits of exhaustion, and his skin was deathly pale. His hair lay plastered to his head with water and darker rivulets that Ulin guessed was blood. A dark bruise discolored his right cheek and a laceration marred his perfectly trimmed beard.

When Kethril saw Ulin's expression, his white teeth flashed in the light in either a smile or a grimace. "Yes, boy. You look as bad as I do."

"My name is Ulin."

"As you say. So what is your next move?"

In reply, Ulin grabbed the chain above his head and hoisted his upper body up so he could have a look at the chain and the roof above their heads. The cave was small, with smooth walls and a low, rough ceiling. Ulin hoped the tide would not fill this cave any more than it already had, or he and Kethril would run out of breathing room very quickly. A quick check showed him the chain was fastened very securely to the ceiling by spikes hammered into the stone, and the chain itself was in good condition. There were no rusty links to break or separate. The collar proved equally as solid. The latch behind his head was locked in a way that defeated every attempt he made to unfasten it. Discouraged, he let himself down into the water and gave his arms a moment to rest while.

"How long have we been down here?" he asked Kethril after a time.

"Hours, at least. Maybe half a day. I'm not really sure. They brought a few others with us, but I haven't seen anyone else since we were put in here."

"Did you see Notwen?" Ulin asked, afraid of the answer. He hoped the little gnome's death had been quick and painless.

"No. He would be nothing but shark bait to the ghagglers."

Ulin let his breath out in a long low groan. "Gods, I wish we were out of here."

Like an answer to his wish, a hideous face emerged from the water beside him. Great staring eyes glared at him and webbed fingers reached for his neck. The creature was big, nearly as tall as Ulin, with a hinged mouth filled with fangs and scaly skin the color of rotting timbers.

It snarled at him in rough Common, "Kill light, magicmaker. Kill it, or we snap your neck."

Ulin recoiled in fear and loathing and quickly obeyed. The light blinked out and plunged the cave into absolute darkness. He could not see the ghaggler, but he could certainly feel and hear him. More sea-sligs surfaced. He felt cold, wet fingers grab his arms and legs, and the collar came loose around his neck. He had just a few seconds to take a quick breath before the monster dragged him under the water. The cold and darkness closed over him. He wracked his brains for something to do, but he could not move, could not breathe, could not think.

The ghagglers seemed to have some purpose in mind, for they hauled him through the water without attempting to kill him immediately. Ulin could not see a thing in the dense darkness, yet his captors had no difficulty maneuvering through the black waters. They swam easily and rapidly through what felt to Ulin was a series of underwater passages. His lungs began to ache. His headache returned in full force as his brain starved for air. He gritted his teeth until his jaw ached, and still the swim continued.

The urge to breathe had turned to a craving when Ulin felt the ghaggler charge upward. Ulin's chest heaved, and suddenly he could not control the urge to breathe. He took a great gasping breath just as his head broke the surface of the water. Gasping and choking, he felt himself pulled to a rock ledge and heaved out of the water. Kethril was dumped beside him like a gasping fish. They lay side by side sucking air into their starved lungs, grateful for the brief reprieve.

Their captors cut the bonds around the men's arms and dived back into the water, leaving the prisoners on the rocks.

Ulin found himself in a cavern where phosphorescent globes provided the only light. Dim and pale green, the globes cast weak shadows against the heavy darkness. Ulin blinked the water out of his eyes and pushed himself to a sitting position. His stomach did a flip-flop and turned cold as the enormity of their danger became clear. He and Kethril had been brought to a huge underwater cavern and put on a rocky outcropping that protruded into a large lake. All around the lake, swimming in the water, perched on the stony shore, or crouched on nearby rocks were ghagglers large and small. Hissing and snapping their fingers, they watched their prisoners like sharks eye their prey. Their shining black eyes glinted in the phosphorescent light. Their fangs gleamed as they jabbered and hissed to each other in their own foul language. Every sea-slig Ulin could see was armed with spears, tridents, or short wicked knives.

Beside him, Kethril rolled over on his belly and vomited a bellyful of seawater. "Oh, mercy," he groaned. "I'm too old for this."

Ulin heard a deep growl behind him and turned his head. "I don't think you'll need to worry about that much longer," he said.

Kethril lifted his eyes and saw the creature crouched on the rocks on the far side of their very tiny island. "Oh—"

His last word was drowned in the roar of a large and very angry sea lion.

Chapter Sixteen

"Don't move," Kethril whispered to Ulin. "Don't draw its attention."

"I think we already have it," Ulin replied. He obeyed, though, and remained motionless on the wet rock, staring at the sea lion. "Look at it! The poor creature is half dead."

"We're going to be dead if it decides to eat us."

Ulin barely listened. He realized, looking at the sea creature, that it was as much a prisoner as they. Sea lions were ferocious and difficult to deal with, and from the old wounds and puncture marks on the animal's face and sides, it had put up quite a fight before it was captured and dragged to this cave. The lion half of its body looked matted and thin; the mane was tangled and streaked with dried blood. The fish half of its body had dried from exposure to the air and had lost its golden gleam. The skin was cracked, oozing, and probably very painful. It snarled at them again, revealing a set of powerful fangs.

"I wonder why it doesn't move," Kethril said, his eyes still on the beast.

Ulin craned his head a little higher and saw a metal fetter around the sea lion's tail. "It's chained to the rock."

A sudden startled exclamation burst from Kethril, and he yanked his bare feet away from the water. Ignoring his own order to remain still, he scrambled higher up the rocks.

"Those brutes!" he cursed. He cradled his foot and examined the bloody gash on his heel where one of the ghagglers had stabbed him with a spear. The sea-slig swam away, sneering at him.

On the opposite side, the sea lion bellowed in similar pain and pulled away from the water. It raised its heavy head and roared in defiance.

"They seem to be provoking a fight between us and the sea lion," Ulin said.

"Winner to eat the loser and then be fed to those sharks," Kethril commented bitterly. "I don't like those odds."

Ulin made no reply. He could see the sharks cruising through the water around the rocky island. Ghagglers often kept sharks in their lairs as guardians, scrap disposals, and deterrents for would-be escapees. He knew with a certainty no one would win a confrontation on this island. Sea lions hated sharks with a passion and often went out of their way to kill one, but this poor creature would not stand a chance in this grotto, and neither would he or Lucy's father.

He was given no more time to ponder the situation. A large ghaggler reared out of the water near the sea lion and gave it a vicious jab in the tail with its trident. The wounded sea lion roared. Maddened with pain and fury, it turned on the first and easiest creatures it could see. It charged toward Kethril and Ulin, its claws unsheathed and the chain flapping behind it. It was only then that Ulin saw that the chain was actually fastened to a rock in the middle of the island, not near the water as he guessed. There was nothing to stop the sea lion's attack, nothing to slow it down. His hand went instinctively to his waist where his sword usually hung and found nothing but a scrap of a loincloth.

"Kethril, move!" Ulin shouted. "Move! Split up!"

The older man scrambled to his feet. He and Ulin stood side by side for a heartbeat while the huge beast lumbered toward them, its small ears flattened on its head, its teeth bared. Around them, the sea sligs hissed and whistled and threw rocks at the stranded men. At the last moment, when the sea lion's claws reached for their bodies, the two men fled in opposite directions, leaving the sea lion to leap on empty air.

Confused, it roared and swung its head to the left and right, trying to catch their scent, then it lunged after the warm, metallic smell of blood.

Kethril bellowed in fear and tried to run to the far edge of the island over the rough rock, but pain lanced up his leg from his lacerated foot, and he stumbled and fell.

Turning around, Ulin saw the sea lion go after Lucy's father. Quick as thought, he scrambled after the lion, grabbed the loose chain attached to its tail, wrapped it around a boulder, then he dug in his heels and braced himself for the impact.

The sea lion hit the end of the chain like a charging bull. The force of its sudden stop nearly ripped the chain from Ulin's hands. It dragged him and the boulder a short distance before the sea lion collapsed on the ground only a few inches from Kethril's bleeding foot. The force of its fall knocked the air from its lungs and for a few minutes it lay still, trying to breathe.

Kethril wasted no time getting to his feet and out of the lion's reach. He crawled around the gasping beast and made his way back to Ulin. "Our odds are not improving," he commented dryly as he fought to stand upright. "I'd start a book on this fight and cover all bets made on us."

"Optimistic, aren't you?" Ulin grunted. He wrapped the chain around the boulder again and kept a sharp eye on the lion. It could attack again at any moment.

The older man tried to smile. "I live by the numbers, not philosophies, boy."

A sudden commotion in the middle of the lake distracted the ghagglers from their sport. Streams of bubbles erupted all around the island until the water appeared to be boiling, and the sharks vanished. Screeching and jabbing their weapons, all but the youngest sea-sligs dived into the seething water.

"What is it?" Ulin asked, but Kethril had no answer.

The sea lion lay quietly and stared at the water as if mesmerized. Perhaps its stunning crash to the rocks had knocked the fight out of it.

Slowly and silently, Ulin dropped the chain and motioned Kethril to follow him. They made their way to the edge of the rocks farthest from the sea lion and stood back to back to await their fate. Without warning, the bubbles stopped and the waters gradually stilled. A tense silence filled the dimly lit cavern while, one by one, the ghagglers slid back into the depths of the cave and disappeared. Before long Ulin, Kethril, and the sea lion were alone in the dim cavern.

Ulin rubbed his aching temples and was about to sit down when the bubbles burst out again. This time they were stained red and were swiftly followed by a seething, struggling force of ghagglers. The sea-sligs fought ferociously against an enemy that followed the sea-creatures up from the depths and into the waters of the lake with equal ferocity and determination.

Kethril stiffened. "I may have to change those bets. We have a new player in the game."

"What?" Ulin demanded.

The gambler winked and pointed. "Sea elves," he said.

Great day in the morning! Ulin thought. Sea elves—the ghagglers worst enemy, a race of sea people sworn to the total destruction of the merciless, bloodthirsty sea-sligs.

The thought had barely registered in his mind when he saw a familiar shapely figure climb out of the water and come toward them at a nimble run. Her lovely face shone with relief, and her sea-green eyes glowed with joy. She threw her arms out with the obvious intent of hugging someone, and Ulin steadied himself for her embrace. She raced right past him and into Kethril's arms.

"Oh, Father, you're safe!" the sirine squealed.

Ulin's eyes bulged. "Father?" he repeated, astounded down to his toes. Lucy was going to love this.

Kethril looked over her graceful blue-green shoulder at Ulin and gave a small shrug. "Her mother is a stunner."

"But, but . . ." Ulin protested. "She looks older than twenty." This just didn't seem right.

"Sirines mature quickly. She's only ten in human years."

The ten-year-old sirine turned her attentions to Ulin. "I am so happy to see you again!" she squealed, hugging him to her ample front. Her skin felt cool and damp against his bare chest, and to his dismay, his face turned red.

This time it was Kethril's turn to be amazed. "You know her?" he demanded. Ulin gently pushed her away and glared at Kethril. Playing the irate father hardly fit the gambler's image. "She helped Notwen and me a few days ago."

Kethril looked visibly relieved. He hopped to a rock ledge and sat, grinning at his aquatic daughter. "That's my girl. Did you bring the elves, too?"

She nodded vigorously. "This clan lives near here. They are my friends. They've been looking for this marauding band of sea-sligs for some time, so after I found the entrance to this cavern, I went to see them."

The chaos in the cavern was slowly subsiding as the sea elves killed the ghagglers and pursued those few that fought their way free. A few corpses floated in the water. All the sharks had vanished.

Ulin sat down on a rock near Kethril and tried not to

shiver. He pointed to the prostrate sea lion and asked, "Is there some way to help him?"

The sight of the pitiable sea lion clouded the sirine's face with sadness. She approached the beast slowly, singing a song in some strange language that sounded to Ulin like a whale's song. The sea lion lifted its head and glared at her, but it made no move toward her as she unlocked the metal fetter around its tail and tossed it aside.

Just then a dolphin popped its head out of the water close by, its bottlenose sleek and gray. The sirine said something to it in her own language, and the dolphin replied in a laughing, low-pitched chitter. It swam back and forth near the sea lion as if assessing the situation, then it ducked under, emerged again, and squirted the lion in the face with a mouthful of water. The lion made an attempt to snarl, but it still did not move. Its mouth curved in a perpetual smile, the dolphin tried again. It had to repeat its squirts three times before the lion rallied enough strength to lumber toward the water. Growling at the persistent dolphin, it slid below the surface. For a minute or two, Ulin and Kethril could see the animal luxuriating in the healing comfort of its natural environment before it gave a deft twist of its massive tail and vanished into the black depths of the grotto.

The sirine waved her thanks to the dolphin and came back. "The lion is weak, but it is free now. It should heal."

Two sea elves climbed onto the island at that moment and bowed to the two humans. The elves were both male, over five feet tall, elegantly built, with skin of greenish silver. Their blue hair was short-cropped against their heads, and their faces bore no trace of a beard.

Ulin pushed himself to his feet and bowed. He greeted them in Elvish and offered his heartfelt gratitude.

They studied him curiously from bare feet to matted, wet hair with no sign of arrogance or condescension, then they struck the butts of their tridents on the stone. "It is our pleasure to kill ghagglers," one replied in heavily accented Common.

"Is there some way out of this damp hole?" Kethril grumbled. "I have things to attend to."

"Yes, like meeting your other daughter," Ulin snapped.

A grimace passed over Kethril's face. "I don't think that's a good idea, not after the, ah, incident in Flotsam. The city council will not be happy to see me. I'm going back to Dead Pirate's Cove to see if anyone is alive."

"On the contrary," Ulin said, his voice like a steel blade. "The council will be delighted to see you." Although he never considered himself to be much like his grandfather Caramon, in that instant his anger kindled the fire in his eyes and tempered the curves of his face into hard planes and angles set with adamant. It was the look many foes had seen on Caramon's face before they died. Kethril read that look and inched back on his seat, but Ulin would not let him back away unscathed. "You took the taxes from Flotsam. You are the reason we traveled halfway across Ansalon. You put Flotsam in danger of being destroyed, and you are the reason your daughter is in a dangerous situation. Now you *will* go to Flotsam to help fix this mess, even if I have to tie you to my back and swim there!" Ulin's voice sharpened with each word until his anger reverberated through the grotto.

The elves watched him with interest. This was none of their affair, but they enjoyed the curious interaction of humans.

The sirine looked worriedly from one man to the other. She sidled close to Kethril and put a hand on his shoulder.

Kethril studied the younger man as if searching for some crack in Ulin's fierce armor. There was none. At last he glanced at the sirine and the grotto beyond, then he said, "Ulin of Solace, if you give me your word that you will grant me safe conduct in Flotsam, I will go with you."

"What makes you think you can accept my word?"

"You have something I have never had, but it is a quality I respect nonetheless. I will accept your word of honor."

The young Majere knew he had little choice. Stuck as he was in an underwater cavern surrounded by disinterested elves, he needed Kethril's cooperation to get back to dry land. There was also the irritating consideration that Kethril Torkay was Flotsam's last hope. "You have it. I will take you to Flotsam and try to convince them not to hang you. But if you try to escape or flee or hide, I will hunt you down and kill you myself."

The gambler sighed and heaved himself to one foot. "I believe you would, young man. I guess we'd better go to Flotsam." In a swift, mercurial change of mood, he slapped Ulin on the back and grinned. "Daughter, my lovely green girl," he called to the sirine, "see if you can find my clothes in the ghagglers' spoils. I'm going to need them if I am to see my oldest."

* * * * *

Notwen hammered away at the spikes holding the new mast to its framework. A few more nails here and there, and the thing just might stay upright—even if the wind blew. He'd been trying for several hours now to find the right configuration of rigging, spars, mast, and sail that would move his flat-bottomed boat. Unfortunately, all his books on sailing ships were on the shelves of his library in Flotsam, so he had to rig this sail from experimentation. He made a mental note to read those books when he returned home and make notes to bring on his next voyage. It was obvious he could not rely solely on his steam engine. It still needed a great deal more work to make it reliable.

While he worked, the *Second Thoughts* drifted placidly westward on the current, warmed by the afternoon sun. The great bay seemed too empty to Notwen. There were no ships or boats in sight, no sign of anyone other than a few birds, a school of passing flying fish, and a curious dolphin who poked its head out of the water, chirped at him a few times, and ducked out of sight. He was so involved in his work that he paid no attention to the progress of the *Second Thoughts* or the time of day or the pod of dolphins that approached the boat toward late afternoon.

The first sound that alerted him to boarders was the pleased greeting of a familiar voice. Things bumped against the side of the boat and the *Second Thoughts* rocked as people climbed over the railings. Notwen cried out in alarm and jumped to his feet, his hammer clutched in his hand. He saw a wet, nearly naked ghost come striding toward him, and terror overwhelmed his stunned mind. His eyes rolled up in his head, and his small body slumped to the deck.

"He fainted?" Kethril said incredulously.

Ulin gathered up the gnome and moved him into the shade of the cabin. "He probably thought we were dead."

The sirine and a group of sea elves climbed onboard and wandered around the small boat touching everything. They examined Notwen's tools, stared at the motionless paddlewheel, and admired the strange little engine, but when they saw the mast and the sail, they gathered in a cluster and laughed uproariously.

It was the sound of their hilarity that brought Notwen to his senses. He lifted his head, saw Ulin first, and grinned from ear to ear. "IamsopleasedtoseeyouUlinhowdidyouescapefromtheseasligsandwhatarethosecreaturesonmyboat?"

"One word at a time, Notwen," Ulin reminded him.

The gnome didn't answer. He bounced to his feet, his fear forgotten, and crowded in among the tall sea elves jabbering and laughing by his mast. "What's so funny?" he demanded. "Hey! Leave that rope alone!"

The elves were laughing too hard to respond. The sirine pointed to the mess of rigging and sail and cobbled-together mast. "They think your sail is a bit overdone." She shook her green hair. "It is a nice try, but it won't work."

He crossed his arms and scowled at the elves. "Why not?"

"I don't know," she replied with a giggle. "I don't sail boats. That's just what they are saying."

Ulin looked up at Notwen's attempts and frowned. "Is something wrong with your engine?"

The gnome gave up trying to reason with the elves and came to join the young mage. "It's broken," he said glumly. "The cogs are cracked, the shaft is bent, and there's a hole in the boiler. I can't fix it without my forge and tools at home."

Two of the sea elves, the same two who had met them in the cavern, detached themselves from the noisy group and walked over to Ulin and Kethril. The elves looked so much alike that Ulin wondered if they were brothers. In the bright light of day, their skin and hair gleamed with the brilliance of sunlight on water, and their eyes shone a dazzling blue.

"The sirine tells us you are in a hurry to return to the place you call Flotsam," one said.

Ulin nodded. Kethril shrugged.

"You will not get there with this sail," the second commented.

Ulin elbowed Notwen before the gnome could sputter a retort.

"If you are willing to trade, we could provide you with dolphins to pull you there," said the first elf.

"Trade what?" asked Ulin.

"Metal. Weapons. Tools." The elf held up Notwen's hammer and winked at the small gnome. "Master Tinker, your work is commendable, but ill-informed. Perhaps we could discuss sails and boats in the time it takes to get you back."

The offer of knowledge evaporated all of Notwen's resentment and won his immediate approval. "I have lots of tools at the laboratory," he whispered to Ulin. "Let them have what they want."

Ulin hesitated before he spoke. There was one more thing he wanted to ask the sea elves, but the thought was not a firm conviction in his mind. He'd had too many failures, too few successes. The small light in the cave had been the first spell to work for him for months, yet somehow he doubted it was the beginning of the return of his magic. The power was gone from his grasp, gone from his imagination. The spell in the cave had worked, but it had not given him the thrill of success that wielding magic once had. Maybe, he thought, his time with magic was over. He tilted his head slightly and rubbed the stubble on his chin. Perhaps if the elves were willing to trade for one or two magical artifacts with him, he could test the efficacy of his power and analyze the results without the emotions of previous failures. It was worth a try. Sea elves loved to delve through sunken ships and old ruins, and they were known for collecting artifacts, trinkets, and treasures from the sea. If nothing else, he could give the artifacts to Palin.

When he mentioned his desire to trade for a few magic artifacts, the two elves exchanged looks and talked together for several minutes.

"It has become dangerous to wield the power of the Istar relics," one elf told Ulin. "The red dragon has hunted our people for years to force us to relinquish our collections. If she learns you have even one magic object, she will send her minions after you."

Ulin met his direct gaze eye for eye. "I know. I am—was—a dragonmage. In the past year my ability to wield magic has disappeared for reasons I do not understand. My father is seeking to learn the truth and to test every possible door still open to us, but we have few left."

The second elf nodded. "We have heard of the failure of magic. There may be one or two small items we could allow you to have." He suddenly brightened and added, "We found a fine Khurish sword among the spoils of the seasligs. Was that yours?" At Ulin's nod, the elf grinned. "We will keep that and see what my chieftain might be willing to part with. Meanwhile, for the use of the dolphins . . ."

He waved a slim hand at Notwen's scattered tools.

While the sirine bandaged Kethril's foot, Ulin, Notwen and the elves finalized their trade of tools for the use of a pod of dolphins willing to pull the *Second Thoughts* back to Flotsam. When they were finished, the sea elves happily collected their tools and called in the dolphins. They rigged half a dozen ropes with loops at the end and tied them to the bow of the boat. Chittering and squealing, the dolphins took the loops over their noses, thrust deep with their powerful tails, and turned the boat toward Flotsam. The *Second Thoughts* gained momentum.

All but two of the sea elves waved good-bye and dived into the sea. In a flash of shining water they were gone into the blue deep. The sirine called a farewell to the elves and made herself comfortable on the bow to watch the dolphins. Ulin watched her, wondering if she planned to go all the way to Flotsam with them. Did she intend to meet her half-sister, Lucy?

Ulin went into the cabin, hung up their wet clothes salvaged from the cavern, and rummaged through his gear until he found two reasonably clean tunics and two pairs of loose fitting pants that might fit Lucy's father, then he took them to the gambler. Kethril was sitting on the deck, leaning back against the cabin wall. His skin was tanned a golden brown from days in the sun, and his muscles were well developed. Ulin wondered what sort of work the man did when he was not stealing from towns or playing at a gaming table.

Kethril's eyes were closed, but he opened one as Ulin tossed a tunic and a pair of pants into his lap. He eyed the younger man for a moment, then closed his eye. "If I look like you, we'd both better get dressed so we don't scare Lucy."

Ulin glanced down at his arms and chest and realized what Kethril meant. Dark bruises, lacerations, and ugly scrapes covered his wrists, arms, chest, and legs. The ghagglers had not been gentle in the transportation or imprisonment of their prisoners. He pulled the clothes on and sat down on the deck beside Kethril. The older man did not move.

Ulin did not mince words or waste time with pleasantries. "What made you change your mind about going to Flotsam?" he wanted to know. "You could have convinced the sirine to help you."

Kethril grunted. His face had relaxed and his breathing was beginning to slow. "Lucy," he mumbled. "She shouldn't have come."

The sun seeped into Ulin's sore muscles like a warm draught. A spreading lassitude wrapped itself gently around him. He thought he should be angry at Kethril's answer, but he could not summon the energy. His own eyelids were becoming very heavy. "She came for you, you know," he said, letting his body slump down against the wall. It had been so long since he had been able to sleep. Somewhere, faintly, he could hear Notwen deep in conversation with the sea elf, and the sirine was singing. He could hear her voice like a soothing continuous sound, as soft as rainfall, as rhythmic as the waves. His eyelids drifted closed, and he heard nothing more.

Chapter Seventeen

Although the holiday was still twelve days away, the preparations for Flotsam's Visiting Day were well underway. For weeks, the town's kender population had been busy finishing the spring ale, pickling eggs for the traditional snack, and baking goodies to share with friends. Pease explained to Lucy that the kender tradition of "Hiyahowareya" in Flotsam had evolved from the old Visiting Day festival once celebrated in Kendermore before the coming of Malystryx. Everyone cleaned their houses on Visiting Day, then instead of visiting friends and neighbors—and often missing them because they were visiting, too—everyone met in the town commonland for a big picnic. That way, no one was missed. Gifts of food and drink were exchanged, borrowed items were returned, and everyone had a good time.

The human population planned to participate as well. Although everyone worried about the dragon and the missing taxes, a spirit of optimism buoyed the citizens of Flotsam.

They had their lady sheriff to handle the crisis, so something would work out.

Only the councilmembers seemed subdued. Saorsha, Aylesworthy, and old Mayor Efrim walked around town looking like doomsayers. Lucy watched them worriedly and tried several times to talk to them, but they avoided her more and more, and when she could corner one or more, they never stayed on the same subject for long. She didn't even have the Silver Fox to talk to. He had vanished completely without a word.

Lucy worried about him. She worried about the elders and the probable return of the Dark Knights. Most of all, she worried about Ulin. He and Notwen had been gone for seven days—days that felt like an eternity. She realized she probably shouldn't worry yet. The trip there and back in the boat would have taken three or four days, and they still had to find her father. It could be another three or four days before she could hope to see them. She yearned for Ulin with every fiber of her being, and she was losing patience rapidly. Why had she agreed to his leaving? Please Ulin, hurry home, she pleaded silently.

Unknowingly, she increased the pressure of her legs against her horse's sides, and he obediently broke into a rough trot. Challie jounced on the horse's broad rump behind her.

"Lucy . . . please . . . slow down . . . there's nothing . . . to hold!" she gasped between bumps.

Lucy quickly slowed the big bay back to a walk. "Sorry," she apologized. "I was thinking of something else."

"Ulin," Challie said. It was not a question. She had seen the worry shadow Lucy's face day by day.

Lucy's shoulders shifted under her blue tunic. "Ever since that strange feeling I had the other day, all I want to do is see his face and know he is safe."

So did Challie. She liked Ulin and respected his abilities. She also admired him for his willingness to help Lucy find her father. Although she would not mention it to Lucy, she thought this business of finding the thief and hauling him back to Flotsam was impossible and a waste of time. The man and the money were long gone. With only twelve days left until tax day, she thought the people of Flotsam should be busy packing to flee, not preparing for a holiday.

Each busy with her own thoughts, Lucy and Challie continued their ride out of the northern hills and down the road toward Flotsam's city hall. They had been visiting the local farms to exchange the news and collect what taxes they could for the dreaded tax collector, and now tired and full of "just a little something before you go" snacks, they rode leisurely through the warmth of the late afternoon sun. A few drowsy flies followed them around and made the horse switch his tail occasionally.

Mayor Efrim was waiting for them when Lucy rode the horse into the back courtyard and tethered him in the shade. The old man's hands shook as he took the small bags she brought. The lines in his face crumpled together like wadded paper, and his rhuemy eyes twitched nervously. "It's not enough," he murmured. His gaze went up to the sky. "Not nearly enough."

Lucy made no answer. What was there to say? She could only collect what the law and the meager resources of Flotsam allowed.

The mayor shook his head sadly and wandered indoors, taking the bags with him.

Challie helped Lucy wipe down the gelding and water him before turning him loose in his pen. Together they strolled around the old barracks to the front steps where they could see the harbor.

It had become a habit for Lucy to scan the waterfront for any new boats, then shift her gaze to the harbor entrance to look for the approach of the *Second Thoughts*. She did it so many times every day that she knew every boat in the harbor, every rock that lined the shores, every curve and characteristic of the small bay. She knew when the tides changed and when the fishing boats went out, but she didn't know when Ulin would come back. She sighed and was about to turn to go into her office, when she saw two small figures pelting along the road toward the city hall.

Challie groaned. "It's the pests," she remarked dryly.

Pease and Cosmo saw them and waved frantically. They shouted something, but their small voices were lost on the wind.

The women waited, curious to see what had excited the kender. Probably some old spoon or a litter of puppies or something equally as thrilling. But it was better than that.

"Lucy!" their voices trailed up the road. "He's coming!"

Lucy stiffened, and before the meaning of their words sank into Challie's mind, Lucy bounded down the steps and raced to meet the kender. They were bouncing up and down around Lucy when Challie finally caught up with her.

". . . saw the boat from the Rock. We have Notwen's farseeing glass. They're just around the headland. Come on!" They ran ahead, their short legs pumping, their top-knots bouncing in their rush.

Lucy and Challie followed as quickly as they could. The kender led them along the waterfront toward the path up the promontory. They dashed past the two docks and a group of fishermen's wives mending nets, past saloons and the gaming houses and the small eatery that smelled of frying fish. They were almost to the foot of the Rock when a new sound rang loud and shrill on the afternoon wind. Surprised by the unexpected warning call, Lucy slowed to a walk.

Pease and Cosmo stopped so fast that they skidded into a rain barrel. People froze in their tracks, and the entire town of Flotsam became deathly still.

"Listen for it," Pease said hoarsely.

Then it came. A second blast, louder and more strident than the first.

"Dragon!" Cosmo wailed.

"Cosmo!" Pease shouted. "I'll take them below. You go find your family!"

Cosmo whirled without a word and ran up the road toward Kenderstreet several blocks away.

Lucy shaded her eyes and looked at the sky. She didn't see anything up there, but around her the town was in an uproar. Screaming and shouting, people ran hither and thither, collecting children and belongings, dragging animals out of sight, shutting doors and shutters—as if that would do any good. It looked like the town was stricken with panic, yet Lucy noticed everyone she saw had a specific job and once it was done, they disappeared inside. There was no purposeless motion or hysterical running, and in a matter of moments, the streets were deserted. Only the dust, the flies, and a few chickens remained on the streets. She wondered how many times Flotsam's citizens had practiced this before.

"Come on! Come on!" begged Pease.

Lucy heard a distant roar like the rush of a whirlwind. From out of the setting sun, a winged shape appeared above the western hills, sending a thrill of terror down her spine. She gasped. "Is that Malys?"

Pease cried, "No, no! Come on! This way!" He took her hand and tried to drag her with him, but she stood staring at the approaching shape in fascinated horror.

The rapid rattle and clop of a pony pulling a cart caused all three to face the street. Saorsha's pony came trotting from the direction of city hall as fast as his short legs could move.

"Oh, Sheriff Lucy," called Saorsha, "thank the absent gods. Come on. You must come with us." She and Mayor Efrim sat in the cart. Both looked as white as sheets.

A spurt of alarm jabbed Lucy's gut. "Come where?" she demanded in a hard voice.

"No time to explain," Mayor Efrim said. He was shaking so hard he could hardly hold on to the seat as he moved over to make room for her.

Saorsha pleaded, "Please, Lucy. We must go meet him. He just wants to talk. Please come with us."

"The red dragon," Lucy paused, grasping for words. "That's Fyremantle? The tax collector?"

Challie took her arm. "Lucy, you don't have to go," she said firmly, her dark eyes on the frightened elders. "They can handle this."

A huge shadow swept over them, swift, dark, and laden with dragonfear. Lucy winced, and the others instinctively ducked as the dragon passed overhead. A hot, acrid wind, heavy with the scent of fire, blasted down around them. The dragon dipped lower. Its outswept wings glowed a fiery scarlet in the late sun. It soared out over the harbor, banked around, and came back. Lowering its head, it expelled a jet of golden fire over a fishing boat moored in the water. The boat caught fire instantly and burned to a cinder in a matter of moments. Any crew still onboard never had a chance.

Saorsha steadied her terrified pony and pulled him closer to Lucy. Her worn face looked ten years older, and the calm self-assurance she had worn with such aplomb was gone. Only her voice was steady as she reached out a hand to Lucy. "Please, come. If we don't go talk to him, he will continue to burn things."

Lucy looked at the flaming hulk slowly sinking into the water and climbed into the cart.

The dwarf rocked forward as if to pull her back. "Ulin's coming. You could wait for him."

But Saorsha snapped her reins and the pony leaped forward into the traces.

Lucy leaned back over the seat, and her voice raised to a shout. "He's on a wooden boat, Challie, about to sail into a harbor under the nose of a dragon. I can't wait!" Her last words were whirled away on the wind as the pony, cart, and passengers turned onto the road up the promontory.

Saorsha drove her poor pony hard almost to the top of the Rock, but the little animal was not accustomed to pulling three adults up a steep slope, and while it did its best, it finally stopped, unable to go another step. Saorsha climbed out, patted its heaving flanks, and tied it in the shade of a rock outcropping. She and Lucy hurried up the rest of the way on foot, and Mayor Efrim reluctantly followed.

The dragon, meanwhile, discovered a fishing boat that had just returned from a profitable day of fishing. Its crew had tied the boat to the dock and had been unloading the catch when the dragon arrived. Gleefully, the dragon landed on the wharf, smashing barrels, crates, rowboats, and anything else that got in its way. The fishing crew saw it coming. One or two jumped off the deck into the water, but the others stood rooted in dragonfear, too terrified to move as the lumbering monster approached them. It snatched the first man it reached, bit his head off, and swallowed the rest of him in two messy gulps. A thin scream ripped across the waterfront from the second man as the dragon grabbed him in its black claws. One by one, the dragon ate four men, then it scooped up huge mouthfuls of fish from the hold of the boat. When it couldn't reach anymore, it tipped the boat upside down and poured the remaining fish into its ravenous maw. Satisfied, the dragon tossed the boat into a small warehouse, set it on fire, then sprang into the air and pulled itself upward on powerful wings. The downdraft of its flight blew objects and dust outward in a cloud of debris.

On the Rock, Saorsha, Lucy, and Mayor Efrim watched the dragon finish its meal and take to the sky. They stood in the open, exposed to view, and waited for the dragon to notice them. It spiraled up from the harbor leisurely and slowly circled the top of the Rock, its wedge-shaped head tilted down to watch them. When it was satisfied, it tucked in its wings and came down to land on the bare rock in front of the humans.

Lucy heard the creak of its massive wings and the heavy thud as its weight settled on the rock. She had never been this close to a dragon, and she never, ever, wanted to again. The terror of its presence overwhelmed her in waves of dark, roiling panic. She wanted to run, to hide from his merciless gaze. Her heart was pounding so hard that she could hear the blood rushing through her head. Her eyes squeezed shut, and her arms clutched each other. She sensed her turban was afraid also, for the edges of it that she could see faded to a dull, dingy tan. Its diamond eyes drew back into folds of the fabric.

"Tyremantle," she heard Saorsha croak. "This is our new sheriff, Lucy Torkay."

A deep, pitiless voice rumbled around her. "I hope this one is more accommodating than the last. Open your eyes, woman, and behold your master."

It took every bit of self-control Lucy had to open her eyes and look up at the dragon. Although he was not as big as Malystryx, Lucy estimated he was over three hundred feet long from tip of dark red snout to the end of his massive tail. His reptile form was covered with scales the size of small shields and the color of brilliant vermilion. Sharp horns extended from his head just behind his smoky eyes, jutting back past his skull nearly ten feet. Wisps of smoke curled from his nostrils as he stared down unblinking at the three humans.

"I came to remind you," the dragon rumbled, "that you have twelve days left. I will expect the taxes to be left here, where I will examine them before I leave. If you fail to pay the *full* amount, I will level this town."

Lucy's throat was sandy dry, and she had to swallow a few times before she could force words past her stiff tongue. "We are collecting the taxes as the law orders," she said, "but this town is suffering. Couldn't you allow them a little more time?"

The dragon's massive head turned toward Saorsha and Mayor Efrim. A thundering chuckle rattled the air around them and fanned their faces with a stink like cremation. "You have not told her of my wrath or of the other towns I have obliterated."

Neither elder could answer.

"You will pay the full amount," the dragon snarled, "on time, and if you fail, this town will be wiped clean from the face of the earth." He lowered his head until his nose was only a few feet away from Mayor Efrim's chest. "If you run, little mayor, be assured I will find you."

Turning swiftly, the dragon moved to the edge of the promontory, unfurled his batlike wings, and swept off into the sky. Lucy and the councilors threw themselves to the ground just as the huge tail swung over their heads.

They lay there trembling as the dragonfear slowly subsided. On the Rock, above the smoke and flame of the waterfront, the sentinels sounded the horn signaling the All Clear.

Chapter
Eighteen

Light and warmth and wind blew away the stink of dragon and returned the Rock to normal. Slowly, cautiously, Lucy pushed herself upright and looked down at the town. The dragon was gone. Only the lingering smoke of the burned wreck and the crushed warehouse marked his visit. Saorsha was climbing to her feet, too. She offered a hand to the elderly mayor.

Anger boiled up in Lucy's mind. Fed by indignation and the release from a hideous fear, her temper rose to a thunderclap. Her face flamed red-hot and her hands began to shake. The turban transformed to a crown shaped of spikes and hard, angular edges. She stood on the Rock and shook her fist at the sky where the red dragon had disappeared.

Mayor Efrim tried to pat her arm, but she would have none of it. Then she saw over the mayor's shoulder a second column of smoke rising from somewhere close to the mouth of the harbor. Her stomach lurched in fear. "Oh, no," she cried softly. "The *Second Thoughts*." Turning her back on the elders, she bolted for the road.

Saorsha sighed bitterly as she watched the young woman run over the rim and disappear. "Efrim, what are we going to do?"

* * * * *

The sound of the warning horn reached out across the water to the *Second Thoughts* just as the dolphins began their turn toward the mouth of the harbor. The first blast brought everyone to the bow to see what the trouble could be. By the time the second clarion call warned the town of an imminent arrival, they had all spotted the red dragon approaching Flotsam.

Kethril snarled a curse. After years of associating with gamblers and thieves, he knew a wide range of swear words and epithets.

Ulin, his hand raised to shade his eyes, studied the dragon a moment and said, "That's not Malys."

"No," answered the sirine. "That is Fyremantle, one of Malys's underlings. One of the most greedy and trouble-some dragons she allows to live in her domain."

"What's he doing here? It's too soon."

No one answered Ulin, for at that moment they saw the dragon incinerate the fishing boat. Kethril pulled his lip thoughtfully. "Want to bet he sees this boat?"

Ulin was not slow to catch his meaning. "Not a bet I'll take. Everyone, into the water!"

The sirine went over the railing before he finished speaking. She swam to the dolphins to warn them of the danger. Kethril quickly followed, swimming through the water after her with clean, powerful strokes. The two sea elves launched themselves into the water and disappeared.

Only Notwen stared at them in amazement. "Jump overboard?" he said, dumbfounded. "Why? I can't leave my boat."

"If the dragon ignores us, we'll swim back and get it," said Ulin, propelling the gnome toward the water.

Notwen dug in his heels. He clamped his hands around the rail and held on for the sake of his beloved boat. "But I can't leave," he wailed. "My engine, my charts, my instruments!"

"Are all replaceable." Ulin tugged at him. "But you are not. Now let go!"

"The dragon won't burn my boat. He won't even see it down here. Look, he's up on the Rock."

"Quit playing around!" Kethril shouted in exasperation. "Just throw him in the water!"

"I can't swim!" Notwen howled.

"We'll help you," Ulin told him. He pried loose one small hand then the other, and before Notwen knew what was happening, he sailed through the air and landed in the water with a splash. Cool saltwater surged over him. He flailed wildly, too panicked to think. His eyes bulged in terror. Then something cool and slick slid under him. A curved fin came into his hands. A long, sleek body rose beneath him and lifted him to the surface where he could breathe. He wiped the streaming water from his face and saw he was astride a dolphin, a wonderfully strong and intelligent dolphin that rolled its eye at him and made a sound like a chuckle. Notwen hugged its dorsal fin to his chest and swore a lifelong friendship to all dolphins everywhere.

Ulin came toward him pulled by another dolphin. The sirine, the two men, the gnome, and the dolphins quickly moved away from the boat and headed toward the bluffs where the afternoon shadows might give them cover from the keen eyes of the dragon. They saw him swoop from the rock and shoot like an arrow out of the harbor. They saw, too, the fiery hot lance of flame that seared from the dragon's mouth and consumed the *Second Thoughts* in the blink of an eye.

Notwen closed his eyes and turned away. He could not bear to witness the death of his creation.

It was a subdued group that swam with the dolphins into the harbor and came at last to Flotsam's small docks. The dolphins left them there and headed swiftly back to the broad waters of the bay, taking with them the sirine's thanks and Notwen's eternal gratitude. Ulin and Kethril climbed up to the empty dock and helped the gnome and the sirine out of the water.

The waterfront was in an uproar. People came out of hiding and formed a bucket line to fight the fire in the warehouse before it spread through the town, while others tried to clean up the blood, mashed fish, broken barrels, and smashed gear where the fishing boat had been destroyed. Relatives of the lost crew searched frantically among the pilings and debris in the hope a loved one had somehow survived. Others stood on the dock and mourned in low, wailing voices.

Ulin heard someone call his name. He felt his heart leap, and he whirled around to see Lucy racing through the crowds of people toward him. Never had he seen anyone so beautiful. His feet sprang forward of their own accord, and his arms flew wide to welcome her. He met her in a delighted collision of arms, lips, and hands that clung and touched and could not get enough. Neither one could say a word at first. It was enough to hold each other and feel the reality of their reunion.

"This had better be Lucy," Kethril said behind them.

Ulin felt Lucy stiffen in his arms. He stood aside so she could see her father standing on the dock, the sirine beside him.

"Is it?" she asked in a voice stiff with ice. Ulin nodded.

All the anger and all the resentment of ten years combined with the tension, rage, and feelings of fear brought by the dragon formed a single brilliant explosion in Lucy's soul. She walked to her father, her green eyes crackling, balled her fist, and punched him in the nose. "You two," she shouted to two dockhands nearby. "Take this man to the city hall and throw him in jail."

The sheer force of her anger and the complete surprise of her punch was enough to topple Kethril Torkay to the planks. He stared at her astounded as the two men hauled him to his feet and bound his hands behind his back. Lucy nodded once to them and stalked away into the crowd of firefighters.

The sirine laughed. "If that was my sister, I think I like her," she commented. "Maybe she'll talk to me." She skipped off after Lucy.

"Come on, Notwen," Ulin said. "We'll go to the Jetties and wait for her. I'll treat you to supper."

Kethril watched the man and gnome head for the street. "Wait a minute. Where are *you* going?" He struggled against his bonds, but the strong dockhands merely grinned and shoved him toward the wharf.

"Supper," Ulin called without turning around.

The gambler struggled forward and caught up with him. "Hold it, boy! You dragged me all the way to Flotsam for this? What about your promise of safe conduct?"

Ulin drew himself up to his full height and coolly cocked an eyebrow. "I'd say—considering the cost, aggravation, physical labor, and time spent getting you here—you're lucky she didn't cut you down on the spot. Believe me, when the townspeople find out you are here, you will be safer in the jail. I will talk to her and the city council."

"You told me the town thought I was dead. I never imagined Lucy would come all this way to identify my body."

Ulin was not moved. "Well, she did, and now she's seen it. I have fulfilled my promise to her. What you do now is up to you." He left Kethril standing on the wharf with his guards, staring morosely at some distant point only the gambler could see.

Notwen looked up at his tall friend and back at the man on the wharf. "He came rather easily, didn't he?"

"For a man facing a noose, he came a little too easily. Maybe he has something up his sleeve besides cards. A day or two in the city jail won't hurt him."

"No." Notwen brightened with his inevitable optimism. "Well, that's good. Maybe you can help me build a new steam engine before you go."

Ulin walked slowly, trying to adjust his long-legged pace to the gnome's shorter legs. "Notwen, just how much do you know about that red dragon?"

"Fyremantle?" Notwen said nervously, tugging at his wet shirt. "He's a greedy, egotistical minion of the Red Queen."

"What was he doing here today?"

Notwen's face paled, and he sputtered a few words before he could answer. "He probably came to remind us about the taxes. He does that sometimes just to keep us upset and frightened."

"Will he come again before Visiting Day?"

"I don't know. Probably not. He has to collect from other villages in this area."

"What else do you know?" Ulin stopped and bent over so he could look at the gnome eye to eye. "You have an investigative mind, Notwen. I am certain you have studied this beast."

"OnlyalittleheterrifiesmeheissobigIcan'thelpit!" Notwen cried.

"I know," Ulin said softly. "He terrifies me, too. But slow down and try to tell me."

The gnome twisted his shirt into a knot. Slowly the words came out as Notwen turned his focus on his knowledge instead of his fear. "Fyremantle is over 250 feet from nose to tail. He is one of the youngest of the red dragons in this realm and one of the stupidest. I'm not sure why Malys puts up with him, except he is in terror of her. He is also greedy, cruel, obnoxious, over-bearing"—Notwen's nervousness fell away as he warmed to his subject—"destructive and merciless. We suspect he has several lairs around this region, but no one knows where." He paused and met Ulin's gaze. "Do you think we can find some way to beat him?"

Ulin straightened and leveled a thoughtful gaze at the smoke from the warehouse fire still curling up to the blue sky. "It's something to think about. We need to talk to Lucy and the city council." He started to walk again, and Notwen had to hurry to catch up. "We'll start at the Jetties. We can talk to Aylesworthy, change our clothes, and have some food. If I don't eat something soon that doesn't smell of fish, I cannot be held responsible for my actions around people who annoy me."

* * * * *

The fire was nearly out in the warehouse, and the waterfront was beginning to return to normal. The people of Flotsam hated dragons, but they were used to the comings and goings of the great beasts. They faced the aftermath of a dragon visit with efficiency and resignation. Ulin guessed Lucy was in the crowds helping where she could, and knowing her as he did, he thought it better to let her work off her anger in useful labor. She would find him when she was ready to talk.

He felt a tug at his sleeve to get his attention. Notwen cleared his throat and looked rather embarrassed. "Um, Ulin, if I tell you something else, will you promise to still help me with my engine?"

Now what? Ulin thought. "If I can."

Notwen ground a toe in the dirt. "Well, there are these . . . no, come with me. It's time you knew about the underground." He took Ulin's sleeve and tugged him away from the docks.

Ulin's eyes narrowed. More secrets? Wordlessly, he followed Notwen toward an old, weather-worn, two-story inn by the road that ran parallel to the wharf. The inn had a stone face of rough-cut granite pitted and patched from years of hard use and a wide porch where the regulars liked to sit to watch the boats in the harbor. A swinging sign over the door identified the inn as the Brown Pelican.

No one sat on the porch that afternoon, and the swinging doors were closed and barred. Notwen glanced in a window then trotted around to a side door that opened easily under his hand. He took Ulin through the empty common room, down a flight of stairs to the basement, and into a storeroom similar to the one in the Jetties.

Ulin was not surprised when an entire rack of wine bottles swung neatly out from the wall and a man wearing a bartender's apron walked through the opening into the room. What startled him were the dozen or so men, a few women, and two children who followed the innkeeper. Everyone nodded or waved to Notwen and welcomed him back. Several greeted Ulin as they passed.

The innkeeper stepped aside to let the others pass. "Notwen, what's happening up top? My boy says one of the warehouses is on fire. Is the dragon gone?"

"Burned to the ground," Notwen said sadly, "and two fishing boats, too. Fyremantle left a little while ago."

"Blasted worm. Wish someone would do something about him. He's more of a pest than Malys these days." The innkeeper shook his head with the resignation born of years of disaster. "Oh, well. Say, he didn't eat the sheriff this time did he? I kinda like her."

"No," Ulin replied dryly. "She's on the wharf fighting the fire."

"Good for her. Glad to see a little dragon trouble won't put her off. Come back sometime, and I'll give you an ale on the house." He waved jovially and went upstairs to reopen his tavern.

"That dragon killed the previous sheriff?" Ulin asked with deceptive coolness.

The gnome scooted into the opening. "Yes," his voice trailed up from a long, narrow staircase.

Gritting his teeth to contain his annoyance, the young man hurried after him. He had to duck his head in the staircase to keep from cracking his skull on the low ceiling. Rough-hewn stones served as stairs in the passage down, but there were no handrails. The only light came from two oil lamps set in niches in the wall.

Notwen waited for him at the bottom of the stairs, two lanterns in his hands. He handed one to Ulin. "This is one of our safe rooms." He held up his lantern so Ulin could see. "We have rooms like this under many of the inns, the city hall, three of the shops, and several other buildings—usually the ones that have survived for many years."

Ulin walked slowly around the room, letting his curiosity take over from his anger for a few minutes. The room was floored with stone and walled with something that looked like stucco. It was not spacious, but it looked big enough to hold twenty or thirty people in a pinch. It had some benches against the wall and shelves that held candles, more lanterns, jugs of water, and other odds and ends. The air was cool and very damp, and Ulin caught the strong smell of mildew.

"Come on this way," Notwen called. He went to a stone door at the opposite end of the room and pushed it open. "These can be barred in an emergency," he explained to Ulin. "It leads to what used to be the old sewer system." He trotted into a tunnel that stretched out before him and vanished into impenetrable darkness. Ulin followed more carefully, for his lanky height did not fit as well as the gnome's in the low stone passage. The smell of damp and rot was stronger here, and stagnant puddles covered parts of the floor.

When Ulin's hand touched the walls, his fingers came away slick and wet.

"There's a lot of water down here," he commented.

Notwen glanced back, his face pale in the weak light. "Seepage. We're very close to the harbor here, and I haven't found anything yet that will stop the moisture from coming in. Here the problem is water. At the other end of town, it's sand."

Ulin's mind went back to some of his journeys—to Palanthas, to Sanction—and a distant memory surfaced to brighten his thoughts. "Have you tried concrete?"

Notwen's ears perked up, and he slowed until he was walking beside Ulin. "Yes, but I could never get a mix I liked. It either cracked or wouldn't stay in place."

"In Sanction the dwarves used a mix to line a cistern. Maybe that would help you."

"Oh! Do you remember what it was?" Notwen asked eagerly. "Did it have any special ingredients or spells or something?"

Ulin laughed, and his voice echoed down the long tunnel. "No. No spells. Only good common sense and some useful ingredients. Can you get some volcanic ash?"

"Ash? Of course! What a wonderful idea!"

They continued along the tunnel discussing combinations of sand, lime, and ash and the chemical wonders of concrete. The old sewer ran straight and true and was joined or bisected by other tunnels, some as old as the original system, some newer and in better condition. They did not meet anyone else, but Ulin saw many signs of recent traffic, including footprints, a broken bottle, and a dropped loaf of bread.

"Where do all these tunnels go?" he asked Notwen when the subject of concrete had been thoroughly covered.

"They run under Flotsam and connect most of the safe rooms. Any time a dragon appears, most of the people come underground. It's the only way this town has survived. We have storerooms and an armory and even a place for a few animals." He broke off, took a deep breath then went on. "These were the tunnels the thieves used to reach the treasury. They expanded one near the city hall and went that way to move the boxes."

Ulin felt his anger stir again. "Were you ever going to tell us about this, or was the council just going let Lucy take her chances with a dragon?"

Notwen sighed. "I'm sorry, Ulin. Really. We would have brought you down here if it was necessary. Unfortunately, we have to be really careful. The people around here know these tunnels are our only chance, but outsiders don't. If Malys found out about this, she would blow this town apart."

Ulin grudgingly accepted that. He knew the red dragon well enough to realize Notwen was right. "So what happened to the previous sheriff?"

The gnome tugged at his beard and did not answer at first. Finally, he told Ulin. "Fyremantle took exception to something he said and ate him. It was too bad, really. Sheriff Gorlain was a nice man."

"What did the man say exactly?"

"I think it was 'Fat chance.' "

"I'll remind Lucy not to say that."

The tunnel came to a junction. Notwen turned right and went down a short passage that ended at another stout door. When he opened it, Ulin discovered they had come to the secret room beneath the Jetties. The room was empty, so they climbed through the barrel into the storeroom and went upstairs to the kitchen. That room was empty, too, although a fire burned in the stove and pots hung over the gleaming coals.

Ulin and Notwen suddenly stiffened, for they heard what sounded like wails. Soft rending cries and hard voices filtered through the door and goaded them onward. Notwen yanked opened the kitchen door. Together they ran toward the common room where the sounds were emanating.

In disbelief they saw Bridget prostrate on the floor, her body racked with uncontrollable grief that tore out of her throat in unending cries of heartbreak. Aylesworthy and Cosmo knelt beside her trying vainly to comfort her. Challie sat in a chair close by, her shoulders slumped and her clothes filthy with mud, smokestains, and what looked like blood. She glanced up when Ulin and Notwen came in, and her usually dour expression crumpled into unaccustomed tears.

"He's dead," she said dully. "Pease is dead."

Chapter Nineteen

Master Aylesworthy closed the tavern in the Jetties early that night to hold a private wake for Pease. The city council came, as well as the Vigilance Committee, many members of the Vigilance Force, the Silver Fox, Ulin, Challie, Lucy, Notwen, and many of Flotsam's kender. Pease had been popular in town, even for a kender, and his death was a blow to them all. Only Bridget did not come out of her small room, for Lucy and Notwen had been forced to give her a syrup to ease her hysterics and put her to sleep. Cosmo sat by his friend's mother and watched her until sleep softened the ravages of her grief, then he came downstairs and sat silently by the bar.

Food was served and toasts were made. Challie told the assembled mourners how she and Pease had taken cover in the warehouse when Fyremantle landed on the dock.

"He was trying to take me to the tunnel under the Brown Pelican," she said, "but the dragon came faster than we thought. He attacked the fishing boat before we could get there, so Pease ducked into the warehouse. He was going to go out the back door the moment the dragon left the dock. Then the boat crashed into the building and timbers and wreckage fell all around us." Challie's voice tightened in her throat. "I was closest to the door. Pease pushed me toward it just as a huge timber crashed on him. I tried to get him, but he was pinned and bleeding so badly. He told me to run. Suddenly the place burst into flames. Someone saw me in the door and dragged me out . . . but we couldn't get Pease." The disbelief was still plain in her voice, and her grief was still very raw. She raised a mug of cider and drank a toast. "He annoyed me endlessly, but I'd give anything to have him back."

The others raised their glasses as well. One of Pease's friends brought out a small lap harp and began to play a lament. Someone else produced a recorder and added accompaniment. Soon the kender had a group in the corner of the room playing drums, the harp, the recorder, and a lute. Before long, the laments ended and the music changed from grief to the celebration of a life. Pease would have loved it.

By unspoken agreement, no one discussed the tax crisis or the internment of Kethril Torkay in the city jail. That, they decided, could wait for later.

Shortly after the music started, another person came into the Jetties. She stood for a moment in the doorway then made her way to the table where Ulin and Lucy sat. Heads turned as she passed, and by the time she reached the table, all eyes were on the lovely sirine.

Giggling at some private joke, the sirine took the extra chair and sat down close to Ulin. "I cannot stay long, I have to go back to the water soon, but I wanted to tell you how wonderful it has been to meet you." It was difficult to tell from her body position and her voice whether she was talking to Lucy or Ulin.

The sirine had met Lucy earlier in the day, and while Lucy had been less than thrilled to know her father had sired other children, she had not been surprised. In fact, she found herself liking the friendly, free-spirited aquatic woman—as long as she did not try to compete for Ulin. A mischievous sprite of a thought popped into Lucy's head, and she found herself scanning the room for Lysandros. Sure enough, he was standing near the bar keeping an eye on their table. She gestured to him to join them.

The debonair resistance leader came willingly and took a chair next to the sirine. While Lucy made the proper introductions, Ulin leaned over and whispered something in the sirine's ear. Her fair face brightened, and like a daisy turns to the sun, she tilted her scantily clad chest toward the half-elf and began to hum something soft and captivating, a tune Ulin remembered all too well. The captain curiously turned at the sound. "Cripes," he said and fell into the spell of her glorious green eyes.

Lucy looked at Ulin and winked.

The wake was beginning to mellow in the late hours of the night, when Lucy and Ulin, the members of the city council, Lysandros, and the Vigilance Committee gathered by ones and twos in the back of the common room. Aylesworthy closed the bar and shooed everyone else out. He had to check three times before he found all the kender, and it took a while to check their pouches and pockets for loose spoons, mugs, other people's pouches, and knick-knacks that had been "found" or "accidentally picked up by mistake." Finally he was able to pour a fresh pitcher of ale and join the meeting at the back of the room.

While the innkeeper closed the tavern, Challie took two of Lysandros's guards to the city jail to fetch Kethril. By the time everyone was settled in chairs and ready to begin the meeting, the magistrate had returned with the prisoner bound at the wrists and chained at the ankles. The tall, fastidious gambler looked less than pleased to be hauled ignominiously before such a large group, but he did his best to hide it.

"A mug of your best spring ale," Kethril called heartily.

The innkeeper made no move to get it. "That'll be one hundred steel pieces," he demanded, his heavy features stiff with displeasure.

The gambler sighed heavily and turned back to his daughter. "Lucy . . . I . . . we got off to a bad start this afternoon. I want to try again."

She gazed at some place over his shoulder. "Why?"

Her abrupt answer took him aback. He didn't know what to expect from this daughter any more. She had become a woman in his absence, and a strong one at that. "You traveled a long way to get here. I thought we could get to know each other again."

Lucy's fingers tightened around her mug, but her distant expression did not change. "I came here for my mother's sake, not yours. She was under the mistaken impression that you were dead. Believe it or not, she was devastated."

Kethril's handsome face assumed an expression of sadness mixed with regret. "Ah, your mother. She was a beautiful woman." He tried to pull out a chair with his foot to sit down at the table.

"Don't." Lucy's refusal was adamant.

Her father looked from her to Ulin, who merely shrugged, and back again to Lucy. "My dear, I—"

Her eyes abruptly focused on his face with the sharpness of a spearpoint. "Do not call me that. I am the sheriff of this town, not some wench you can charm. Now that we have you here, you are to stand trial for the theft of Flotsam's annual taxes."

He recoiled from the intense animosity in her voice and expression. Something flickered through his green eyes. "Here? Now? This is no public trial."

"Be thankful it isn't," Mayor Efrim declared, on the verge of anger. "Most of the people in this town wouldn't hesitate to lynch you on the spot."

The old man drew a chair to face the group and pointed to it. Kethril's guards set him in the chair with quick efficiency, chained his ankles to the chair legs, and took their places on either side of him. Challie stood to his left. The mayor found another chair and sat to his right.

Kethril fired a glare at Ulin. "Is this your idea of safe conduct?"

"You haven't been injured yet," Ulin answered reasonably.

"Safe conduct?" Lucy repeated, her full mouth tight with disapproval.

"I gave him my word I would insure his safe conduct in Flotsam if he would come of his own will to face the city council and the sheriff."

"You gave *your* word, Ulin," Aylesworthy said loudly. "I say hang him."

Protestations, agreements, and arguments of all kinds burst from the inhabitants of the room. The noise quickly grew to a chaotic babble.

Lucy rose slowly to her feet and faced the group, her round face etched with determination and fine lines of tension. "Silence!" she shouted at them all. It was a measure of their respect for her that everyone fell quiet at her demand and gave her their full attention. "This is an inquiry. We need facts and honesty before we can decide what to do. There will be no sentencing of the prisoner until we are all in agreement. Is that understood?"

At their nods of assent, she resumed her seat. Mayor Efrim called the inquiry to order and went immediately to the point. "Kethril Torkay, you are accused of stealing the treasury of the city of Flotsam and thereby endangering the inhabitants who are unable to replace that money. How do you plead?"

Every head swiveled to look at the culprit who sat chained to his chair, his handsome face posed with a half-smile. "Not guilty, of course," he said as if it should be obvious to everyone.

The mayor did not give the spectators a chance to react. "Magistrate," he ordered with a strength that belied his infirm age. "Present the evidence."

Chalcedony bowed to the mayor. From a satchel she had stowed under a table, she withdrew a sheaf of parchment, some flat pieces of what looked like broken glass wrapped in a scrap of linen, and a strange flat rectangle of dried plaster.

"I would like to show the court this"—she pulled out a piece of paper and held it up for everyone to see—"the signed death-bed confession of Bernic, a cutpurse who admitted to aiding Kethril Torkay in the theft of the Flotsam Treasury. Only an untimely explosion stopped the theft before it could be completed—and mortally wounded the witness. He identified himself and his ringleader, Kethril Torkay, before he died." She slapped the paper on the table and laid out the pieces of broken glass and the plaster. "Notwen, if you please, will you identify these two items?"

The gnome came forward, shooting nervous glances at the people clustered around. He wasn't used to so much avid attention. "Um, before I explain the significance of this glass, will everyone take a look at the tips of their fingers?"

Curious and willing, the people lifted their hands and scrutinized their fingers. Ulin, who knew the significance of Notwen's request, kept his arms crossed. Behind Lucy, he sat quietly in the shadows and watched the faces of the Flotsamites and of Kethril Torkay. He added nothing to the proceedings, for he was aware that his silent, mysterious appraisal was as powerful an addition to Lucy's authority as her own reputation.

Notwen went on to explain. "If you look closely at your fingertips, you will see there are patterns of whorls and lines in the skin. No two patterns are identical." He paused as the onlookers studied their fingers and compared them to those of others.

"All right," the blacksmith said testily. "So what?"

"These patterns can be used to identify a person. Have you ever noticed the marks or prints yours hands or fingers leave behind on flat shiny surfaces? How many times have you had to polish a blade or wipe marks off glass or jewelry or brass or silver?"

Aylesworthy nodded his understanding while the others around him looked on in dawning comprehension.

Kethril seemed frozen in his chair. Nothing moved in his face but his cold green eyes as they flicked from Notwen to the glass on the table to the people around him before finally settling on Lucy's accusing stare.

Notwen picked out a piece of glass and held it up by the edges. The thin piece gleamed in his hand and reflected back the light of the lamps. "This is from a mirror, a brass framed mirror I found in the tunnel under the ruins of the treasury room. It was close to the collapsed entry into the room near the debris pile. I know it was originally part of the collected tribute, and you will find it on the inventory list."

Challie held up a second piece of parchment and laid it beside the first.

Notwen was more confident now as he delved into a subject he enjoyed. "I have a powder that makes fingerprints more visible. When I dusted this mirror with my powder I found several prints on the glass and I made copies of the patterns." Once again Challie held up several papers, these marked with the swirling patterns found on human fingertips. "Two prints did not match the accused, but one is an exact match of his thumbprint," Notwen said. "So we must ask, if he did not handle the mirror, how did his print come to be on its glass?"

Kethril shifted in his chair as if he suddenly found its seat uncomfortable. "That's ridiculous," he tried to laugh heartily. "Even if there were fingerprints on that mirror, how could they survive the explosion?"

Notwen's brown face lit with a grin. "We were lucky there. You must have dropped the mirror after the explosion, and when it fell, it landed upside down on a piece of board."

"Fascinating, Master Gnome," Mayor Efrim said patiently—the patience of a cat waiting at a mousehole to pounce. "Please go on."

Notwen put the glass down and picked up the plaster. "This is a mold I made of a bootprint I found in the newly dug tunnel leading to the treasury." He held it up over his head. "As you can see I cannot positively identify the wearer of something so common, but after a number of calculations, I can tell you the person who made this print was a man, about six foot plus several inches, who weighed about two hundred pounds. This boot was worn slightly at the heel and had a slight crack across the ball of the foot. There were several other prints in the dirt that fell after the tunnel collapsed, all leading out, but this is the only one clear enough to make a mold."

Lysandros spoke up. "To be fair, Notwen, many men besides Kethril fit the description you just gave. Is there any way to be more certain?"

"Not without the original boot," Notwen replied. "All this does is strengthen the circumstantial evidence."

"Which is nothing!" Kethril blurted out. "You have no clear evidence that I took that money."

"Maybe not," Ulin said from the back, "but I have your exact words: 'Oh, departed gods, I don't believe this. Flotsam. They'll kill me.' Now why would you say that unless you truly feared some consequence if you returned to Flotsam? According to these people, they hardly know you. Why would they want to kill you . . . unless they knew what you knew: that you stole their treasury?"

"Hogfeathers!" Kethril said loudly. "I haven't been in Flotsam in years."

"Of course you have," Notwen said, waving the plaster mold. "You stole our taxes."

The gambler tried to bound to his feet only to be pulled backward by the chair and his guards. "This is a frame-up! All of you are trying to prove I'm guilty to cover your own failings."

For a blink of an eye, Ulin hesitated, slowed by a flash of doubt. Could it be possible that Kethril was right? The city council had never proved they'd had the money. What if they had blown their own treasury to hide that fact and then tried to pin it on an innocent man? After all, they had lied to Lucy several times, manipulating her into the position of sheriff and Ulin into finding Kethril Torkay. They "lost" the body of the alleged thief, hidden information from Lucy, and, except for the very real presence of Fyremantle, had proved none of their tale through anything except circumstantial evidence. What if Kethril was right?

Then Notwen said in his matter-of-fact voice, "Actually, we saw you in the Oracle Glass."

The energy seemed to drain from Kethril Torkay before their eyes. He sagged back into his chair. "You went to see Janira?" he said softly.

Notwen nodded. Ulin watched the gnome in amused respect. He never thought Notwen would try a bluff. Technically, they hadn't seen the image of Kethril, nor was it as specific as Notwen inferred. But if Kethril knew the red-haired woman as well as she hinted, perhaps he believed in the power of her oracle and would fall for the gnome's small trap.

Lucy walked to Kethril, put her hands on the arms of the chair, and looked into his face. "Where's the money? If you give it back so they can pay the dragon, I'm sure we can negotiate a fairer punishment than the noose."

A heavy quiet settled into the common room. The fire crackled softly in the fireplace. A sea wind moaned around the roofline outside. Someone's chair creaked when its occupant shifted slightly in the seat. Kethril sat so still that he seemed made of clay. His fingers were wrapped around one another and his handsome face looked gray.

"It's gone," he said at last. "I spent it."

The words fell heavily in the silence then burst a dam of words that crashed through the room like a tidal wave. People leaped to their feet, gesticulating and shouting.

"Hang him!" Aylesworthy shouted furiously.

"Burn him at the stake!" cried the blacksmith.

"Feed him to Fyremantle! Maybe the dragon will sicken and die!"

"Do you realize what you have done?" Saorsha said to Kethril. "Fyremantle will level this town."

Ulin moved swiftly to put himself between the prisoner and the furious Flotsamites. Lucy and the mayor gradually quieted the group and had everyone resume their seats.

Saorsha covered her face. "What do we do now?" she moaned.

"Does he know about the tunnels?" Notwen asked worriedly.

Master Aylesworthy replied, "We don't think so, but it won't do us much good if everything in the town is in little bits."

Lucy looked around at the speakers. "What tunnels?"

"There is a system of tunnels and saferooms under the town where everyone goes when the dragons come," Ulin told her.

Challie said sadly, "That's where Pease said he was taking me."

Lucy crossed her arms and looked disgusted. "Nice. Were you planning to tell me? Your hired sheriff?" She snorted indelicately. "Tell me again, why did you hire me?"

"For the reasons we told you," Saorsha replied. "After the money disappeared and Fyremantle ate Sheriff Gorlain, the three of us were terrified. We had no idea how to find that much treasure. We don't have that kind of money ourselves. So we have been collecting what we can and . . . I guess we hoped something would happen or someone would come who could help us with this. When you appeared with your magic and your courage and your willingness to help, we thought you were the answer to our prayers."

"So why didn't you tell me about all of this in the beginning?"

The old mayor lifted his hands in a small gesture.

"Would you have taken the job? No, of course not. No one in their right mind would have. We were hoping that if you worked in the town for a while, you would learn to like Flotsam and its people. This place is rough and gets a little wild sometimes, but there are good people here and they need help."

"We were going to tell you about the tunnels as soon as Ulin returned," Aylesworthy explained, "because we don't want you to leave us. Not yet. We have seen how well you two work together. Now that we know Torkay can't help, you two are our only hope."

Lucy said nothing for a moment while she studied the people in front of her. A loud voice in her mind told her to quit, to pack up and go home. Her father had been found, and her mother did not need to worry about a burial. The quest had been successful. She and Ulin could go home and resume their lives.

Not quite, said another voice in her heart. Her own personal quest was not complete. She had taken this job for reasons of her own, and the job was not yet finished.

But they lied to you, argued the first voice.

Only partially, the second voice came back. *They were trying to protect their town.*

And none of that changed the fact that she still wanted to do something useful. She had to admit, too, that the council's tactic of letting her get to know Flotsam had been partially successful. While she would never want to live here, Flotsam was beginning to grow on her—kind of like a fungus. She did like the people . . . and they had more to fear from Fyremantle than she.

This is a red dragon they're talking about, insisted the first voice, *the nastiest, cruelest, most greedy of dragons. What do you know about fighting dragons?*

Who said we had to fight it? Surely there is some way to meet its demands, or better yet, just get rid of it, said the voice of her heart.

Saorsha rose slowly to her feet. "Lucy, I don't know

how to apologize enough for our lies. We handled this badly. We didn't mean you any harm. We just didn't know what to do. I guess we were hoping you could give us a solution and leave before anyone got hurt. Not terribly realistic, is it?"

"No," Lucy replied, her tone wry. "Do you have any plans at all to satisfy this dragon?"

Aylesworthy answered, "We have collected part of the tribute, but it won't be enough. Fyremantle said he will count every coin."

"So, you either need to find the full amount of the treasure and pay off the dragon until the next time he decides to blackmail you, or you need to figure out a way to prevent him from doing this again." Lucy stated.

"In eleven days," Saorsha added.

"Lucy," Kethril said at last. "I might have an idea that will help."

"You?" she sneered. "Why would you help? Why would you do something like this in the first place?"

He looked down at his lap, at the worn, dirty fabric of his once-fine Khurish robes. "I needed the money for a venture."

"What venture?" Lucy snapped. "What sort of venture is worth endangering an entire town?"

He did not look up. "I did not give it that much thought, to be honest. Possible consequences to other people are not something I include in my calculations."

"Of all the half-cocked, stupid—" someone started to say.

Lucy cut the speaker off with a sharp gesture. "Well, maybe it's time you start thinking about it," she said in a voice of steel. "Because I will suggest to the city council that they stake you out beside the empty boxes and leave you to explain to Fyremantle."

Kethril blanched. "If I can help you, will the council agree to release me?"

Lucy glanced around at the elders of the city. For the

first time in days she saw a gleam of hope in their faces. "Yes."

"But how can we trust him after what he did?" Lysandros asked.

"Release him to my custody," Ulin answered. "I have already given my word to protect him and my promise of what I will do if he tries to flee."

"Release him?" Saorsha gasped.

Ulin put it simply. "If he stays, we can decide if his idea is valid and if he earns his reprieve. If he flees, he dies."

The half-elf lifted his hands in a gesture of agreement. "How far can he go when the entire city is watching him?"

At a nod from the city council, the captain gestured to his men to release the prisoner. "Now, what is this idea of yours?" he asked Kethril.

"Not tonight," Lucy said. "It's late. Let's get some sleep and talk about it in the morning. Meeting adjourned." Without a glance at her father, Lucy took Ulin's hand and led him from the room.

The others looked at one another in surprise, then in ones and twos they finished their drinks, bade farewell to Aylesworthy, and left the inn. Lysandros said something to the sirine, who giggled and took his arm. They left together. At last only Cosmo and Kethril were left with the innkeeper. Cosmo helped clean up the common room, wash the dishes, and turn out the lamps. Kethril did not move from his chair. He sat, staring into the darkest shadows until Aylesworthy cleared his throat.

"I have a room, if you want it."

"No, just a jug of spirits." He fumbled in his pockets until he pulled out two steel coins and flipped them on a table. "The strongest you've got."

Wordlessly, the innkeeper fetched a jug and a flagon, set them on the table, and pocketed the coins. He set a lamp on the bar and left Kethril to his thoughts and his jug.

* * * * *

Outside the door, Ulin caught Lucy's arm and stopped her. His golden eyes blazed with something Lucy had not seen in a long while. "You are going to stay, aren't you?" he asked.

She tilted up her chin so she could look into those eyes. By the gods, they made her tingle all over. "Yes," she said rather breathlessly. "I don't know why. It's probably suicide, but I—"

He put a finger over her lips. "That's what I thought. Then you'd better marry me."

She giggled softly. "I already said I would."

"No." He leaned close to her ear so his breath warmed her neck. "I mean tonight."

"Tonight! That's so soon!" A delicious heat began to spread through Lucy's veins. Oh, praise Mishakal, it has happened, she thought. She pulled away a little and looked at him sideways. "Why tonight?"

His hands slipped around to the small of her back and pulled her close against him. "Because I want you so much it is burning me, and if we're both going to die fighting, I want you for as long as I can."

"We can't get married now. It's very late. Where would we find someone in this town to marry us? Besides, my mother and your mother would never forgive us if we married without them."

Ulin grinned and waved at the front door. "They'd probably say it was high time." He hugged her. "I'm sorry, Lucy. I should have asked you months ago."

She leaned against him. "You don't need to apologize. I understand why you waited. Besides, I am greedy. I would rather have all of your attention than share it with a ghost."

His voice was husky in the dim light. "Well, you have it now. When I was in that cave and thought I'd never see you again . . . Please, marry me."

Lucy laughed and shook her head. "Not here. I want to be married in Solace with your family and mine in attendance."

"All right, you win." He started to move away from her, the disappointment plain in his voice.

A giggle escaped the Sheriff of Flotsam. She pulled Ulin close again and framed his face in her hands. "We are betrothed. The wedding vows merely make the promise official."

Ulin felt a tremble run through his body as he picked up Lucy and carried her down the hall and into his room. This was right, his body and mind had known it months ago—it had just taken his heart that long to catch up. He laid her on the bed and felt himself enveloped by the love he saw in her face. He knew from now on he would have to work very hard to make up for all the time he'd wasted.

Chapter Twenty

Kethril was still sitting in the common room when Ulin and Lucy came down the next morning. He sat in his chair, his upper body sprawled over the table, his head buried in his arms.

Aylesworthy jerked a thumb in his direction. "He's been there all night."

Lucy laughed. She felt infused with joy from the delights of her night, and she was not going to let anything, not her father or elders or dragons, ruin her happiness. "At least he didn't run."

A long, low groan issued from the man at the table. "Be quiet, I beg you. Leave the mortally afflicted in peace."

"Oh, Father, don't exaggerate so," Lucy said sweetly. She took a mug of cider from the innkeeper and with an evil glint in her eye, she slammed it down on the table beside Kethril's head. "Have something to drink, Father. You don't look well."

He flinched, moaning in misery. "Wicked child," he

mumbled. "Go away. There's someone trying to die here."

"No, going away is your action of choice. I stay and finish the job. Something I learned from my mother. Innkeeper, call the elders."

Aylesworthy lifted his chin at her request. He gestured to a serving girl he had working in the kitchen that morning. "Run and fetch Saorsha and Mayor Efrim," he ordered quietly. As soon as she left, he set about preparing a large breakfast of turnovers, fruit, fried ham, and eggs, and for Lucy, kefre, hot and black. When he brought the tray into the common room, Lucy and Ulin were sitting at Kethril's table grinning at each other like a pair of mischievous children. Kethril was not in sight, but the sound of someone being noisily sick by the front door explained his whereabouts.

Aylesworthy set down the tray and stood back to watch. It had been a long while since he had seen two people so totally happy and so appreciative of his food. They ate ravenously and asked for seconds. As he walked back to the kitchen, Kethril staggered back in.

Ulin studied his father-in-law then snapped his fingers. "Of course! Tika's remedy, just the thing!" He hurried into the kitchen. Under Aylesworthy's amused and interested observation, he mixed together his grandmother's well-known remedy for hangovers: Warm milk to coat the stomach, feverfew for headache, anise and cinnamon for nausea, and a dose of nux vomica for whatever those didn't relieve. He sniffed it once and grimaced. He liked the smell of anise about as much as he liked chicken and dumpling soup. Carrying it out at arm's length, he put it down in front of Kethril. "Hold your nose and drink it down," he ordered.

The gambler slumped in his chair and glared at the younger man through bloodshot eyes. "If you weren't engaged to my daughter, I'd knife you where you stand."

To their amazement tears gathered in Kethril's eyes and slowly trickled down his stubbled cheeks. He sniffed loudly.

"He's still drunk," Lucy observed. The kefre pot had some black at the bottom, so she dumped the dregs into Ulin's remedy. The results did not look or smell as bad as she thought it would. In fact, it smelled almost drinkable. She pushed the mug toward Kethril and said in a gentler voice, "Drink this, Father, it really will help."

He ignored it. "Gods, I should never drink that blasted dwarven swill. It always make me feel maudlin."

"You're not maudlin, Father. You're nauseated. You were never maudlin."

"I know when I'm maudlin," he stated formally. Unfortunately the effect was lost in a series of hiccups. "It's when I think about your mother and you girls, and Mauvrin, and the sirines, and Gwendolin, and Janira with her oracle glass, and—"

"We get the point, Father," Lucy said sharply.

"Beautiful women, all of them." He stared off into the distance and heaved a grand sigh—whether one of contentment or regret, Lucy could not tell. "I just never could stay with one for long." Oblivious to what he was doing, he reached for the mug and took a deep swallow of the tonic. The warm liquid slid down his throat and settled peaceably into his rebellious stomach. "Hmmm, that's not bad," he mumbled. "Didn't know I liked this stuff."

"Ulin, I want your recipe," Aylesworthy requested. He could make money on a good hangover remedy. He brought his tray over to their table and refilled their plates. Kethril looked at the food and buried his face in the mug.

The innkeeper's timing was excellent, for just as he slid three more empty plates onto a nearby table, Saorsha, Notwen, and Mayor Efrim came in through the front door.

"Aylesworthy, you might want to send someone out front to clean up your walk," Saorsha suggested.

"Ah, the city council has arrived," Lucy announced.

"Give 'em some kefre," Kethril roared, waving his mug. "Drink to the health of my ladies fair."

A tight smile lifted Saorsha's mouth. "He's drunk."

Ulin corrected her. "No, he's just maudlin."

Mayor Efrim sat at the table with the plates, put one in front of him, and said, "We understand you've decided to stay."

Kethril leaned forward, buried his head in his arms, and began to cry. "Oh, gods, Lucy, I'm sorry!" He sobbed. "I'm sorry I've been such a terrible father. It's not because of you. It was never because of you or your sisters, or even your nagging mother. I loved you all. I'll make it up to you."

Everyone watched him in amazement. Ulin, who had seen his own father break down, felt his heart twist. The confession might have been spurred by the aftereffects of too much drink, but the emotions were real.

Lucy did not know what to feel. For years she had harbored the very fear he mentioned, that he had left their family because of her. She was not beautiful like her mother or talented like her sisters or anything a father could be proud of. As a little girl she agonized that she must have done something wrong or been inadequate for his love. It wasn't until she came to the Academy and met Ulin and his family that she realized the fault was not hers. Now she looked at her father's heaving shoulders and came to the conclusion that there really was no fault involved. Kethril Torkay was a rogue and a wanderer and no one was going to change that. It was probably those very characteristics and the hint of danger and adventure about him that had drawn Lucy's passionate mother to him in the first place.

She patted him awkwardly on the shoulder. "It's all right, Father."

He raised a rumpled, wet face. "No. No, it's not. This forsaken town can't raise the tribute, and you're going to have to face that blasted dragon."

"True," Lucy prompted, hoping to ease her father into a more useful state of mind. "You said you had an idea that could help."

"Yes! Help!" Kethril said loudly. He drained the contents of his cup and set it on the table. "A plan. We need a plan."

Lucy looked skeptical. "Such as?"

"I know something you don't." He leaned forward until he was looking blearily into his daughter's face. "Fyremantle is stealing from Malys. Has been for years. He raised your taxes so he could skim some for himself."

A stunned silence fell over the people in the room. The thought of anyone, even another red dragon, stealing from the merciless overlord was almost inconceivable. Almost.

"Why that nasty, greedy . . ." Saorsha said indignantly.

Mayor Efrim drew a deep breath and let it out noisily. "That's it. We could tell Malys what he is doing! She would kill him!"

"And probably put a worse dragon in his place—if she even believed you in the first place," Notwen pointed out. "Fyremantle may be greedy and cruel, but he is predictable and fairly stupid. We know this dragon."

Aylesworthy shifted impatiently in his chair. "So what about this idea, Kethril? How is this knowledge going to help us?"

"Ah, his treasure. I found it," Kethril informed them. He patted the front of his robes, the robes he had carefully retrieved from the ghagglers' cave and worn ever since. "I know where some of it is. I have a map."

The others looked at each other, thoughts and ideas running through their minds.

"Yes, and what do you plan to do with it?" Lucy prompted again.

Kethril was still under the strong influence of the dwarven spirits, but he was not so drunk that he could not think. "Oh, we could steal it. Like a game of Dragon's Bluff." He paused to hiccup again. "Lots of treasure." He rested his head on his arm, closed his eyes, and his features slowly relaxed. "We could blackmail the brute," he murmured before his breathing eased and his body sagged into sleep.

* * * * *

At Lucy's insistence, they let Kethril sleep off his hang-over in a back room of the inn. As she pointed out, they needed him lucid and coherent in order to explain more about the treasure. Until he woke and could tell them where it was and how much was in it, there wasn't much they could do to finalize their plans.

While he slept, Lucy donned her "uniform" and the turban and, taking the council members with her, went to the city hall. If the news of Kethril's capture had spread through the town, she thought there would prob-ably be people coming in asking for answers and infor-mation, and she felt the city council needed to be there to explain.

People were lined up at the door when Lucy and her small group arrived, and while the citizens did want their questions asked and their fears calmed, Lucy was surprised to learn that most of them came to be assured that she was still acting sheriff.

"Wouldn't blame you at all for leaving," a fisherman told her, "but we're glad you're sticking with us."

His words, if nothing else, convinced Lucy she had made the right decision to stay.

Notwen appeared at the city hall a little before noon, carrying a large portfolio with him. He looked worn and tired but pleased with himself, and he happily showed the portfolio to Lucy.

She laughed when she saw it. It was stuffed with tech-nical equations and drawings that meant nothing to her. "Show it to Ulin," she said, giving the gnome a quick hug. "He's out in the stable with the horse."

Notwen's face turned red as a strawberry from her hug, and he trotted out, muttering to himself about the ability of females to make him feel so silly. He found Ulin currying the bay gelding in the shade of the stable. With the portfo-lio tucked under his arm, he stood well clear of the horse and asked, "Before you go home would you be willing to help me with a new engine?"

"We're not leaving yet," Ulin told him from behind the big bay's flank. "We've decided to stay past Visiting Day."

Happiness and worry crowded into the gnome's small face. His blue eyes shone brighter than ever, but a frown turned down his mouth. "But if you stay, you might . . ." He couldn't finish.

"I hope not. I plan to have a long and happy life with Lucy. We just have to deal with this dragon first." Ulin's thoughts returned to the conversation that morning, and he told Notwen about a new idea that had occurred to him.

The gnome quickly caught Ulin's line of thinking. "We found him upriver of Dead Pirate's Cove, yet he had not been seen in the settlement for some time. So it is possible Fyrcmantle's treasure is somewhere near there, which means . . ."

"To retrieve the treasure in time to bring it back here, we need a new steam boat, probably a bigger one," Ulin finished for him. He moved around the horse and saw the portfolio under Notwen's arm. "What do you have there?" he asked as he put away the brushes.

For once the gnome looked embarrassed about one of his inventions, and he shuffled his feet a minute before he carried the drawings over to a stone wall and spread them out for Ulin to see.

The man studied the calculations and drawings for what seemed a very long time to Notwen. "What is it?" Ulin asked.

"It's a plan for a dragon trap."

Ulin could scarcely believe his ears. "A trap? For *dragons*? Why?"

The gnome gently touched the papers of his work. "It's just something I've worked on over the years—a conundrum I guess you'd call it. Something I designed but never intended to use. Do you think it might work?"

"For Fyremantle?" As much as the thought scared him, it caught his imagination, too. Capture a dragon . . . the idea had possibilities. He gathered up the plans and walked through the city hall, Notwen close on his heels.

"We're going to the laboratory to build a boat," Ulin called to Lucy as they hurried past the sheriff's office. "Call me if Kethril wakes up."

"Did that make sense to you?" Saorsha asked Lucy, watching the tall man and the short gnome trot out the door and down the road toward the docks.

Lucy thought for a moment and said, "Actually, I think it does. They want to have a boat ready to fetch the treasure—if it exists. At least it gives them something to do."

The older woman put her hand on Lucy's arm. "I just hope Kethril remembers his offer when he wakes up."

"So do I." Lucy sighed. "So do I."

* * * * *

Later that afternoon, Challie and Cosmo came walking down the road together. Bridget was better, they reported. She was subdued and still fighting her disbelief, but since she had missed the wake the night before, she insisted on rising and fixing a meal—a feast from the length of the shopping list—of Pease's favorite dishes. The work, Challie told Lucy, would do Bridget good.

"We're helping her," Cosmo said. "We have to go to the market."

"Your father is still asleep," Challie said, her disdain plain to hear.

"Good," Lucy replied. "Ask Aylesworthy to invite the usual crowd. We're going to work out a plan, even if I have to hang Kethril up by his thumbs to get some answers."

The dwarf and the kender soon left to visit the market for Bridget, and Mayor Efrim, looking tired and strained, went home at Saorsha's insistence, leaving the two women in the sheriff's office. The half-ogres stood outside as usual, but the visitors had gone and the interior of the building was empty and quiet in the late afternoon. It was, Lucy decided, like the quiet before the storm.

Chapter Twenty-one

At sunset Ulin came to accompany the two women to Bridget's dinner. For a while they walked without talking along the streets of Flotsam, all three lost in their own thoughts.

"How is your boat progressing?" Lucy asked when they were nearly to the Jetties.

Ulin chuckled in the twilight. "We've had to cobble much of it together on an old boat Notwen has, but we made some improvements in the paddle wheel and the cogs, and the engine is almost ready to be assembled." He squeezed her and said, "I'm sorry, but it may mean we will have to work all night."

"I understand, but when this is over—"

"When this is over—" and he leaned closed and whispered in her ear.

They were laughing together when they walked into the inn. A large group had already assembled in the common room, and the people clustered together, drinking the new spring ale and talking intently. They quickly made room for Lucy and her companions. Aylesworthy poured his best white wine into a pair of goblets for the sheriff and her escort, and Lucy and Ulin drank a toast to each other and then to the guests. Everyone took a seat at one of the many tables.

Kethril came in last. He looked surprisingly hale and energetic, back to his normal self, as if the drunken crack in his facade had never opened. With a flashing grin at the room, he took an empty chair beside Ulin.

Bridget had outdone herself for the feast with her best recipes and favorite dishes. There were platters of stuffed capons roasted to a golden brown, mountains of fluffy mashed potatoes delicately seasoned with herbs, spring peas fresh from the garden, freshly baked bread filled with pockets of melted cheese, bowls of preserves and candied fruits, and for the sweet, a marzipan cake filled with chopped almonds and a delicate white cake. Lucy and Ulin ate until they were stuffed. When the feast was over, they called Bridget from the kitchen and cheered for her, then everyone drank a toast to Pease. Bridget stood with tears running down her cheeks until the toast was over. Mopping her face with a handkerchief, she fled back to the kitchen.

Lucy stood and called for everyone's attention. She looked over the faces she had come to know so well in such a short period of time, and she fervently hoped they could keep their minds open and their wits sharp. The city councilors were there, as well as Lysandros and some of the Vigilance Force. Notwen, Challie, and Cosmo sat close by. The blacksmith and other prominent kender and humans she had befriended were scattered around the room. It was time to get to work.

Aylesworthy wasted no time. "What about this treasure? Is Kethril going to give us that treasure he found?"

All eyes turned to the gambler. Under the scrutiny of so many people, Kethril could hardly say no and still remain in good health. He squirmed and looked at the ceiling as if beseeching divine guidance. He rubbed his aching temples. "That is the last time I drink that swill at your place," he grumbled to Aylesworthy. The owner of the Jetties only glowered at him.

Kethril slowly climbed to his feet and faced his daughter. When he spoke, he talked directly to her as if there was no one else in the room. "You asked me yesterday why I stole the city's money, and I told you I needed it for a venture. I did. The biggest heist this side of Sanction." He pulled a small dagger from his belt, removed his outer robe, and began to cut a careful slit in the quilted front of his inner tunic. From the slit he withdrew a piece of oilcloth carefully wrapped around a piece of coarse paper. He unfolded the cloth and laid the paper out on the table. "This is the work of several years," he said. "I have been tracking Fyremantle, learning his habits, and looking for his lairs. As far as I know he has three. I have found two of them—one even Malys does not know. The other is well hidden. I was looking for that when Ulin caught me."

She looked at him without expression. "So what was the money for?"

"Spies to track the dragon, new clothes for my disguise, bribes, horses, equipment, and ah, to pay off a few gambling debts that were getting uncomfortable."

"What do you propose we do?" Lucy asked.

He leaned forward, his hands flat on the table. "Steal the treasure from one of Fyremantle's secret caves. A lot of it's come from Flotsam anyway. You could pay Malys with that and blackmail Fyremantle into leaving the city alone—at least for a while. I will lead you to the treasure, if the city lets me go."

His words hung in the silent room. All eyes turned back to Lucy to wait for her answer.

She studied her father for an uncomfortably long time, then she nodded. "It's a deal."

All at once she crossed her arms in a copy of her father's stance, and a brilliant smile transformed her face.

Kethril looked slightly startled at the change in her features, then he matched her grin for grin.

Ulin, sitting at the table beside Lucy, recognized the resemblance in an instant. They were almost identical down to the wrinkles in the corners of the eyes—the way the full mouths spread open to reveal even, white teeth, the glint of humor and a light of mischief that burned like lights behind the color of the eyes. To Ulin it was remarkable. There was more of Kethril in his daughter than either one of them knew.

The entire gathering had sat silent through Kethril's speech and listened with what Lucy assumed was stunned horror. But they surprised her. As soon as she accepted, a chorus of voices began talking, not to condemn the idea as she feared, but to offer ideas, advice, and suggestions.

"Where is this treasure you want us to steal?" Ulin asked when Kethril sat down.

"The closest cache is here"—the older man pointed to a spot on his map—"in the caves of an old volcano just north of Secar's Point. It's well camouflaged and only lightly guarded. We will not need many men, In fact, the fewer who know of this part of the plan, the better." Like many people with no morals, Kethril did have certain standards. His map was detailed, well drawn, and accurate. His plans to infiltrate the lair of the dragon were careful, organized, and efficient.

Lysandros moved to the table and studied the map. "I have enough men in the Vigilance Force to do this. Their discretion has already been tested." He shifted over to make space for Notwen, who crowded in beside him.

"I know this place," the gnome said excitedly. "We can use the boat to go along the coast to the Point. The new boat is big enough to haul cargo."

"But where do we put this treasure?" Mayor Efrim wanted to know. "Is there enough to pay Malys's taxes?"

Kethril laughed. "There's enough to pay Malys for several years and buy this town a decent gaming house. That dragon has been skimming taxes from you and several other places for years. He keeps his ill-gotten gains in this cave and one other so Malys won't realize what he's doing."

"But where do we put it?" The mayor quavered again. "How do we keep it safe from Fyremantle, or the likes of you?"

"Hide it." Kethril's disarming smile lit his face. "Hide it and don't tell me about it."

Aylesworthy heaved his bulk to his feet and crowded into the group around the table. "Look, this money is all well and good, but Fyremantle will be furious. He'll burn this town to the ground before we ever get a chance to talk to him."

More voices joined his argument.

"We could kill him," the blacksmith suggested.

"Yes, then Malys would kill us and scorch this town to ash."

"What if we—"

Lucy threw up her hands for quiet. On her head, the turban shimmered a brilliant shade of yellow and watched the proceedings with sparkling eyes. The noise slowly simmered down.

"Actually, Lucy," Ulin said in the quiet. "Notwen has invented a trap that just might subdue Fyremantle long enough to convince him to cooperate."

She turned to the gnome. "Honestly? Is that what those drawings were?"

Notwen nodded, pleased that she would take him seriously.

"Then that's what we'll do," said Lucy. "We'll lure Fyremantle into the trap and convince him that it would be in his best interest to restore the original tax level and leave Flotsam alone."

"And how do we convince him?" someone asked.

Kethril hooked a finger around his mug of ale and pushed it gently back and forth. "That's where the blackmail comes in. What would Malys do if she even suspected one of her underlings was stealing money meant for her treasury?"

"Eat him," Lysandros answered, "and take his collection."

"Exactly—and he knows this. So we tell him we have a messenger on the way to Malys with names and locations and amounts."

Aylesworthy shuddered. "Who would be stupid enough to face Malys in her lair?"

A wicked smile beamed on Lucy's face. "Someone who does it regularly. The Dark Knights."

"Venturin? That harpy?"

"For a bit of gold, I'll bet that harpy would sing like a lark," Mayor Efrim remarked acidly.

"I'll talk to her," Lucy said. "She's due back any day. I'm sure I can convince her to help the town—for the sake of her iron backside."

A smattering of chuckles met her suggestion, and the business of the meeting continued. Before the evening ended, a plan of sorts was put together, and the people agreed it was the best they could do given the circumstances. It was not perfect, and it depended on many things happening at the right time, but with luck and some hard work, it just might work. Lucy thanked everyone for their help and commitment, and she waited until most people had left. At last she could not keep her eyes open another minute. She kissed Ulin goodnight and went upstairs to bed.

Ulin and Notwen talked to the blacksmith for a while, then all three left to work on the boat. Eventually, only Kethril and Lysandros were left in the common room. The resistance leader rose, stretched, and moved toward the door. He paused and turned back to Kethril. The gambler sat alone at his table staring morosely into his empty flagon. The half-elf picked up a pitcher and poured a stream of golden ale into the man's cup.

"Don't stay up too late, Kethril. You have a treasure to fetch in the morning." He chuckled softly.

Kethril glanced up at the half-elf. "So where are you off to? Patrols? A Thieves' Guild meeting?"

"To see the sirine. I think she and her people might help Notwen and that boat of his. At least they won't let him drown."

"She'll leave you, you know. They all do."

The captain shrugged. "And I may die tomorrow. But in the meantime I have enjoyed the love of an exquisite woman."

It was Kethril's turn to chuckle. He slapped the half-elf on the arm. "I knew there was something I liked about you."

Lysandros started to say something, changed his mind, then said it anyway. "What I don't understand is how you managed to have a daughter like Lucy. She is incredible."

Kethril stared down at his long, supple hands and absently twisted an ornate silver ring on his thumb. "She is, isn't she?" he replied, his voice distant. "She's her mother's own."

* * * * *

The boat was ready soon after the sun rose, a red-gold disk in the eastern sky. Ulin, Notwen, the blacksmith, and three dwarves who were friends of Notwen had worked all night to adapt the paddlewheel to an old blunt-sterned fishing boat and fit the steam engine into the hold. They loaded the boat with cords of wood, enough supplies for a few days, shovels, picks, ropes, and this time they brought a rowboat, oars, and an extra sail.

Kethril offered little help. He stood on the dock, his arms crossed, and watched the loading with a jaundiced eye. Why, in the name of Krynn, had he ever thought to steal from Flotsam, and why did this dump of a town have to have a council with some imagination and dogged determination? And why, after all these years, did his wife still love him enough to send their daughter after him? Numbers, odds, the fall of the cards . . . these he could understand. Emotions of the heart were incomprehensible to him.

"Are you ready to go?" Lucy asked behind him.

"No." He didn't move as she came up beside him and stood an arm's length away. "Why did you come to Flotsam, Lucy?" He hadn't planned to ask her, but the words blurted out before he could take them back.

"You know why," she replied, her words deadpan.

"You could have said no. Most people would have."

"Most people do not have you for a father." She paused, and a hint of that smile teased her mouth. "Although there are more of your children around than I thought."

"I never intended to involve you in any of this. I never thought you'd come to Flotsam."

"The council did offer us a quarter of your estate."

"Only a quarter? I'd have held out for at least a third." He tried a smile, but the cold glint in his daughter's eyes evaporated the expression. "That might have persuaded your mother, but you still haven't answered my question. Why did *you* come?"

She cast an oblique glance in his direction, and for the first time she realized how old he looked. The image she remembered of him from ten years ago was of a vibrant young man with a smooth face, a strong body, and an exuberant, restless energy. This man who stood beside her had aged. His face had darkened and creased from years of travel. His light hair was more gray than blond. His charm was still evident, but the fiery energy of youth had faded to a cooler, more calculating ember. The only thing Lucy remembered about him that hadn't changed at all was his perception. He still saw himself as the center of the universe.

Lucy tucked a strand of hair up under the turban and finally answered. "I spent years trying to decide if I loved you or hated you. I guess I came on this journey because I needed to prove to myself that I loved you, that in spite of everything I could travel halfway across Ansalon just to see my father's body. I wanted to put an end to the debate so I don't go into my own marriage with a burden of hate."

Ulin hailed them at that moment and jumped onto the dock from the boat. He strode toward them, the wind ruffling his chestnut hair, his head thrown back, and his eyes on his beloved.

Her face lit with an answering joy. She turned to her father and winked. "I guess it worked," she said, and ran to meet Ulin.

They had to make a quick farewell so the boat could catch the morning tide. Notwen, the blacksmith, the three dwarves, and five of Lysandros's most trusted fighters waited for Ulin on the boat, and smoke was already puffing out of the new engine.

Lucy gripped Ulin's elbows in her strong hands. "Nothing will go wrong. You have help this time and strong backs to dig or row or whatever you need. And if I'm not mistaken, my blue-skinned sister is waiting at the mouth of the harbor for your boat." She hugged him tightly and moved back to let him go.

He nodded once. "You have the instructions Notwen left for you. Good luck." He kissed her. "Keep that turban on. Come on, Kethril!"

With a face like a martyr, the gambler climbed into the boat. Dockhands cast off the ropes, and for the second time, Ulin and Notwen churned out of Flotsam harbor and headed for the east coast of Blood Bay.

* * * * *

That evening in the lingering sultry heat, the Flotsam Vigilance Committee called a town meeting and summoned a full muster of the resistance fighters. Except for a few drunkards, some visitors, and babies, the entire population of the town arrived in the large mess hall of the Dark

Knights' old barracks to find out what was going on.
People from Ulin and Lucy's dinner meeting had spread
some chosen bits of the news, but rumors abounded, and
meanings were often twisted. Everyone wanted to hear the
facts for themselves. Several hundred people crammed into
the room and sat on stools, pillows, or rugs they had
brought. Those with nothing to sit on lined the walls three
or four deep.

Aylesworthy, flanked by Saorsha and Mayor Efrim,
explained in his calm bass voice what had happened
with Kethril Torkay and what the council planned to
do. As soon as he finished, an uproar burst the silence
in the hall.

Twenty or thirty people—Lucy couldn't tell exactly
how many in the milling, gesticulating crowd—abruptly
left the hall. She guessed they would probably pack their
belongings and flee. Not that she blamed them. If she had
an ounce of common sense and little less of her father's
blood, she would pack her gear on the bay horse, take Ulin,
and show this rat-trap of a town her heels. Yet she couldn't,
and neither could the remaining people who had made this
place their home and had stuck with it through fair
weather and foul, Dark Knights and dragon attacks, and
some of the toughest conditions on Ansalon. The people of
Flotsam were tough, and they were about to be asked to
prove their mettle again.

Lucy moved from her place by the empty fireplace and
came to stand beside Saorsha. Challie went with her, and
the Silver Fox, in his tan pants and tunic, seemed to mate-
rialize out of nowhere to join her. She held up her hands.
The sight of such a united front gradually stilled the
troubled voices, and everyone grew quiet.

On Lucy's dark hair, the turban shifted to a shimmering
silver like a polished helm. Its diamond eyes glittered in the
torchlight.

"People of Flotsam," she called, "you have been put in a
dangerous situation!" Loud catcalls and shouts interrupted

her until she chopped her hand down for silence. "That is hardly new to you."

"Yeah, but a trap?" a storekeeper yelled. "And a gnome invention at that! It'll never work!"

"Notwen is not like most gnomes," Lucy responded. "I believe with his idea, our hard work, and some luck, we can succeed."

"The festival will have to continue. We'll want things to look as normal as possible," Mayor Efrim said.

"But we should send quite a few of the youngsters, babes, elders, and sick ones into the hills," Saorsha added. "We shouldn't trust everyone to the tunnels."

Loud and stunned discussion broke out again. Lucy let the crowd talk to work off some of their surprise and fear, then she held out her hands again for silence. "As you can see, we need help. The Vigilance Committee cannot do this alone. "

An old man is the back of the room pushed forward. "You're not shoving me into some dank cave! I'm staying right here. This is the damndest game of Dragon's Bluff I've ever seen, and I want to see who wins! I'm with you, Sheriff."

Lucy glanced around the room and saw acceptance begin to dawn on the faces of the crowd. "All right. Good." She spread her arms wide to include everyone. "This is what we're going to do. . . ."

Chapter
Twenty-two

Three long, busy days passed in Flotsam while the townspeople sweated and worked to prepare for Visiting Day and the arrival of the dragon. Only seven days were left, and there was still no sign of Notwen's boat and the treasure seekers—not that Lucy really expected them back this soon. Notwen had told her the trip to the Point would take a day by the new steamboat, so she was counting on seeing Ulin and his company late on the fourth day. But that knowledge did not make the waiting much easier. Too many things could go wrong. What if Fyremantle visited his cave while they were removing the treasure? What if it was heavily guarded? What if some mishap happened on the way back? Oh, gods, what if . . . what if . . . what if? Lucy knew she could make herself crazy with worry if she let it loose, so she tried to keep a tight seal on her fear and distracted herself with work.

There was certainly plenty to do. Notwen had not explained any of his crazy instructions in the note to her, only that he wanted certain things done—certain things that made no sense to her or anyone else. But since no one could suggest anything else to try, and no one dared alter his instructions for fear of fouling his plans, Lucy and the townspeople followed them to the letter.

The first thing they had to do was find a level place close to town to hold the "Hiyahowareya" gathering. Notwen requested the location be near some old buildings and away from the tunnels that honeycombed the sublevels. Mayor Efrim suggested a derelict block at the southernmost edge of town. The few buildings still standing were abandoned, in ruins, and worthless. People quickly set about cleaning out the overgrown street, pulling down the most dangerous ruins, and doing what they could to make the place look like the site of a festival and picnic.

The second thing they had to do was dig out a hole at the site two feet deep, a hundred feet long, and as wide as the street. The workers looked appalled at the amount of work.

"Two feet isn't deep enough to catch a deer, let alone a dragon!" one man complained to Lucy. "How does Notwen expect that to hold Fyremantle?"

Since Lucy could not answer that with any truth, she shrugged, grabbed a shovel, and started to dig.

The hole was well underway when the Dark Knights rode into town. A sentry by the caravan road spotted them late in the afternoon and sent word to the sheriff. Lucy swiftly dusted off her clothes and sent a boy to the closest tavern for a pitcher of ale and a couple of mugs. Her workers vanished into the alleys and ruins of the derelict street.

By the time the Dark Knights rode into sight, the street was empty and Lucy was sitting in the shade of an old abandoned shop, sipping her ale and waiting. Up the road from the docks rode Knight Officer Venturin and four Knights. Their black armor and horses looked like dark stains against the colors and bright light of the afternoon. Light glinted off their swords and the maces hanging on their belts. They were riding directly for the festival site.

Knight Officer Venturin hid her surprise well when she stopped her horse at the edge of the large pit and looked around. Finally she leveled a glare at Lucy. With deliberate care, the Dark Knight dismounted. She clucked her tongue and walked slowly to Lucy. She paced around the seated sheriff, studying her from turban to boots. Her lips parted to reveal the tips of her long teeth, and she grinned like a feral cat. Without warning she clamped a hand around Lucy's neck and hauled her to her feet.

"I came to be sure the tax collection is going smoothly. Visiting Day is only week away, and I would hate to report to Her Majectic Queen that you have failed in your duties."

Lucy twisted out of Venturin's grip. "The taxes are being collected," she said, ignoring the pain in her neck. "All of them. As required by law." Instead of backing away from the Dark Knight, she picked up another mug, filled it, and handed it to Venturin. "So tell me. How much tax does Malys require?"

The Knight Officer's dark eyes narrowed, and her hand tightened around the mug. "Six hundred steel pieces or its equivalent—no less, as you well know."

"Actually, I don't," Lucy paused and filled her own mug. "This town has been paying a thousand steel pieces to Fyremantle for the past five years. They have it on record."

"What?" The word came out sharp as a dagger.

"Fyremantle has been doing some creative collecting at Malys's expense. He told the council Malys raised the taxes. Did you know about this?"

Venturin took a swallow of her ale as if her throat was suddenly dry.

"Yes," Lucy went on. "The town might have gone on in blissful ignorance if someone hadn't stolen the taxes a few months ago. When we finally caught up with him, he told us about the padded taxes. Now, maybe Malys doesn't care if her minions indulge in a little theft and extortion, but if one does it, they might all decide to help themselves, and then where would the Overlord get her revenues?"

"How do we know you are not shorting the taxes yourselves and trying to blame it on a faithful servant?" Venturin snarled.

"Why would we be that stupid? Flotsam has faithfully paid its taxes to Malys's coffers for years and will continue to do so if Fyremantle does not level the town," Lucy pointed out.

Venturin made a rude noise. "And what do you plan to do about him? Drop him in this little hole?"

"Offer him a deal. He continues to serve Malys as usual, but he stops skimming off our taxes and leaves us alone."

The Knight Officer's curiosity was piqued. "What makes you think he'll accept that?"

"Because I am going to tell him you are on your way to inform Malys, and only a secret, coded message from me will stop you. From then on, you are in on the secret, too."

"Why should I bother? Deal with him yourself."

"How would it look to Malys if someone else told her? Someone besides her loyal watchdogs?"

Venturin bristled. "Are you threatening me?" Her voice was cold and smooth as ice.

"Of course not," Lucy said. "I am authorized to make you a deal."

A sharp cry and a scuffling sound caused Venturin to whip around, her hand reaching for her sword. She gaped at the five riderless black horses milling around in the dust of the street. There was no sign of the other four Knights. Furiously, she turned back, her hand pulling out her dagger. Swift as a striking snake, she snatched a handful of Lucy's hair and the turban and shoved Lucy back against the stone wall of the building.

The turban unwound in the blink of an eye and whipped its length up the Dark Knight's arm. She cried out in disbelief, "Get this thing off me!" She tried to stab the flying end of the turban, but the creature was too fast for her. It twisted itself around her wrists and her head, effectively binding her. The dagger fell to the ground.

Now it was Lucy's turn to take control. She pushed the woman around and into the stone wall and said, "Listen carefully. Your men will be our guests for a few days. If you make any move to rescue them, they will be killed. If you act as our messenger and we tell Fyremantle you are going to Malys's lair to inform her of his transgressions, then I will release your Knights unharmed and turn over five percent of the monies we are gathering to pay Malys."

The Knight Officer was breathing heavily, her face cold with anger.

"Release her," Lucy told the turban. Like a whisper, it unwound from the Knight's head, flowed back to Lucy's arm, curled up on her chestnut hair, and stared malevolently at Venturin.

The Dark Knight shook her head as if to be sure the thing was gone. She studied Lucy for a long moment and glanced back at the street where her Knights had been Finally she picked up her dagger and shoved it back in its sheath. "All right. Ten percent." Venturian's mercenary bent took over. "And if you so much as bruise one of my Knights, I'll burn this town myself."

"Seven," countered Lucy. "With luck you won't have to go far."

"Eight will buy my silence about this little affair."

"So will fear, but it's a deal."

"How do I know you are not lying about all of this?"

"You don't. But what is there to lose? If our plan fails, you go to Malys about Fyremantle. We will provide the information you need and the location of his lairs. You will have done your duty in bringing a malefactor to her attention. If we succeed, you will be rich."

"Where is this alleged money coming from?"

"Ah," Lucy said with a slight smile. "We can't tell you everything."

The Dark Knight shot a quick look at the turban, then she turned on her heel and strode to her horse.

"Be here at dawn on Visiting Day," Lucy called after her.

Venturin did not respond. Stone-faced, she collected the reins of the loose horses and mounted her own. She spurred her mount to a canter and led the riderless cavalcade away. The sound of hooves pounded on the road and dwindled away toward the west end of town.

Lucy leaned against the wall and took a deep breath. As the dust settled, the workers warily poked their heads out from the windows, doors, and ruinous gaps of the old buildings.

Challie came out the doorway of a gaming house several blocks down the road and joined Lucy. A faint smirk tilted up her mouth. "They're trussed like chickens and spitting mad. Lysandros's men have the Knights in a safe room under the Game Cock. He says his guards will keep an eye on them."

The sheriff grinned, remembering the look on Venturin's face when she realized her Talon had vanished. "That should sour her wine for a while."

Challie picked up a shovel and drove it into the dirt. "I just hope this works, because if it doesn't, there's going to be some dragon-sized trouble."

* * * * *

The paddleboat arrived later than expected. It came chugging into the harbor under full steam, pulling a laden raft and aided by teams of powerful, sleek dolphins. Ulin saw Lucy and Challie standing on the wharf and waved to them. He was off the boat and running toward Lucy before the boat had come to a complete stop.

Lucy took one look at the eagerness on his tired, haggard face and melted into his arms. "Oh, thank goodness, you're here," she gasped. "I was getting so worried."

"Hello to you, too." Kethril strode up the dock. "We got the treasure. It's all there—every chest, box, and bag. We cleaned out the lot. We'd better hurry if we're going to unload it."

Lucy's face took on a look of wary determination. "Oh, no, not you. You come to the Jetties with me." She took her father's arm and steered him toward the wharf.

"Daughter, you wound me with your mistrust," he said mournfully.

"The Magistrate, Notwen, and the dwarves are going to handle this one," she said. "Ulin, are you coming?"

He nodded wearily. "We need some food, then we're going to get to work on Notwen's trap. We didn't expect to take so long."

The three of them began the long walk to the Jetties. Behind them, the chugging sound of the steam engine filled the small harbor as the boat cast off and headed for whatever place Challie and Notwen decided to hide the dragon's cache.

Walking between the two men, Lucy looked at them carefully and saw that both of them were dirty, tired, and worn. Kethril's expensive robes were gone, replaced by an old tunic and tattered pants that had seen a great deal of work but very little soap. Her father was limping slightly, and Ulin moved as if every muscle hurt. She did not ask any questions, keeping them to herself until she could get the two men to the Jetties, seat them at a table, and bring them a pitcher of ale. Aylesworthy took one look at them and yelled at Bridget to bring platters of stew and freshly baked bread.

While the two men ate, Lucy and Aylesworthy curbed their impatience. Lucy told the innkeeper the treasure had been secured, but both of them wanted to hear about the dragon's lair and the theft.

At last Ulin pushed his ale aside and asked for wine. When it was brought, he stretched out his long legs and took a long, appreciative sip.

"So?" Lucy prompted. "What happened at Fyremantle's lair?"

"It wasn't technically a lair," Kethril answered. "It was only a stash of his stolen goods. He could not keep it at his known lair for fear of Malys finding it."

Ulin chuckled and glanced at the gambler with something akin to respect. "Your father may be a thief, a gambler, and a morally poor example of a man," he told Lucy, "but he has courage, imagination, and a lot of gall. His observations of the hiding place were accurate up to the small matter of booby-traps."

"Booby-traps?" Lucy and Aylesworthy said together.

Pulling the map out of his tunic, Ulin tapped a finger on the spot marked *Secar's Point.* "The stash was exactly where the map is marked, in a dormant volcano just to the west of the Point. It was down in an old volcanic tube that you could not see unless you were standing right on top of it. Malys would never have seen it from the air. We would never have found it if Kethril hadn't known where it was. He was right, too, about the guards. There were none. I guess Fyremantle didn't trust anyone with the location of his secret hoard."

Some of the other customers in the inn, hearing Ulin's voice, moved their chairs closer to listen to the tale. Aylesworthy hurriedly refilled Ulin's wine goblet.

"We arrived at the Point shortly after sunset and hid Notwen's boat in a small cove. At daybreak, we hiked up to the volcano to find the cave and determine what was needed to remove the treasure."

"Fyremantle was there," Kethril interrupted him. "That greedy little worm was adding to his stash from taxes collected at one of the Khur settlements. He stayed there all day, counting and gloating. It was disgusting." He broke off and saw Lucy, Ulin, and Aylesworthy staring at him. "What?"

"You're a fine one to talk about counting and gloating," Lucy said.

Ulin took up the tale again. "We had to wait until Fyre-mantle left before we could enter the cave. One of the Vig-ilance fighters found the first booby-trap when he tried to open the stone that blocks the entrance. A cloud of acid burned his lungs and ate his skin. His death was slow and agonizing. That made us think twice about moving too quickly, so we waited until the next day when we could use the daylight to help us see. It was a good thing we did. Once we got the stone door open, we found the tube was infested with cave lizards." He stopped and shuddered. "I don't know if you've ever seen one, but they're nasty creatures. These were about three feet long, mottled gray, and very aggressive. They scooted over the ceiling of the tube and were on us before we even knew they were there. They use their long tongues to grab a victim and pull him in range of their teeth. One of those lizards isn't too difficult to beat off, but five or six of those things chewing on your arms or legs is very frightening. They almost killed one of the dwarves before we got to him."

"What did you do?" Lucy asked, wide-eyed.

"Light," Ulin replied. "They hate light. The sunlight drove them from the entrance and I used some magnesium flashpowder in the interior."

"The tube is quite long," Kethril added. "And there were scorpions and several pitfalls and a sand trap. Fyre-mantle was taking no chances. It was hours before we fi-nally found the chamber where he hid his stash. We worked for a full day to neutralize the booby-traps, crate up the goods, and haul it out of there. By the time we finished, there wasn't so much as a coin to toss to the lizards. It was a beautiful operation," he finished enthusiastically. Like most thieves, he enjoyed a good heist.

Ulin gave Lucy a slow weary smile. "It was a successful attempt. Except for Lysandros's man and the wounded dwarf, we got out of there with little injury or loss."

"So what do we do now?" Aylesworthy asked as he topped off Ulin's wine.

Lucy looked at her father and her betrothed and said, "Sleep. We can work tomorrow."

"No, no. I need to help Notwen," Ulin said, but he made no move to stand up.

"He probably needs sleep as much as you. I will go check on him. Aylesworthy, if you could see these two to bed, I would appreciate it."

"Absolutely, Miss Lucy."

Kethril started to argue, but the food, the ale, and the lack of sleep finally caught up with him. He sagged back in his chair and grinned at nothing. "It was a good heist," he murmured.

Chapter
Twenty-three

T he eve of Visiting Day came on a brisk
wind and a warm sun. While the kender
prepared for the picnic and festivities, the Vigilance Force
set quietly about removing the elderly, the lame, the sick,
and the younger children to safe camps in the dusty hills.
The number of sentinels on the Rock and around the town
was doubled. Most of the fishing boats moved out into the
bay and sailed east for the open waters of the sea, leaving
behind a few older and damaged boats tied at the docks.
Traveling merchants, visiting Khurs, and other transients
quickly abandoned the town, as did a few dozen of the permanent residents.

Those who remained swallowed hard and went to
work creating a new festival ground on the south side of
town around the large area of bare ground where the large
hole had been dug. The hole was prepared and filled in
now, and Notwen's dragon trap was carefully camouflaged among the abandoned buildings. In and around the

open street and buildings the men scythed the scrubby grass and the weeds and cleaned out the debris. They put in a large fire pit at the edge of the trap, and at Notwen's direction, the women set out trestle tables over the tamped earth of the excavation. The plan, he said, was to lure the dragon between the buildings and onto the trap. Other folks cooked food and hung lanterns and decorations of flowers, dried grasses, and ribbons. Two large oxen were butchered and left to roast overnight in the fire pit. The smell of roasting meat soon filled the town, and Lucy thought that alone would distract Fyremantle and lure him from his perch on the Rock.

Meanwhile, Ulin and Notwen remained hidden in Notwen's laboratory, poring over plans and working on concoctions only they could understand. The trap was as ready as they could make it, but they spent hours double-checking figures and thinking of more ways to slow the huge beast.

Lucy retreated to her room and spent that evening perfecting half a dozen spells until she could cast them in her sleep. Most of them were spells she had done years ago at the Academy. A few were new ones she devised to protect herself or others from the dragon, and one was a special spell Ulin asked her learn. Her spellcasting was flawless, but to her dismay, even with the help of the turban, the spells went awry or failed more than half the time. Exhaustion finally forced her to stop, but she was frustrated at her failures and deeply worried. She could not afford to fail tomorrow when the red dragon appeared for his tribute.

Challie woke her the next morning with a mug of cooled cider and two hard-boiled eggs. "There's more if you want it, but if your stomach is like mine, you won't be able to eat it."

Lucy quickly found Challie was right. As soon as she got out of bed and went to the small table, the enormity of their task for that day sank in its claws and twisted her stomach into knots. She drank the cider, ate one egg, and had to give up. "Do you want the other?" she offered.

Challie shook her head. "I've tried to eat, too, and can't. Bridget is in the kitchen fixing these enormous meals, and no one can eat them. Even Cosmo is off his feed."

The dwarf sat on the edge of her chair, twisting her hands. She wore the blue tunic and baggy pants that made up her uniform, and her silver axe hung at her belt, but her face was pale, and the dark blue of the tunic only enhanced the dark circles around her eyes. "Lucy, I'm nervous," she admitted. "I never thought I'd admit this, but that dragon terrifies me. I have never been so close to a dragon before. What if I can't do what I am supposed to do?"

Lucy stood by her friend's chair. "I know," she said. "All of us are terrified. I won't hold you to this, Challie. If you want to leave, one of the Fox's men can take you to one of the camps in the hills."

"No," the dwarf said vehemently. "I will not run. I made an oath to serve you and this town, and I will, but . . . I will be very glad when this is all over."

Lucy couldn't agree more. To occupy her mind, she put on her clothes, meticulously brushing the dust from her pants and tunic, donning everything so it all hung just right. She fastened her belt around her waist and slid her dagger scabbard to her right side. Her leather boots slid on easily, and she tucked her pants' legs into the soft cuffs. Last of all, she picked up the turban from its resting place on the table and gently set it on her head. The moment when the creature returned to its preferred place never failed to amaze her. It wrapped itself happily about her chestnut hair like a cat snuggling into its bed for a nap, and the pleased mental thoughts of its consciousness settled around her in a comforting aura. Taking a deep breath, she half-bowed to Challie, and the two of them left the inn to face the day together.

Shortly after sunrise, the familiar figure of Knight Officer Venturin was spotted riding along the road into town. A sentry quickly steered her to the festival site where the sheriff was waiting for her. When she reached the street, she slowed her horse and looked around in surprise at the picnic preparations.

Lucy barely nodded to her as she handed Venturin a packet. "It's all there: a map, tax records, and signed statements. Keep riding until our messenger catches up to you. I will not reveal your name to Fyremantle, but keep the information in case you need it in the near future."

Venturin glowered down at her from the saddle. "My men?"

Lucy whistled loudly and pointed down the street. From the Game Cock, two men led a Dark Knight out the door. It was quite obvious, even from a distance, that he had been enjoying himself. He waved drunkenly to his commander. "As you can see, they're fine."

"Who is this messenger? How will he be able to catch up with me?"

"The messenger is on loan from a friend. It is a hawk, specially trained to deliver messages. It will find you."

"One of the Silver Fox's?" Venturin demanded. "Is he involved in this?"

"I wouldn't know."

"I'm not surprised." The Dark Knight snatched the packet from Lucy's hand. "Don't try to cross me, Sheriff." She spurred her horse around and galloped southeast toward the Desolation.

Mayor Efrim had told Lucy that the tax collection in Flotsam usually occurred around midafternoon on Visiting Day. Fyremantle collected the taxes from several places and usually needed the day to cover all his obligations. This day, they hoped, would not be different.

Everyone who volunteered to stay behind gathered in the new festival ground. Most of the kender were there with their containers of pickled eggs and their faces unclouded by fear. The city council, Mayor Efrim, and those of the Vigilance Force not guarding the camps made their appearance. There were enough people there, Lucy hoped, to give the dragon the impression that the whole town had come for the festival.

At her request, the firepits were uncovered and the sides of meat on their spits were raised and set to keep warm over the coals. Sniffing appreciatively, Ulin pulled out a leather bag and sprinkled the contents liberally over the roasting meat. He and Lucy watched as the white powder blended with the meat juices and slowly disappeared.

"What will that do?" Kethril asked curiously.

"With luck? Buy us some time. It is supposed to make the dragon drowsy for a short while. Don't let anyone touch that meat. And the same with these barrels of beer." He pried off the lids of three large kegs of beer and poured the contents of a second bag into the golden liquid.

Notwen tugged Lucy's sleeve. "Sheriff, I've been meaning to tell you. The reason we had to make these powders . . . ?" He hesitated and looked at Ulin then back at Lucy. "Well, I did some calculations last night, and I've rechecked them dozens of times. My, uh, trap will hold, but not for long. I estimate you will have about fifteen minutes before he breaks out."

Appalled, Lucy stared at him. She had thought they would have ample time to convince the dragon to see things their way. "Fifteen minutes?" she gasped.

"It was the best we could do in such a short time," Ulin said apologetically. "You and Kethril will have to talk fast."

"*Me?*" Kethril exclaimed. "Why me?"

"I have to handle the rockets and the ropes and be close by in case the trap doesn't work properly. You started this whole mess." Ulin said pointedly. "You can help finish it."

Lucy's father nodded gloomily. His fingers went to the silver ring on his right hand and began to twist it around and around.

Challie and a guard arrived, driving a laden freight wagon covered with a tarp. They parked it near the fire pit and unhitched the horses.

Around noon people brought out the rest of the food prepared for the feast and set it out on tables under fly-proof screens. No one ate very much. Almost everyone stood around and watched the sky. A few musicians set up their instruments and played dance tunes, but no one danced. Lucy, as she walked around the grounds, thought the festival did not look very festive. The day was very warm for spring, and the heat rose in wavy sheets above the dry hills. The wind stirred dust into tiny whirlwinds and sent them spinning through the streets of the town. A large tumbleweed broke loose from its dry stalk and rolled through the festival grounds, enticing the kender to chase it. Notwen checked his trap for at least the thirtieth time and made sure the lamps were lit.

An hour after noon Lucy, Saorsha, and Aylesworthy climbed the path to the top of the Rock to wait for the dragon. In the meager shade of the hidden guard post, they sat without saying a word. Lucy kept her eyes to the west where the sky remained maddeningly empty.

"There he is."

The guard's soft words did not penetrate Lucy's thoughts at first. She tore her eyes away from the sky and said, "What?"

Instead of answering, the guard lifted his horn to his lips and blew the first signal to the town below. In the festival field, the people froze in place and waited, their hearts pounding, for the second signal.

"There," Saorsha said, pointing to the north. "There he is."

They could all see him now, a dark shape against the summer sky, coming fast on his beating wings. The guard blew the second signal.

"Here we go," Saorsha muttered. The three of them

climbed out of the guards' post and walked across the windswept stone.

Fyremantle flew over the last row of hills and swept down over the town. He circled once, twice, his head lowered to see the buildings and streets. He curved south and angled over the festival. The people below screamed and shouted and ran in all directions. Huffing his pleasure, Fyremantle beat his wings and soared over the Rock.

Abruptly the sun was blocked out on the headland. Lucy tried to look up, but fear of the dragon nearly overwhelmed her, and she screwed her eyes shut and tried to stifle the scream that gathered in her throat. She heard the heavy rustle of his leathery wings and the scratch of his claws on the rock as he came in to land. A rush of wind blew the sulfuric stench of his body around her and made her gag.

"Mighty Fyremantle!" she heard Saorsha say. The older woman's voice was tight with strain, but at least she could say something. Lucy forced her eyes to open and looked up into the face of the massive dragon. His scales gleamed like blood in the hot sun and radiated heat in shimmering waves.

His smoldering eyes were fastened on the empty stone where the barrels and boxes were supposed to be. His blackened nostrils curled in disdain. "This is all you were able to scrape together?" he said in withering scorn.

Mayor Efrim and Saorsha quickly fell to their knees and bowed low. Lucy followed suit. "Oh, no, inestimable lord. The taxes are here as required," Mayor Efrim explained. "The boxes are still below. We had to make a final accounting to be sure everything was accurate. It is being loaded as we speak."

"Below!" the red roared. His voice pounded at them like thunder. His anger sparked little flames around his teeth. "I gave you ample time to gather my tribute. Why should I bother to fly down into that dung heap of a town? Bring it up here this instant."

"Of course, of course," Saorsha said hastily.

Fyremantle suddenly cocked his scaled head. "What is that I smell?"

"We have prepared a feast for Visiting Day, your magnificence," Lucy said. "If you will be patient, we'll have the taxes—"

"Why should I be patient?" he rumbled. "You have disobeyed me."

"Oh, no! No, lord. We have only been delayed. The treasure will be here any minute."

He snorted a blast of hot, scorched breath. "It had better be." He lifted his head and gazed toward the festival ground. He sniffed the air appreciatively. "Perhaps I will wait for a short time." Abruptly he leaped to the edge of the headland and dropped off. His wings stretched out to slow his descent, and he glided down to the field. His massive weight landed with a shuddering thud. His crafty eyes gleaming, he snaked between the old buildings.

No one waited for him. Even the kender had disappeared into the grass or the nearest buildings. With a bound he landed amidst the trestle tables and crushed them under his body. His tail swept back and forth like a scythe, demolishing everything in its path. He snatched up the bowls and platters of food and dumped everything down his insatiable maw as he made his way toward the fire pits. Two of the sides of meat vanished between his jaws in just a few bites. He used a claw to pry open three beer barrels left standing near the fire pits. Each barrel was emptied down his throat. When he was finished, he looked around in satisfaction. The festival was in ruins; only the two remaining sides of beef were left.

On the headland, the sheriff ran down the road toward the festival, leaving the councilwoman and the mayor to follow in the pony cart. The hidden townspeople peeped nervously through cracks to see what he would do next. Not even Ulin knew for certain how quickly the sleep potion would affect a large dragon, and the greatest fear was that Fyremantle would leave before the trap could be sprung. A small fire had already started near the firepits where the wind from his wings had sent embers from the cooking fire flying into the dry grass. To their relief the dragon did not seem to notice the fire, nor did he try to start any of his own.

"Come on," Ulin whispered urgently. "Stay and eat that last bite of meat. Take your time, you blasted worm."

Lazily, Fyremantle stretched out his limbs and settled down on top of the wreckage to finish the last of the beef. His great body dropped to the ground, and his wings furled against his sides.

"Get ready," Ulin hissed to those around him.

The red blinked his eyes. His tail flicked a few times then lay flat on the newly dug earth. His head snaked down and reached for the last haunch of beef.

"Now!" Ulin bellowed.

Fyremantle's head snapped up with an audible "Huh?" sound.

Behind the old ruins, Notwen, Kethril, Challie, and Ulin sprang into action. Lighted wicks in hand, Challie and Kethril lit the fuses to two cloth bags filled with flash powder and hurled them into the firepit. A heartbeat later two brilliant flashes exploded like stars only a feet away from the dragon's startled gaze.

He roared in fury, but the dazzling light and the clouds of smoke that issued from the pit momentarily blinded him to the frantic activity of the people around him.

Ulin felt his heart pounding in his chest. The dragon-fear emanated in cold, palpable waves, causing his hands to shake and his entire body to tremble as if stricken with a fever. For a sickening moment his eyes watered with tears, and he felt his knees buckling. He looked around and saw Kethril clinging to a doorframe. Others fell to their faces, groveling in terror.

Fyremantle began to rise from the ground. His wings, though hindered by the buildings, lifted from his back.

Ulin turned his thoughts to Palin and his twisted hands, to his wife dead of a plague, to the Academy lying in ruins, and to his hatred of all evil dragons that caused such misery in the world. Anger raw and hot seared back his terror and stilled the trembling in his limbs. "Notwen!" he bellowed. "Do it now!"

The strong, powerful voice of the mage galvanized the trembling gnome. Ulin lit the fuses on a series of long pointed tubes placed strategically on one side of the street while Notwen lit the fuses of another.

The results were spectacular.

Like arrows of fire, the tubes rose above the street, jetting pink sparks and clouds of smoke. Attached to one set of rockets was a light-weight net strengthened with wire. The others carried ropes at their tails. They soared to their apex and arched down over the dragon, the net falling first and the ropes coming down on top. They were so carefully aligned that most of them crossed each other perfectly and laid their lines over the dragon from his neck to his tail.

Fyremantle squalled in confusion and rage. The powders Ulin had sprinkled on the food sapped his strength and left him lightheaded and weak, but the big red was not easily overcome. He struggled to stand, his head whipping back and forth, and his tail lashed at the buildings on either side. Spurts of fire blew from his jaws. His claws raked the ground and tore great holes in the road until he reached the grid of iron that sat just below the surface.

The rockets, having done their work, fell sputtering to the ground, and the citizens of Flotsam jumped to grab the ropes. One end of the net had been hidden in the dirt and was fastened to the iron grid beneath the dragon, but the other edge was loose and had to be tightened down. Shouting and screaming, the men and women tied the edge of the net and ropes down to rings Notwen had embedded in the ground and to anything that might hold the dragon in place.

While they struggled to hold him, Lucy, charging ahead of Saorsha and Mayor Efrim, worked her way around the buildings and came up behind him. At the edge of the net, her father met her.

"Don't worry about fire," Kethril yelled over the uproar. He tapped the ring on his hand. "It's an artifact from Istar I picked up years ago. It will protect both of us, if we are touching."

Lucy squeezed his hand gratefully. That took one problem off her mind. She had thought she'd have to make a mage shield to protect herself from the dragonfire, but with her father there to protect her, that was one less spell she had to worry about.

She placed her hand on the heaving net pinning the dragon and began the incantation that Ulin had taught her. The turban squirmed with delight, its crystal eyes glowing in the surge of magic that flowed through them both. Lucy tightened her hand around a strand of the net. She felt the magic fill her mind and body, its familiar warmth a welcome invasion. Carefully, precisely, she shaped the magic to her will, all the while praying in a small part of her mind that nothing would take her magic away. She sensed something close by, something odd, and for a second she thought she felt something tickle her skin.

The magic started to slip out of her control. Lucy's thoughts gathered in one passionate objection: *No!* The turban responded and used its own power to bolster hers long enough to complete the spell. Lucy felt the net change under her fingers. From a stiff, unresponsive inanimate thing, it became supple as a vine and strong as steel.

The dragon felt the change, too, and his efforts to escape increased to sudden terror. But he was too late. The net molded neatly around his body and pinned his wings to his sides. Drawing power from the metal grid beneath the road, Lucy's spell instantly hardened the net and turned it as rigid as the iron bars. Fyremantle was now trapped beneath an unyielding cage. He thrashed his head up and down and blew gouts of fire from his cavernous mouth, but he could not move.

Lucy fell back into her father's arms, gasping for breath. "Notwen's estimate of fifteen minutes may be optimistic," she shouted to Kethril. "The spell is weak. I don't know how long it will last. We'll have to hurry."

The sheriff and the gambler worked their way around the trapped dragon. Everyone else stayed out of sight.

"Fyremantle!" Kethril shouted over the dragon's furious rumble. "Fyremantle! We want to talk to you!"

"How dare you!" roared the red, and he breathed a viscous stream of fire directly at them.

Lucy cringed close to her father as he raised his fist and the silver ring of Istar. The dragonfire bounced off the power of the ring and splashed around the two people in streams of yellow and orange.

"Stop it!" Lucy yelled before the dragon could take another breath. "Your fire will not harm us. Nor do we intend to harm you. We just want to talk."

Fyremantle paid no attention. He fired another jet of scorching flame and watched furiously as it fell harmless around them.

"I said stop it! If you don't, I will shrink this net and cut you to pieces," Lucy cried. She wasn't sure she could do that, but it didn't hurt to threaten.

Kethril pointed to the freight wagon close by. "And if you aren't careful, you will burn that wagon that holds Malys's tribute, then you will have to explain to her why your delivery is nothing but a molten blob."

Fyremantle hesitated, his black eyes malevolent but thoughtful. Steam curled from his nostrils. "Whatever you have to say will not save this town. When I escape from this cage, I will incinerate everything."

"I would think about that very carefully if I were you," Lucy said reasonably.

The dragon lowered his head until his nose was only a

few feet away. "Why?" he said in a long, drawn sound that was almost a snarl.

Lucy kept her hand clamped on her father's. The reek of the dragon was almost more than she could bear. It took all her self-control to say, "We want to make a deal."

Kethril pulled his map out of his tunic and held it up for the dragon to see. "A map of this region. Do you recognize anything on it?"

The dragon had to tilt his head to look at the map. He studied it for several minutes before the significance of several marked places snatched his complete attention. Without warning he snorted a gust of flame that caught the map and reduced it to ash.

Kethril merely shook his fingers and pulled out another map. "The advantages of living in a town full of forgers."

"It has come to our attention," Lucy said before the dragon could respond, "that you have hiked up Flotsam's taxes without Malys's knowledge so you could steal some of it for yourself. We want you to stop."

"I am lord of this region. I will do as I please," Fyremantle replied. He tugged fiercely at the net around him then sank back, panting.

"Indubitably. However, we believe Malys will not appreciate your efforts at self-enrichment. She does tend to be rather jealous and unreasonable."

The dragon stilled, his glittering eyes fastened on Lucy and Kethril. "I am loyal to my overlord," he protested.

"So she must think, too," Lucy said. "It would be a shame to tell her otherwise."

"You will never tell her!" bellowed the dragon. "You cannot prove it!"

"Of course we can," Kethril said, his tones cool, "and we will unless you leave Flotsam alone."

"I will burn it first. No one will escape to tell my queen."

"Too late," Lucy said. "We already have a messenger on the way, and if she does not receive a message from us, she is instructed to deliver our letter and proof to Malys."

Fyremantle bellowed and threw himself against the constricting net. Lucy and Kethril scrambled back and watched breathlessly as the huge dragon struggled and thrashed until his scales were scored and his head hung in exhaustion. Still the ensorcelled net held.

When he had been still for a moment or two, Lucy and Kethril eased forward to continue the conversation.

Lucy went on. "The only way you can stop the messenger is to agree to our proposal. You will continue to collect the taxes from the town, but we will only pay the original six hundred pieces of steel. And you must give your word to leave the town alone. It cannot make its contributions to Malys's treasury if you burn it."

Kethril waved the copy of the map. "Just to ensure your good behavior, we also included one of these maps."

"Why?" hissed the dragon. "Malys already knows the site of my lair."

"Lairs," corrected Kethril. "We found your lairs." He drew Lucy to the freight wagon with him and pulled back the tarp to show the contents to the dragon. "When the Flotsam city taxes were stolen, the people had to look elsewhere for the money. One of your lairs is now empty. You can pay Malys Flotsam's taxes this year to make up for all the years you were stealing from the towns around here."

"No!" Fyremantle growled. "You're bluffing!"

Kethril reached into the wagon and pulled out a large doublehandled king's cup cast in gold and encrusted with garnets. "Remember this? And how about this?" He pulled out an elegant cutlass and waved it in the dragon's face.

Dragons can remember every item of their hoards down to the last coin, and Fyremantle was no exception. He was so angry he sputtered sparks.

"If you try anything against these people," Lucy warned him. "We will tell Malys about your other lairs."

"I will hide them again," he steamed.

The gambler tossed the sword back in the wagon. "We found them once, we can find them again."

Fyremantle raised his head and stared to the southeast as if fearing to see some sign of Malys. "All right. I agree."

"You agree to what? I want to hear you say it loudly so the whole town can hear." Lucy insisted.

Fyremantle hissed, but after a moment, he bellowed in a voice heard all the way to the Rock, "I agree to leave Flotsam alone and collect only the taxes due to Malys!"

"Now that wasn't so hard, was it?" she said sweetly.

"Release me!" he roared. The powders were slowly wearing off, and Fyremantle felt his full strength returning.

Lucy realized it, too, and she knew it would be far better to have the dragon trap remain a dangerous and mysterious thing in Fyremantle's mind than to allow him to break loose himself. Swiftly, she reached out, touched the net, and nullified her spell.

The strands returned to normal. Behind the wall of the building next to the dragon, Challie drew her axe and swiftly sliced through the ropes holding down the net.

Fyremantle shrugged and felt the net slide off his shoulders. He bounded out of the trap and halted long enough to shake out his wings. "I will find a way to make you pay for this," he snarled to Lucy and Kethril.

In that instant of silence, they all heard the faint sound of pony's hooves and the rattle of a small cart coming along the road. Lucy turned cold. From a side-street several blocks down she and Kethril saw Saorsha's pony cart turn onto the street and abruptly stop. Its two occupants gaped at the loose dragon crouched in the middle of the road.

"Saorsha, back up!" Lucy heard Ulin yell.

The ex-legionnaire pulled frantically on her reins, but the pony, already terrified by the smoke and strange smells, panicked and reared.

Fyremantle roared a great thundering bellow of rage. "You!" he howled at Saorsha and Mayor Efrim. "You have been a stone in my claw long enough. Flotsam! Find yourselves a new mayor!" He blew a long blast of yellow fire at the cart and the two people. Neither had time to scream.

The dragon snorted at his small satisfaction, then he snatched the freight wagon in his front claws and leaped into the air. His wings swept downward, pushing him high into the warm air. He roared once and turned away to fly south and east toward the ruined lands of Malys's lair.

Chapter
Twenty-four

A hideous hush followed the departure of the dragon. Every person in the smoke-filled block stared horror-stricken at the blackened remains of the mayor and the woman who had cared for Flotsam. The corpses were blackened and burned almost to the bone, yet everyone walked slowly into the street and gathered around the bodies.

"Why did she do that?" Lucy mourned. "Why didn't she look first?"

"Blasted dragon. I thought for a few minutes we might actually get away with it freely," Ulin said.

Lysandros squatted down by the old mayor, gently touched a burned hand, and offered a eulogy Efrim would have appreciated. "He did his best for this town." He looked up at Lucy. "Do I send the hawk after Venturin?"

"Yes," she replied. "They worked too hard for this for us to fail them now."

Beside her, Kethril stared at the two bodies and said nothing.

Someone brought two blankets from the Game Cock and covered the bodies. Later they could be buried with proper respect in the hillside cemetery where Saorsha's family already rested.

For now though, a new concern demanded their attention. Several fires had started from the dragonfire and the remains of Notwen's rockets. They were spreading rapidly around several buildings. Fed by the dry grass and pushed by a steady wind, the fire could be almost as dangerous to the town as the dragon. Fortunately, fires were a familiar danger in Flotsam, and the populace was used to fighting them. Instead of panicking, men and women grabbed buckets and shovels and went to work to stifle the fires before they could get completely out of control. Mule-drawn wagons soon arrived with barrels of water to douse the ground and buildings, and a firebreak was quickly dug.

The flames consumed most of the old, ruinous buildings, and a few still in use, like the Game Cock, were scorched around the edges. To everyone's relief, the wind shifted to the north in the late afternoon, and a damp seabreeze prevented the fire from spreading any farther.

The townsfolk were so busy fighting the last of the fires and dousing hot spots that they did not hear the signal horn sound a third time. The first warning Lucy had was from Lysandros who poked her in the ribs and pointed down the road. Just cresting a hill cantered the black horse of a Knight of Neraka.

Firefighters scattered as the Dark Knight rode her horse heedlessly into the crowd. Lucy stood her ground, waiting for Knight Officer Venturin to find her. The Knight saw her immediately and reined her horse over. She did not dismount at first but sat on her tired, sweating horse and eyed the smoke-grimed people around her.

Venturin waved a negligent hand at the smoke and flames. "Problems?"

Lucy shrugged with equal disdain. "Nothing we can't handle."

"I see." The Knight Officer ran her gaze over the destruction in the street: the smashed tables, the overturned barrels, the empty trap, and the covered bodies. "You've had an interesting day." She dismounted, her narrow face expressionless, and removed the packet from an inner pocket in her black tunic. "This made interesting reading. It also frightened Fyremantle enough that he came looking for your messenger."

"Did he see you?"

Venturin's gaze turned contemptuous. "Of course not. I assumed he would search, and I took cover shortly after noon. I will keep this information. If Fyremantle does not hold to his word, I will give it to the overlord."

Lucy nodded her thanks. She waved Challie over and held out her hand. The magistrate wordlessly untied a heavy bag from her belt and dropped it into Lucy's hand. It fell with a satisfying chink. "Eight percent plus a bonus," Lucy said, handing it over to Venturin. "Fifty steel coins."

The Dark Knight shoved the bag into her belt without counting it. "My Knights?"

"Of course. Challie, where is the Talon?"

The dwarf jerked a thumb toward the gaming house. "When the Game Cock caught on fire, they came out to help. I think they're still there."

As the Knight Officer remounted, Lucy noticed for the first time that the Dark Knight had no other horses. "What about your men? Didn't you bring their mounts?"

Venturin sneered. "They allowed themselves to be taken by surprise and captured. For that they will walk to camp." She yanked her horse around, missing the smothered sound that escaped from Challie's tightly clamped mouth.

"What is it?" Lucy asked in concern. The dwarf looked about to choke.

Challie waited until the Dark Knight was out of earshot

before she released her breath in a gasp of laughter. "Their camp is ten miles away, and those Knights have been helping themselves to the proprietor's stock. It ought to be a pleasant journey back for them."

With the fires nearly out and the Dark Knights gone, it seemed that the plan had finally reached its conclusion. The dragon trap had been a success. A cheer rose up somewhere in the midst of the lingering smoke and weary people. It quickly spread until the entire block rang with shouting voices. The euphoria of success was sweet beyond words.

Lucy found Notwen, Kethril, and Ulin by the ropes and churned earth of the dragon trap. In a burst of relief, she caught Notwen up in a hug and swung him around until he was breathless, then she embarrassed him beyond all measure by kissing him on the forehead. Ulin grinned then knelt beside him and solemnly shook his hand.

"That was an excellent invention, my friend," he said.

The small gnome grinned. "I couldn't have done it without Lucy and you. When you go, I shall have to work on some improvements. Fyremantle probably won't behave for long."

"One thing I want to know: where did you get the fuel for those tubes?" Lucy asked. "I thought you weren't going to make that firepowder anymore."

Ulin slipped an arm around her and turned her slightly away so Notwen couldn't hear.

"That's not my black powder. Notwen refined that from the residue of the explosion your father caused. I, ah, toned it down somewhat."

Lucy's mouth dropped. She knew her father had some talents, but she hadn't thought he knew alchemy. "Your powder blew up the treasury?" she asked Kethril.

He shrugged with little regret. "It was supposed to be a time-delayed blast that would collapse the tunnel as soon as we left. A Khurish alchemist made it, but it went off too early."

She reached out and tapped his ring. "And this is what saved you."

Kethril studied the ring for a moment. "That and some luck. I've had this ring for years. It has come in handy." He patted his daughter's arm rather distractedly and wandered off into the crowd.

Twilight drifted into Flotsam by the time the fires were completely out, the mess cleaned up, and the bodies of Saorsha and Mayor Efrim collected for burial. Sometime in that wild afternoon, Kethril Torkay cleaned out the cash box at the Jetties and disappeared.

Lucy was not surprised, but in her heart she was disappointed. She knew her father now—the rogue who lived by the numbers and followed the wind, yet the child in her had hoped he had liked what his daughter had become and would care enough to say good-bye. Obviously, she had been wrong.

All the food Bridget had prepared that morning was quickly devoured that night by the hungry firefighters. No one stayed late. They were all too tired, and there was much to do in the morning. Aylesworthy treated Lucy and Ulin to free baths in his small bathhouse, then bid them both a good night.

Ulin was waiting for Lucy when she came in, still drying her hair. He pointed at a small pile of drawstring bags left propped on their bed.

Lucy cocked an eye at the pile. "Where did those come from?"

"Kethril left it."

"He didn't find the treasury, did he?" she asked sharply.

"No. Notwen hid it in his laboratory. No one else but Challie knows where it is. He probably took this while we were moving the cache from the dragon's den."

She hefted a heavy bag. "I wonder how much more he took for himself."

Ulin handed her a scrap of paper. "This was with it."

She fingered the paper a minute before she read aloud,

" 'I believe the council promised you twenty-five percent of my estate. It won't make up for ten years, but maybe it will help you now. You made me proud, Lucy. You're the one good thing I've done in this life.' "

She tucked the note away, more for her mother's sake than its sentimental value. Its words were already burned into her memory. He loved her—as much as he could love anything that didn't spend—and he was proud of her. Nothing else he might have given her could ever equal that. Her hate and bitterness were gone, replaced by a deep gratitude for the few days she'd had with him. Now she could go home and tell her mother, in all honesty, that Kethril Torkay was gone.

* * * * *

Two days later, a Khurish caravan came into Flotsam and injected a new spirit into the marketplace. The townspeople were exhausted, grieving, and trying to adjust to the changes. The arrival of the Khurs with their goods and money and desire to wash away the dust of endless miles was like a breath of fresh air. The entire town snatched at the excuse and threw a huge party. That same night the citizens elected Innkeeper Aylesworthy the new mayor and Bridget, the blacksmith, and Challie the new city council.

The position of sheriff would soon be available, too, but no one wanted to take the job until Lucy left.

"We'll find someone," Challie said. "We take what we can get when we can get it."

The next day Ulin bought a small traveling wagon for the bay horse to pull and made arrangements with the caravan master for the journey back to Sanction. Their job was done in Flotsam, and he felt a strong urge to go home.

The day before they were due to leave, Lucy resigned as sheriff and turned her office over to the new city council. She tried to return the turban to Notwen, but he would have none of it.

"You are and always will be the Sorceress in my mind," he said, screwing up enough courage to kiss her hand. "The creature is yours now."

Mayor Aylesworthy tried to give her payment in full. She smiled and gave it back, explaining that her father had already given her part of his "estate."

"Just be sure and keep that treasure of yours safe, and if my father turns up dead again, don't come get me. Just bury him."

The city council laughed.

Lucy and Ulin left Flotsam early the next morning amidst the raucous confusion of the Khur caravan. Almost the entire town turned out to see them go. They waved and said good-bye to everyone, especially Challie, Aylesworthy, Bridget, and Lysandros. All too soon the whips cracked, the horses neighed, and Lucy and Ulin had to climb into their wagon and join the caravan.

Lysandros and some of his men escorted the caravan out of town. The Silver Fox saluted them both before he turned his troop aside and rode back to Flotsam.

On the hill where they had seen Flotsam for the first time, Lucy turned around and waved one last time.

> "Wreck upon the water
> Washed up on the sand
> Make a town of sea wrack
> We'll call it Flotsam."

Ulin snorted. "Where did you hear that?"

"Pease taught me." Lucy hesitated then kissed Ulin's cheek. "Thank you for coming with me."

Ulin glanced at the woman beside him and thought how incredibly beautiful she was. "It was an honor," he told her.

THE DHAMON SAGA
Jean Rabe

THE EXCITING BEGINNING TO THE DHAMON SAGA

— NOW AVAILABLE IN PAPERBACK!

Volume One: *Downfall*

HOW FAR CAN A HERO FALL?
FAR ENOUGH TO LOSE HIS SOUL?

Dhamon Grimwulf, once a Hero of the Heart, has sunk into a bitter life of crime and squalor. Now, as the great dragon overlords of the Fifth Age coldly plot to strengthen their rule and destroy their enemies, he must somehow find the will to redeem himself.

Volume Two: *Betrayal*

All Dhamon Grimwulf wants is a cure for the painful dragon scale embedded in his leg. To find a cure, he must venture into the treacherous realm of a great black dragon. Along the way, Dhamon discovers some horrible truths: betrayal is worse than death, and there is something more terrifying on Krynn than even a dragon overlord.

June 2001

CLASSICS SERIES

THE INHERITANCE
Nancy Varian Berberick
The companions of Tanis Half-Elven knew of their friend's tragic heritage—how his mother was ravaged by a human bandit and died from grief. But there was more to the story than anyone knew.

Here at last is the story of the half-elf's heritage: the tale of a captive elven princess, a merciless human outlaw, a proud elven prince, the power of love, and how tragedy can change a life forever.

May 2000

THE CITADEL
Richard A. Knaak
Against a darkened cloud it comes, soaring over the ravaged land: the flying citadel, mightiest power in the arsenal of the dragon highlords. An evil wizard has discovered a secret that may bring all of Ansalon under his control, and it's up to a red-robed mage, a driven cleric, a kender, and a grizzled war veteran to stop him before it's too late.

DALAMAR THE DARK
Nancy Varian Berberick
Magic runs like fire through the blood of Dalamar Argent, yet his heritage denies him its use. But as war threatens his beloved Silvanesti, Dalamar will seize the forbidden power and begin a quest that will lead him to a dark and uncertain future.

MURDER IN TARSIS
John Maddox Roberts
Who killed Ambassador Bloodarrow? In a city where everyone is a suspect, time is running out for an unlikely trio of detectives. If they fail to solve the mystery, their reward will be death.

New characters,
strange magic,
wondrous creatures.

ADVENTURE THROUGH THE HISTORY OF KRYNN
WITH THESE THREE NEW SERIES!

THE BARBARIANS
PAUL THOMPSON & TONYA CARTER COOK

Follow a divided brother and sister as they lead rival tribes of plainsmen amidst the wonders and dangers of ancient Krynn.

Volume One: *Children of the Plains*
Volume Two: *Brother of the Dragon*
August 2001

THE ICEWALL TRILOGY
DOUGLAS NILES

Journey with an exiled elf to the harsh, legendary land known as Icereach, where human tribes battle for life and ogres search to reclaim lost glories.

Volume One: *The Messenger*
February 2001

THE KINGPRIEST TRILOGY
CHRIS PIERSON

Discover for the first time the dynastic history of the Kingpriest and how his religious-political rule of Istar influenced the world of DRAGONLANCE® for generations to come.

Volume One: *Chosen of the Gods*
November 2001

STORIES FROM
THE CHANGING FACE OF KRYNN

Bertrem's Guide to the Age of Mortals:
Everyday Life in Krynn of the Fifth Age

NANCY VARIAN BERBERICK,
STAN BROWN,
AND PAUL B. THOMPSON

Countless legends, histories, and sagas have told of the great heroes and villains of Krynn. Now, delve into the life of Ansalon in the Fifth Age as seen through the eyes of the common people, through articles on everything from arms and armor to festivals and clothing!

TALES FROM THE WAR OF SOULS

Don't miss this new collection of short stories detailing the era of the War of Souls, newest chapter in the continuing saga of Krynn. Contains stories from Richard A. Knaak, Paul Thompson & Tonya Carter Cook, Jeff Crook and other popular Dragonlance authors.

October 2001

BERTREM'S GUIDE: A WAR OF SOULS JOURNAL

The War of Souls has begun, and Ansalon will never be the same again. See how these world-changing events affect the lives of the everyday people of Krynn. Includes articles from Nancy Varian Berberick, Mary H. Herbert, John Grubber, and Jeff Crook.

September 2001

Venture into the
FORGOTTEN REALMS
with these two new series!

Sembia
GET A NEW PERSPECTIVE ON THE FORGOTTEN REALMS FROM THESE TALES OF THE USKEVREN CLAN OF SELGAUNT.

Shadow's Witness
Paul Kemp

Erevis Cale has a secret. When a ruthless evil is unleashed on Selgaunt,
the loyal butler of the Uskevren family must come to terms with his own
dark past if he is to save the family he dearly loves.

The Shattered Mask
Richard Lee Byers

Shamur Uskevren is duped into making an assassination attempt on her husband
Thamalon. Soon, however, the dame of House Uskevren realizes that all is not
as it seems and that her family is in grave danger.

JUNE 2001

Black Wolf
Dave Gross

The young Talbot Uskevren was the only one to survive a horrible
"hunting accident." Now, infected with lycanthropy, the second son
of the Uskevren clan must learn to control what he has become.

NOVEMBER 2001

The Cities
A NEW SERIES OF STAND-ALONE NOVELS, EACH SET IN ONE OF THE MIGHTY CITIES OF FAERÛN.

The City of Ravens
Richard Baker

Raven's Bluff — a viper pit of schemes, swindles, wizardry, and
fools masquerading as heroes.

Temple Hill
Drew Karpyshyn

Elversult — fashionable and comfortable, this shining city of the heartlands
harbors an unknown evil beneath its streets.

SEPTEMBER 2001